Sheila w_____ lives in
Chelmsf_____ ese cat
Charlie.

She has three grown-up daughters _____led
plenty of inspiration for her boo'____

She works a_____ospital and
writes in her_____e. She ha__ __tten avidly since childhood, and her __ __ng career took off when she won two
short story awards in the early 1990s. Her short stories
have since been widely published, mainly in women's
magazines.

When not busy working or writing, Sheila enjoys travel,
swimming, contemporary fiction, rock and pop music,
playing the piano (badly!), pubs and restaurants, and high
street fashion. She doesn't believe 'middle age' has to be a
time for slowing down or growing up – and hopes this is
reflected in her writing!

Sheila is also the author of *The Trouble With Ally, Other
People's Lives, Body & Soul* and *The Travel Bug* also
available from Piatkus

Sweet Nothings

Sheila Norton

PIATKUS

꧁ *Visit the Piatkus website!*

Piatkus publishes a wide range of bestselling fiction and non-fiction, including books on health, mind, body & spirit, sex, self-help, cookery, biography and the paranormal.

If you want to:

- read descriptions of our popular titles
- buy our books over the internet
- take advantage of our special offers
- enter our monthly competition
- learn more about your favourite Piatkus authors

VISIT OUR WEBSITE AT: www.piatkus.co.uk

Copyright © 2006 by Sheila Norton

First published in Great Britain in 2006 by
Piatkus Books Ltd.,
5 Windmill Street, London W1T 2JA
email: info@piatkus.co.uk

The moral right of the author has been asserted

A catalogue record for this book is available from the British Library

ISBN 0 7499 3774 2
ISBN-13 978 0 7499 3774 4

Typeset by
Action Publishing Technology Ltd, Gloucester

Printed and bound in Great Britain by
Clays Ltd, St Ives plc

For Alan. As you always like my bread pudding!

Sweet Nothings

Michelle

Two things happened on the twenty-fourth of October 2003 to make it a date I'm never likely to forget. One was that my mum started to become famous. And the other one was that I lost my boyfriend.

Oh, it's OK; don't reach for the tissues. This isn't going to be some horrible weepy tragedy about death and heartbreak. When I say I lost him, I mean it literally. One minute he was there, and the next, he was gone. If I'd believed in abduction by aliens, I'd have been quite prepared to think they'd popped down from Mars while I was in the Ladies, and whisked him off. He'd have liked that. He was always moaning on about wanting to go travelling.

'We never go anywhere,' he'd been saying, only that morning, before he disappeared.

'For God's sake, Robbie.' (That was his name, by the way. Robin, really, but he liked to be called Robbie on account of Robbie Williams being cooler than Robin Williams. Not that his name was Williams, you understand. It was Nelson.) 'For God's sake – not this again,' I said, pulling a face at him. I was pissed off with him, you see, because of the washing machine. He hadn't phoned the landlord about the washing machine, because he said he could fix it quicker himself – and then it'd flooded all over the kitchen floor, the landlord was away for the week, there

1

were no washing machine repair men in the Yellow Pages who didn't have a year's work already lined up and could even discuss the problem without having their palms crossed with silver, and I was having to do all the washing by hand. He was supposed to be helping by wringing out the clothes ready to go in the dryer, but was he? No, you guessed it; he was sitting at the breakfast bar, staring out of the window, whingeing away about going travelling.

'If you want somewhere to go,' I told him, quite cleverly I thought, 'you can put the rest of this lot in a black bin bag, stick it in the car and drive it to the launderette in Duffington.'

And he sighed; this huge, deep sigh as if he had all the troubles of the world on his shoulders (as my mum would say), stood up, stretched himself and said:

'Look at us, Chelle. Both got the day off work, and we're stuck in the fucking kitchen doing fucking washing.'

Correction. Only one of us was doing the fucking washing, actually. And anyway, *I* had the day off work. Robbie hadn't, not legitimately, anyway. He'd decided to take a sickie that morning when he woke up, because 'I don't see why I should go to work when you're not.' His boss probably wouldn't have seen it quite like that so he'd developed some sudden and terrible symptoms that probably frightened everyone at his work, just to hear about them.

'We could go out somewhere,' he said, putting his arms round my waist and kissing the back of my neck. It was kind of hard to stay really mad at him when he did that (and he knew it, which was irritating), but I tried to stick to my guns.

'If you'd called the landlord straight away. . .'

'Never mind. We'll call him next week.'

'But we won't have any clothes left by then!'

'Wear them dirty. Who cares?'

'*I* care, Robbie! I can't go to work in smelly knickers.'

'Mmm!' He smiled suggestively, and that was it.

It annoyed me, really. It always ended up like that. I mean, it didn't always end up with us having sex on the kitchen floor on the pile of dirty laundry, no, but you know what I mean. Having sex didn't get rid of the problems or the arguments. It just shelved them till another day.

'Tell you what we'll do, then,' he said as soon as we'd finished (almost before I was quite finished to be perfectly honest, but I think he was getting bored so he started chatting to pass the time), 'We *will* put the washing in the car, and take it to the launderette, if you like.' If I *like*? What was there to like about it? 'Then, while we're in Duffington, we'll go and have a drink in the Grey Mare. Yeah? Maybe we'll get a pub lunch.'

That was one of the short-term benefits of having sex with Robbie. He was always extra nice to me afterwards. He knew I liked the Old Grey Mare. It's the only half-decent pub in Duffington. The others are the ones he goes to with his mates. You don't get women in them. They have football twice a week on the big screens, and they don't do food, unless you count pork scratchings. The toilets smell and the carpets have strange stains on them. Robbie didn't normally like going to the Mare because he thought it was poncey, but why is it poncey to have clean carpets and nice toilets with silk flowers on the windowsills? Those are the things that make a difference at the end of the day. My mum and I went to the Mare together sometimes on Saturdays when we were shopping, and had a nice prawn salad and a glass of wine. I didn't go there with Nicole and Kim and the others, though. We normally went to Purple Cloud or Club Rouge – although it wasn't quite the same going there now that I wasn't single and available any more, and sometimes Robbie used to get a bit arsey about me going. But it's important to keep up with your girl-friends, isn't it?

So, anyway, as I was saying, we put the washing in the car, and drove into town and took it to the launderette, and there we were, sitting at one of the window tables in the bar of the Grey Mare with our drinks, waiting for the girl to bring us our chicken and salad rolls (with side serving of crisps and sour cream dip), when I thought maybe I should go to the loo before eating (otherwise you know what happens – you always need to go right in the middle of it, don't you). And I'm sure I could only have been gone two or three minutes, because I remember thinking it was cold in the toilets so I didn't hang around in there. And when I went back in the bar, Robbie had gone.

I waited quite a long while, thinking he'd gone to the gents or maybe gone out to the car for some reason or seen someone he knew, out of the window, and gone out in the street to talk to them. I wasn't worried. Then our lunch turned up, and I thought I might as well get started on mine as Robbie always ate much faster than me anyway. It wasn't really till I'd finished my roll and was dipping the last few crisps in what was left of the sour cream dip that I started to think it was a bit odd. In fact, I was getting narked. Trust him, I thought. Isn't that just like a man, to bring you out for lunch and then get chatting to one of his mates and leave you sitting on your own with a chicken roll. I got up and went to the bar, and peered across where you can see into the other part, where the pool table is. I had a feeling he might have wandered in there and got involved with someone who fancied a game of pool. But no, he wasn't there. So I put my coat on and went outside, looked up and down the street, went round into the car park and checked the car. No sign of him. I was worried now, and the more worried I got, the more cross I was getting too. What was he playing at? Where the hell had he buggered off to? I went back in the pub and asked the barmaid:

'Excuse me, but you know my boyfriend, that was sitting here with me earlier on? Did you see him go out?'

She shook her head, looking me up and down as if she thought I might have a screw loose.

'Did anyone see my boyfriend leave?' I called out to the rest of the bar staff.

They all shook their heads and one guy said, 'Sorry, love. Didn't see him. Must have been kidnapped.' And they all laughed as if this was absolutely hilarious.

But it wasn't. Because I was beginning to think that was exactly what had happened.

Anyway, I thought I might as well eat his chicken roll. Waste not, want not, as my mum always says.

The reason I'd taken the day off work was to hear my mum being interviewed on the radio. It was the most exciting thing that had ever happened to my mum. How it came about was that she'd got herself involved with this group that were protesting about the lorries going through our estate, using it as a short cut to the A12. They called themselves the Peace for Panbridge Park Pressure Group, and they spent a lot of time in Mum's sitting room planning things like petitions to the local council, and letters to the papers, and protest meetings. Mum said it had given her a new interest in life since I'd left home to live with Robbie, which I thought was nice for her, really. Not that she didn't have enough on her plate. She worked part-time as a receptionist at the vet's. She'd been there for about two years, since being made redundant from the tractor factory, and she liked it much better at the vet's. She said the work was more interesting because animals have a lot more going for them than tractors, and are more varied. One minute she could be seeing a dog brought in through the door, and the next minute it might be a rabbit or even a gerbil, whereas tractors are pretty much the same all the time, of course. And when she wasn't working, Mum was, more often than not, lumbered with Jessica.

I don't mean that to sound horrible. Jessica is my brother Adam's little girl, and obviously I love her to bits, she's my niece and everything, but I'll be straight with you: I didn't think it was right. My mum wasn't getting any younger – she was fifty-two at the time – although I have to say she didn't look bad for her age. She kept herself nice and slim, and although her hair was a bit grey by now, she used to get it highlighted down at Cutting It Fine next to the Co-op. And she always dressed nicely – not like some of the women of her age you see round about here, always wearing jogging bottoms with all their spare tyres wobbling about. Mum looked nice in trousers, and her legs were still all right to wear straight skirts to work, with high heels, if she wanted to.

Anyway – she'd done her bit with bringing up children, hadn't she, with me and Adam when we were little, and now, just as she'd got us both off her hands, Adam was dumping Jessica on her whenever he couldn't get a child-minder, which was, like, almost every day if you ask me. Fair enough, I felt sorry for him when Julia left him (stuck-up cow), although he should have known better than to get involved with someone like her in the first place, and we all told him so at the time. And how she could walk out on her own baby, her own flesh and blood – well, it's just not natural, is it? What kind of a mother could do that, and leave the poor little mite with only a father to bring her up? Especially someone like Adam, even if he is my own brother. But there you go. Water under the bridge, as Mum would say.

So anyway, Mum was getting right into this Peace for Panbridge Park thing, and good for her, I told her. It was like a kind of hobby for her, something a bit more exciting than looking after her fuchsias. And it got her out meeting some new people, because apart from her friend Maureen she didn't really go out with anyone else, and let's face it, working with dogs and cats every day is all very well but you don't get a lot of conversation out of them. And when East Coast Radio got in touch with them, wanting to interview one of their group about the protest they were planning, where they were going to stand in the middle of the road waving banners at all the lorries to slow them down and piss them off big time, someone suggested Mum did it. And she said yes. I

6

couldn't believe it, actually. I was completely gobsmacked when she first told me about it.

'Bloody hell, Mum!' I said. 'The radio! Are you sure?'

And she was all kind of giggly and excited about it, so I said:

'Well, good for you. Be an experience for you, anyway.'

Privately, to be honest, I was thinking: 'Rather you than me!' I wouldn't have done it, myself, not for all the money in the world. I'd have been shitting myself with nerves, thinking about all those people out there listening to me. But my dad really annoyed me, because he just looked up from his paper and said, very dismissively I thought:

'She wants her bleeding head examined.'

And that was why I thought: I'll take the day off, and listen to her.

The radio interview was supposed to be on at quarter past three. I didn't really know what to do. By the time I'd looked outside again, and asked one of the guys behind the bar to go and look in the Gents, in case Robbie had been taken bad in there or something, and collapsed, and no one had seen him, in a cubicle or behind the door – well, you never know, stranger things have happened – it was nearly quarter to three and, obviously, I didn't want to miss my mum on the radio. It was her big day! We were supposed to be meeting up at Mum and Dad's at three o'clock at the latest – so we could get ourselves a cup of tea ready for when we sat down to listen to the interview. It was going out live, you see. That was the really scary thing about it. I don't know how she got the guts to do it, I really don't. Anyway, the thing was, it was going to take a good twenty minutes to get from Duffington back to Panbridge Park, always supposing I had the spare car key on me, because needless to say, Robbie had not only buggered off, he'd taken the bloody car key with him, which was typical. So there I was, running out of time, and calling Robbie all the names under the sun as you can probably imagine, tipping

7

my handbag upside down on the pub table trying to see if I had the spare car key. Which, luckily, no thanks to bloody Robbie Disappearing-Man Nelson, I finally found in the zip-up bit at the side which is where I normally keep my mobile phone so it was the last place I looked. Typical. At the end of the day, I'm very sorry if I did the wrong thing in taking the car and pissing off out of it, but where was he when I needed him, that's what I want to know?

And my Mum was about to become famous. So really, I had no choice in the matter, did I? That's the way I saw it, anyway.

Penny

The trouble was, everyone thought I wasn't nervous. I don't know why they thought that. It only stood to reason, didn't it, that I was absolutely terrified. I was shaking in my shoes. Everyone kept saying, 'Ooh, Penny, you're so brave, I could *never* do that! Going on the radio, with all those people listening, aren't you scared you're going to say something silly?' Of course I bloody was. But someone had to do it, and no other bugger volunteered, so I thought – well, Penny, let's see what you're made of. It can't kill you.

Archie was about as much help as an ice cube in an oven, but that was nothing new.

'You want your bleeding head examined,' he said when I told him.

I took no notice, but Michelle had a go at him.

'Why don't you try supporting Mum for a change?' she said.

I know it annoys her, the way he talks to me sometimes, but I tell her – Chelle, I say, there's no point taking any notice of him. Just leave him be. He's no use to man or beast – well, none of them are, are they? – so you're only getting yourself worked up for nothing. You'll never change him.

'That's right,' I said to him. 'I know I want me bleeding head examined. I wanted it examined thirty-two years ago.'

That's when I married him: August 1971. I was twenty years old and almost a virgin. We'd kind of done it a few times in the back of his car, but it wasn't very satisfactory so we got married so that we could do it properly in bed. Unfortunately, it carried on being not very satisfactory. We were sort of brought up to expect nothing better. But I must admit, I'd learned a lot since, from TV programmes and some of the books I'd read, and I reckoned I wouldn't say no to trying it all over again with a toyboy if one came my way. Maureen used to say it was all bravado when I said that, but I said: You watch me; chance would be a fine thing.

'I'll support you, Mum,' said Michelle, and she pulled a face at her dad behind his back. 'I'll take the day off work next Friday so I can listen to it.'

'That'll be nice, love. Maureen's coming round, and some of the others from the PPPP.'

That's what we call our pressure group. Peace for Panbridge Park Pressure Group – PPPP. It always sounds more impressive if you call it by initials, like that, don't you think?

'What do you mean, coming round?' said Archie, waking up a bit and tearing his eyes away from *EastEnders*. 'Who's coming round? What's the point, if you're at the radio place being interviewed?'

'We're gathering together, Dad,' said Michelle, 'to support Mum. So that she can think of us all here, listening together, while she's being interviewed.'

'And that's supposed to make her feel better?' he muttered.

Like I say, really, it's best to just take no notice of him.

'Don't worry, Mum,' said Michelle, who was learning fast. 'I'll be here.'

The day before the radio programme, Archie was even quieter than usual. I got home from work at lunchtime and he was already home, slumped in front of the TV, watching some golf.

'What's up with you?' I said, dumping the shopping in the kitchen and going through to the lounge to look at him. What a state. Half his trouble was, he was only fifty-six but he'd taken early retirement from his job in the Renault dealership and was doing odd jobs for local pensioners – gardening, painting and decorating, DIY, you know. He was good at that kind of practical thing. The pensioners liked him because they knew he wasn't going to rip them off and he'd do little jobs for his regulars for almost nothing. But now, I think he was kind of missing his old job sometimes. I think working for elderly people all day every day, he was beginning to feel like one himself. And act like one, although I suppose I shouldn't say it.

'Nothing. Just finished early, if that's all right with you,' he said, without taking his eyes off the golf.

I felt like turning the bloody thing off. How are you supposed to have a conversation if Tigger Wood or whatever he calls himself is just teeing off the green or peeing down the fairway?

'Well, as you're finished early, you can give me a hand unpacking this shopping, can't you. Only I need to spend a bit of time looking through my notes.'

'Notes?' He got to his feet reluctantly and followed me back to the kitchen. 'What notes?'

'For my interview. I don't want to be unprepared, do I? I don't want to be flustered and go er, um, er, all the time, to every question they ask me.'

'Oh, yes. The *interview*,' he said sarcastically as he started taking tins out of carrier bags and plonking them on the worktop. Why not put them straight in the cupboard? Why make it two jobs instead of one? Unless, of course, he still didn't know where the baked beans were kept after only twenty-three years of living in this house. 'When is it again, the *interview*?'

And why such a nasty, sarcastic tone? Why was it necessary, do you think? Unless, of course . . . could it be that Archie was jealous?

11

'It's tomorrow. What's the matter? Are you jealous, or something?'

'Jealous!' he snorted, almost dropping the eggs as he plonked them on the worktop along with the tins and the vegetables and the packets of cereal. 'What the hell would I be *jealous* about?'

But I hadn't known him for thirty-odd years for nothing. He was feeling jealous, and resentful, and left out, and neglected. And he was just a little boy at heart, like them all, with simple needs, just wanting Mummy to show them a bit of attention. I'd make him his favourite pudding and everything would be hunky-dory. It was worth it, to get him in a better mood. I put some bread to soak in a bowl of water and started weighing out raisins and sultanas.

'Mm!' he said, his eyes lighting up as he saw what I was doing. 'You making bread pudding for tonight, Pen?' And he started moving the butter and cheese and things from the worktop into the fridge. And even found where the baked beans went. 'Tell you what. I'll make us a cup of tea, and when you've finished out here, I'll read through your interview notes with you, if you like. Pretend I'm the bloke at the radio, yeah?'

See what I mean? Amazing, isn't it.

I left in plenty of time for the interview. I didn't want to get held up in traffic, and get myself in a state, and turn up all sweaty and cross from rushing. So instead, I arrived there nearly forty minutes early, which was absolutely ridiculous. I parked and sat in the car park for what felt like ages, looking through my notes again, practising my answers to all the questions I thought they would probably ask out loud. When I looked at my watch it was still half an hour to go. If I sat there any longer I was going to change my mind about the whole thing, so I went into the building and told the receptionist who I was. I was trembling with nerves.

'Oh, yes, Mrs Peacham,' she said, giving me a huge

smile that showed all her teeth and most of her tonsils. 'You're for the Darren Barlow show, aren't you. The lady from the ...' (she looked at some paperwork on her desk) 'from the *Panbridge Park Peace Group* ...'

'Peace for Panbridge Park Pressure Group,' I corrected her. My voice was shaking.

'Lovely,' she smiled, dismissing this with a wave of her hand. 'Now then, you're a *little* bit early, so if you like to take a seat—' she waved again, in the direction of a plump leather sofa and a coffee table strewn with fancy magazines – 'there's a coffee machine in the corner if you want to ...'

'Actually,' I said, leaning closer to her and dropping my trembly voice to a whisper, 'what I really need is the toilet.'

'Sorry?'

Obviously dropped my voice too far. I tried again.

'The toilet?'

'Oh, the *toilet*!' she shouted, so that everyone in the reception area turned round and looked me up and down as if I was in the act of peeing my knickers on the spot. 'Just along the corridor here, first on the left.'

I sat in the Ladies and wondered what would happen if I just walked out now and went home. I didn't suppose Darren Barlow or his listeners would care. He'd probably just play a couple more records. But what about Michelle and what about Maureen? They'd be disappointed in me, and, more to the point, so would all the others from the PPPP. And Archie would take the piss out of me for months. He'd love it. He'd have a field day.

No. I stood up, flushed the loo and straightened myself up. I wasn't going to run away from this – I was going through with it. I looked at myself in the mirror and patted a stray bit of hair into place. At least, thank God, it was radio and not TV. Even if I sounded like a prat, I didn't have to worry about looking like one.

13

'And this afternoon, ladies and gentlemen, our guest here in the *Daytime with Darren* studio is Mrs Penny Peacham, who's here with us this afternoon to represent the ... Peace for Panbridge Park Pressure Group. Is that right, Mrs Peacham?'

I nodded timidly.

'Mrs Peacham's nodding at me, everyone. It's radio, Mrs Peacham – we're going to need you to speak – ha, ha!'

'Oh! Yes, yes. Sorry. Yes, that's right. Peace for Panbridge Park Pressure Group.'

'That's an awful lot of *P's*, isn't it! Ha, ha!'

'Yes, I suppose ...'

'And *you're* Penny Peacham! Tell me, Penny – can I call you Penny? – she's nodding again, ladies and gentlemen! – Tell me, Penny, did you join the group because of your initials? Ha, ha!'

'Sorry?'

I stared across the studio in confusion at Darren Barlow. He was probably about forty, and had shaved his head the way men do when they start going bald early but hope no one will realise and just think they're fashion leaders. He was wearing a bright yellow T-shirt with Darren on the front. Why would anyone over the age of seven want to have their own Christian name on the front of their shirt?

'Well, *Penny Peacham* from the *Peace for Panbridge Park Pressure Group*,' he said, in the same sarcastic tone that Archie had used the previous day, 'you've come here today to talk to us, I think, about the *peaceful protest* your group's holding next Monday week in Panbridge Park. Is that right?'

'Yes,' I said, breathing a sigh of relief. This was more like it. Now I could start using the stuff I'd prepared. I straightened out my crumpled notes. 'The Peace for Panbridge Park Pressure Group,' I began, a bit breathlessly, 'believes that there must be an answer to the problems of traffic congestion in the centre of Panbridge Park. And we believe the answer is a bypass. We believe—'

14

'A *bypass*!' interrupted Darren Barlow, yelling it out as if it was a new word he'd personally invented. 'So: what your group believes, Penny, if I've understood you right – what your group *believes*, as well as needing to have a lot of P's in their name – ha, ha! – is that Panbridge Park deserves a *bypass*. Is that what you're saying?'

'Yes,' I said quietly. I wished he'd shut up and just listen. I'd only read the first two lines of my notes. But maybe this was what radio presenters were supposed to carry on like, how they filled out the time. 'Yes, that's what I'm saying. Panbridge Road wasn't built to take the sort of traffic that's using it nowadays. Articulated lorries and trucks and—'

'What was it built for, then, Penny? Horses and carts? Ha, ha!'

I was beginning to want to thump him. Was he taking the piss, or was this all a normal part of the interview?

'I ... er ...' *Sod* it. I didn't want to say *er*. I'd practised so hard not to. 'I ... um ...' *Sod* it! 'I don't really know. I'm not quite old enough to remember horses and carts.'

Aha! That was better! Darren smiled, and flashed me a kind-of encouraging look, as if to say 'One to you!' So was this what it was all about? Were the listeners of his *Daytime with Darren* bloody programme only tuning in to see if he could get one up on a silly woman who wanted to talk about a dangerous traffic on a B-road through a housing estate? Were they hoping to hear me stammering and stuttering and being made a fool of by Darren Barlow and his witty ripostes?

'So what exactly *are* you old enough to remember, then, Penny?' he prompted.

'Peaceful lanes,' I retorted. 'I've lived in Panbridge Park ever since my husband Archie and I got married over thirty-two years ago, when it was a new estate; we started off in one of the little houses just off Park Lane. Our children used to be able to cross the road without being

15

terrified of getting run over, and I used to push them in their prams without having to jump out of the way of lorries and tankers, and we didn't have to breathe in diesel fumes when we went to the local shops to get a loaf of bread.'

I took a deep breath. I didn't realise it till later, but I'd stopped looking at my notes.

'But Penny, Penny . . .' he said soothingly, 'surely that all belongs to a bygone era now? I mean, with all due respect – and, ladies and gentlemen, Penny hasn't told me her age but she's told us that she and her husband have been married for thirty-two years, which is a *heck* of a long time. I think it would be fair to say, Penny, that neither of us is a spring chicken – ha, ha! – Is that fair to say? And with all due respect, life has to move on. We can't live in the pages of a history book! We can't expect time to stand still, and the fact is that we now live in an age when lorries, and tankers, and diesel fumes, as you say, are all part of life, and—'

'Yes! And so are motorways, and bypasses! And *we* believe that this traffic using Panbridge Road as a shortcut should be redirected by—'

'A bypass. So the Panbridge Park Peaceful Pressure People won't be happy, ladies and gentlemen, as I understand it from talking to Penny Peacham here, who – as their chosen representative (in case you've just tuned in) – is with us in the *Daytime with Darren* studio here at East Coast Radio to tell us all about their Peaceful Protest . . . . as I understand it, Penny, your group is *demanding* a bypass for Panbridge Park, and in fact, on Monday week, you're planning to take up your banners and *stand* – actually *stand* – in the middle of the road, stopping the traffic from flowing along Panbridge Road at the busiest time of the morning rush hour.'

'That's right. We've tried other ways to get the council to listen, but so far . . .'

'And tell me, Penny. Tell the listeners, now – because you're going out *live*, don't forget, Penny – tell the listeners

16

of East Coast Radio, for me, why you think it's fair for your group, the Panbridge Park Peace Protesters, to take away the right of ordinary, decent, working people, trying to earn an honest buck, just trying to exercise their right, as citizens, as taxpayers, to get to their place of work on time in a peaceful and law-abiding manner . . . '

'I will! I will tell you, if you'll let me get a word in!'

Well, it was either that, or get up and thump him. He smiled again and gave me a thumbs-up. It was obviously what he wanted. Maybe the listeners were expecting a fight.

'We're not doing this to stop anyone getting to work. We're not trying to upset people, or take away their rights. We just want to publicise our cause. We want people to stop, and look at what we're saying, and then drive on and hopefully think about it.'

'But people *are* going to be late for work, Penny, aren't they. And deliveries are going to be held up, and children are going to be late for school. And maybe – and I don't want to suggest, ladies and gentlemen, that the Peaceful Protest for Panbridge Park Group has overlooked health and safety issues – but has it occurred to you, Penny, that just *maybe* there might be an ambulance somewhere in that traffic jam, with an innocent victim maybe in pain, bleeding, maybe even losing their tragic fight for life because of . . . your little protest? Just a thought.'

'Don't be ridiculous! Of course we'd let ambulances through! The police are going to be there. And if people don't want to be late for work, or school, or whatever, then they can take another route. That's the whole point! That's why we're publicising the protest!'

'Well, Penny, you've certainly given us something to think about today, here on the *Daytime with Darren* show . . . '

'Is that it?'

'Sorry, Penny?'

'I said, is that it? I've prepared six pages of notes. I've

17

spent every evening for a fortnight practising for this interview, and I've even got my husband standing in for you, pretending to be you, asking me serious, sensible questions about road safety issues and why this protest is so important. And after all that, you've hardly let me say a word!'

'Ladies and gentlemen – Penny Peacham of the Panbridge Park Peace ...'

'Peace for Panbridge Park Pressure Group!' I snapped.

'Penny Peacham has been with us this afternoon in the studio, talking about her group's concerns about the traffic in Panbridge Park, and the *peaceful* protest planned for next Monday morning. If you've got any questions for Penny ...'

I froze. Questions? Questions from real people out there on the other side of the radio waves? I didn't know about this! I wasn't prepared for it!

' ... call us after *this* by Dido.'

Darren Barlow sat back and took off his earphones as one of Dido's records began to play.

'Well done, Penny. You were excellent,' he said coolly.

'What! I haven't said anything ... you wouldn't let me!'

'Always better not to say too much. Just a few snippets, then let the listeners come back with their questions. They always like to listen to a bit of banter between me and my guests. Makes them laugh, gets them interested.'

'And I didn't know there would be people phoning in! What am I going to say? I haven't prepared for this!' I wailed.

Dido was drawing to a close. I could feel a hot lump of panic rising up in my chest. What if no one phoned in? What if they *did* phone in?

'Ladies and gentlemen,' Darren was saying as the final notes of the record were fading out, 'that was Dido with 'White Flag'. Now, for those of you who've just joined us, I have with me in the *Daytime with Darren* studio today. Mrs Penny Peacham of the Pressure for Peace in Panbridge Park group, who's ready to answer your questions about

18

their protest next Monday – holding up the rush-hour traffic – maybe holding *you* up as you try to make your way to work on Monday morning, maybe holding up your bus, as you wait in the rain at the bus stop – do *you* think that's right? John, from Duffington, on line one – what have you got to say to Penny about her peaceful protest, John?'

'First of all,' said a surprisingly loud and confident voice – must have been a regular caller – 'I'd like to say to Penny: Well done, Penny, for standing up to old Darren. He needs to be kept in check from time to time – ha, ha!'

'Well, thank you, John, ha, ha!' joined in Darren.

'Thanks,' I echoed faintly.

'And also,' went on John, 'I'd like to say I agree with Penny about the roads when we were younger. It used to be a pleasure walking along the road, or going for a bike ride with a pack of sandwiches in my saddle bag, not a care in the world, no bloody great lorries coming up behind, no traffic jams and—'

'Yes, but as we've said, John, times have changed, we live in a world where speed of transport, speed of communication, are what count, so we have to— '

'We still need to think about *people*, though, Darren, don't we. Children growing up in an environment of concrete jungles, never seeing a blade of grass or hearing birds sing . . .'

'Thank you, John. Who's on line two? Carol? Carol, from Great Ridsbury, what's your question for Penny Peacham, please?'

Not that I seemed to be needed here. I might as well have packed up and gone home. This seemed to be a Darren Barlow fan club phone-in programme. The guest appeared to be irrelevant.

'Hello, Darren. Yes, I've got a question for Penny. Penny, how come you've managed to stay married for thirty-two years?'

There was a startled silence in the studio during which Darren and I blinked our surprise at each other. Then he

19

started to laugh and was just about to say something, probably something sarcastic, to Carol from Great Ridsbury, when I thought: No! I'm not letting him get away with this! He invited people to phone in with questions for me – for *me* – and I'm bloody well going to answer them.

'Well, Carol,' I said, sitting up straight and talking very firmly into the microphone, 'Although this hasn't really got anything to do with the Peace for Panbridge Park Pressure Group, I *will* answer your question. I've managed to stay married because my husband loves my bread pudding!'

I don't know what made me say it. It was just on my mind, I suppose, because of how it had put Archie in a better mood the day before. But obviously, it was meant to be a joke. Darren realised it was a joke. He went into one of his guffaws.

'Ha, ha, ha! Bread pudding, eh! Would you say your bread pudding has some very *special* ingredients, then, Penny?'

'Oh, definitely.' And can we get back to the subject of the bypass, now, please?

'What kind of ingredients, Penny?' asked Carol from Great Ridsbury, sounding a bit breathless. 'Can you tell me the recipe?'

'Oh, no, I'm afraid not. It's a family secret, handed down through the generations.' I was talking crap, but I just wanted to shut her up and get on with what I'd come here for. 'But if you've got a question about the protest next Monday . . . ?'

'Well, we've got Jane on line three now, from Hopfield village,' said Darren quickly, cutting Carol off before she could ask any more questions about bread pudding. 'Jane, you're calling to tell us about how much better life in Hopfield is since the bypass was built there . . . how many years ago, now, Jane?'

'Three years ago, Darren. And I was part of the Bypass Hopfield! Committee, at the time. But what I really want to know now is: how long has Penny been making her bread pudding?'

'What!' I couldn't believe this. What was the matter with people? I tried to ignore her. 'I think the way the Bypass Hopfield! Group fought for their bypass was marvellous, actually. We'd already asked the county council about a Panbridge Park bypass, and we were watching your campaign with a lot of interest. And then . . .'

'But did you start making the bread pudding as soon as you got married, Penny? Or only . . . you know, once the romance started to wear off?'

'Come on, Jane, I think we all know the romance wears off sooner or later, in any marriage, don't we,' said Darren, who'd obviously decided if you couldn't beat them it was better to join them and forget about bypasses. 'Bread pudding or no bread pudding.'

'But you *are* happily married, Penny?' persisted Jane from Hopfield village. 'After thirty-two years?'

I thought for a minute before I answered. I'd have liked to say, in all honesty, that Archie and I rubbed along OK together most of the time. That we had our ups and downs. That sometimes we had huge, flaming rows and sometimes we didn't talk to each other for days on end. That he drove me round the bend with his dirty shoes on the lounge carpet and his wet bath towel dropped on the bed, with his tendency to shout at me when I was driving, and his rustling of the newspaper to show he was in a bad mood. That I hated the way he whistled through his teeth, and the way he slurped his tea, and belched in public. That we hardly ever had sex any more, and when we did, I pretended he was George Clooney or one of the young vets from my work. But I couldn't, could I? I was on live radio, with everyone listening to me. My daughter, my son, all my friends from the PPPP. And they'd have the radio on at the vets'. And all our neighbours would be listening; all the little old ladies who thought Archie was wonderful when he fixed their leaky taps and pruned their roses, all the elderly men whose ceilings he painted, and let them think they were helping by holding the step ladders so that they could

21

keep their pride. And Archie would be listening himself too. It wasn't right that he should find out from a local radio phone-in show that his wife fantasised about other men and wanted to murder him when he slurped his tea.

'Yes, I'm *very* happily married, of course,' I said, trying to avoid looking at Darren, who seemed to be staring at me as if he knew exactly what I'd been thinking. 'But as you know, I'm really here to discuss the protest next week about Panbridge Park and the traffic ...'

'And on line four, Penny, we've got Stanley from Duffington, who wants to know if you'd like to make *him* some bread pudding ...'

'And coming through now on line one, Margaret of East Pearling, says she could get the recipe published in the East Pearling parish magazine for you ...'

'And Hazel from Birmingham, on holiday here in the East Coast area – Hazel's phoned in to say she's going to try making bread pudding for her husband when she gets back from holiday to see if it revives their sex life ...'

'And now we've got Graham, on line five – Graham, you say your marriage has recently broken up – sorry to hear about that, Graham – and you think if your wife had made you bread pudding every night you might still be happy together, is that right, Graham?'

And I sat back, and shook my head, and folded up my notes about the traffic on the Panbridge Road and the peaceful protest about the need for a bypass, and I looked at my watch. In less than half an hour, I'd somehow managed to turn a serious debate about road safety into a fiasco of calls for marriage guidance and pudding recipes.

As far as local radio was concerned, I was a dismal failure.

Michelle

My brother Adam opened the door when I got to Mum and Dad's place.

'Hi, Chelle,' he said, standing in the doorway and looking behind me down the road. 'Where's Robbie?'

'I don't know. I couldn't find him. Why?' I tried to get past him into the house, but he was still staring over my shoulders as if he was expecting Robbie to jump up out of the hedge.

'I thought you said he'd got the day off. I thought you said he was coming?'

'Yes, but he disappeared, in Duffington, so I had to ...'

'Disappeared?'

Jessica came hurtling down the hallway, pushed herself between Adam's legs and threw herself at my knees, making me stagger backwards.

'Chelly! Chelly!'

I suppose it doesn't really matter, but I think he could have taught her to say 'Auntie Michelle'. I was dead excited about being an auntie, and I *am* her godmother too, and I think it would have been nice to be called Auntie, but maybe I'm just being old-fashioned, as my mum would say.

'Come see my picture! Come see ...'

She was pulling at my legs, trying to drag me into the house, but Adam was still in the way.

'What do you mean, he disappeared?'

'Never mind that now. Come on, get inside. Mum's going to be on the radio in a minute.'

'I know. But I thought, if I left Jessica here with you, me and Robbie could go down the pub for a little while.'

Sometimes, men – even my brother – really make me sick. In fact, he's one of the worst, in a lot of ways. I don't know who he takes after because my dad's not like that. He never used to piss off down the pub all the time when we were little, and leave Mum to look after us, or dump us with other people. Not that Dad hasn't got his faults. The way he talks to Mum sometimes, if I was her I'd want to smack him one. I think she's got used to it. She doesn't seem to take any notice. All she ever says is: *Leave him be, Chelle*, even when he shouts at her for stupid things like taking the wrong turning off the motorway. I'd never put up with being shouted at like that, but I suppose when you've been married as long as my mum and dad, you just put up with anything.

'Adam,' I said, 'you are *not* going down the pub today. We're here to listen to Mum on her radio show, and you need to keep Jessica quiet so that everybody can hear it. Are we going in, or are we standing on the step all day?'

I saw him mouthing 'Bossy cow' to himself as he turned to go back down the hall, but I pretended not to notice. No point having a row, today of all days, I thought to myself, although what with losing Robbie, and now Adam showing off, I'd had just about enough, I can tell you.

In the living room there were four other people from the pressure group, who I recognised from some of their meetings, but I didn't really know them properly to talk to. Sitting in the armchair next to the radio, with her hand on the volume switch and obviously in charge of controls, was Mum's best friend Maureen. And that's a funny thing. I didn't get called 'Auntie' by my three-year-old niece, but up until only a few years back, I'd still called Maureen 'Auntie Maureen', even though she wasn't my auntie at all. In fact my only real auntie was my mum's sister Shirley who lived in Germany, so I didn't often get much of a chance to call her anything. It was really difficult and embarrassing to stop calling Maureen 'Auntie', and sometimes I still thought she might turn round and tell me off for not saying it.

'Hello, Maureen,' I said. 'I'm not too late, am I? Only we were having lunch at the Mare in Duffington and Robbie went missing . . . '

'Ssh!' said Maureen. 'It's just about to start. Where's Robbie?'

'I was just saying: we were in the pub, and when I came out of the Ladies . . . '

'Ssh!'

'Be quiet, Michelle, when your Auntie Maureen tells you,' said my dad, who was sitting at the table reading the paper.

Honestly! He still talked to me as if I was ten years old, sometimes! I reckoned there were still a couple of minutes left, so I went out to the kitchen and made myself a cup of tea. Otherwise I'd probably have thumped him.

When the radio presenter introduced my mum, everyone in the room kind of gasped, and we all grinned at each other, and so many people went 'Ssh!' at Jessica, even though she was just sitting on the floor scribbling with her crayons quietly, that she screwed up her face and started to cry, and Adam had to take her out to the kitchen and get her a biscuit.

'Stupid man!' muttered Maureen as Darren Barlow kept interrupting Mum, and the four PPPP people started shifting in their seats and looking uncomfortable, probably feeling sorry for Mum and wondering if she was ever going to get a chance to talk about the bypass. But I knew my mum, and I could tell she was getting mad, and any minute now she was going to snap, and bloody good for her, too. That twat Darren Barlow needed someone to have a go at him and make *him* feel silly, for once. So when Mum came out with all this stuff about how she'd written all those pages of notes and practised her interview with Dad and everything, Maureen and Adam and the others were all closing their eyes or holding their heads and looking pained and embarrassed, but I wasn't.

'Bloody right, too!' I said out loud. '*Bloody* right!'

'Ssh!' went everybody at once.

But I caught my dad's eye and, for once, I could see he agreed with me.

During the Dido record, we all started arguing amongst ourselves.

'She should have been more forceful,' said one of the blokes from the pressure group. His name was Roger, he was about seventy-five and kind of thin and wispy-looking, and I doubted whether he'd ever been forceful about anything in his life. 'She should have just kept on saying what she wanted to say about the bypass, and not let him interrupt her.'

'That's very easy for you to say!' snapped Maureen. 'Maybe you should have volunteered to do the interview!'

'I wish *I'd* volunteered, now,' said this very posh woman called Elizabeth (never shortened to Liz). 'But I thought poor Penny should be given a chance.'

'You could get on the phone now, if you want to give her a chance,' I suggested crossly. 'Go on, phone up the radio station and ask her a question!'

It all went very quiet then. Funny, that.

I won't even try to describe to you what it was like when the whole bread pudding thing started. Most of us were kind of stunned into silence. Adam took Jessica out to get her a drink of orange, but I think it was just an excuse really because he couldn't bear to listen any more. My dad retreated behind his newspaper again.

'Well,' I said, when it was all over and a Coldplay record was on, 'shall I make us all another cup of tea?'

'It's nice that she said all that about being happily married, though,' I said to Adam while I was waiting for the kettle to boil.

'Not exactly appropriate, though, was it. Not exactly what she went on the radio to talk about.'

'No, but it was Darren Barlow's fault. He got her all flustered.'

'Fucking idiot.'

'Ssh!' I nodded towards Jessica, sitting at the kitchen table with her orange juice. 'Adam, if you keep swearing in front of her she's going to come out with something at nursery, and they'll stop her going.'

'Save me some money, wouldn't it!' He grinned.

Yeah. And who'd look after her on the days she normally went to nursery, I wonder?

I was expecting Robbie to be at home when I got back. I was expecting him to have got a bus home, and to have a go at me about taking the car. What else was I supposed to do, I was going to say, with my mum being on the radio and everything? And anyway where did you bugger off to, without even eating your chicken roll?

But he wasn't there. I wandered around the flat, not sure whether to be worried or annoyed. He'd probably gone out on the piss with some of his stupid mates and he'd be too drunk to get home. He'd more than likely stay at one of their places and turn up the next morning, feeling like shit, and serve him right.

I put the TV on to keep me company, and went into the kitchen to see what I could cook myself for tea. And that was when I remembered. I'd left the bloody washing at the launderette. I had to turn everything off again, and drive back to Duffington to pick it up, otherwise I wouldn't have had any clean knickers for the next day. And the washing machine still wasn't working. And it was all Robbie's fault.

The next day, when he still didn't come home, I reported him missing, but the police didn't really want to know.

They said that with adults, unless they were mentally disturbed, it was usually assumed that they'd disappeared because they wanted to.

'Why would he want to?' I said, but this policeman just sort of coughed and changed the subject. I don't think he knew the answer.

On Monday night, when I got in from work and he still hadn't come back, I phoned Kim and Nicole and they came round with a bottle of wine.

'What are you going to do?' said Kim.

'I don't know. I suppose now the landlord's back from his holidays I'd better phone him to get someone round. Otherwise I'll have to keep using the launderette.'

'Not about the washing machine, Michelle. For God's sake! About Robbie!'

I shrugged.

'What else *can* I do? I've told the police, and they're not really interested.'

'When our cat went missing,' said Nicole, 'my mum put an advert in the local paper. And she phoned the RSPCA.'

'Did that work? Did she get the cat back?'

'No.'

'What are you two on about?' said Kim. 'Robbie's not a fucking cat! You can't phone the RSPCA and tell them your boyfriend's gone AWOL!'

'I was just *saying* ...'

'I think I'll just leave it, for now,' I said, pouring myself another glass of wine. 'I expect he'll turn up.'

'But what if he doesn't?' said Nicole gloomily. 'What if you never see him again?'

We all stared at each other. I sipped my wine and thought about this. What if he never *did* come back? What if he'd disappeared forever?

'Well,' I said eventually, 'I suppose one thing about it is that we could go to Club Rouge on a Friday night again. Couldn't we?'

*

I was working as a health care assistant at Duffington General Hospital. I was ever so proud of my uniform. I worked in the outpatient clinics, changing people's dressings, cleaning up their wounds and all that. The nurses told me what to do. Most of the patients thought I was a nurse, anyway.

'Thank you, Nurse,' they used to say, and I didn't bother to put them right. It's easier to say than 'Thank you, Health Care Assistant,' isn't it. Not that I was pretending to be a nurse, but sometimes I used to daydream about it. I'd have quite liked to be one, but I didn't get enough GCSEs.

I liked talking to the patients. Some of the elderly people were really funny, they enjoyed telling me their whole life stories and they never got impatient and stroppy like some of the younger ones when they were kept waiting. One or two of the old blokes would flirt with me, too. They were harmless. I didn't mind.

'How's my lovely girl today, then?' said this old Mr Garrety, grinning at me with all his false teeth hanging out.

'Leave her alone, Jack,' said his wife, laughing and giving him a nudge. 'She's spoken for – she's got a nice young man – haven't you, love?'

'Yes,' I said vaguely.

But I was thinking: Well, have I? Or haven't I?

It was a bit of a peculiar situation.

I was round at my mum's on the Wednesday, when the local freebie paper was delivered. My dad picked it up and started reading it while Mum and I were playing with Jessica, with her Lego.

'Bloody hell!' he said, all of a sudden. 'Christ al-bloody-mighty, woman, you're in the bloody paper!'

'What! Let me see!' Mum took the paper from him and I could see her hands were actually shaking as she was reading it. She went bright red. I thought for a minute she was going to cry.

'Show me!' I said.

'Show me! Show me!' squealed Jessica, jumping up and down all over the Lego on the carpet.

'No, Jessica. Nanny's reading it, and I'm reading it afterwards. Now look what you've done! You've knocked all Nanny's castle down!'

'Don't want a castle!' She stamped on the Lego.

Mum folded the paper up, really roughly, and passed it over to me without saying a word.

'What?' I said. 'Is it about the interview? Is it that bad?'

'Read it!' she said, and she went out to the kitchen.

I looked at my dad.

'It's all about the bloody bread pudding,' he said.

'You're joking. Jessica, stop showing off or Nanny won't do you sausages for tea. You know what she said.'

'Be a good girl, Jessica,' said Dad. 'And Nanny might make you some bread pudding!'

'Dad! It's not funny!' I couldn't believe he was laughing about it. 'Mum's very upset about this. She wanted them to do an article about the protest on Monday, not about ... bloody hell.'

I'd opened the paper, and there was a picture of my mum with this great big headline: PENNY'S RECIPE FOR A HAPPY MARRIAGE. I skimmed through the article quickly.

Mother-of-two Penny Peacham, 52, of Panbridge Crescent, Panbridge Park, intrigued listeners to the *Daytime with Darren* show on East Coast Radio on Friday. Happily married to husband Archie, 56, a retired car salesman, for 32 years, she revealed that the secret of their successful relationship was a special recipe for bread pudding, handed down through the generations of Penny's family. 'It has some very special ingredients,' said Penny, a receptionist at Tail Waggers Veterinary Practice in Panbridge Road South. 'My husband simply loves it!' Penny refused to divulge the secret ingredients to which she attributes their happiness. However, our own cookery editor

Moira Sweetlove says: 'The all-important thing with bread pudding is the combination of fruits and spices. I'd guess that Penny probably uses nutmeg in her pudding, which creates calmness and a sense of well-being, and raisins, which are a very high-energy food. A perfect combination for a healthy and active sex life well into old age!'

'Hey!' I said, as Mum came back into the room and started picking up Jessica's Lego. 'What's all this about an active sex life? You didn't say that on the radio!'

'And what's that about old age!' said Dad. 'Who are they calling bleeding old?'

Mum was very red in the face.

'I wish I'd never mentioned it,' she said. Her voice was quite shaky. She was really upset. 'It was only meant to be a joke. If he hadn't made me so cross ... if that woman hadn't phoned up and asked such a stupid question ... '

'Don't worry, Mum.' I went over and gave her a hug. 'Dad – stop laughing. It's not funny. Mum wanted publicity for her protest group.'

'I didn't *want* publicity at all,' she said. 'And now I've got my photo all over the local paper, thanks to Roger thinking he's so clever.'

Roger, apparently, was the group's press officer. He'd told Mum it would be a good idea if he sent her photo to the paper and told them there was going to be a radio interview.

'And not a word about the protest!' she said miserably, throwing bits of Lego into the box. Jessica watched her, her thumb in her mouth.

'Want to play with my Lego,' she mumbled through her thumb, but Mum didn't take any notice.

'Yes, there is,' said Dad. 'There's a little bit at the end of the article, look. After Moira Whatsername's bit about the nutmeg and stuff.' He picked up the paper again and read it out loud:

'"Penny Peacham will be taking part in a protest meeting on Monday (3 November) at Panbridge Road, near the junction with Sutton Avenue, to publicise the need for a bypass for Panbridge Park."'

'It's almost like an afterthought!' I said indignantly. 'Like it doesn't even matter!'

'Well, in the scheme of things,' said Dad, folding up the paper again, 'I don't think it's half as important as your mum's bread pudding, Chelle.'

Robbie still hadn't reappeared by Friday night when Kim and Nicole called for me to go to the club.

'Do you miss the sex?' said Kim, staring around our flat like she was expecting it to look different without Robbie there. Well, to be honest, it did. There were no dirty cups on the coffee table, no old newspapers lying on the floor, no biscuit crumbs, no shoes in the middle of the bedroom floor. No mess.

'Give over. He's only been gone a week!'

'Yeah, but – you must have got used to having it regularly, living with someone for – what – two years?'

'Eighteen months. We didn't move in together till we'd been going out for six months. I didn't want to rush into anything.'

'OK, eighteen months. Eighteen months of regular shagging, and then, suddenly – nothing.'

'Join the club,' said Nicole gloomily. Nicole didn't often seem to get a boyfriend. I couldn't understand why. She was pretty, and she wore some lovely clothes. Robbie used to say she was OK till she opened her mouth, but that was just him being mean. He always thought it was funny to be mean about my mates.

'Anyway, we weren't shagging *all* the time, were we!' I said. 'We'd got past that stage.'

'Maybe that's why he's gone,' said Kim.

'Shut up!'

32

'Yeah, shut up, Kim – that's not very nice,' said Nicole. She put her arm round me. 'Don't worry, Chelle. He'll come back.'

But I wasn't worried, not really. And I quite liked having the bed to myself, to be perfectly honest.

We got chatted up by some blokes in the club. There were two of them. One of them was quite good-looking and I had a dance with him. His name was Kevin and he said he fancied me, but I didn't snog him because I kept thinking: Have I got a boyfriend or haven't I?

'What's the matter?' he said. 'Don't you fancy me?'

'You're all right,' I said. 'But I'm kind of with someone.'

'Kind of? What, you're not sure?'

'Well, we kind of live together, but ... '

'Fuck that, then,' said Kevin. 'I'm not getting into that. I did that once before, and this bird's bloke gave me a black eye. Sorry, love.'

Like I cared.

He snogged Nicole instead, 'cos his mate had already got off with Kim. I was pleased for Nicole. But I felt a bit left out, really, and I thought – fuck it, next time, I'll keep quiet about Robbie.

It was his own fault, after all. I didn't *ask* him to disappear. But I was already kind of getting used to it.

Penny

I was worried about my Michelle. All this business with Robbie disappearing – it was very unsettling.

'She doesn't seem that bothered, Pen, if you ask me,' said Archie.

Isn't that just like a man? Any fool could see that Michelle was putting on a brave front. She's like that. She takes after me, in that respect – she doesn't ever like to make a fuss, bless her, whereas Adam – well, like father like son, is all I can say. If either of them gets so much as a sniffle, you'd think they were dying. Anyway, I said to Archie:

'So how do you think *I* would feel if *you* suddenly disappeared? D'you think I'd not be bothered?'

'That's different,' he said, shaking his paper grumpily. 'We're married.'

'Yes,' I said.

He looked up with a frown at the way I said it, but I just ignored him and went on with the ironing.

The protest meeting was that Monday morning, at eight o'clock. I normally started at the vet's at half past eight, so I'd asked for the day off, and worked on the Saturday instead.

'What is it you're up to on Monday, Penny?' asked one of the vets as he was leaving after his clinic. His name was

Chris Filbey, he was only about thirty-five – not very many years older than Adam – and slim, dark, and very good-looking, and I was quite shocked by how much I fancied him. Sometimes it was really difficult to sit there and talk to him about a cat's pregnancy, or a guinea pig's bowel movements, just for instance, without going off into a fantasy in my mind about being on my own in his consulting room with him and getting frisky over the examination table. I know it might not have been practical, what with dog hairs and the smell of urine, but in my fantasies nothing like that ever came into it.

'I'm ... er ... taking part in a demonstration, actually, Chris,' I told him, watching him shrug himself into his jacket and wondering whether he realised how sexy he was.

'A demonstration!' He paused and gave me a quizzical look. 'What? A cookery demonstration?'

I felt myself blush bright scarlet.

'Oh, no! You haven't read that awful thing in the paper?'

'Of course I have!' he laughed. 'I thought it was a very good picture of you, actually, Penny.'

If it was possible to blush even redder than bright scarlet, I was now doing it.

'It was terrible! And I did *not* say all that stuff, on the radio! All that about bread pudding ingredients ...'

'What, the stuff about the active sex life?' He was grinning at me now, a wicked teasing grin, obviously knowing how embarrassed I was. 'Oh, I thought that was the best bit.'

I flapped around with some papers on the desk, pretending to be suddenly terribly, terribly busy, and wishing the phone would ring and some annoying client, like Mrs Murphy with the incontinent Pekinese, would demand to speak to him so that he had to stop grinning at me like that. 'Yes, well, it was *supposed* to be a serious interview, and a serious article in the paper, about this protest demonstration we're doing on Monday morning. But I got kind of sidetracked by the stupid radio presenter, and the stupid

35

people who called in ... '

'Never mind,' he said. 'It's probably done you a favour. More people will have read that article than a serious one about the protest. They'll probably all turn up tomorrow to gawp at the lady who makes the sexual healing pudding.'

'Very funny!' I muttered, still looking at the papers on my desk.

'Good luck, anyway,' he said as he went out. 'See you on Tuesday.'

I looked back up just in time to get a sneaky last glance at his backside as he went out. Nice.

'D'you think it's normal, having thoughts like that about a vet?' I asked Maureen when we met to go shopping in Duffington after I finished work

'Why not? What's different about vets? Don't they do normal sex, with women, like other blokes? Do they prefer horses or something?'

'No! Listen! I mean – he's my boss. And I'm old enough to be his mother.'

'So?'

'Well, it's not very *comfortable*, getting hot and bothered over someone when you've got enough trouble already with the hot flushes.'

'Still, life would be very boring without getting hot and bothered occasionally, wouldn't it, Pen. Make the most of it. A few more years and we probably won't even notice if we go home and find George Clooney posing nude in our kitchens. We'll be past caring.'

She stopped, and looked at me sideways, giving me a quick smile. 'Unless, of course, we keep eating your bread pudding to keep our sex lives good and active ...'

I tried to hit her with my handbag but she ducked. Cow! Still, I must admit I did laugh to myself. I suppose I was beginning to see the funny side of it. A bit.

It was absolutely pissing it down with rain on the Monday

morning. I have to say, I could think of dozens of things I'd rather have been doing, than going out and standing in the middle of Panbridge Road holding a banner saying, BYPASS PANBRIDGE NOW! and getting soaking wet into the bargain.

'You want your bleeding head examined,' said Archie encouragingly as he went off to put a new toilet seat on for Mrs Wrenn at number sixty-three.

'I know,' I said crossly.

I wasn't just cross about the rain. I was cross because Adam had asked me to have Jessica. He knew I wasn't at work, and it wasn't one of her days at the nursery, so he just brought her round and expected me to have her.

'But I'm doing the demonstration today!' I said.

'I know. That's OK. You can take her with you, can't you?'

'But Adam! It's not really the kind of thing ...'

'Come on, Mum!' He looked at his watch, wanting to get off to work. Jessica was already in the lounge, watching the TV. 'Only I can't have any more time off work, and the childminder's still got the flu.'

'She's always got the bloody flu. You want to get someone more reliable. Or get her into the nursery five days a week.'

'It's a nightmare trying to get childminders. And I can't, Mum – I can't make her go to the nursery any more than she does already. You know how she screams when she has to go.'

Yes, and I know how easy it is to say, all right, Jessica, you don't have to go today, I'll ask Nanny to have you instead.

But she was my granddaughter, at the end of the day. What was I supposed to do?

'Put her wellies on her, Pen,' said Archie before he slammed the door behind him. 'Or she'll get her socks soaking wet in the puddles. It's terrible out here.'

Thanks for nothing.

*

37

I dressed Jessica up in her raincoat and wellies and strapped her into her buggy. She was yelling her head off.

'Not the buggy! Not a baby! Big girl now!'

'I know you're not a baby, Jessica, but you've got to sit in the buggy today. There's not going to be anywhere to park the car.'

'Want to get out! Want to walk! Want to go home! Want a biscuit! Want to watch the telly! Want my daddy!'

Then she gave up yelling, as I wasn't taking any notice, and started crying instead – a loud, despairing, gasping, sobbing cry as if her whole world was coming to an end. I pushed her past the newsagent's, past the queue at the bus stop, where everyone turned and stared at me as if I was a child molester at the very least, and round the corner into the main road where the lorries that I'd committed my spare time to complaining about thundered past us, splashing my legs and Jessica's buggy with nasty black oily water out of the gutters, and sprayed a fine coating of smelly residue over my umbrella and raincoat that dripped off my fringe with the rain.

'Sorry, Jessica,' I told her without very much feeling. 'Sorry, darling, but I really don't have a lot of choice. It's not much fun for you, I know, but it's fuck-all fun for me, either.'

I said that last bit under my breath because I didn't want her picking up obscenities from me. Bad enough the language my son used, without me making matters worse.

'OK,' said Elizabeth Baxter-Simpson, who was Chairman of the PPPP since we'd had our AGM a couple of weeks before and Reg Cartwright had stood down on account of his varicose veins. 'OK, Penny – if *you* stand on this side of the road, facing the oncoming traffic ...'

She was having to shout because the noise of the rain, coming down like stair-rods and bouncing up off the road again, was drowning out all attempts at normal conversation. That, and the noise Jessica was making.

'Sit here,' I told her, parking the buggy on the pavement, well away from the kerb. 'And don't move.'

'I'll mind her, dear,' said an elderly man with a walking frame who just seemed to be hanging around for the fun of it. Didn't these old folk have anything better to do at half past eight on a rainy Monday morning? I couldn't understand why they were out. I was bloody sure that, when I retired, I was going to stay in bed every morning until at least half past nine, and probably later if the weather was like this. What was there to get up for?

'Well ... er ... that's very nice of you,' I said cautiously. Should I leave her, yelling and trying to undo the straps on the buggy, with someone who might or might not be a pervert but certainly didn't look as if he'd be able to bend down to help her if she injured herself, and might well come off worse than her in a fight? 'But I don't know whether I really should.'

And then, thank God, round the corner, orange umbrella blowing inside-out in the wind, high-heeled brown suede boots splashing dirty black rainwater right up as far as her red tartan miniskirt, came my Michelle.

'Chelly!' shouted Jessica, stopping her bawling with a surprised hiccup.

'Hiya, Mum! Hiya, Jessi-baby!' called Michelle, running to join us. 'What's up with you, little one? I could hear you all the way from the shops!'

'She's got the hump 'cos she couldn't stay in and watch the telly,' I said. 'And 'cos I made her sit in the buggy. How come you're not at work, Chelle?'

'Thought I'd come and watch the fun. I don't have to be at work till half past nine and if I'm a bit late I'll just say it was your fault, holding up the buses!'

It was nice to see her, though. She brightened everything up, like it suddenly didn't matter about the rain. Even Jessica was bouncing about in the buggy, smiling again.

'It's OK, thank you,' I told the potential pervert with the walking frame. 'My daughter's here now,' and, picking up one end of the banner, with Dodgy Roger holding the other end, I stepped out into the road in front of a Tesco delivery truck and made my little bit of history for Panbridge Park.

'Well, hello! It's Mrs Many-P's, I do believe!'

The demonstration had gone well. We'd made the 14B bus thirty-seven minutes late, caused twenty-one cars and a milk float to do three-point turns and head back in the opposite direction and, most effectively, made several large trucks, a petrol tanker and a car-transporter queue for over half an hour with their windscreen wipers going and their drivers sighing and leaning out of their cabs watching us with resentful eyes while the police patrolled at a discreet distance in case of any trouble.

'May I be permitted to speak to you, Mrs Many-P's, now that you're such a celebrity?'

It was Stupid Darren Barlow, with a dripping wet baseball cap covering his bald head and a brown leather bomber jacket covering whatever infantile T-shirt he'd chosen from his wardrobe today. From what I could see at the neck, it was purple.

'What are you doing here?' I asked him, ignoring his sarcasm. Tell you the truth, I only just about managed not to tell him to piss off.

'Why, Mrs Many-P's, I've come to do a live broadcast for East Coast Radio about your protest demonstration, of course,' he replied, smirking.

'Oh! Oh, well. I see.' There was a yellow and blue East Coast Radio van parked half-up on the pavement, just out of our banner-waving range. 'Well, the chairperson of our group is Mrs Baxter-Simpson, over there in the green raincoat – maybe you should ... Elizabeth! Elizabeth – they want to do a broadcast for the radio.'

'I don't want to talk to Elizabeth,' said Darren. 'I want to talk to *you*, Penny Peacham. It's *you* everyone's been phoning in about – ever since your interview the other week

40

'– and especially since that bit in the paper.'

'That,' I said, trying desperately to attract Elizabeth's attention, 'was a *ridiculous* story in the paper. I think I should sue them for ... for defamation of character!'

'I think they actually did a really good PR job for you. And the photo wasn't bad, either. Did you get it touched up?'

'What!' I gave up waving at Elizabeth, who was chatting earnestly to a guy from the county council who'd come along as a goodwill gesture, and turned back crossly to give Darren Barlow a piece of my mind – only to see that he was laughing.

'I'm only joking, Penny,' he said. 'It really *was* a good photo. And while we're at it, I think I probably ought to apologise for the hard time I gave you on the show. I should have warned you that's the kind of thing my listeners like. It gets them all indignant, and then they phone in – usually to tell me what a bastard I am. You actually did very well.'

'Oh!'

I was so surprised by his change of tone, I didn't really know what else to say. But he wasn't listening to me, anyway. He was listening to his earpiece, and as he listened he reached out a hand to touch my arm, and raised an eyebrow at me, and mouthed silently at me: 'Five ... four ... three ... two ... one ...'

'Yes, ladies and gentlemen, Darren Barlow here, and I'm here at Panbridge Road, Panbridge Park, where as most of you know, the Peaceful Protest for Panbridge People have been holding their demonstration today about the need for a bypass. And here with me, on a very miserable, rainy morning in Panbridge Park, ladies and gentlemen, is Penny Peacham, looking – if I may say so, Penny! – every bit as lovely as she does in her photograph in the *Duffington Echo*. Penny, how's the protest been, this morning? Would you say it's been worthwhile? Or has the weather been a bit of a downer?'

41

He thrust the microphone up to my chin and nodded at me. Bugger it. I'd had no time whatsoever to prepare this time and, knowing Darren, he'd probably do his utmost to embarrass me. But how was I supposed to get out of it now that he'd announced my name to the whole world?

'Um ... yes, it's definitely been worthwhile,' I stumbled. 'If anything, the rain's made it even more effective. More people using their cars, you see; so more of a traffic jam than there would have been otherwise.'

'I see. And tell me, Penny, how did people react to being stopped, on their journey to work, by a group of – well, they *could* be forgiven for thinking you were a group of *nutcases*! – standing in the middle of the road waving banners at them? Were there any problems with that? Did anybody get nasty?'

'Not at all. In fact, we found people were quite support-ive. Most people driving through Panbridge Park find it a difficult part of their journey; it's congested with parked cars and delivery vans, they get stuck behind buses at bus stops and they've got the traffic lights and school crossing patrols to contend with. They all support the idea of a bypass. They'd get to work – or wherever they're going – much more quickly!'

'So you think people were happy to be late for work today, so that you could make your point, and hopefully get the plans for the bypass approved by the county council?'

'I don't say they were *happy* to be delayed. But they understood the reason. We handed out our leaflets explain-ing our group's aims ...'

'Yes – ladies and gentlemen, I have one of the Panbridge Peace Protesters' leaflets here, and—'

'Actually, Darren, it's the Peace for Panbridge Park Pressure Group. You keep getting that wrong, don't you!'

He raised both eyebrows up to the brim of his baseball cap, grinned at me in surprise and paused for a moment before going on:

'Yes, as Penny's just pointed out, it's actually the *Peace for Panbridge Park Pressure Group* – thank you for correcting me there, Penny! – and I've got one of their leaflets in my hand, which does in fact tell you all about the group, and their aims, and how long they've been actively pressurising the county council for the bypass to be approved. Can East Coast Radio listeners get copies of these leaflets, Penny? Yes, Penny's assuring me she's got plenty of the leaflets, so if you'd like to know a bit more about *where* the bypass would go – which of course is very important, isn't it, if you live in the area – or indeed, if you're one of the people who've had their journey to work disrupted this morning, ladies and gentlemen, and you're listening to your radio in your car now, or your lorry, or whatever, and you're trying to make up time now and wondering what on earth all that was about – send for one of these leaflets – they're called *Panbridge Park Bypass: the Facts.*'

He paused again, glanced at his watch, then turned to me with a truly horrible smile and added, 'Well, that's all from the protest demonstration here at Panbridge Road, but of course I can't finish without saying a quick word to Penny about her famous bread pudding, can I!'

The bastard. I'd been feeling good about it up till then. I was thinking how much better it'd gone than the *Daytime with Darren* show. He'd actually given me a chance to say my bit. I'd stopped feeling nervous, and remembered all the important things I wanted to say. But he just couldn't resist it. I shook my head at him. *No! No!* I mouthed. But he wasn't having any of it.

'We've been *inundated* with callers phoning in to ask about your pudding, Penny! And is it true what we've all been reading in the paper? About the *special* properties of some of the ingredients?'

'I really don't think I want to answer that ... '

'Well, ladies and gentlemen, it seems like Penny Peacham's keeping her pudding recipe a closely guarded secret. But I *can* tell you that, for thirty-odd years of marriage, she's looking remarkably good on it! Thank you, Penny – and back to the studio!'

Darren gave me another one of his wicked grins.

'Well done, Penny. That was great. You're a natural!'

'It was *not* supposed to be about the bloody pudding! Why did you have to ... '

'Penny, Penny! They *love* to hear about your pudding! I've had people phoning from Liverpool, from London, even from Scotland, about your pudding! And at the end of the day, it *all helps* to publicise your bypass!'

'Do you think so?' I said uncertainly.

I still wasn't sure whether he was taking the piss. I'd have said a bit more, only just then I caught sight of Michelle, on the other side of the road, talking to someone at the bus stop.

'Michelle!' I yelled. She turned and weaved her way through the traffic towards me. Don't hurry yourself, love. 'Where's Jessica?'

'I left her with some old guy with a walking thingy. He was singing her nursery rhymes. She's OK.'

'Oh, Chelle, you said you'd look after her ... '

'I did! He's all right, he's at least ninety-five, he's not going to run off with her. Mum, I've got to get the bus to work now, all right? Well done, it was great, wasn't it!' She leaned over and gave me a kiss on the cheek. 'I'll come round later, OK?'

'OK,' I said, vaguely, scanning the thinning crowd for a ninety-five-year-old singing nursery rhymes. 'Thanks for coming.' I turned to Darren Barlow. 'I've got to go now. I need to find Jessica. She's only three. I shouldn't have brought her.'

'Your daughter?'

'No, my granddaughter.' Idiot. As if I'd have a three-year-old, at my age!

'I meant *her*, actually,' he laughed, following Michelle with his eyes as she darted back across the road, her short skirt waving gaily around her thighs. She was beautiful.

Her long blonde hair swung behind her, shining through the rain. Any man would look at her. Any man would fancy her, wouldn't he. My hackles went up protectively.

'Yes, she's my daughter, and she's spoken for,' I told him tartly.

'Thank you,' he said, still watching her. 'So am I.'

Jessica was watching her newly appointed childminder with eyes like saucers as he leaned on his walking frame and sang: 'Three Blind Mice! See how they run!' in a voice so unexpectedly high and warbly, I felt my own eyes growing round with shock too.

'Thank you,' I told him. 'Come on, Jessica – time to go home.'

'Don't want to go! Want more songs!' she cried.

He grinned a gummy grin at me.

'Don't know any more, missus. Only that one.'

Thank the Lord for that.

'Can *he* come home too?' asked Jessica in a shy little voice, pointing at her new friend.

'Not today, darling. Let's go back now and I'll make you some hot chocolate, shall I?'

Not that I'm bribing you or anything. But I want to get away from here *now*.

It wasn't just because of the Ancient Mariner. I didn't want to face anyone else, either. I was so embarrassed by the whole thing about the pudding being heard on the radio, I didn't want to go back to Elizabeth Baxter-Simpson's house, with everyone else from the group, for the planned debriefing meeting and buffet lunch. I'd made my excuses about having to look after Jessica. For once, I wasn't sorry that Adam had chosen to leave her with me today. The others could find out about the pudding broadcast all in their own good time. They certainly wouldn't hear about it from me.

45

Michelle

I was late in to work on the day of my mum's bypass demonstration.

'Sorry,' I said to Sister as I ran to dump my coat and bag in the staff room. 'The traffic was terrible, because—'

'I know,' she said a bit snappily. 'Most of the staff and half the patients have had the same problem. Some bloody protest group holding up the traffic. In the rush hour – I ask you! No consideration for other people. Take Mrs Green to X-ray, will you, and then there are two patients waiting to have their dressings taken down. But maybe you'd better phone Haematology first for Mr Swan's blood tests results. And when you've done that, the doctors will be wanting their coffees.'

Thoughts of sticking a broom up my arse to sweep the floor at the same time did cross my mind, but to be fair I enjoyed my work, I enjoyed being busy and being needed by lots of people to do lots of different things. My friends who worked in offices used to ask me how I stood it, what with the blood and everything, and patients moaning at you sometimes about being kept waiting. But I told them: the thing was that it was never boring, I never looked at the clock wondering how soon I could go home – and I met all kinds of people. Sister was all right really, she just got stressed and ratty when the clinics were running late. And most of the patients were lovely; it was only a few who got

46

arsey, and I never argued with them, I just thought to myself: Let them have their moan. One day, when they have a heart attack because of their bloody bad tempers, they're going to really need the NHS and they'll be grateful to people like me then.

But best of all, I got to meet the doctors. Before I started going out with Robbie, I was seeing this medical student called Craig. He was younger than me but he was absolutely gorgeous. When I went to Purple Cloud with him, all the other girls' eyes were out on stalks. But he was only at our hospital for six weeks and he never phoned me after he moved on. Mum said let that be a warning to me, that doctors were notorious and I shouldn't trust them. And she might have been right, but he wasn't even a proper doctor, was he. He was only practising.

Some of the real doctors were ever so nice. Not the consultants – I was a bit wary of them. They sometimes used words I didn't understand, probably thinking I was a proper trained nurse, and I had to say, Sorry, what are you talking about? And then they'd sigh and repeat it in normal English. But I was beginning to learn stuff, like for instance when I first started, I wouldn't have understood what Haematology was. You see? It was a learning curve, as my mum would say.

No, it was the junior doctors I liked. They'd have a laugh with me, and say, 'What are you doing tonight, Michelle?' and wink at me, and some of them used to tell me dirty jokes or talk to me about their girlfriends. I think they thought they could trust me, kind of thing.

'Late this morning, Michelle?' teased Dr Willoughby as I went into his consulting room with some blood results. He was a registrar, specialising in Medicine for the Elderly, and I loved the way he talked to the old people, never talking down to them, even if they were completely senile and hadn't got a clue what it was all about.

'Yeah. Got held up in the protest demonstration in Panbridge Park,' I said.

47

'Oh, yes. Sister was having a rant about that, earlier.'
He grinned.

'Well, I didn't want to say anything to Sister,' I
confided, 'but actually my mum was taking part in it.'

'Was she? Well, good for your mum! A right little rebel,
then, is she?'

'I wouldn't say *that*. She wants the traffic to get bypassed
out of Panbridge Park, that's all. She's even been on the
radio about it,' I added, as he was looking so interested and
impressed, '*and* in the *Echo*!'

'Really! Blimey! A famous mother, eh!' He smiled at me
again. 'How does that make you feel?'

'Me?'

I stopped dead, staring at him, thinking about this. How
did it make *me* feel? I hadn't even given it any thought up
till now.

'Proud, I suppose.' I nodded. 'Yes, I'm proud of her for
doing it, especially the radio show, 'cos that was a bit
nerve-racking, and Darren Barlow was a bastard to her. But
it's embarrassing about the bread pudding.'

'Bread pudding?'

'I'll tell you another time. I've got two dressings to take
down.'

I hadn't told anyone at work about Robbie disappearing.
But that lunchtime, I was sitting with some of the nurses in
the canteen and they were talking about the Christmas
party. Which was ridiculous, really, because it was only the
third of November, and the party wasn't until the twelfth of
December, but if you ask me, some people don't seem to
do anything much with their lives from one Christmas party
to the next. As soon as the posters go up in the hospital
announcing the date, they start talking about what dress
they're going to wear and when they're having their hair
done. By the week before the party they're practically
wetting themselves with excitement. Then, on the night,
they get completely off their heads, snog everything in

sight, and spend the whole of January trying to find out what they said that was embarrassing, and where they left their shoes. Anyway, as I say, this was only the beginning of November but already it was starting. As if it wasn't bad enough with all the Christmas cards and presents in the shops already.

'Are you bringing your boyfriend, Michelle?' said Julie, one of the staff nurses.

'Who?' I wasn't really listening. I'd been watching Dr Willoughby and a couple of other registrars, coming into the canteen, and talking very seriously to each other while they lined up for their dinners, and thinking how nice it must be to have serious things to discuss like the life or death of your patients, instead of sitting with this lot talking about whether to wear red dresses or black trousers.

'Your boyfriend! Robbie!' She was laughing. 'Have you forgotten who he is?'

'Well, yes, kind of,' I said. 'As he's been gone for nearly two weeks, I'm beginning to wonder.'

There was a shocked silence. Then Julie said, putting her hand on my arm and looking very upset, 'God, Michelle, I'm so sorry. I didn't know. You didn't say ...'

'Have you split up, then, Michelle?' asked one of the others. 'Was it mutual, or what?'

'Are you OK, love?'

'Don't worry. You're better off on your own – isn't she, girls? They're all bastards, in the end ...'

'I'm never living with anyone again, me. It never works out. Just shag 'em and shove 'em, I say ...'

'Don't take him back, love, however hard he begs. Get yourself a cat instead.'

I let this go on for a while, everyone putting in their two pennies'-worth on the subject, while I got on with my lunch and watched Dr Willoughby and his friends sitting down at the table opposite and carrying on their serious conversation over their lasagnes.

'So what was it – another woman?' asked Julie eventu-

49

ally, when everyone had finished with the all-men-are-bastards bit.

'No. He didn't exactly leave. I just kind of lost him.'

'Lost him?' They'd all stopped eating now and were staring at me. Well, I suppose it does sound a bit careless. 'Lost him where?'

'In the Grey Mare. While we were waiting for our chicken rolls.' I shrugged. 'I looked everywhere, but I couldn't find him. And I had to go round my mum's, so I needed the car.' I shrugged again 'I told the police, but they didn't really want to know.'

'And he hasn't even phoned, or anything?' demanded Julie.

I shook my head.

'What about his mobile?'

'Switched off.'

'What about all his stuff? His clothes, and things? Hasn't he been back for them?'

'No. Not even his DVD player. And I'd have thought if he was going to leave, that'd be the thing he'd definitely come back for. That and the car.'

'So what will you do?' asked one of the older nurses gently. Her name was Claire and she reminded me of my mum. 'What will you do if he doesn't come back?'

'I'll move back in with my mum and dad, I suppose,' I said a bit gloomily. I'd been putting off deciding about it, really. I liked the flat, but I couldn't pay the rent on my own for very long. It was OK before when I lived with Mum and Dad, except for when my dad started throwing his weight around, talking to me like I was still a kid. That's when we used to argue a lot; to be honest, it was great moving in with Robbie for that reason. I'd left home once before, when I was only nineteen, and I moved into a flat with Kim. We were best friends at school, but living with her wasn't so easy. She wanted to go out drinking every night and never did any washing up. And when the rent was due, she was broke. So it didn't last very long.

But when Robbie and I moved in together, it was different, because for one thing we were both twenty-four by then and obviously much more sensible, and for another thing, of course, we were in love, so things like washing up didn't exactly come into it.

'Do you have no idea at all where he's gone?' asked Claire, in that same gentle voice that made me feel like crying. 'Has he not got a mother or a sister, or even a cousin somewhere, that you could ask?'

Claire was Irish, you see. I think they have a stronger idea of the extended family. The truth was that Robbie had left his home in Liverpool when he was sixteen and moved down south, and as far as I knew he never had any contact with anyone in his family. It was really sad, if you ask me. I used to get upset about it, thinking if we ever got married, what were we going to do about the wedding photos? It would be all lopsided, with all my lot on one side and no one on his. That kind of thing can really unbalance a wedding. And then, if we had kids, there would be no grandparents on his side, no aunts and uncles, no godparents. I just had this feeling it wasn't exactly fair. But I didn't used to talk to him about it, because it pissed him off.

'There isn't anyone,' I told Claire sadly. 'I've phoned some of his mates. They haven't seen him, either. Muggs is upset because Robbie hasn't paid his Lottery.'

'Muggs?' she queried faintly. The other girls had gone back to talking about the party, fortunately, so we had a moment to ourselves.

'His best mates are Muggs, Farty, Johnson and Killer. I've phoned all of them, but they're all even more pissed off with him than I am. Killer was saying something about a loan for the car. But I don't really know what he's going on about. Robbie bought the car from my mate Kim's dad. I lent him the money. So it's got nothing to do with Killer, has it?'

'Did you get the money back?' asked Claire quietly.

51

'Money? What money?'

'The money you lent him for the car, child.'

Claire says that sometimes – 'child'. She says it to all of us, as if she was our mum. Actually I don't mind it, really.

'No. He's kind of paying me back monthly. But he can only afford it if he gets the overtime.'

'And does he normally get the overtime?'

'He hasn't done recently. Not since we moved in together. It's been a bit hard for him, one way or another.'

She nodded slowly.

'I see.'

'What?'

'And tell me, child. What are his other friends *pissed off* with him about?'

'Oh, I don't know. The Lottery, and something about his football season ticket. Boy things!' I laughed.

'Hm,' said Claire. 'And tell me: have you spoken to his bosses at his job? What do they make of him disappearing like this, do you think?'

'They're not very pleased, either,' I admitted. 'They're going on about him being paid sick. But that's a load of crap too, because he hasn't been off sick. Well, at least, not until the last day – the day he ... went.'

'And he's been at work every day up till then, has he, so?'

'Of course! Every day, regular as clockwork, we got up at half past seven, and I got the breakfast while he was having his shower, and we'd leave the flat at the same time, and when I got home, bless him, he was already in, so he had the potatoes peeled all ready for dinner, and the kettle on. Not many men would do that. My dad wouldn't, I can tell you! My mum was very impressed. "Michelle", she said, "You've got a good one there. You want to hang on to him."'

It was a bit embarrassing really, but before I could stop myself I was blubbing into my soup. The thing was, up till then I hadn't really cried much about Robbie going. I'd kept telling myself he was just being an arsehole and he'd be back any day now. But Claire was giving me this look. It was a very *kind* look, but I didn't like it. It was telling me things I didn't want to hear.

'He's gone, hasn't he,' I blubbed, giving up on the soup and putting my spoon down on the table in a messy splodge of orange. 'He's run away. He's not coming back.'

'I think you knew that really, didn't you, bless your heart.' Claire put her arm around my shoulders and made a gesture at the other girls – who'd stopped their debate about black evening sandals versus suede cowboy boots and were gawping at me with undisguised curiosity – implying that they should look the other way and pretend they hadn't noticed anything. 'He's got his problems, child, and he's taken himself away and done you a favour, so he has. Thank God for small mercies.'

Thank God? I couldn't even remember which God I was supposed to believe in. Mum used to take Adam and me to Sunday school when we were little, so it wasn't like I was completely atheist or anything like that. I just hadn't kept up with it. You know how it goes, when you get older, you forget all the hymns and what the special days are for. Whitsun, for instance, and Pancake Day. But I thought maybe I'd have a go at remembering the Lord's Prayer that evening, and see if it did any good. Crying obviously wasn't going to bring Robbie back.

'Hello,' said a voice behind my shoulder as we were going back to work. 'Good lunch?'

It was that nice Dr Willoughby.

'Oh! Yes, thanks. How about you?' I hesitated, wondering if it was the right thing to say, but he was smiling encouragingly and nodding yes, yes, very nice lasagne, thank you very much, so I added, 'It must be nice to sit and talk to the other doctors about important things at lunchtime.'

He laughed out loud. Not a horrible laugh that made me

feel stupid, but a nice, friendly laugh, and he put his hand on my shoulder as if we were great mates, and whispered to me:

'Actually, don't tell anyone, but we were talking about your mum and her bread pudding!'

'Oh!' How embarrassing. 'And there was me thinking you were probably making life or death decisions about patients' drugs and operations and stuff ...'

'Sorry!' He looked a bit sheepish. 'Dr Ahmed happened to mention the traffic hold-up this morning, so I said I knew what it was all about because you'd told me about your mum. And then Peter – that's Dr Turner – said he'd been listening to the car radio, on the way in, and heard someone being interviewed and bread pudding being mentioned ...'

'How embarrassing!' I said out loud, feeling myself blush on my mum's behalf. She didn't tell me she'd been interviewed again. So that must have been that stupid Darren Barlow she was talking to – the one with the ridiculous baseball cap.

We were walking along the corridor together now, and I noticed some of the other girls turning their heads and staring.

'I'd better catch the others up, or I'll be late for the clinic,' I said, suddenly feeling very awkward.

'OK. But don't forget to let me know the full story on the bread pudding some time.'

'OK.'

'And – Michelle?' he called after me as I walked away. 'We do sometimes talk about life and death stuff as well!'

I shouldn't have been smiling to myself, really, when Robbie had gone missing and I'd been crying into my soup over him only ten minutes ago. But like I said, crying wasn't going to help, was it? And I felt much happier smiling, really, at the end of the day.

Mum got a bit flustered when I asked her about the interview.

54

'I didn't know he was going to turn up today – that Darren Barlow – never mind getting me doing another live interview.'

'You never said anything! I only found out 'cos one of the doctors at work heard it!'

'I just wanted to bring Jessica home and try to forget about it, to be quite honest. It was embarrassing.'

'It wasn't,' said my dad, very surprisingly, looking up from his paper. 'It was good. It was better than the other one. Although he still managed to get a bit in about the pudding!'

'Yes! Stupid man!' said Mum crossly. 'I don't know what Elizabeth and the others from the group are going to say when they find out.'

'They'll be pleased with the publicity,' he said. 'I mean, if even people like doctors at Michelle's hospital are listening, it can't be bad, can it?'

'That's what Chris Filbey at my work said,' admitted Mum.

I thought she looked a bit funny when she mentioned this Chris Filbey. Kind of even more flustered, a bit pink-looking. My dad didn't notice, of course.

'There you go, then,' I said. 'Vets *and* doctors. Mum's getting famous, isn't she, Dad?'

'She certainly is,' he said.

And the funny thing was, he didn't sound too pissed off about it, either.

Penny

Michelle came straight out with it, as soon as I opened the door to her.

'Mum,' she said, 'I think I need to move back home. If you and Dad don't mind.'

'Mind?' I said. 'Don't be bloody ridiculous, girl. This is your home. You know that. There'll always be room for you here. What's up? Still no word from Robbie?'

I knew there wasn't, of course. She'd have told me if there was. She'd have been straight on the phone, all excited, instead of turning up here on the doorstep looking like the world was coming to an end.

'No – nothing. And it's been nearly two weeks, hasn't it, and to be quite honest, Mum, I don't think he's going to come back.'

'Oh, come on, love! You don't know that.' I gave her a hug and signalled to Archie to put the kettle on. 'No news is good news, they say.'

'I don't think so,' she sniffed. 'I think no news means he's fucked off ...'

'Michelle!' said Archie, raising his eyebrows at her.

'Sorry, Dad. But if someone had fucked off and left *you* in the lurch, with the rent to pay, and owing you money for the car, *you'd* feel like fucking swearing, wouldn't you.'

He went on filling up the kettle without any further comment. But fair enough. I felt like fucking swearing

56

myself, and it wasn't even me that had been left with ...

'What do you mean, money owing for the car?'

'I used the money out of my savings account to pay Kim's dad for the car. Robbie was paying me back. *Supposed* to be. A bit at a time.'

'Oh, Chelle!' I said. 'You never!'

I couldn't believe it. We'd always told her not to touch the money in her savings account. We'd been putting it away for her since she was a baby. We did the same thing for Adam, and he used the money to set up home with Julia. Waste of money *that* turned out to be, too!

'Well, the answer to that is easy,' said Archie, dropping tea bags into the mugs. 'The car belongs to Michelle. Until such time as he comes back and pays her what he owes her.'

'It's not as simple as that, Archie. There are such things as the registration document, and ... '

'It's registered in my name. But he's got the key. I've only got the spare,' pointed out Michelle. 'He could just come back one day when I'm at work and drive off with it.'

'Drive it to work, then, instead of using the bloody bus! Get as much use out of it as you can, if that bastard doesn't — '

'Archie!'

'It's all right, Mum. Dad's right. I think he *is* a bastard, to just go off like that without telling me why. It's not as if we'd had an argument or anything. He even left me to pay for the chicken rolls.'

'I'm sure there's an explanation, love,' I told her. I didn't like seeing her upset. And to be honest, I couldn't make head nor tail of it. Robbie had always seemed such a nice young man, not at all the type to just up and leave in the middle of a pub lunch.

'Well, I've tried to think of one, but I can't. And I won't be able to pay the rent, and there are two nurses at work who want to take over the flat, so I'm going to let them have it. Can I move my stuff back into my bedroom at the weekend?'

It was a crying shame. She'd been so happy when she moved into that flat. Like a little mother hen feathering her nest, she was. And I'd used her bedroom for my fuchsias, so they'd all have to be moved before the weekend.

There was a strange kind of silence in the vets' when I arrived at work the next morning. It was that kind of silence you get when everyone's been talking, and the person they're talking about suddenly walks in.

'What?' I said.

Chris Filbey, and the other vet, Glenn, were standing at the reception desk with Debbie the nurse, looking over her shoulder at something. Debbie stood up, looking embarrassed, but Chris and Glenn were both grinning at me.

'Morning, Penny!' said Chris. 'Have you seen the paper?'

'Oh, not that again! I thought you'd all seen it already . . .'

'No, not the *Echo*,' said Glenn. 'The *Sun*! Didn't you know? You're in this morning's *Sun*!'

They didn't find it quite so funny when I came over so faint with shock, I had to sit down and have a sniff of the stuff they use to bring dogs round after an anaesthetic.

Well, it was the ridiculous headline, quite apart from anything else. Quite apart from the shock of it even *being* in the national paper in the first place. I mean, you'd have thought they'd have asked me first, wouldn't you? Glenn said no, they just look for good stories in local papers – and they'd obviously phoned up Elizabeth Baxter-Simpson to get the full facts about the protest demonstration, because there was a little bit about that, and even a photo of us all standing there in the rain holding our banners. I didn't remember it being taken, but it wasn't a very good one, although you could just see Jessica's pushchair at the edge

58

of the picture. And you'd think the headline would have been about the bypass, wouldn't you? Wrong. Staring at me from the middle of page twenty-four was:

BREAD PUDDING – THE KEY TO A SUCCESSFUL MARRIAGE?

I grabbed the newspaper and folded it roughly, pushing it out of sight under the reception desk.

'Aren't you going to read the article?' teased Chris. 'It's very good ...'

'No, I'm not. I'm going to get on with my work.'

'We thought you might have brought us in a bit of your bread pudding, Penny,' said Glenn.

'Stop it, you two,' said Debbie. She was quite nice really, in spite of the purple hair and the eyebrow rings. 'Don't be upset, Penny. It's really good publicity for the bypass, isn't it.'

'Yes, at my expense,' I muttered.

'Well, I think it's very clever of you,' said Debbie stoutly, 'being able to make things like bread pudding. We never have puddings in our house. I can't even make custard. It always goes lumpy, even if I buy the one in the can and heat it up.'

'How can it?' began Chris, but it was a mistake to ask.

'Oh, you can shut up, too. You're just like my Phil. I've told him – unless you want to cook the bloody dinners, just eat your baked beans and—'

'But they come in a tin, too. Don't they go lumpy?'

'Always bloody criticising!' she sighed. 'Honestly, Penny, I think you must be a saint, making puddings as well as everything else.'

I didn't feel like a saint. Not in the least, unless saints get pissed off and feel like wringing everyone's neck. And it was going to get worse.

By the end of the day, I was beginning to dread the phone ringing or clients walking through the door.

'Oh, hello Penny!' it went. 'Have you seen that bit about

your pudding in the *Sun* this morning?'

Never a mention of the protest, or the bypass. Just the pudding, the bloody pudding, over and over again. I was beginning to be sick of the subject. Everyone seemed to be so obsessed with my pudding, they were forgetting what they'd phoned up for. I kept having to remind them – was there something wrong with their rabbit or their cat? People came in with their dog on a lead, started yakking to me about the pudding, and next thing you knew, the dog was crapping on the waiting room floor or trying to mount Mrs Murphy's incontinent Pekinese, and they hadn't even noticed. It was leading to a complete breakdown of discipline in the surgery. One woman even turned up for her appointment about her guinea pig's constipation without bringing the guinea pig with her. Debbie was a bit sarcastic to her, asking her how she thought the vet was going to treat him when he was still in his cage at home, but she just laughed and said she'd been so excited about seeing the 'local media star' she'd completely forgotten him.

'Why don't you give him a bit of bread pudding,' I said, rather sourly I must admit. 'It's turning *my* stomach, just talking about it.'

'Oh! Do you really think that'll work?' she squealed.

You just can't help some people, can you.

'How does it feel being the local media star, then?' asked Chris Filbey when we were both walking out to our cars to go home.

'I'm so sorry,' I said, fumbling with my car key and not wanting to look at him. 'I had absolutely no idea this was happening. I know it was very disruptive today, but I expect all the fuss will die down tomorrow ...'

'Don't be silly. I've quite enjoyed it!' I could hear the laughter in his voice. I sneaked a quick glance at him and he flashed me a grin. 'It's brightened up the day, having everyone talking about your culinary skills. Makes a change from the weather, or the TV, or the cost of pet insurance ...'

'It's all just really silly ...'

'Why?' He slid gracefully into the driving seat of his MG, pausing for a moment to look me up and down before adding, 'I think you should be quite proud of your new reputation, Mrs Passion Pud!' – with which he slammed the car door shut and roared off.

I didn't read the article until I got home.

'This is *so* embarrassing,' I complained to Archie when he came back from giving old Mr Stokes' ceiling a second coat of emulsion. 'Look at it! They're calling me *Mrs Passion Pud*! I ask you! I wouldn't mind if they'd even asked me if I wanted to be in the *Sun*!'

'Oh!' He kicked off his shoes and looked at me a bit shamefacedly. 'Well, actually, I meant to tell you. Someone did phone, the other day, when you were at work. They wanted your work number, but I didn't think you'd want me to give it to them. They said they'd try again later, but perhaps they couldn't wait.'

'Someone called from the *Sun*? And you didn't even think to tell me?!'

'Sorry. Jessica was here, wanting her tea, and then Michelle came round, and you know how it goes ...'

'No, Archie, I don't, not really. It's not exactly what you might call a normal phone call, is it? I'd have thought you might have remembered it at some point, about a national newspaper wanting to write an article about your wife! Going on about bread pudding as if it was some sort of ... some sort of ...'

'Aphrodisiac.'

'What?'

'Aphrodisiac. That's what you call it, when a food has ... well, has ...' He was grinning from ear to ear. 'Certain *sexual* properties.'

'Archie Peacham! Have you taken leave of your senses?

What on earth are you going on about – sexual properties? You're as bad as ... as bad as ... ' The memory of Chris Filbey's mischievous grin came uncomfortably to mind. 'As bad as everyone else,' I finished lamely.

'No. Everyone else is different,' he said, still grinning. '*They're* all wondering what's in the bread pudding, Pen. I *know* what's in it!'

'Yes, you stupid great dollop!' I exploded. 'You know what's in it – bread, and eggs, and fruit, and spices. Nothing whatsoever with sexual connotations – unless you count the bread being squeezed, and the eggs being beaten!'

'Phwoargh!' he said, pretending to shudder with excitement.

I couldn't believe this. Archie, my husband of over thirty years, who for the last ten or twelve of them had shown about as much interest in sex as he had in coal mining, was suddenly and inexplicably turned on by the thought of the pudding he'd been eating regularly nearly every week. And all because of a bit of publicity! How pathetic was that?

'You're off your head,' I told him calmly, starting to peel potatoes for dinner.

But it was funny. We had sex that night, for the first time for ages, and it wasn't bad. But I kept thinking he was looking at me kind of differently. Like being in the paper had changed me somehow. Or maybe the bread pudding really did have something in it – something that even I didn't know about.

'What are you doing?' asked Maureen on the Friday afternoon when she came round to find me up to my ears in fuchsia plants and cuttings.

'What does it look like? I've got to get all of these out of Michelle's room before she moves back in, tomorrow. I was going to overwinter them in here because it's nice and warm, what with the airing cupboard. But they'll have to go in Adam's room.' I lifted a couple more pots and started carrying them across the landing. 'You can help if you like. Or at least put the kettle on.'

'Adam's just pulled up outside, with Jessica in the car,' she told me, picking up a tray of cuttings from the windowsill. She paused, watching out of the window. 'He's got a lot of her stuff with him. Buggy, coat, bags, toys ... and Jessica's running around like a mad thing, waving her arms in the air. She's got ... '

I came back into the room and joined Maureen at the window. She glanced at me and finished cautiously:

'She's got Red Bed-Ted with her.'

Maureen knew what this meant as well as I did. Red Bed-Ted was an ancient teddy bear, so ancient that he'd been relegated to bedtime use only, as even Jessica understood that he was too delicate to withstand regular daytime throwing around. He used to be Adam's favourite teddy bear. He was threadbare, eyeless, had had more restoration of amputated limbs than was good for anyone of his age, and leaked stuffing like an unpleasant old man dribbling bodily fluids. The presence of Red Bed-Ted meant only one thing. Jessica intended to stay the night.

'So where do we put the fuchsias now?' asked Maureen helpfully.

'I can't leave plants in Michelle's room,' I told Adam firmly. 'It isn't fair. She's allergic.'

'Not to fuchsias, she isn't, surely? You've always had bloody fuchsias in the house, Mum, and I don't remember Chelle having a problem before. It was only daffodils.'

'It's *all* flowers, Adam. Some worse than others. You never did take any notice. Your own sister!'

'Well. She wants to get herself some tablets from the doctor's, if she's that bad.'

'Tablets! She *takes* bloody tablets! Antihistamines! She has to use a puffer when she gets really bad. You've got no consideration ... '

'Hang on, hang on! How is this suddenly my fault, that

63

Michelle's allergic to bloody fuchsias? Did I ask you to grow bloody fuchsias?'

'It's your mum's hobby, Adam,' pointed out Maureen, depositing a cup of tea on the table in front of him. 'You can't deny your mum her hobby. One day, you'll understand. When you get older, there isn't much else left in life, and hobbies suddenly become more important ...'

'Hey! What's all this about getting older?' I turned on her. 'What's all this about not much left in life!'

'Yeah – Mum does *so* have other things in her life – don't you, Mum?' put in Adam, smirking as he lifted his cup to his lips.

There was a silence in the room. Silence, apart from Jessica counting out the toys from her bag – 'One, two, five, *tenty*!' and counting them back in again – 'One, tree, four, *six*!'

'What's *that* supposed to mean?' I asked my son quite pleasantly.

'Well, you know.' He put down the cup and tried, unsuccessfully, to wipe the smirk off his face. 'You know, Mum. Like it said in the *Sun*. "According to Penny Peacham, from Panbridge Park, near Duffington in Suffolk, who's known locally as 'Mrs Passion Pudding', the special ingredients in her bread pudding are the secret of her long and happy marriage to husband Archie."'

'Yes, well. Stupid newspaper, stupid story!' I snapped.

'Be fair, Mum,' said Adam, still grinning. 'It goes on to say how you took part in the protest ...'

'Yes, almost like an afterthought. Like: "Here's a picture of Penny – who just happens to be waving a banner in the middle of the road but don't worry about that – the real news is about this pudding ..."'

'It's just a gentle bit of journalistic humour,' said Maureen, finding the page in the paper and smiling at it.

'I wouldn't mind if people took it as humour. But you know what happens. Stupid men like ... like Adam, and Archie ... read it and think there's some truth in it!'

64

'Stoopid men!' shouted Jessica, 'Stoopid men!'

'Yes, darling,' agreed Maureen. 'Absolutely right.'

Adam was going away for the weekend. He was a bit cagey about where.

'It's not on, really, is it, Mum?' said Michelle. 'I mean, he's probably on a promise with some bird ...'

'You don't know that! You've got no reason to think—'

'Oh, come off it. What – do you think he's gone off on a weekend break with one of those coach tour companies? Autumn in the Cotswolds, or whatever? Get real, Mum. He's met some woman, and it's more important to him to get his leg over than to be at home with Jessica. It's not fair, just expecting you to have her.'

'I don't mind, really,' I said honestly. 'It wouldn't be a problem if it wasn't for the fuchsias. Only, I can't let her sleep in the same room as the fuchsias. I don't think it's healthy for one thing, and for another thing, if she gets out of bed like she does sometimes, she'll probably break all the stems. You can't blame her. She hasn't exactly been brought up with fuchsias.'

'Don't worry about it,' said Michelle. 'I'll sleep on the sofa.'

'Are you sure, love? It's only for the weekend.'

'Yes, it's fine. Honestly, Mum, don't fuss. Only I'd better take all my stuff upstairs, out of the way, before Dad comes in and starts moaning.'

'He's not moaning so much, lately,' I said thoughtfully. 'He's even been singing a bit, around the place, and doing the washing up without me asking him.'

'Blimey! Is he feeling all right?'

'Gandad sing to me!' said Jessica. 'Gandad sing like the funny man!'

'Let's not push our luck, Jessica,' muttered Michelle.

That's right. Let's not. Because I wasn't going to tell anyone, but what Archie had taken to singing around the house was 'I'm in the Mood for Love'. And he'd taken to kissing me suddenly in the middle of *EastEnders*, too, which was very unnerving, trust me. It was a good job Michelle was coming home to live, really, otherwise next thing I knew he'd be wanting sex on the sofa again, like we used to do sometimes before the children were born. And that was a long time and several sofas ago. I wasn't sure I was up for it these days, to be quite honest. I'd have to consider my back very carefully first, for one thing, because I'd read something recently in a magazine (a true story) about a woman who injured her back very badly having sex in an unusual position (she didn't specify which position, but possibly it could have been on a sofa – though I'm not sure if that's unusual enough these days) – and she ended up in a wheelchair.

Really, at the end of the day, I don't know whether it would be worth it, do you?

Michelle

'What's it like being back with your old folk?' asked Nicole when we were on the bus into town on the Saturday night.

I shrugged and stared out of the window.

'Dunno, really. Only moved back in last night, and I've got to sleep on the sofa at the minute 'cos my little niece is in my room. And Mum's got her fuchsias in the other room.'

'Oh!' giggled Kim. 'Do you think they're trying to tell you something, Chelle?'

'No!' I snapped. 'Fuck off! It's cool!'

'Yeah, fuck off, Kim,' said Nicole. 'Chelle's mum probably likes having her back, doesn't she, Chelle? Someone to talk to. That's what my mum says. She says if I left home, she'd have no one to talk to. My brothers have their headphones on the whole time. And there's no point talking to my dad.'

Up till now, I'd have agreed with her. There's never been any point talking to my dad, either, what with the sport on TV and his nose in the paper all the time. But it's funny, there's something different going on at home now. I can't explain it really, but it's just like Dad seems to be listening to my mum more, and looking at her a bit differently. And the night before, after Jessica had gone to bed, I went into the lounge and they were sitting on the sofa together, and I got this feeling I'd interrupted something.

Like they'd been ... well, I know it sounds ridiculous, when you think how old they are and how long they've been married and everything ... but like they'd been having a snog or something and they'd quickly jumped apart when I came in. I sat down on the other sofa and didn't know where to look, I was so embarrassed, and we all just kind of pretended to be terribly interested in what was on telly after that.

So I was feeling a bit awkward now, and wondering whether I'd done the right thing coming home to live.

'It's all stupid Robbie's stupid fault,' I grumbled. 'If it wasn't for him, buggering off like that, I'd still be in my nice flat.'

'Never mind, Chelle,' soothed Nicole, putting her arm through mine. 'Forget about him. You've still got us – hasn't she, Kim?'

'Yeah, and we're going to have a good time tonight, aren't we? Eh? Forget about Robbie Nelson, yeah, Michelle?'

Yeah. Why not.

I had three Bacardi Breezers within the first half-hour we were in Purple Cloud. We'd already had a bottle of white wine between us while we were doing our make-up round at Kim's place. I wouldn't put it quite so strongly as to say that I was on a mission, but yes, I'd made up my mind that tonight was going to be the night I moved on. No point waiting around for someone to come back when you didn't even know where they'd gone, or why.

We were on the dance floor early that night. We were all in the mood for a good boogie, and I'd already got my eye on someone I fancied. He was tall and black and dressed completely in white – white trousers, white T-shirt and white shoes – and he was the most fantastic dancer. All the girls were looking at him, but I kind of thought I might be in with a chance, 'cos a couple of times I caught him smiling at me. I was just concentrating on making my dance moves as sexy and meaningful as I could, and giving him the odd sneaky smile back, when all of a sudden my view of him was blocked out by someone else. Someone standing right in front of me.

'Hello, Michelle,' he said.

'Sorry,' I said, trying frantically to catch sight of my Man in White over this guy's shoulder. 'Do I know you?'

'Darren Barlow. From the radio station. I interviewed your mum. And I saw you at the protest demonstration.'

'Oh. Oh, right. Hi.'

True, he looked completely different. For a start he wasn't wearing the stupid baseball cap, or the bright purple T-shirt that made him look like a character from *Rainbow*. But also, I didn't really want to look at him. I wanted to look at the Man in White, and he was right in my way. I didn't want to be rude, but really, couldn't he just piss off?

'Great dancer, isn't he?' said Darren, closer to my ear than I would have liked.

'What?'

'The guy in the white trousers. Natural talent. I always envy guys like that. Always gets the girls going, a guy that can really dance.'

'Yes.'

Except that I can't see him at the moment, with you standing right in my face like this.

'Excuse me,' I said. 'I think I need another drink.'

'I'll get you one.'

Oh, great. So much for shaking him off.

He followed me to the bar.

'It's OK, honest,' I told him as he started to get his money out. 'I'll buy my own. I'm getting my mates a drink too.'

'No problem. What do you all want?'

Call me shallow. But the drinks in Purple Cloud are very expensive, you know, and if someone offers to buy all three of us a drink, especially when he's only drinking Coke

69

himself – well, I'm not going to refuse, am I?

'Thanks very much,' I said as he brought the drinks over to the edge of the dance floor. I scanned the floor quickly. Shit. No sign of the Man in White.

'So how do you feel about having a famous mother?' asked Darren Barlow.

I sighed. Suppose I had to be polite, what with drinking his Bacardi and all.

'I don't think she'd like to be thought of as *famous*,' I said. 'Mum really was only interested in publicising the bypass, you know.'

'But all the same. Whether she likes it or not, she's a bit of a media star now, isn't she. *Mrs Passion Pud*! Does she make her passion pud very often at home, Michelle?'

Creep.

'She used to make bread pudding all the time. But I think she's gone off it a bit now, with all this fuss.'

'Shame.' He took a mouthful of his Coke and gave me a very direct look. 'Still, maybe you could learn to make it yourself, eh? Keep it in the family?'

'I don't think so. I'm not much of a cook. I mainly just have ice cream for afters.'

Kim and Nicole had joined us while we were having this scintillating conversation and were giving me very funny looks.

'This is Darren Barlow,' I told them. 'He bought us our drinks. He's the radio pre—'

'The radio presenter!' shouted Kim. 'Darren Barlow!'

'Wow! Darren Barlow! *Daytime with Darren* and *Darren on Sunday*!' enthused Nicole.

Darren smiled condescendingly.

'That's right, girls. Maybe I could play a song for you tomorrow?'

'Ooh, yes please!' they both crooned together. And they were so busy and excited going through a possible list of songs he could choose from, and a list of people they wanted mentioned in the request, from their granddads to the kids next door and their second cousins in Australia, that I managed to sneak away without making it too obvious. And found the Man in White on the other side of the dance floor.

'Hi.'

He was leaning against the wall, drink in hand, looking down at me with a lazy smile. Like he'd been expecting me.

'Hello.' Now what? 'I ... er ... I was watching you earlier. Dancing.'

'I know. I was watching you watching me.' He put his beer down, slowly, and nodded towards the dance floor. 'Want to?'

'Sure. Why not?'

'Thanks very much!' exploded Kim when she caught up with me in the Ladies a bit later. 'Leave us with Darren Barlow and go off with ... '

'Luke,' I said dreamily. 'His name's Luke.'

'Go off with some *Luke* ... '

'He's gorgeous. Have you seen him dancing?'

'Yes, we've all seen him dancing, Michelle. Right show-off, isn't he.'

'Well, *I* think he's gorgeous. And he's just gone to get me another drink, then we're going to dance some more. Anyway, I thought you were both dead chuffed about meeting Darren Barlow?'

'Yeah. We were. But we couldn't get rid of him for ages. And all he wanted to talk about was your mum.'

I had a snog with Luke at the end of the evening. It seemed a bit strange at first, kissing someone else instead of Robbie, but then he pulled me really close to him and we were swaying with the music, and I could feel him hard against me, and it was getting me excited and I thought: Sod Robbie. Time to move on.

71

But he didn't ask to take me home, or anything.

We were waiting for a taxi when this car pulled up and the window slid down, and Darren Barlow put his head out of the window and said:

'Want a lift, girls?'

'Come on,' I said to the others. 'Might as well.'

There was a long queue for taxis. We'd have been there all night.

So we piled into his car, and he drove us back to Panbridge Park, talking the whole way about how he was going to play these requests for us in the morning. And he dropped Kim off first, then Nicole, and then it was a bit quiet in the car heading back to my place.

'It's been good to meet you again, Michelle,' he said as we turned into my road.

'Well, thanks for the lift. And the drinks, earlier.'

'My pleasure.' He pulled up outside my house. 'And maybe ... perhaps we could meet again – some time – and you'd let me buy you another drink?'

I was a bit taken aback by this. I mean, all the way home, while I was half listening to them all going on about their favourite bands, I was fantasising to myself about having sex with Luke. Even though he hadn't offered to take me home, or asked to see me again. I reckoned that next time I saw him at Purple Cloud he'd probably ask me to dance again, and I'd make sure next time I was wearing a very short skirt and a tight top. I'd end up getting off with him, if I had anything to do with it. So it was a bit unexpected, to put it mildly, having Darren Barlow suddenly ask me out like that. For one thing, he must have been at least forty. For another thing, he was quite strange. But he was a celebrity, and to be honest I was flattered.

'Or I could take you to a nice restaurant,' he went on. 'Perhaps the new little Italian in Duffington? Would you like that?'

Would I? Oh, would I!

Robbie would never have dreamed in a million years of offering to take me to the new little Italian restaurant in Duffington. His idea of a big night was a Chinese takeaway and a video.

'That'd be lovely,' I said before I'd had time to think about it any more. 'Thank you. Yes, that'd be lovely.'

Eat your heart out, Robbie Nelson.

I didn't tell Mum about Darren Barlow. I nearly did, mind you – I nearly just came out with it over Sunday lunch, just as I was passing the gravy across to my dad, and Mum was cutting Jessica's meat up for her.

'Guess who I met up with last night at the club?' I said.

But then, in the few seconds it took for Mum to put her knife and fork down, pass Jessica's plate back to her and nod to her to pick up her little baby fork and get on with her dinner, I thought to myself: What am I doing? It really, really, is not a good idea to tell Mum about Darren Barlow! And Dad! Dad would so *not* like the idea of me going out with someone of Darren's age, probably nearly twenty years older than me. Not that it was any of their business, you know, but now I was living back at their place I felt kind of awkward about things. Like I was a teenager again.

'Who?' said Mum, smiling at me a bit vaguely, her mind probably still half on Jessica and what she was doing with the potatoes and the gravy on her plate.

'Er ... um ... ' I took a mouthful of my drink. 'Er ... a guy called Luke,' I finished desperately.

'Luke? Luke who? Do we know him?'

'No, but he's ... ' Shit. Why have I started this? 'He's a really, really good dancer.'

'Oh. That's nice, dear,' said Mum. 'Jessica, eat that properly. You're not a baby now!'

'Don't *want* carrots. Don't *like* carrots!'

'Eat them up, Jessica. Make you see in the dark!' said Dad.

Blimey, all the same old things they used to tell me when

73

I was little. I used to eat up all my cabbage because they told me it would make my hair curly, and look at me now. Dead straight. Lucky thing straight hair is back in fashion, really – at least I don't have to eat cabbage any more.

'Don't *want*!' shouted Jessica, pushing her plate away so the gravy slopped all over the tablecloth. She folded her arms across her chest and pouted at Dad. 'Don't *want* dark! Don't like dark!'

'See?' said Dad as if there had already been a conversation about it, 'What she needs is a firm hand.'

Mum sighed and gave him a filthy look.

'Adam does his best,' she shot back, 'Considering.'

'And anyway,' I put in, 'Does it matter if she doesn't like carrots?'

They both looked at me in surprise as if this hadn't occurred to them.

'Don't *like* carrots!' confirmed Jessica mutinously, her lower lip beginning to wobble.

Well, at least it got us off the subject of Luke. Or Darren. Phew.

Adam didn't get back till late. He was whistling as he walked up the front path.

'Wotcha!' he shouted when I opened the door to him. 'All right, Chelle?'

'Ssh! Jessica's asleep!'

'What? I said I'd be back to take her home to bed tonight, didn't I.'

'Yeah, but look at the time. She was getting tired and ratty, so Mum put her in her pyjamas and she's gone to sleep on the sofa. So try not to disturb her, yeah?'

I opened the lounge door and pointed to where Jessica was snuggled up asleep under a duvet on the sofa, Red Bed-Ted tucked under her arm, looking angelic.

'OK!' he whispered. 'Great. Any chance of a coffee, then?'

Mum and Dad, on the other sofa, both looked liked

they'd nodded off, too, watching some 'spectacular costume drama' on BBC. Obviously not so very spectacular.

'Yeah. Come and sit in the kitchen,' I whispered back.

We sat at the kitchen table, mugs of coffee in front of us.

'So.' I looked at him through the steam from my mug. 'Good weekend?'

'Great, thanks.' He didn't meet my eyes. 'You?'

'Me? Oh, it was all right. You know. Went up the Cloud last night with Kim and Nic. Nothing special.'

'D'you pull?' he asked with a grin.

'What?' I felt myself going red. 'Don't be silly. No. Of course not.'

'Still. I don't see why not. What with Robbie buggering off.'

'So what about *you*? You're the one that goes off for mysterious weekends away. Are *you* on the pull, then, Adam?'

''Fraid not, Chelle. Chance would be a fine thing.'

'Yeah, right!'

He just shrugged at this, and picked up his coffee mug. Adam's always been a bit like that. If he doesn't want to tell you something, he won't. He doesn't even seem to find it difficult, like I do. He just shrugs and goes quiet and that's the end of it, no matter how many questions people ask. He'd probably be good as one of those secret agents. You'd never get passwords or codes or anything out of him, not in a million years.

'Well,' I said, giving him a serious look that I hoped would Make Him Think, 'Just as long as you remember who your first priority is, Adam, that's all.'

'Who?' he said.

'Who? Jessica, you total prat. Who do you think?'

'Don't you worry about that,' he retorted, draining his coffee cup and putting it back down on the table with a thump. 'I know what my priorities are, thank you very much, Michelle. I don't need you to remind me.'

You can't win, can you? Now it looked like I'd offended him. But let's face it, it had to be said, didn't it, whether he liked it or not.

A couple of days later, I was taking down a dressing on an elderly man who'd cut off the tip of his finger with an electric saw (bit of a mess, that – he didn't seem to be healing very well), and I was totally engrossed, really, trying not to hurt him, and listening to him telling me all about his life history, how his wife had died of cancer and he liked doing a bit of DIY in his little bungalow when it was too cold to get out in the garden, when all of a sudden there was a tap on the door and that nice Dr Willoughby came into the room and just stood there behind me, watching me, and listening to the patient going on and on about his DIY, until eventually I felt a bit uncomfortable and looked up at him and said:

'Is there anything you wanted, Dr Willoughby?'

'Yes, Michelle. Thank you,' he said. 'The surgeons have asked us to come and have a talk to Mr Partington about his asthma.'

'I'm all over the place with it,' admitted Mr Partington, waving his partly amputated finger at us. 'I was all right till I got brought into hospital after the accident. But now I keep getting short of breath and I wake up in the night coughing and gasping. I haven't forgotten to use my puffers, Doctor!' he added, looking a bit anxiously at Dr Willoughby.

'Sure. We may need to adjust the amount you use your inhalers, Mr Partington. Or possibly give you a short-term course of oral steroids. Probably the stress of all this,' he nodded at the patient's injured hand, 'has made your asthma worse.'

Mr Partington nodded and looked suitably reassured.

'If you like to stay here,' I told him, 'Dr Willoughby can have a chat to you while you're waiting to see the surgeons.'

'Thanks, Michelle,' said Dr Willoughby, walking to the door of the consulting room with me and holding it open for me as if I was someone important. He dropped his voice and added, 'We'll have to run some lung function tests. I just hope it isn't anything more serious than an exacerbation of his asthma.'

Exacerbation was another word I didn't used to know when I first started this job. I felt very proud now, having a doctor talking to me and using words like that instead of *getting worse*, and expecting me to understand.

'I hope so too,' I said, smiling at him. 'He's a nice old man.'

And he looked at me for a minute, with his head on one side, as if he was considering something, and then, very strangely, he suddenly blurted out:

'Are you going to the canteen for lunch?'

'What? Today?' I asked, a bit flustered. 'Well, I expect so. Only it's chicken curry on the menu, and normally we do all like their chicken curry ...'

'Good!' He said. 'I'll see you there. You never did tell me the whole story about your mum and the bread pudding.'

'Oh! All right. See you later, then.'

How bizarre was that? I never would have thought he'd have remembered it.

Generally, in the hospital canteen, visitors sat at tables on their own, keeping their worries to themselves, and nurses sat with other nurses, managers with other managers, and doctors with other doctors. That Tuesday lunchtime Dr Willoughby and I changed the course of history. He was two in front of me in the queue to pay for our dinners, and when he'd paid for his, and got his knife and fork, he looked back at me and said:

'I'll nab us that table over there by the window before anyone else gets it.'

There was a shock-wave reaction all the way down the

77

queue. All the nurses who were behind me, holding their trays with their chicken curries or their salads and yoghurts, kind of gasped out loud, all together, and I heard a couple of whispers:

'Table over there by the window? What, him and *her*?'

'What's going on *there*, then?!'

I tried to ignore it, but my heart was thumping right up in my throat, and my hands were trembling as I picked up a knife and fork, and a serviette in case I needed to wipe the curry off my mouth, and took my tray over to the table by the window where he was sitting watching me with a smile on his face.

'What?' I said, nervously, putting my tray down on the table and pulling out the chair opposite him.

'Does it bother you?' he asked.

'Does what bother me?'

'You know what I'm talking about. The other nurses will be watching us the whole time we're eating, and by the time we've had our lunch they'll have assumed we're having a full-blown affair.'

I shrugged and picked up my fork to start my curry, but inside I was trembling with nerves and bewilderment. What was this all about? Did he really just want to ask me about my mum and the pudding? Or was it something to do with Mr Partington's asthma? Had I done something wrong? Was he going to report me?

'It's up to them what they think, really, isn't it.'

'I'm glad you see it that way,' he said, looking chuffed. And proceeded to tuck into his dinner.

'But what about me?' I added.

'Sorry?'

Well, I couldn't just get on with my dinner. Not even though it smelled delicious, and I was starving, and watching him eating was making my mouth begin to water. I couldn't relax and eat, without knowing what was going on here.

'What am *I* supposed to think?' I said. 'I don't know why

you wanted me to sit with you. I mean, it's not normal, is it. Is it just because of my mum, and the pudding? Or is there something you want to tell me?'

I meant – like I've messed something up with his patients. Or I've lost a blood result. Or whatever.

But he put down his knife and fork and smiled at me across the table, across our two plates of curry, and said quite casually:

'Yes, Michelle. Yes, there's something I want to tell you.'

I held my breath and waited for the telling-off.

'I'd like you to come out for a drink with me. Tonight, or tomorrow night, if you're free. Would that be all right with you?'

Bloody hell, I thought, taking a quick look over my shoulder at the table where all my colleagues were sitting together probably gossiping about the Christmas party again. This is a turn-up for the books, as my mum would say. I can't believe it! It's like overnight I suddenly seem to be attracting men left, right and centre. Maybe Mum really *is* putting something in her bread pudding, eh?

Penny

I thought all the fuss had died down, at work, about the so-called 'Passion Pud', so it was a bit of a shock when Chris Filbey suddenly started on about it again. The embarrassing thing was, we were the only two left at the surgery, the clinic having run late and Debbie having had to go because of getting her bus and buying a cauliflower, and I'd been fantasising, while I was waiting for Chris to finish with his last patient so that I could take their money and make their next appointment or whatever – my usual fantasy about being stripped naked on the table in his consulting room – without any dogs or cats on there of course – when he put his head round the door and asked me if I'd mind popping into the room for a minute. I didn't mind, but I did have to avoid looking at the examination table, which in fact had a dead gerbil on it.

'Penny,' he said to me very quietly, 'I wonder if you'd mind taking Michael to sit in the waiting room and giving his mum a call? I think he'd like her to come and take him and ...' He glanced at the dead animal on the table. '— to take him home.'

There was a boy of about twelve or thirteen sitting on the floor of the surgery, with his head in his hands, looking as though he'd fainted and slid down the wall.

'Come on, Michael,' I told him gently, touching his

shoulder. 'Come and sit somewhere a bit more comfy. I'll get you a drink of water.'

He looked up at me and I saw there were tears streaming down his face. He wasn't making any noise at all, just sitting there, against the wall, silently crying buckets. It brought a lump to my throat. I've seen lots of people lose their pets and it's always terribly sad, but some react worse than others. Some go hysterical. But this lad looked like he was in deep shock, and he was all on his own with his dead gerbil on the table. It wasn't right.

'Come on,' I said again, and I helped him to his feet and led him out of the consulting room, past the sad little corpse of his pet, and sat him down in the empty waiting room. I got him a drink and I found the family phone number on the computer and dialled it quietly from the back office.

'Mrs Crisp?' I said when a woman answered the phone.

'Yes. Who's this?'

'It's Penny Peacham here, Mrs Crisp, from Tail Waggers Vets' Practice. We've got Michael here in the waiting room, and he's a bit upset ... '

'Michael? At the vet's? What's he doing there? He's supposed to be doing his paper round.'

'Mrs Crisp, he brought his gerbil in. It's passed away. He's very upset.'

'That nasty gerbil of his? Dead, is it? Good. I kept telling him to get rid of it.'

I took a deep breath, and tried again.

'I'm ringing you because Michael's very upset, Mrs Crisp. I wondered if you could pop over to the surgery to take him home? I'll wait here until you arrive'

'No. He'll have to walk back. I'm doing the dinner. Tell him to bring a pint of milk in with him, can you? Thanks, love.'

The line went dead and I stared at the phone for a minute before hanging it up. When I looked up, Chris was standing in the doorway, watching me.

'I'll drive him home,' I said flatly.

'No. I will. I need to ask his mother ... or father ... what they want me to do with Joey.'

'Joey?'

'The gerbil. Michael's in no state to decide. They might want to bury it in the garden or— '

'I doubt it,' I said crossly, imagining his mother getting on with cooking her dinner and telling her son she was glad his pet was dead.

'Life can be tough,' Chris said to me abruptly.

'I know. I'm not stupid. I know not every family is like the bloody Waltons.'

'Yeah. OK, well, I'll take him home, then.'

'I'll come with you,' I decided, grabbing my coat. 'In case his mum gets funny about it.'

You know – strange man giving a boy a lift in his car. Some people will read something into anything.

'Thanks, Penny.'

After we dropped Michael off at home, carrying Joey the gerbil in a box and pretending he hadn't been crying, we drove back to the surgery in silence.

'Cheer up,' said Chris as we turned into the car park. 'He'll probably get another gerbil next week. Go home and forget about it. Go and make some of that famous passion pudding of yours, yeah?'

I know he was only trying to cheer me up. But I felt myself going hot with embarrassment.

'Actually I don't make it any more,' I told him. 'And it never was a passion pud.'

'Shame. I'd have liked to try it.'

'Are you taking the piss?' I asked him.

Well, you couldn't blame me, could you? I know he was my boss, and also he was very gorgeous and fanciable and everything, but he was making me feel stupid and uncomfortable, and also I still felt upset from thinking about Michael and his gerbil.

He turned and looked at me sharply.

'No. No, I'm not taking the piss, Penny,' he said very seriously. 'I'm sorry. I was just having a little joke with you to try and cheer you up. But I really mean it about the pudding – I would like to try it, if ever you'd consider making it again. And I really admire you for the way you've handled all this stuff – the radio, and the papers – all the publicity. I'm not joking now. I mean it.'

'Do you?' I squawked. 'Oh! Well! Thank you!'

'And I really appreciate you coming with me to Michael's place tonight, too.'

'Oh, it was nothing. I didn't mind at all. I wanted to.'

'And while we're at it ....'

'What?'

We were still sitting in his car. I was very, very aware of how close together we were, and how the windows in the car were beginning to steam up, and how much I'd like to touch his thigh. He looked at me for a full minute or two without saying anything. I found myself counting the stripes on his shirt. Fourteen stripes across, from the shoulder to the neck. Fifteen from the neck to the other shoulder. Funny, that.

'Nothing,' he said eventually, making me jump. 'I'd better not say any more. Good night, Penny.'

And with that, he got out of the car and came round to open my door for me. As I stepped out he leaned forward and kissed me on the cheek – a light touch of the lips like the brush of a powder puff, the kiss of a cousin or an old platonic friend.

'Good night, Chris,' I said.

I got into my own car and started the engine. All the way home, I had to keep taking my hand off the wheel to touch the place on my cheek where he'd kissed me. I expected it to feel burning hot but, surprisingly, it didn't. By the time I got home I thought I must have imagined it.

'Penny? It's Darren Barlow here.'

'Darren ...? Oh. Hello.' My heart sank. I was in the

middle of making bread pudding, for the first time in ages. I was rushing to get it in the oven while Archie and Michelle were watching TV, so they didn't start asking questions about why I'd suddenly started making it again. 'What do you want?' I asked ungraciously.

'I wondered if you'd like to be on the show again.'

'No,' I said. 'I wouldn't. Are you joking? After last time?'

'Penny, Penny! You were *great* last time! I keep telling you – everyone loved you. And now that you've been featured in the *Sun* ...'

'Look, I keep telling you, I never wanted all that stuff about the pudding. I only wanted—'

'I know, I know. The bypass. The protest. Listen, Penny: what I'm suggesting is this: You have the first part of the interview to talk about the bypass. The protest. Serious stuff. No interruptions. OK? Then after the break, we throw it open to the listeners. Let them call in and talk to you, and you answer their questions. If they ask about the bypass, fair enough. But if they ask about the pudding, you talk about the pudding.' He paused, waited, and when I didn't reply, he added: 'Is that a deal?'

'I suppose ...'

What was I saying? What was I thinking about? I must have been mad. I guess I was tempted by his promise that I could talk seriously about the bypass for the first half of the interview – but look what happened last time! How could I possibly trust him? If I hadn't been rushing to get the pudding in the oven, I'd never even have considered it.

'Great!' he said quickly. 'Shall we make it this Friday afternoon? Same time as before? How does that sound?'

'Well, I don't know. I'll have to see if I can get the time off work. It's not always easy, especially if there are any dogs being neutered that day. I can't expect one of the nurses to cover for me, you understand, if there are dogs being neutered.'

'I understand,' he said seriously. 'But you'll find out and get back to me? Tomorrow?'

Oh, shit. How did I get myself into this? I put the dish of bread pudding onto the middle shelf of the oven and slammed the door shut.

'Yes,' I sighed into the phone. 'I'll call you back tomorrow. But I'm not promising anything, OK?'

I phoned Roger from the PPPP and told him about Darren Barlow's suggestion.

'Would you prefer someone else to do it?' he asked. Not that he was going to volunteer, you can bet your sweet backside.

'Yes. Really, I would prefer that, Roger, but I think Darren Barlow only wants me back on condition I answer questions about the bloody ... about my bread pudding, as well as about the bypass.'

'Well, I suppose it's all publicity, Penny. But I can't help thinking it does trivialise the subject somewhat. As you know, PPPP is a community-centred pressure group. It's not about making a media star out of any individual member.'

I had to bite my tongue hard to stop myself from telling him to go and fuck himself. He was so far up his own arse he must have had trouble walking.

'It's up to you,' I said stiffly. 'I don't particularly want to do it, but if you think it would be good publicity for the bypass, I will. But we've only got till Friday, so I don't think there's time for a full committee meeting and referendum.'

'Right. OK. What I'm going to do, Penny, is to phone Elizabeth and consult with her, and call you back. OK?'

Good plan, Rog.

He called me back less than five minutes' later. Elizabeth Baxter-Simpson, apparently, had pretty much told him to stop farting about and let me get on with it. Suddenly, it seemed I had an ally. Or maybe Roger just

85

got on Elizabeth's nerves as much as he did mine.

'Bread pudding!' said Archie, coming into the kitchen while I was washing up. He stood with his nose in the air, sniffing like a bloodhound on the scent. 'Mmm! Lovely! When will it be ready, Pen?'

Silly me. How the hell did I expect to be able to keep it a secret and smuggle it into work tomorrow?

'Not till late,' I said, guilt making me snappy. 'Too late to eat it tonight.'

'It's only nine o'clock. I can have a bit for my supper, can't I?'

'No. I don't think you should, Archie. It's bad for you to eat stodgy stuff just before you go to bed.'

He came up behind me and put his arms round my waist. I tried to shake him off. I was up to my elbows in washing-up and it was irritating having him suddenly starting to paw me like that. What was the matter with him these days?

'Leave off!' I said. 'Get a tea towel and help dry up, if you want something to do with your hands.'

'I wasn't thinking of drying up,' he said with a chuckle, but when I didn't laugh he picked up the tea towel anyway. 'Come on, Pen, don't be mean. The pudding will be cooked by the time we go to bed. A nice hot bit, straight out of the oven, would be just what the doctor ordered.' He flicked the tea towel at me playfully. 'We could eat it in bed. No knowing what it might lead to!'

'Archie, I'm beginning to think there's something wrong with you! Next time you go past the surgery, make an appointment for Dr Carnegie to give you a check-up.'

'Nothing wrong with *me*, darlin'!' he retorted with a wink. 'I'm in perfect working order, thank you very much. I'll give you a demonstration later on, if you like!'

I wasn't too sure whether I'd like, or not.

But in the event, I just closed my eyes and thought of ... Chris Filbey.

*

'Is this your famous pudding?'

I'd been hoping Chris would see it first. I'd left it in the dish, in the little kitchen out the back past the urine samples, and he normally made himself a cup of tea before he started surgery. But Debbie had gone in there before him.

'Yeah. Sorry about the bit missing. Archie helped himself to a large portion.' In more ways than one. 'But there's still plenty for everyone.'

'Cool! Can we have it with our coffee later on? Will it make us wild and passionate?'

'What's all this? Who's wild and passionate?' asked Chris, strolling in just at the appropriate moment and giving me a smile that made my toes tingle.

'Penny's brought us in a dish of her passion pudding,' said Debbie.

'Oh, really?' He raised an eyebrow at me. 'I thought you didn't like making it any more?'

'Well, I had a lot of bread left over, so I just ...'

'And her Archie pinched a big bit.'

'Yes. I'm sure he did,' said Chris, nodding slightly and looking me up and down so that I flushed red hot and had to turn away. 'Well, I'll look forward to pinching a big bit myself, later on, then!'

'Where's the rest of the bread pudding, Pen?' shouted Archie.

I was in the lounge with Michelle and Jessica. We were playing 'Kerplunk' and Jessica was getting very over-excited. I froze. Shit. I'd planned to make another one to replace the bread pudding I took to work.

'Your turn, Nanny! Your turn, your turn!' shouted Jessica.

'Where's the bread pudding?' called Archie again, louder. I heard him slam the oven door, open the fridge door, slam that, and start opening cupboards. 'There was loads of it left!'

87

'Nanny! Nanny! Your turn, Nanny!'

'Calm down, Jessica,' said Michelle. 'Don't shout, or you'll have all the neighbours running round here to see who's being murdered.'

Jessica's eyes opened wide.

'Who's murdered?'

'Don't tell her things like that, Chelle. She'll have nightmares now.'

'Where's the rest of the bread pudding?' demanded Archie, appearing in the doorway. 'Who's eaten it all?'

'Who's murdered?' repeated Jessica, tugging at my arm. 'Who's murdered, Nanny?'

'Your granddad, in a minute,' I muttered. 'Sorry, Arch. I took some into work. I'd promised the girls there they could have a bit.'

'Oh.' He looked at me thoughtfully. 'That was a good idea.'

It was?

'Did they like it?'

'Well.' I thought briefly of the way Chris Filbey had grinned at me while he was eating it. And the way he'd jumped up and pretended to chase me round the waiting room after he'd finished, shouting that he'd turned into a sex-crazed beast. Luckily it was after the end of the morning clinics so there wasn't anyone waiting in there. As it was, the Alsatian in the post-op recovery cage started whining and pawing at the ground. We were glad really, because he'd been taking a long while to get over the anaesthetic. 'Well, yes, I think everyone liked it,' I said with a shrug.

'That's good.' Archie nodded, still looking at me as if I was a very interesting new picture hanging on the wall. 'That's very good. Maybe you should start making it more often again, and maybe Michelle could take some into the hospital, and I could take some round to the people I work for . . .'

'What! What do you think I am, a bread pudding

machine, all of a sudden? What on earth are you on about – making it for all and sundry?'

'Yes, Dad. Mum's got enough to do already, without making puddings for the whole town.' Michelle shook her head, obviously as bewildered as I was by this whole turn of conversation. 'You make them yourself if you think it's such a good idea.'

'Maybe I would if your Mum would teach me the recipe!'

'Oh, don't be so ridiculous, Archie! You've never made a pudding in your life. You wouldn't know where to start. If you want to do something useful, go and put the kettle on.'

He sighed and turned back to the kitchen.

'What was all *that* about?' whispered Michelle, staring after him.

'God knows. I think he's at a very funny age. I can't make head nor tail of him lately,' I whispered back.

'Nanny,' said Jessica, climbing onto my lap and putting her arms round my neck. 'Why you gone all quiet?'

'It's OK, darling. We're just talking nice and quietly for a change.'

'But Nanny,' she carried on whispering. 'Who's murdered?'

'See what I mean?' I said crossly to Michelle. 'You shouldn't joke like that with children. You don't realise how they pick things up and worry about them.'

'Sorry, Jessica. Nobody's really getting murdered. We were talking about a TV programme.'

'Can I see?' she shouted at once, jumping down off my lap and running to sit in front of the TV. 'Can I see who's murdered? Is it now? Are there guns?'

'I don't think she's too traumatised, then,' said Michelle.

Maureen was getting a bit shirty with me.

'It's all very well, Penny,' she said, stirring her coffee aggressively, 'as long as it doesn't get out of hand.'

89

'What do you mean? What gets out of hand?'

'All this about Chris Filbey. I've been round here half an hour, and you haven't stopped talking about him yet. And you're getting all fluttery.'

'Fluttery? What's that supposed to mean?' But I could feel myself getting fluttery, just saying it.

'You know very well what I mean.'

'Well, I'm so sorry if I'm boring you,' I said, offended. 'A little while ago you were encouraging me. *Good for you, girl*, I think you said, or words to that effect.'

'Yes, absolutely, good for you, as long as it's just a fantasy we're talking about.'

'Well of course it—'

'As long as you're not taking it seriously. Like, seriously considering *doing* anything.' She was stirring so hard, she looked like she was going to make a hole in the cup. 'Only, as your friend, I think I ought to tell you.'

'Tell me what? What are you talking about? Don't be silly. Of course I'm not taking it seriously. Like I said, he's about twenty years younger than me, and he'd never give me a second look.'

'But if he did?'

With that, she stopped stirring, suddenly, and threw her spoon down on the kitchen worktop. She took a sip of her coffee and stared at me over the rim of the cup, her eyes drilling into mine defiantly. I shook my head.

'Don't be silly. He ...'

'I'm asking you. Just suppose. Just say, he did fancy you, never mind about the twenty years, why shouldn't he fancy you? Just say he came on to you. Come on, Penny, don't just stand there shaking your head – ask yourself. What would you do if he came on to you?'

'Nothing,' I said moodily, looking away from her. 'Like I say, this is silly. You're making a mountain out of a molehill. He wouldn't fancy me anyway, and it's just a fantasy, OK?'

'OK,' she said. But she was shaking *her* head now, as if

I was being deliberately awkward and she was fed up with me. 'If you say so. But I still think I should tell you ... '

'Tell me what? You keep saying you should tell me – tell me what? What's the problem? Can't I have a little fantasy? Isn't it allowed, now I'm over fifty? Is that what you're saying?'

'No, Penny, of course not. What I'm saying is, what I'm trying to tell you is – I think you're becoming obsessed. That's all.'

That's all? That's bloody all?

We spent the next ten minutes or so, while we finished our coffees, making polite conversation about the weather and what we were both going to cook for dinner that night. We'd been friends for a long time but I don't think Maureen had ever offended me like that before. How dare she say I was obsessed? I was beginning to think, to be quite honest, that she was a little bit jealous. Where she worked, in the office at Duffington Crematorium, she didn't really get to meet very many people, and when she did, they were either dead, or they were very upset and tearful, so it wasn't a whole lot of fun for her really. Sometimes when I talked to her about my job she got this kind of faraway look in her eyes, like she was imagining how it would feel to work with nice people, and dogs and cats, instead of sitting there all day taking phone calls about people dying. To be honest I often thought she'd have been better off looking for a new job. I'd told her about a vacancy I'd seen advertised in the *Echo*, in the lingerie department at Marks & Spencer, but she said she didn't see any future in knickers.

Anyway, I wasn't going to get a chance to worry about Chris Filbey and whether (or *not*) I was obsessed with him, because it was Friday morning, and I'd got the day off work, and this afternoon I was going back to the radio station to have another go on *Daytime with Darren*. After Maureen went, I sat down on my own in the lounge and had another read through the notes I'd made for my first interview. I imagined what kind of stupid comments Darren Barlow might make, and I pencilled a few things in the margins that I could say if he did. Better to be prepared, I always say. I was a Girl Guide years ago, and that was always drummed into us, although to be fair that was more about carrying a penknife and a compass with you, and knowing how to tie knots with ridiculous names like the Sheep Shank and the Round Turn and Two Half Hitches. I often think about them when I'm tying my fuchsias to their support sticks, but quite honestly I just use a normal reef knot every time.

This time, I didn't get to the radio station quite so early, and although I still felt nervous when I walked into reception, I only had to sit down for a few minutes and pretend to read a magazine, and before I'd even moved on from a headline saying: WHY TOM CRUISE LOVES IRONING, they took me into the studio.

'Hello, Penny, darling!' said Darren.

The 'darling' threw me a bit, but I just nodded at him and sat down. There was an old U2 track playing – 'I Still Haven't Found What I'm Looking For'. Darren hummed along with it, nodding his head to the beat.

'How are you, my darling?' he called out when I'd got myself settled.

'OK, thank you.'

I stared at him. He really was the most ridiculous-looking person. He was wearing a lime green sweatshirt today, with a picture of a pig across the chest. He had two big hoop earrings dangling from one ear, and he'd grown back some of his hair, just around the sides – and it was a very unusual colour. Red. Not auburn, or ginger, but really red.

He caught me staring, gave his head a little shake and bowed towards me.

'Like it? The new me?'

'Um, er ... very nice,' I said, awkwardly. 'It's a shame we're not on TV, isn't it?'

You see, I couldn't understand the point of all this over-the-top dressing, all these bright colours, when none of the listeners could actually see him. But I'd obviously said the wrong thing, because he just nodded to me that the song was just about to finish, and I immediately got all nervous again and picked up my notes and started scanning through them quickly, but what I was thinking to myself was: He's gutted that he isn't on TV. That's what's the matter with him. He's only doing radio because he can't get into TV.

I don't often get these flashes of insight, but when I do, I'm usually right, you know.

I was amazed at how the interview went. I didn't have to use the sarcastic comments in the margins at all. Darren was perfectly well behaved; he let me talk about the bypass and describe the protest demonstration properly, and he asked me to update the listeners about the latest response from the county council, and he didn't take the piss or mention puddings one single time.

And after we had the next bit of music, he started taking calls from the listeners, and to my surprise the first two were serious, sensible questions from people who agreed with the campaign. One of them was a lady who lived in a flat over the shops in Panbridge Road, right by the zebra crossing, and she was saying how awful the traffic was and how only the week before, she'd seen an accident where a boy had been knocked off his bike by a lorry reversing out of the delivery area behind the shops onto the main road, and it was a miracle he wasn't killed. I thought this was great publicity for the bypass, although fair enough, it wasn't so good for the poor boy, who apparently got a broken leg and his bike was a complete write-off with nothing of any use left of it apart from the saddle and one pedal.

So I was feeling quite cheery and confident when the next caller came on, a housewife called Wendy from Sorrel Bay.

'Hello, Penny,' she said. 'Are you the same Penny Peacham that was in the *Sun* the other week? About the pudding?'

Oh, shit. I felt the cheeriness and confidence draining away from me. Still, Darren had kept his side of the bargain so I supposed I'd better keep mine.

'That's right,' I said, more calmly than I felt. 'But I'm also involved in the Peace for Panbridge ... '

'Yeah, I heard. But what I wanted to say to you was, I really admire you, Penny!'

'Oh. Oh, really? Well, thank you ... '

'You see, I noticed in the paper that you're in your fifties.'

Thanks, Wendy.

'And you see, I'm only thirty-six, but I have to be honest, Penny: my sex life is not really what I would like it to be.'

She paused, obviously expecting me to give her some advice. How are you supposed to respond to total strangers who announce to the whole of the East Coast that they're not happy with their sex lives? I glanced at Darren. He was grinning.

'Well, er ... I'm ... sorry to hear that, Wendy,' I stammered. 'Maybe you should try ... well, I don't know. They say you should try spicing things up a bit, don't they?'

What the hell was I talking about? How did I get myself into this? The only kind of spicing up I understood was adding two spoonfuls of cinnamon to the mixture instead of one spoonful!

'That's it, exactly!' said Wendy, with rather more enthusiasm than I'd expected. 'That's what I'm going to do, Penny. I'm going to follow your example, and make my Douglas a nice spicy pudding, and see if that'll get him going! All I need is the recipe.'

To my surprise, before I could reply, Darren jumped in to interrupt:

'Penny doesn't share her secret recipe with anyone, I'm afraid, Wendy.'

'No. I ... it's an ancient family secret,' I agreed.

'Oh, please, Penny,' whined Wendy the Unsatisfied. 'Just tell me the Secret Sexual Ingredients! Do you add brandy to the mixture? Is that it? Or is there ... something more ... well, some *illegal substance* in it?'

'What!' I exclaimed, shocked. 'No, definitely no illegal substances!'

I couldn't even think of any, offhand.

'No brandy?' she insisted.

'I think that's all Penny's prepared to say on the subject, Wendy,' Darren cut in again. 'Thank you very much for calling. Now on line four, we have Teresa from Duffington Common, who has *this* to say to you, Penny ... '

'Hello, Penny!' said a very breathless voice. 'I think it's *great* that you're still making your Passion Pudding, at your age ... '

'Hang on a minute!' I snapped. I'd had just about enough of all this stuff about my age. 'I'm only fifty-two, not a hundred and two!'

Oh, I know. I should have kept my mouth shut. But I think it was just the last straw, after Maureen going on at me about Chris Filbey earlier.

'There's nothing wrong with having passionate sexual feelings at the age of fifty-two, Teresa – or even a hundred and two, if you like. Age is no barrier! In fact, I think we often get more passionate and more sexual, the older we get!'

Teresa from Duffington Common, who sounded like she was either mid-shag, mid-asthma attack or in the middle of hanging a very gluey and very awkward-shaped piece of wallpaper from the top of a badly balanced stepladder, said goodbye and thank-you so fast, I spent the rest of the afternoon wondering whether we should have called an ambulance to her address. Darren took over again, spent a few ingratiating minutes praising me to the heavens, and

95

finally as a *coup de grâce*, announced the next song, which was 'Love Potion Number Nine'.

'Very funny,' I said, still feeling rattled.

'Well,' he laughed, looking pleased with himself, 'I couldn't find a song about love pudding.'

'I don't know why you let me make such a complete arse of myself,' I told him crossly. 'You should have cut me off.'

'Nonsense, Penny. You were wonderful! Amazing! People love you! They look up to you! You're their sex guru!'

'Oh, for God's sake—!'

'Seriously, Penny. That was great. Thank you. Just one word of advice?'

'What?'

'Don't ever tell anyone the recipe. No one, not even your closest friends. Don't tell them a single ingredient. Keep the mystique.'

I stared at him. The man was off his head. Mystique be buggered. It was just a bloody bread pudding.

But all I could think about on the way home was the fact that Archie would have been listening to me shouting my mouth off on the radio about being passionate and sexual. And more to the point – so would Chris Filbey.

Michelle

I hadn't exactly forgotten about Darren Barlow coming out with that stuff about going to an Italian restaurant. I'd just kind of put it to the back of my mind, because let's face it, blokes say things all the time, don't they, and then completely forget. Also, to be honest, it was the Italian restaurant I was interested in, not Darren Barlow.

So I was a bit taken aback on Saturday afternoon when I answered the phone and it was him.

'Hello, Michelle,' he said, 'How are you? D'you fancy trying out that new restaurant tonight, then? I could pick you up about eight.'

Talk about jumping straight in. He hadn't even given me a chance to answer.

'Well, no, actually I can't tonight. It's Nicole's birthday, and we're all going into Lowestoft, having a Chinese and doing a couple of clubs.'

'Very nice too. Make sure you don't overdo it and miss the last train back.'

He sounded like my dad. But then again, he was probably almost old enough to be. I didn't answer. I couldn't think of a single thing to say to him.

'Well, maybe I could have a word with your mum, then, please? If she's in?'

'Mum!' I yelled into the kitchen, 'Darren Barlow on the phone for you!'

97

She came rushing in, drying her hands on a tea towel, and I went back to watching the TV and painting my nails. After a while I became aware that Mum was talking very strangely into the phone. She'd turned away from me and was bending over the phone as if that would keep it quiet, but I could hear her going: 'Oh, Darren! Darren, really!' – and giggling. I sat up and stared at the back of her head.

'What was *that* all about?' I demanded when she finally hung up.

She looked flushed and jittery like she'd had a shock.

'Nothing, nothing,' she said, smoothing down her cardigan and her hair and fluttering her eyelashes as if there was something very irritating getting into her eyes. 'He just phoned to thank me again for being on the programme yesterday, that's all.'

'Actually,' I said, '*Actually*, he phoned . . .'

But I couldn't, could I? I couldn't very well tell her he'd phoned to ask me to go to the Italian restaurant with him at eight o'clock, when she was fluttering about, all pink and pleased because he'd been flirting with her and making her giggle like a teenager.

And then again, was he only asking me out because he really wanted to get in with my mum? My hand shook momentarily as I was applying the second coat of Aubergine Dream to my right little fingernail, and I ended up with a big splodge on the next finger. Shit. I really ought to talk to Mum about this. I didn't trust Darren Barlow an inch, and the thing is, Mum had been with Dad for so long, she'd probably forgotten what men are like. You know what I mean? I didn't want her falling for his flattery, getting taken in by all his crap, and not realising where it was leading. Before you knew it, he'd be propositioning her. And Mum wouldn't really know how to handle that, would she? Not after all those years being married to my dad.

Nicole was twenty-five that day. It's a big one, isn't it. I felt a lot more grown-up as soon as I reached twenty-five (a couple of months previously) – like I'd completely left my silly younger self behind and joined the adult world. There were a couple of bars in Duffington that I actually stopped going to once I turned twenty-five, because they were full of seventeen- and eighteen-year-olds.

We didn't very often go into Lowestoft for the night. It took half an hour on the train, you see, and there was always the panic about getting the last train home, especially if we'd had a few drinks. But it was a much better night out than just going into Duffington. Me and Robbie (before he buggered off) sometimes used to drive up there for the evening and go in the Amusements, and get some fish and chips and eat them on the front – especially in the summer.

Anyway, there was a whole crowd of us going there that night, on the train. Me, and Nicole and Kim, and Kim's younger sister Lisa, and a couple of the girls from Nicole's work, and her next-door neighbour and her cousin, and two or three others we used to go to school with. We were all in a party mood, and by the time we'd had our Chinese, with a couple of Becks each before the meal, and several glasses of white wine during it, we were probably getting a bit lairy, although to be honest I don't remember an awful lot about it. The reason I don't remember much is the number of vodkas and Red Bull I had later in the club. And the reason I had so many of them was that Luke was buying them for me.

I couldn't believe it really. I mean, the other week was the first time I'd ever seen him up at Purple Cloud, and then when we go to Lowestoft he turns up in the club there. He told me he lived in Lowestoft and he was only in Duffington the week before because he was with a friend from work who lived there. He bought me a drink, and we danced together. Then he bought me another drink, and we danced again. I remember Kim coming over and having a go at me because I wasn't staying with them, when it was

99

Nicole's birthday, and I think I told her to fuck off, which isn't like me really. And because I was a bit upset that she was pissed off with me, Luke bought me another drink and we danced some more. And then I don't remember anything else, until I woke up on the train back to Duffington.

Opposite me was Kim, staring at me with a face like thunder, and Nicole, asleep with her feet on Kim's lap and her head hanging off the end of the seat. She had something round her head that looked like a suspender belt and something down the front of her cardigan that looked like candyfloss. The other girls were sitting across the aisle from us, singing 'Ten Green Bottles' very badly.

'Oh,' said Kim. 'So you're awake, are you?'

'What happened?' I said, holding onto my head. It felt wobbly and delicate.

'We found you passed out, outside the club. We had to carry you back to the station.'

'Oh,' I said in a pathetic little voice that was all I could manage.

'I hope you realise,' said Kim fiercely, 'what could have happened to you, on your own, passed out and drunk, outside in the street like that ...'

'Oh,' I whimpered again.

'Leave her alone,' muttered Nicole surprisingly, without opening her eyes. 'She wasn't in the street; she was just in the club doorway. And she wasn't on her own.'

'I wasn't?'

'Well, he was probably going to *leave* you on your own, after he'd finished with you,' spat Kim.

'Luke?' I said, trying hard to remember something, anything, other than the pain in my head and the nausea rising up to my throat.

'He was trying to hold you up,' said Nicole, opening one eye and giving me a drunken, lopsided grin.

'Oh,' was all I seemed to be able to manage again. And then: 'Oh, oh, I think I feel sick.'

Pushing Nicole's feet off her lap with a heavy thump,

Kim jumped up and shoved me along the train to the toilet, which was luckily only at the end of our carriage. And which was where I discovered, eventually, the reason I felt kind of strange and cold under my skirt. My knickers were screwed up in my jacket pocket.

'So did you have sex with him?'

Nicole and I were talking on the phone the next day, after I'd finally got out of bed at about half past eleven and managed to drink a cup of black coffee. I'd phoned her to apologise for getting drunk on her birthday, but she didn't remember much about the journey home herself either.

'I don't know,' I said miserably. 'I don't *think* so. I'd have remembered it, wouldn't I?'

'Well surely you can tell? I mean, well, you know. Isn't there any *sign* of anything?'

'The only thing I know is that I didn't have my knickers on. I don't think I would have just stood in the middle of the club and taken them off, would I?'

'The state you were in,' she giggled, 'you might have done anything.'

'Oh, God. I feel so awful. What a tart I must have looked. And what a pig *he* must be, to get me drunk like that and just ... well, just ... whatever he did ...'

'He looked like he was looking after you, to be fair,' she said. 'Ask Kim. She was more sober than me.'

'No, I'm not asking Kim!' I wailed. 'She hates me! She had to carry me to the station, and take me to the toilet, and she thinks I'm disgusting!'

'Don't be daft. She's just jealous.'

'Jealous? Kim?'

'Of course! You should have seen her face when you were dancing with Luke! She fancied him really badly herself!'

Well I'm buggered. There's a turn-up for the books, then, as my Mum would say.

I didn't have his number. I didn't even know his surname. It wasn't going to be any use phoning some 118 Directory Enquiries number and asking some person in India for the number of Luke from Lowestoft. And anyway, what would be the point of talking to him? What was I going to say to him? 'Hello, can you just remind me whether or not I had sex with you last night?' sounded just a little bit insulting, whether we'd done it or not. And 'Hi, have you got any idea how my knickers came off?' didn't really sound like the start of a sensible conversation.

No, I was just going to have to try and forget about it. And forget about him. And despite what Nicole said about him looking after me, I did feel quite annoyed with him for continually buying me all those drinks when he must have been able to see that I was already out of it. What if he'd put something in one of my drinks? That was another thought, and it wasn't funny. My mum would go mad if she knew about all this. She was always, always going on at me about not letting people buy me drinks. The more I thought about it, the more I decided it was all Luke's fault, and the more I decided I hated him. In fact, thinking about my experiences over the last few weeks, what with Robbie pissing off and everything, I decided I hated all men. All of them. Forever.

'Hello, Chelle,' said Adam, leaning towards me to give me a kiss as he came in the front door with Jessica skipping up and down beside him. 'Cor, bloody hell! Your breath stinks of booze! Where've you been?'

'Out, last night, for Nicole's birthday,' I said crossly. 'Like *you* never go out on the piss, I suppose?'

'Ooh, tetchy, aren't we?' he teased. 'Still feeling rough, eh?'

'Shut up.' Adam was just as bad. He might be my brother, but he was just another man, and I expect he treated girls badly too, if the truth be known. 'Leave me alone.'

102

'Chelly!' sang Jessica, still skipping up and down like a demented puppet, 'Going to the beach! Going to the beach! Going to the beach!'

'No, we're not, Jessica,' said Adam, suddenly looking embarrassed. 'Not today.'

'Going to the beach, *you* said, Daddy!' she retorted, tears coming into her eyes. 'You *said*!'

'I don't think so, Jessica,' I told her, frowning at Adam as I led her, starting to cry properly now, into the kitchen to see what kind of biscuit might pacify her a bit. 'I don't think Daddy would have meant that. It's winter, and it's cold, and raining, and it'll be getting dark soon.'

It was only one o'clock and he'd brought Jessica round for Sunday lunch, but well, it was only stretching the truth a little bit. It would be getting dark by the time we'd had dinner, by the look of the sky, what with all those clouds up there. Definitely not a day for the beach. What was Adam thinking about? He must have mentioned it. Little kids of Jessica's age don't make up things for no reason.

'Daddy *said*,' she sobbed as if the world was coming to an end. She batted away the chocolate biscuit I offered her. 'If I'm a *good* girl, I can go to the beach!'

'Not *this* time, Jessica,' Adam called out above her crying. 'I didn't mean *this* time.'

'What nonsense have you been telling her?' said my mum, looking up all red and cross from putting the potatoes in the oven. 'She's not going to the beach this time of year. You know what it's like down there. She gets mud all over, from her head to her toes.'

Jessica started howling even louder.

'*I want mud! I like mud! I want to go to the beach!*'

'I was just suggesting, that's all. I didn't mean today. I was just saying *maybe*, if she was a good girl, another time when perhaps I go away and she stays here ...'

At this, Jessica stopped crying with a hiccup, stared at Adam and shook her head wildly.

'Don't go away!' she yelled, stamping her feet. 'Stay here, Daddy!'

Knocking the biscuits out of my hand completely, she threw herself at Adam's knees, punching him in the legs, yelling and crying, until Mum slammed the oven door shut and took hold of her hand, pulled her away into the lounge and left her lying on the sofa screaming, with my dad complaining that he couldn't hear the TV.

'*Now*,' said Mum, looking at Adam across the kitchen and wiping her hands on the tea towel. 'What is this all about? What have you been telling her, Adam? It's not fair, making promises to her.'

'I didn't say ...'

'Don't give me that!' Mum still talked to Adam like he was ten years old when she got cross with him. 'Jessica hasn't had temper tantrums like that since last Christmas at least! There's got to be a good reason for it.'

'It might be something to do with you going away for your weekends,' I told him bitchily. 'She doesn't want you to go away, Adam. Maybe you should be listening to her.'

'Maybe *you* should keep your big fucking nose out of it!' he retaliated.

There was a shocked silence. Mum has never liked to hear *fucking* in the kitchen, and Adam knew it.

'Sorry, Mum,' he added sulkily.

Mum stayed very dignified, with her back to him, chopping carrots on the worktop. We could still hear Jessica crying on the sofa, and Dad saying, 'Ssh, Jessica,' in an irritated voice every couple of minutes, but she was getting a bit tired now and gradually going quieter.

'Sorry, but it's none of Michelle's business,' he said, giving me an evil look.

I shrugged and went into the lounge to sort Jessica out, but I could still hear what they were saying in the kitchen. I was leaning towards the door so I didn't miss anything.

'She got upset about me going away next weekend,' Adam was saying. 'So I was kind of trying to cheer her up.'

'Bribing her, you mean,' said Mum, banging a saucepan down on the cooker.

'Just trying to make her feel better. "Look, Jessica," I said, "Remember how much fun you have when you stay at Nanny and Granddad's? Remember when you went to the beach and collected shells in your bucket?"'

'That was in August, Adam. It was hot. It hadn't rained for weeks, but she still got covered in mud. There's no way, this time of year ...'

'All right, I know! I didn't think she'd take it that she was coming to the beach the next time she came round here, did I?'

'No, you *didn't* think. That's your trouble, Adam, you don't think.'

'That isn't fair, Mum. I do my best. It's not easy, on my own.'

Oh, spare me the bloody violins. It made me sick. It was always the same – whenever we got to the point where I thought Mum was actually going to sit him down and say: Look, Adam, I'm fifty-two, I've had enough of bringing up children, I've got a job and a life of my own and you need to sort out some proper day care for your daughter and stop expecting me to look after her ... every time, he turned on the sob story about how hard it was for him, bringing her up without her mother, and Mum gave in. She felt guilty and ended up saying nothing.

I sat Jessica up and gave her a cuddle, wiped her nose and told her I'd read her a story till dinner was ready.

'The one about the wolf and the pigs?' she asked, sniffing and shuddering the way children do when they stop crying.

'I don't think we've got the book here. Will your Caterpillar book do?'

She nodded and put her thumb in her mouth. I got her book out of her bag of things and settled down with her on my lap. Adam looked in sheepishly and gave me a thumbs-up. I ignored him. Arsehole.

*

105

I was round Nicole's on the Tuesday night, and we were having a glass of white wine and a moan about men in general, when suddenly my mobile rang and it was a number I didn't recognise.

'Hello, Michelle,' said this not-very-friendly voice. 'It's Killer here. Robbie's mate.'

'Oh!' I said, completely gobsmacked. 'How are you?'

I hadn't expected to hear from him again. He was Robbie's mate, not mine, and to be honest I found him a bit off-putting. He wasn't as bad as Farty, not in his habits, but there was something about the chains he wore hanging off his clothes, and the size of his boots, and the way he cleaned his nails with a knife, that made me kind of uneasy.

'I'm not feeling too good, actually, Michelle,' he said. 'In fact I'm feeling, shall we say, very *sick* at the moment, as a matter of fact.'

'Oh dear. Why's that, then, Killer? Not this flu that's going around, I hope?'

'No, I don't think it's the flu. I've got this bloody great *hole* you see, Michelle. A huge, great big gaping hole. Right in the middle of my bank balance. And it's really, really, beginning to piss me off.'

'I can imagine. But what's that got to do with—'

'Still not heard anything from that fucking stupid boyfriend of yours?'

'Robbie?' I said, my voice wavering a bit. Like I knew of any other fucking stupid boyfriend.

'Robbie Fucking Nelson. Mister Robbie Disappearing Act Fucking Nelson,' he said, beginning to sound really nasty about it. 'No sign of him creeping back into your nice warm cosy bed yet, then?'

'No,' I said. 'And to be honest with you, Killer, if he came creeping back, I'd throw him out again, because—'

'Well, that's a pity, Michelle. I'm very sorry to hear that.'

'Why? What do you mean, you're sorry? What do you want, anyway, and how did you get my number? Only I'm round my friend's, and we're just about to watch a video, so if you don't mind ...'

'Oh, I don't *mind*, Michelle. Little Michelle,' he sneered. It made me shiver. I could picture him, in his big boots, swinging his chain. 'I don't want to spoil your evening, with your *friend* and your *video*.'

'Good. Well then, if that's all you want ...'

'No, it isn't all I fucking want!' he shouted, so suddenly I nearly dropped the phone. I grabbed hold of Nicole's arm in fright. 'I want my *fucking* money, Michelle! Do you understand? I want the two grand he owes me for the fucking car! And I want interest on top! And if I don't get it off fucking Robbie, I'm going to come round and get it off you, darlin', so if you know where he is you'd better let him know.'He stopped for a minute. I'd started crying at about the time of the second *fucking* and I was aware he could probably hear me snivelling in the silence. 'Keep yer knickers on, darlin',' he said. 'Leastways till I get round there, eh?'

He was laughing really nastily when he hung up.

'What am I going to do?' I cried into Nicole's arms. 'He's coming after me, Nic! You don't know what he's like! He's big and ugly and he's got a beard!'

'He can't be that bad,' she soothed me. 'He's probably just pissed off at Robbie ...'

'He wears huge boots and chains and he's got spider's webs tattooed all over his arms ...'

'He's just trying to frighten you. Don't take any notice.'

'He's got massive studs in his ears, and red hair growing out of his nose ...'

'Blimey. That does sound a bit scary.'

'Oh, Nic! What am I going to do? He wants two thousand pounds plus interest! I haven't got it! He's going to kill me!'

'No, he won't. Have another glass of wine. I thought you said *you* lent Robbie the money for the car?'

'Yes,' I said thoughtfully, staring at her through the yellow of the cheap wine she was holding out to me. 'Yes, that's right, I *did* lend him it. And the bastard never even paid me back. Like my dad said, it's my bloody car, isn't it. So it hasn't even got anything to do with Killer.' I took a gulp of my wine. 'What's he on about?'

'I don't know, Chelle. Take no notice of him.'

'No. I don't think I *will* take any notice of him, Nic.' The wine was making me feel braver. Another glass or two and I'd feel completely calm again. 'Men, eh?' I said a bit shakily. 'Bloody idiots, the lot of them.'

'Bloody idiots, and bloody bastards,' she agreed, clinking her glass against mine. 'Let's just forget about them, Chelle, and watch the video, eh?'

'Yeah, let's!'

'Yeah, let's!' She giggled as she switched on the TV and slid the video into the slot. 'But by the way, Chelle. You know what I think?'

'What do you think, Nic?'

'About Saturday night. Don't take this the wrong way, like. But maybe you should have taken the morning-after pill. Maybe, just in case, I think you ought to get a pregnancy test done. Don't you?'

108

Penny

My poor Michelle. She pretended everything was all right, because she probably didn't want me or Archie worrying about her. But I'm her mother, and I know her. I think she'd just about started getting over Robbie disappearing, and let's face it, that's quite a big shock in your life when you're only twenty-five, even without a mortgage or babies to worry about. And to be quite honest, I wanted her to have a little bit of a breathing space in her life. Do you know what I mean? I didn't think it would be good for her to go straight into another relationship. What we used to call 'on the rebound'. I was worried she'd meet someone at the Club Rouge or the Silver Cloud or whatever they call it, when she went out with her friends, and just because she was missing Robbie, she'd get drawn into having a relationship with someone unsuitable, much too quickly, and end up regretting it. And if anyone was unsuitable, it was that bloody silly Darren Barlow.

I knew it. I just knew he'd come sniffing around her if he got the chance. I knew it as soon as I saw the way he was ogling her legs on the day of the demonstration. Well, I wasn't having it. He was much too old for her, and he wore silly T-shirts. And anyway, he'd told me he was already attached. She didn't need anything like *that*, thank you very much.

He'd already phoned a couple of times, pretending he

109

wanted to talk to me first, and then saying casually, 'And is Michelle home tonight, Penny?' He asked me to give her messages that he'd called, but I never told her. You might think badly of me for this, but remember, she may have been twenty-five but I was still her mother, and I knew what was best for her. I was only being protective.

But then he phoned on that Saturday afternoon, and she answered the phone. I didn't realise it was him she was talking to, of course, until she passed me the phone and said 'Darren Barlow for you!' He started off by thanking me for the interview the day before, but he quickly moved on to Michelle. 'What a lovely daughter you've got, Penny', and 'Oh, Penny, you can't be old enough to have a daughter of her age!', and 'It must run in the family, like mother like daughter, both as beautiful as each other'.

It was making me feel sick, but Michelle was watching me really closely so I just kept giggling and pretending to flirt back with him.

Anyway I was glad she was going out with her friends that night, so she didn't have time to think too much about it. It was that nice little Nicole's birthday and all the girls were going up to Lowestoft together on the train – lovely little outing for them all. I liked to see them all dressed up for their nights out. Although I say it myself, my Michelle was always the prettiest, what with her long blonde hair and lovely figure. I would have preferred her to wear slightly longer skirts, but what could I say? I was the first girl in my class to wear miniskirts in the Sixties, and I always made sure I wore knickers to match my skirts, in case they showed when we were dancing at parties. So I know what it's like to be fashion-conscious. It's just that it was quite a cold night, and there's generally so much *less* of their knickers nowadays. Still, at least she had her long boots on.

'Michelle,' I told her before they set off, 'just hold onto your purse, and watch no one puts anything in your drinks. That's all.'

'All right, Mum,' she said, giving me a kiss goodbye. 'If

110

we can't be good, we'll be careful!'

They all went off giggling, and I had to smile to myself. It was better for her, being out and having fun with her friends, than sitting at home moping about Robbie. Or talking to that awful Darren Barlow. He phoned several more times the following week, and I was beginning to be pissed off with it.

The trouble was, after the birthday night out, Michelle seemed to get more and more moody. It made it difficult to talk to her. We'd always been able to talk about things before.

'It's still early days,' I told her. 'I expect you're still upset about Robbie, but ...'

'Who?' she said.

'OK, look, I know how you must be feeling, but you can still go out and enjoy yourself with Kim, and Nicole, and have a lovely time.'

'What? I know I can.'

She wasn't looking at me. She was staring at the TV but I don't think she was really watching it, either.

'You don't have to worry about getting another boyfriend just yet,' I went on.

'Boyfriend?' she repeated as if I was talking Swahili. 'What boyfriend?'

'Well, look, Michelle. I don't want to sound interfering, but I don't think it's a good thing, that Darren Barlow keeping on phoning up.'

'Neither do I!' she said, really crossly, turning to give me a look like it was *my* fault. 'Maybe you should tell him!'

'Well, I will, then. If you want me to. But don't you think it should come from you?'

'I don't care. If that's what you want, yeah, I'll tell him anything you want me to tell him. But I'll wait till after he's taken me to the Italian restaurant, if that's OK with you. I was looking forward to it.'

'Oh, Michelle!'

'What?' She looked at me irritably. 'What do you mean, Oh Michelle? What have I done now?'

'You're not going out with him, are you? Come on, love, he's much too old for you. And I don't like to tell you this, but—'

'It's not really me he's interested in. I know that, Mum. I'm not bloody stupid. I'm only going to the restaurant with him because I like pasta. Is that all right with you?'

'Well, really, dear, it's not up to me, is it? But I don't like the idea of two-timing. I might be old-fashioned ...'

Michelle gave me a very funny look.

'*Two-timing*, is it, Mum?'

I wasn't sure about the way she said *two-timing*. I didn't like her tone of voice. *Obviously* it was two-timing, wasn't it, if she knew he already had someone else. But I didn't want to have a row with her – not while she was still feeling so low about Robbie. So I just shook my head.

'I hope Dad knows about this,' she said, still sounding very cross.

'I'll tell him, if you like,' I said. 'But to be honest, I thought you'd want to keep it quiet. I doubt whether he'd like it.'

'No!' she snorted. 'No, I doubt very much whether he would! You can't blame him, can you!'

I was beginning to think all the stress and worry about Robbie was making her go a bit daft in the head. I sighed. The last thing she needed in the world was to get tangled up with someone like Darren Barlow who already had a wife or a girlfriend.

'If you *must* go out with someone,' I sighed, 'why don't you find a nice young man of your own age? What about that Luke you were telling me about, that was a good dancer?'

But to my amazement, she just burst into tears at this, and ran upstairs to her room. Must have been her hormones.

*

112

'Who's Chris?' asked Archie when I was cleaning my teeth in the morning. I stopped mid-brush. He was standing behind me in the bathroom and I caught his eye in the mirror and had to look away, feeling suddenly sick and giddy like I'd just stood up too quickly.

'Chris who?' I said, trying to sound cool. I could hear my voice echo inside my head.

'I don't know. You were mumbling something about Chris this morning. When I was trying to wake you up.'

'Was I?'

Shit. I remembered it now. Since he heard me say all that crap on the radio about being sexual and passionate, Archie had been getting more and more randy every day. This morning he'd been trying to wake me up by stroking the inside of my thigh, obviously hoping I was going to respond in time to have a quickie before we had to get up. I must have thought I was dreaming.

'Must have been dreaming,' I said, going back to brushing my teeth. I knocked the toothbrush against my gum and winced. 'Can't think who I know called Chris,' I lied.

'Well, let me know if she's pretty,' he laughed. 'If she is, I'll join you in the dream next time! Threesome! Nice!'

Everyone in my house seemed to be going through some kind of hormonal crisis.

My gum was bleeding now. And I was going to be late for work.

There was a hamster waiting for me, and a cocker spaniel with a weak bladder. Already there was an unpleasant smell of urine in the waiting room, and it was only twenty to nine.

'Chris is seeing the rabbit with the abscess early,' said Debbie, coming out of the consulting room in a fluster with a syringe in her hand, 'being as he couldn't sit down.'

'Chris couldn't sit down?' I echoed. Even the mention of his name was making me feel hot, thinking about his hand on my thigh this morning in bed. But no – wait! It wasn't his hand, was it. It was Archie's.

'Not Chris! Digby! The rabbit! With the abscess in his rectum!'

'Lovely.' I smiled. 'And who's next? Oh dear.'

The spaniel had done it again.

'Sorry,' said his owner, looking round helplessly. 'She's always worse when she's nervous.'

'Not to worry. I'll get a cloth and . . . look out!'

Too late.

A frisky Labrador puppy, first through the door, pulling his reluctant owner behind him, had leapt with great enthusiasm into the puddle of urine in the middle of the waiting-room floor and was now happily spreading it around on his paws and tail.

'Sometimes,' said Debbie tonelessly as she hurried back in to help Chris with the abscess in the rabbit's rectum, 'I wonder what I see in this job.'

It was twelve o'clock before the last patient, a cat with one ear bitten off in a fight, was stitched up, dosed up, and sent back out into battle.

'What a morning!' exclaimed Chris, finally emerging from his room, stretching and yawning. 'Jesus! Every one a problem. What's happened to all the nice easy vaccinations and wormings?'

'They don't test your skill enough,' said Debbie, giving me a grin and a wink. 'They're a waste of all those years of training.'

'So . . . we don't do them any more?'

'Yeah. We give them to Glenn,' I said, grinning back. 'He's older. He needs to take it easy.'

'Cheeky mare!' laughed Glenn, who was still probably ten years younger than me to be fair.

'Yes, she *is* getting a bit cheeky, isn't she,' said Chris, turning to me and fixing me with a slow, sexy stare that felt like it went straight through me. 'I think she's asking for a good *spanking*!'

114

'Hardly appropriate behaviour for the surgery, really,' I said haughtily, trying to keep my voice steady.

To be honest, I liked the idea of it, but I was having trouble getting over the image of the cat's blood on the table, and the remains of his ear.

'Well, you surprise me,' said Chris, not taking his eyes off me. 'I thought I heard you announcing to the whole of the county, on the radio the other day, that you were more sexual and passionate these days than ever?'

I felt myself shiver under his gaze. Shit. He was doing my head in, not to mention other parts of my anatomy. I was really, really, bothered by how much I suddenly wanted to get hold of him and kiss him. And maybe let one thing lead to another ...

'You can't believe everything you hear on the radio,' I said in a kind of demented squeak, looking away quickly and rummaging in my drawer for something, anything, that might take my mind off kissing him. Found a stray paper-clip. That'd do.

'That's a shame. I guess we'll just have to leave it to our imaginations, then.' He paused, and then added quietly. 'Leave that poor paperclip alone, Penny. You've made a complete mess of it.'

'Talking of which,' said Debbie briskly, giving me a slightly puzzled look, 'There's blood and guts to clear up next door, and I'm starving.' She took a bite out of a huge doorstep cheese sandwich and added, 'Did anyone dispose of the rest of that cat's ear?'

I had a phone call during my lunch break. I was a bit taken aback. I didn't normally get personal calls at work. I was in the middle of eating a ham and pickle roll and reading my stars in the paper.

'Is that Mrs Peacham? Penny Peacham?' asked this rather posh female voice.

'That's me. Who is this calling?'

'Penny, I hope you'll forgive me calling you at your

115

work. Your husband kindly gave us the number. It's Fantasia Topping here, from *Woman Today* magazine.'

It took me a good few minutes of rigid shock to get over her name, before I even moved on to where she was calling from.

'*Woman Today*?' I repeated weakly.

'Are you familiar with the magazine, Penny?' asked Fantasia, who sounded kind of breathless with excitement, as if she'd just heard she'd won the Lottery, or met George Clooney in an alleyway.

'Yes. Yes, I've ... seen it.'

Seen it, but hadn't ever bought it. It was thick and glossy and usually turned up in doctors' and dentists' waiting rooms. Not in ours. Anything that turned up in ours ended up on the floor soaking up cocker spaniels' accidents.

'Marvellous, marvellous!' breathed Fantasia. 'Well, Penny, I'll come straight to the point. We're planning a feature on passionate older women, and I'm looking for women who have full and interesting lives, to tell us about how they keep vitality and excitement ...'

'Excitement? Oh, well, look, I don't really know where you got my name, but ...'

'Well, Penny!' She was beginning to sound like she was only seconds away from orgasm. 'Well, we've *actually* been sent a copy of a recent article in the *Sun* about your *Passion Pudding*!' The word *passion* obviously having sent her over the edge, she went into a paroxysm of pealing laughter, which was quite honestly so embarrassing to listen to that I had to hold the phone away from my ear till she'd calmed down.

'It wasn't supposed to be an article about pudding,' I told her without much hope of being listened to. 'It was supposed to be about a new road. A bypass.'

'We thought the article was *wonderful*!' Like I say, no hope of being listened to. 'And we think you're *just* the kind of person we're looking for, Penny.'

'What kind of person is that?'

116

Well, I might have been an axe-murderer for all she knew.

'Mature,' said Fantasia, suddenly sounding more businesslike. Maybe the drugs were wearing off. 'We need mature women with sexual vitality!'

I was just about to tell her that I might be mature, but I had about as much sexual vitality left in me as a worn-out old slipper with its fur hanging off, when the outside door opened and Chris Filbey came back in from his lunch. It was raining outside and as he stepped into the waiting room he shook himself after the manner of a rather special golden retriever, then ran both hands through his hair, looked up and gave me a smile. My sexual vitality score suddenly jumped so high up the scale, it hit the bell at the top and left the air vibrating.

'That certainly sounds like me!' I found myself agreeing with Fantasia, staring at Chris and giving a silly little giggle for his benefit.

'That's *marvellous*, Penny!' Fantasia yelled at the top of her voice. 'Absolutely *marvellous*! I think you'll be just *perfect*! I can't *wait* to *meet* you!'

'Meet me?' My silly giggle died in my throat. 'I thought you were just going to write a little bit in the magazine?'

'This is going to be a full-colour quality *feature*, Penny,' she rebuked me. 'We're featuring four lovely ladies! We already have a gorgeous grandmother with ten grandchildren, who teaches Judo and recently did nude headstands for charity, and we also have a sixty-five-year-old with pierced nipples and a motorbike, and ...'

'*Nude headstands*?' I queried wonderingly. Chris was looking at me with puzzled interest.

' ... and a Latin teacher who sleeps in the garden with her husband every night because she believes it's more healthy for his testicles ... '

'*What*?'

Did I *want* to get involved with these madwomen?

'... and you're the fourth, Penny!' she finished in triumph.

117

'So let me get this straight. It's me, a naked grandma, a Hell's Angel pensioner, and a teacher with an outdoor-sex fetish?'

Chris sauntered over and leaned on the desk, watching me, smiling broadly.

'That's right!' squealed Fantasia with a fresh burst of excitement. 'And what we need, Penny, is a convenient date for you all to come up to the *Woman Today* offices . . .'

Oh, I don't think so! Forget it, sunshine. You can count me out of your sad little freak show.

'. . . for a lovely, *lovely* morning in our *makeover* studio; for a facial, manicure, hair styling, make-up . . . and then, when you're *completely* beautiful, you'll all have your photographs taken by our *wonderful* photographer Bernard,' (judging by the way his name was being pronounced, Bernard was evidently either very foreign or very pretentious) 'and then!' (excitement reaching fever pitch now) 'a *wonderful* lunch with our Beauty Editor and our Features Editor!' Fantasia took a well-deserved gasp of breath. 'Doesn't that sound marvellous, Penny?'

Not bad, actually. I've always fancied one of those pampering days at a spa resort, but they seem to cost not only an arm and a leg but most of the feet, ankles and bum too.

'What about the interview?'

'Oh, we do that on the phone,' she said dismissively. 'Nothing to worry about, Penny. One of our writers will call you to establish a convenient time for the telephone interview, and you can get yourself settled in your favourite armchair with a gin and tonic, and it'll only take about twenty minutes or so of your time. OK, Penny?'

Why did I suddenly feel distinctly patronised?

'OK, Fantasia,' I said between my teeth. But only because I want the pampering, OK, yah? 'So what do I have to do now?'

'Just give me a *teeny* little idea of your availability

118

during the next couple of weeks, please, Penny. Then I can get my PA, Charisma, to do some *juggling* of dates and confirm everything to you in writing. How does that sound, Penny?'

Fantasia and Charisma? They could do a double-act advertising body lotions or intimate feminine deodorant sprays.

'Yah. I mean ... yeah, fine. Tuesdays and Wednesdays are normally good for me. I'll look forward to hearing from Charisma, then.'

'*Marvellous, marvellous!*'

I hung up the phone and met Chris's eyes across the reception desk.

'Penny,' he said in tones of great awe, 'I don't believe it! You're not going to be a porn star, are you?'

Michelle

Every time I saw that nice Dr Willoughby at the hospital, he gave me a little wave, and a smile that had a question mark in it. I know what he wanted to ask me. Was I going to go for a drink with him like he'd suggested over the curry in the canteen? But I just kept waving back at him and rushing off as if I had important things to do and couldn't possibly stop to talk to him. Normally I'd have felt a bit mean, keeping him waiting for an answer like that. But to be honest, nothing personal, I was just sick of the whole of the male species. And I had more worrying things on my mind, such as whether or not I'd had sex with Luke and was going to end up as a single mother without even knowing his surname, and whether or not I was going to have a visit from Killer that led to me being found tied up, gagged, blindfolded and dead in a ditch somewhere because I couldn't give him two thousand pounds plus interest.

I hadn't told anyone about Killer, apart from Nicole. But when Adam brought Jessica round that Friday night, he gave me a funny look and just said:

'You all right, Chelle? You're a bit quiet.'

Mum was at one of her PPPP meetings, and Dad was washing up, whistling away to himself in the kitchen like there was something to be happy about, so Adam and I were just sitting in the lounge having a quick cup of tea together before he went off for another one of his secret weekends.

'Just a bit pissed off, really, Adam,' I said, blinking back a tear.

I felt really sorry for myself. I mean, there was my mum being interviewed on the radio and photographed for newspapers and flashy magazines and everything as if she was a film star, and my dad coming over all cheerful all of a sudden, and Adam having nice weekends away while we looked after Jessica for him – and what about me? Great! All I had was a missing boyfriend, threatening phone calls from his scary friend, and the mysterious removal of my knickers without even knowing whether I'd had sex or whether I'd enjoyed it.

'Never mind,' said Adam, patting my hand as if I was a nice little dog waiting to go for a walk. 'Maybe he'll just turn up one day, Chelle, you never know, large as life and twice as ugly. Eh?'

'Who? Robbie?' I said, pushing his hand off mine. 'Get out of it. I don't want him back. He can get stuffed. It's his mate Killer I'm worried about.'

I *so* wasn't going to tell him. But it all kind of came out in a rush, and Adam just sat there staring at me, listening without saying anything – and the longer he didn't say anything, the more I just went on, repeating everything Killer had said on the phone, and about his tattoos and chains and his nose-hair and all.

'I'm scared of him!' I snivelled. 'I try not to be, but it only works when I'm drinking. I'm scared he's going to come round here and murder us all in our beds. But I won't let him touch Jessica,' I added as an afterthought. 'Don't worry. I'll hide her in the cupboard under the stairs.'

'I reckon you're being a bit overdramatic,' he said, but he was still staring at me like he was thinking about it. 'I don't think he'll come round here. He's all mouth. He thinks he's big, threatening innocent women, but he's pathetic really.'

121

'Really? You think so?'

'Yeah. He's just annoyed at Robbie. He probably thinks you know where he is and if he scares you, you'll get onto him about paying him back his money.'

'But Robbie doesn't even owe him money for the car! I paid for the car! He owes *me*!'

'Hm,' said Adam. He stood up and walked to the window, staring out at the garden. 'Hm, right.' He shook his head, and when he looked back at me I thought he looked really angry. I wondered if something out in the garden had upset him, but it was dark out there.

'Anyway, I've got to get going, now, Chelle. OK?'

Well, thanks very much. So much for caring about *me*.

'Sod off, then,' I said moodily. 'See you Sunday.'

Mum and Dad were both like dogs with two tails about the *Woman Today* feature. I could understand Mum being excited – who wouldn't like the idea of a free makeover, never mind having your picture all over a glossy magazine? I was pleased for her. All right then, yes, I suppose I was a bit jealous, too, especially the way Kim and Nicole went 'Ooh' and 'Aah' about it and kept on and on about how lucky I was, having a famous mum. But to be fair, the way I looked at it was, Mum only had a few more years really before she was too old to do anything like that. I mean, fifty-two was bad enough, but when you get to about sixty, probably nobody ever looks at you again, do they? Whereas at least I still had a lot of years in front of me to maybe get noticed by someone from a magazine myself, or even a modelling agency – stranger things have happened, as Mum would say. No, it was my dad I couldn't make out. What did *he* have to get excited about? Anyone would think it was him that was going to be in the magazine, the way he was hopping around, singing to himself and chatting to Mum about when she might be going down to London for her big day.

'Maybe I can come with you,' he said. 'We could make it a day out together.'

'Hm,' said Mum. 'Maybe.'

But she caught my eye and I could see her thinking *maybe not*. And I didn't blame her, either. It was her day, wasn't it, not Dad's. It'd be just like him to try and get in on the act, giving an interview to the magazine himself, talking about her bread pudding and how it kept their marriage spiced up, or something equally gross.

'Elizabeth Baxter-Simpson thinks it's great publicity for the pressure group,' she said that evening, after her meeting. 'Roger and some of the others are a bit huffy about it, but do you know what she said? "Penny's the only one here who's doing anything whatsoever to promote our group to the media. Unless the rest of you can come up with anything better, you should all stop sniping and damn' well congratulate her!" Wasn't that nice?'

'Lovely, Mum,' I said. 'Do you want to go up and say goodnight to Jessica?'

'Oh, yes, of course!' said Mum, going a bit pink and rushing upstairs. 'Hello, Jessi-darling! Nanny's home!'

I know this sounds horrible, but I had a feeling she might have forgotten Jessica was here at all. I suppose that's what happens when people start getting famous.

I didn't go to the Cloud on Saturday night.

'What's up, then?' asked Kim on the phone. 'Worried you'll get pissed and end up losing your knickers again?'

'Fuck off,' I told her. I didn't need reminding about it. 'I'm just not in the mood, OK?'

'Suit yourself. I'll give your love to *Luke*, then, shall I, if I see him?'

'You won't see him. He lives in Lowestoft. He never normally comes clubbing down this way.'

I wanted to say, And you're only being nasty like this because you fancy him yourself, but do you know what? I couldn't even be bothered.

'Not going out tonight, Chelle?' asked Dad as I settled down in front of the TV in my old jogging bottoms and

123

dressing gown.

'Does it look like it?'

'Well, I just thought, you know, now that you're single again, you'd be out *bopping* every Saturday night with your friends, eyeing up all the lads ... what's the matter, love?' He stopped and looked at me a bit more closely. I was trying not to cry. 'What's up? Had a row with your mates?'

'No, not really,' I said, wishing he wouldn't ask. 'Sometimes Kim gets on my nerves, that's all. I just feel like a night in. Got any good videos I haven't watched?'

'Well, how about *The Sound of Music*?' he said, 'Or *Mary Poppins*? They seem to cheer your mum up if she's had a bad day.'

Can't imagine how. Looks like it'll be *Saturday Night Fever* for the nineteenth time, then.

'Tell you what, Chelle,' added Dad suddenly just as Mum came downstairs from tucking Jessica into bed, 'If you're just having a quiet night in, then, how about you babysit for Jessica, give your mum a break, and I can take her out for a nice dinner?'

Mum stopped halfway into the room, her mouth a big round 'O' of surprise, and no wonder, either. Dad never normally suggested going out for nice meals, not unless it was their anniversary, and even then Mum usually had to remind him, or drop hints for about a fortnight, and then he'd tell her to book something herself.

'Well!' she said, smiling. 'Well!'

'Would you like that?' he asked, smiling back at her.

Something about their smiling made my toes curl.

'I was going to phone for pizzas for us all,' I said grumpily.

'That's a nice idea, love,' said Dad happily. 'Phone for one for yourself. I think we'll try that new Italian restaurant in Duffington, shall we, Pen?'

'Oh, lovely, Archie!' said Mum. 'I'll just run and change.'

'*Bollocks*!' I said out loud to myself after the front door shut behind them. '*Bollocky bollocking bollocks*!'

Didn't want to go to that Italian restaurant anyway.

I was only a little way into *Saturday Night Fever*, and still waiting for the pizza delivery man, when the phone rang.

'Michelle, darling!' said a horribly familiar voice. 'Not out clubbing tonight, then?'

'Not tonight, Darren, no. I'm babysitting for my little niece.'

'Oh, dear. That's a shame, isn't it?'

Is it?

'I was going to suggest I take you to the Italian restaurant. Like I promised.'

'That's funny,' I said, although to be honest I didn't think it was, not at all. 'Mum and Dad have gone there tonight.'

I wanted to make him understand, you see, that not only was my mum a married woman, but she was *not* the type of married woman to take an interest in other men, however much she might giggle and flirt with them on the phone. Far from it, she was actually the type of married woman who went off to nice restaurants with her loving husband – see? So stick that up your airwaves, Mr *Daytime with Darren*, and leave my mum alone!

'Well, how about that, then, Michelle. What a coincidence! We could have made up a foursome!' he said, laughing.

'No, we couldn't!' I retorted, shocked.

'But threesomes are much more my style, of course!'

'Don't be disgusting,' I told him. 'Anyway, I'm looking after Jessica, so I can't go out. And there's the doorbell, so I've got to go. It'll be my pizza.'

'Shall I come round and share it with you? I could bring us a nice little Chianti.'

'No. And I don't think you ought to keep calling, OK?'

I put down the phone, with only a little pang of regret about the Italian restaurant. It was a sacrifice I'd have to

125

make, to keep him away from my mum. She'd thank me for it one day.

I hadn't even finished eating my cheese and garlic pizza when Jessica started crying.

'All right, baby, Chelly's coming!' I called up the stairs. Normally Jessica was really good at night; she only cried if she had nightmares.

'Nanny!' she screamed. 'I want Nanny!'

'What is it, darling?' I put the bedside lamp on and sat down on the edge of the bed. 'Did you have a bad dream?'

'Nanny!' she yelled again, trying to push me off the bed. 'Want Nanny!'

'Nanny's gone out, Jessica. Chelly's here. D'you want a nice drink of water?'

'No! No drinka water! Don't want you! Want Nanny!'

As if I hadn't been feeling bad enough already. Even Jessica didn't want me now. She sat up in bed, pushing me harder away from her until I gave up and got up off the bed.

'What is it? What's the matter?' I asked her as she threw the duvet off her and started scrabbling around in the bed like a little animal digging its shelter.

'Where's he gone? Where's he *gone*?' she sobbed. 'Where's my Red Bed-Ted gone?'

'Oh, baby, don't cry! He must be here somewhere. Let's put the big light on and have a proper look.'

Fifteen minutes later, I'd had the duvet off the bed, taken it out of its cover, turned the cover inside out, shaken out the pillows, pulled the mattress off the bed, pulled the bed out away from the wall, crawled underneath it, moved the bedside table and looked behind it, even looked under the carpet, and all the while Jessica's wails and cries for Nanny were getting louder and more desperate.

'Are you sure you had him when you went to bed?' I asked. 'Why don't we both go downstairs and have a look in the lounge just in case?'

126

While Jessica sat on the sofa still crying her lungs out, I turned everything in the lounge inside out and started on the kitchen.

'This is silly,' I said eventually. 'Jessica, how about taking one of your other toys to bed with you just for tonight? What about Tommy the Tiger? He's lovely and cuddly.'

'NO!' she screamed, shaking her head so hard I thought she'd do herself an injury. 'Don't WANT Tiger! Want Red Bed-Ted! I WANT NANNY!'

'Well, Nanny wouldn't know where Red Bed-Ted is, either,' I said a bit irritably. Could you blame me, really? Suddenly my mum was Superwoman and I was just useless all round, it seemed to me.

'Nanny! NANNY!' yelled Jessica even louder. She was starting to get hysterical. I'd have the police knocking on the door in a minute.

'OK, Jessica,' I said, sitting down next to her. What the hell could I give her that was going to distract her? 'Want a bit of my pizza?'

'NO pizza!'

'Want to watch a nice video with me? *The Sound of Music*? It's Nanny's favourite!'

'NANNY! I want NANNY!'

'If you're a good girl and stop crying, you can stay up till Nanny comes back. Yeah? Stay up really, really late with Chelly, till Nanny and Granddad get back from the restaurant?'

'I want Nanny NOW!'

This went on for about another ten minutes. I was kind of hoping she'd cry herself out, maybe even fall asleep out of exhaustion, but no such luck – every suggestion I made, everything I offered her, just set her off yelling even louder. I was actually thinking maybe I should give Mum a ring on her mobile and ask her and Dad to come home, but how would that make me look? How pathetic is that, if I can't even quieten down a three-year-old and get her back to bed without her teddy bear?

Then suddenly, in the middle of a particularly ear-splitting I WANT NANNY!, I thought of it. It wasn't going to be a lot of fun, in fact it would be an absolute pain in the arse, but I was pretty sure it'd do the trick.

'Come on, Jessica,' I said, picking her up and carrying her, kicking and yelling, out into the hall. 'Let's get your coat and boots on over your 'jamas. And your hat. Wrap you up warm.'

She looked at me in surprise as I shook off my dressing gown and pulled my own coat on, and, thank God, at last she took a deep shuddering breath and stopped yelling.

'Where we going?' she asked hoarsely.

'To the beach, Jessica. We're going for a ride in Chelly's car. To the beach.'

Despite what my brother told Jessica about her nan and granddad's house being at the seaside, it was really about a ten-minute drive to the nearest beach, and to be honest Duffington Sands wasn't even a particularly *nice* one. It was more like Duffington Muds if you ask me. But I wasn't about to drive her all the way up the coast to where the nicer beaches were, not at half past nine on a cold, dark, November evening when (just my luck) it was starting to spit with rain too. If I'd stopped to think about anything beyond the fact that the word 'beach' had shut her up, I'd have had a bit more sense than to take her out at that time of night anyway, least of all to the bloody beach – but there you go. I'm not a mum. I haven't got that instinct thing, that they say kicks in when you give birth, that starts making you sensible and stops you killing the kid with daft ideas.

Jessica was completely silent in the back of the car for the first few minutes of the journey. I started thinking maybe she'd gone to sleep, and I could just do a circular trip and take her back home to bed without her noticing. No such luck. Eventually this little tiny voice, not much more than a whisper, floated across to me:

'Are we *really* going to the beach, Chelly? Really, *really*?'

See? Even she thought it was unbelievable.

'Yes, really, as long as you've stopped crying and you're going to be a good, quiet girl from now on.'

'I *am* a good girl, Chelly. I *am* stopped crying, for ever and ever!'

Promises, promises! She fell silent again, probably completely overcome with amazement at her luck and thinking it'd be a good plan to lose Red Bed-Ted and have a screaming turnout every night if this was the result.

'Here we are, then!' I said gaily, pulling into the beach car park. It was completely deserted. Not even a steamy-windows courting-couple's car in sight. Everyone else had somewhere warmer to go, like in front of the TV watching *Saturday Night Fever* and eating pizza.

'*Not* the beach,' accused Jessica, staring around her at the dark, deserted car park.

'Yes, it is – listen! Can't you hear the sea?'

I was being a bit optimistic. The loudest sound was the rain now pelting down at full strength and beating off the roof of the car.

'*Not* the sea!' said Jessica very suspiciously. 'Where's sea? Where's sand? I want sand!'

'The beach is just over the sand dunes here, Jessica. Come on, hold my hand. I don't want you falling in the puddles.'

This was definitely, definitely, not a good idea. Why didn't I bring an umbrella? Why didn't I bring a torch? Why didn't I just stay at home in the warm and bribe Jessica with sweeties till she fell asleep? Holding her hand tightly, I trudged up the dunes and down the other side, pulling her behind me, feeling my feet sink further into the cold, wet sand at every step and wishing I'd got sensible welly boots on, like Jessica, instead of my best Nikes.

'Can you see the sea now, Jessica?' I said hopefully.

'*Not* the sea,' she said grumpily. 'Can't see the sea.'

'No, well, it's a bit too dark.' I screwed up my eyes and stared at the big black space in front of us where the sea should be. There wasn't even any moonlight to give a little bit of a shimmer to the waves. I could quite understand Jessica, really, thinking it wasn't there. I was beginning to have doubts myself. 'Let's walk a little bit closer, and then you'll be able to hear the waves. Only the rain's making so much noise, isn't it! It's like that song you sing at nursery, Jessica. Shall we sing it together? "Pitter-patter raindrops, pitter-patter raindrops ...."'

Good job nobody was listening. I was beginning to feel like Postman Pat with his black-and-white cat. Jessica wasn't even joining in, I was singing it all on my own like a prize prat.

'There!' I stopped, crouched down next to Jessica and pointed. 'Look! See that light out there? Watch it moving! It's a little boat, see?'

'Not a boat,' she retorted. 'Can't see a boat. No flag!' It wasn't really the right time to get into any sort of explanation about boats not always having flags. '*Not* the sea!' she added crossly. 'Don't like it! Want to go home!'

I was getting pissed off now. OK, OK, I know it was my own fault. It was bad enough having brought her here. But if I'd ruined my new trainers in the mud and it wasn't even going to cheer her up, then I'm sorry, but maybe I wasn't cut out for looking after little children. Maybe it was a good job nobody loved me, nobody stayed living with me for long enough to marry me or get me pregnant without pissing off with no explanation over a pub lunch.

'Jessica!' I said, quite snappily I admit, 'Chelly's getting cross now. I've brought you to the beach for a Very Special Treat, and you promised to be a good girl!'

'Go 'way, Chelly! Don't like you! I want Nanny!'

'Well, you can't—' I stopped dead, listening carefully, my heart suddenly giving a lurch of fear. 'Hello? Is anyone there?'

I thought I'd heard someone behind me. Someone coughing, or clearing their throat. I needed my bloody head examined, as my dad would say, coming out here in the pitch dark with just my jogging bottoms and old pyjama top on under my coat – anybody could knock me over the head and rape me without even having any struggle to get my clothes off. It didn't bear thinking about. And what about Jessica? Terrific auntie *I* was, dragging a three-year-old down the beach in the pouring rain and telling her off because she didn't like it.

'Hello. I recognise that voice. Is that you, Michelle?'

'Dr Willoughby! Oh, thank God it's you!' I almost fell into his arms with relief. 'I thought you were going to tear off my pyjamas and rape me!'

'Hm,' he said. He might have been smiling but it was hard to tell in the dark. I could only see his teeth and the whites of his eyes. 'Interesting idea, Michelle, but not really the weather for it, is it? Should I ask why you're out on the beach in your pyjamas, or would you rather not say?'

'Oh, it's just that Jessica wouldn't stop crying because of losing her teddy, you see, so . . .'

'Red Bed-Ted,' put in Jessica, in a pathetic little sad voice. 'Red Bed-Ted gone! Want to go home now. Don't like it here.'

'Yes, all right, Jessica.' I sighed. 'So much for cheering her up.'

'Kids, eh!' he said lightly. 'Is that your car up in the car park? Shall I walk back with you?'

'OK. That'd be nice. What are *you* doing here, anyway?' I asked him as we started to climb back up the dunes.

'Oh, just walking, listening to the sea. Chilling out.'

'Funny weather for chilling out on the beach, isn't it?'

'Well, maybe I'm a funny bloke,' he said with a little laugh. 'I often come here, after I finish a shift at the hospital. Feel the sea breeze, smell the ozone. Helps me unwind.'

'Lovely,' I said.

'Most people think it's crazy,' he added.

'Most people would probably think I'm crazy too, bringing a three-year old here in the pouring rain,' I admitted. 'My mum will throw a fit.'

'Still, it's not your mum that's having to stop her crying, is it?' he said quite gently. 'You mustn't worry too much what other people say, Michelle.'

'No, that's true. You're right.' After all, Mum went out, didn't she, and left me in charge. Why should I feel bad about it? I did what I thought was best. I'd tell her that, too, when she flew off the handle about the mud all over Jessica's pyjama legs. 'Thanks, Dr Willoughby,' I added, feeling better.

'Fraser,' he said. We stopped at my car and he waited while I fished around in my pockets for the car key. 'Call me Fraser, please, Michelle.'

'OK. Thanks, Fraser.'

'And we really must have that drink together. What about Wednesday night? I'm off duty then.'

Well, now. On the one hand, I'd gone off men completely, for ever and ever, as Jessica would say. On the other hand, he was quite a nice, quiet, *gentlemanly* kind of man – not like my normal type at all. And besides which – he was a doctor. I had a few issues I wanted to discuss with a doctor, you see.

'That'd be nice. Yeah, that'd be really nice. Thanks ... Fraser. 'Bye, then.'

''Bye, Michelle. 'Bye, Jessica!' He patted her on the head.

'Nice man,' said Jessica as I started the car up. 'Nice man, horrid Chelly.'

God. I don't think I'm ever having children. They do absolutely nothing for your self-esteem.

Jessica was back in bed before Mum and Dad came home. She'd fallen asleep in the car and was so completely zonked out, I managed to carry her up to bed, change her pyjama trousers and get her under the duvet without her waking up.

'Why've you got the washing machine on, at this time of night?' was the first thing Mum said as she came in the door.

'Jessica and I went to the beach and got covered in mud, so I had to wash our clothes.'

'Oh, very funny, ha ha,' said Dad mildly, rubbing his stomach and burping. 'That was a lovely meal, Michelle. You should go there some time.'

'Yes, I'd like to,' I said between my teeth. 'In fact, I got invited there tonight, but—'

'Oh, and guess who we saw in the restaurant?' interrupted Mum, giving me a very pointed look. 'Darren Barlow! With ... his girlfriend, I suppose.'

The bastard. I turn him down, and he takes some other bird instead.

'Yes, but he was giving your mother the eye all night,' said Dad, smiling at Mum and seeming quite happy about it.

'Oh, of course he wasn't, Archie!' Mum retorted with a silly little giggle. 'Don't be ridiculous!'

I tripped on Red Bed-Ted when I went in the bathroom to clean my teeth. He was lying just inside the door. If I didn't know better, I could have sworn Jessica had planted him there deliberately.

Penny

I didn't know what to make of him. Darren Barlow, I'm talking about. I couldn't work out what he was playing at. Asking my Michelle to go out with him, when he already had a girlfriend! It really made my blood boil. And you should have seen her – he was with her in the Italian restaurant – she was an absolute stunner. Not as pretty as my Michelle, you know, but – well, the type any bloke would go for. A bit obvious. All red lips and red nails. Big eyes, big boobs, tiny little waist and her bum wiggling inside a skirt so tight I was watching to see if it would split when she sat down. Why was he messing around flirting with Michelle when he already had someone like that? And why was he .... well, I'm not being funny, but why was he looking at *me* in that way, too? Why, when I was sitting enjoying a nice meal with my husband, and he was sitting across from me, enjoying a nice meal too, and a lot of high pitched giggling with that woman, was he grinning at me over her shoulder, winking at me and licking his lips in a very embarrassing and disgusting way? I thought I was imagining it at first, but I don't think, even if I tried, I would have come up with something like that in my imagination.

Archie looked round at one point, and caught him smiling at me.

'That's Darren Barlow,' I explained quickly.

'Oh. The stupid radio presenter,' he said, staring at him. 'He can't take his eyes off you, Penny.'

'Don't be silly.' I felt myself going all red. 'He fancies Michelle, if anything. That's probably why he's looking at us. And he's got a girlfriend. She might even be his wife, I don't know.'

'Well, that's as may be. But if you ask me, Pen, he fancies the pants off you. Not that I can blame him!' he added, giving my thigh a squeeze under the table.

I nearly dropped a whole forkful of tagliatelle, I was so shocked.

'Archie Peacham!' I hissed at him. 'Stop it – everyone will be looking at us!'

'Let them look!' he laughed. 'We're married, aren't we!'

Exactly. Not really the way you carry on when you've been married over thirty years. I was beginning to think I should buy something to put in Archie's tea and calm him down.

'Honestly,' I said to Maureen a couple of days later, when we were in Marks & Spencer together. 'Honestly, my whole family is acting very strange. What with Adam going off for these secret weekends, and Michelle moping around crying ...'

'Crying?' she said sharply. 'What's your Michelle got to cry about?'

'What do you think? Her boyfriend went off and left her without so much as a—'

'Come off it, Penny. She got over that quicker than you could blink. Her pride was the only thing hurt. She was out clubbing with her mates five minutes after he'd gone ...'

'I know, and bloody good luck to her!'

'Absolutely. You can't blame her, can you. I said that to Cynthia Matthews. "Cynthia", I said, "You can't blame her for having a bit of fun with the boys. Poor girl got dumped by her boyfriend, didn't she. No wonder she wants to have a drink and have a bit of fun now ..."'

'Bit of fun? With the boys?' I squawked. 'What boys? What are you doing, talking to bloody Cynthia Matthews about my Michelle?'

Cynthia Matthews was Kim's mother, and I'd never liked her. Her tongue was so poisonous, she gave herself a belly-ache just sucking on it, judging from her expression.

'She was only saying about that night they all went up to Lowestoft.'

'Nicole's birthday.'

'Yes. Your Michelle had a right skinful, apparently.'

'Well, I expect they all had a few ... '

'She said Kim was worried about her. They thought they'd lost her at the end of the night. She was outside in the—'

'Maureen!' I snapped. I seemed to keep on snapping at Maureen lately. She seemed to be going out of her way to annoy me, somehow. 'I don't want to hear it, all right? I don't want to hear a single word that bitch Cynthia has to say about Michelle. If she starts it up again, you can just tell her to shut up and mind her own business.'

'Well, I was only telling you, Penny, because I'm concerned about your Michelle ... '

'No, you're not. You're telling me because it's a bit of gossip and you want to find out if it's true.'

And if you had kids of your own, you wouldn't spend so much time interfering in the lives of other people's.

I nearly said it. Shit, I so nearly said it, I had to literally bite my tongue, and it bloody hurt, too. I've thought it for over twenty years, to be perfectly honest – but you can't say things like that to your best friend, can you.

'Well, I'm sorry, I'm sure,' she said huffily, pretending to get very interested in some pink bath towel sets.

I sighed.

'Forget it. I'm worried about Michelle myself, but I don't want other people saying things about her. I expect she just feels a bit fed up, you know. Maybe Christmas will cheer her up.'

136

'Maybe.'

'And anyway.' I was gabbling away, frantically trying to make up for what I'd nearly said, trying to be nicer on the outside than my thoughts were being inside my head. 'Anyway, I wanted to tell you about this makeover day I've been invited to, at *Woman Today*. It's really bizarre! They've got a woman who makes her husband sleep in the garden, and one who does handstands in the nude, and ...'

'And *you*?' She was still looking at the pink towel bales.

'Yes, and the feature's supposed to be about mature women with sexual vitality – can you believe it?' I giggled, nudging her, trying to be friends again. Trying to stop her staring at the bloody towels.

'Huh!' she snorted, which annoyed me all over again. She might at least make an effort to be interested.

'And we've all got to be interviewed, but Fantasia thinks that will probably be done over the phone, and—'

'Fantasia?!' said Maureen with another snort. At least she'd turned round from the towels now.

'Fantasia Topping, she's the Features Co-ordinator, and—'

'Sounds like a bloody instant whip dessert.'

'Yes, I know, and we all have our hair and make-up and everything done, and our photos taken, and—'

'Photos, eh?'

'And we have lunch with the Beauty Editor and the Features Editor, and then—'

'Oh! The *Beauty* Editor and the *Features* Editor, eh?'

I didn't like the way she was saying it. She didn't sound as impressed as I thought she'd be.

'I thought,' I added, tapping her arm to make her look at me. I gave her a smile to show we were still friends. 'I thought you might like to ... they said I could take someone with me. I thought maybe you might like to come?'

I was expecting this to change everything. I thought she'd stop looking sour and disapproving. I thought she'd

137

forget how I'd snapped at her and forget the whole thing about Cynthia Matthews, and forget how we'd argued the other week about Chris Filbey when she said I was obsessed. I'll admit it – I thought she'd be beside herself with excitement, and she'd hug me and say how grateful she was, and what a good friend I was, and how lucky she was that I'd chosen her to go on my day out to London.

I thought wrong.

'Sorry, Penny,' she said very dismissively, turning back to the towels and picking one up as if she was considering buying it (which I knew she wasn't, because her bathroom was blue, and she'd rather have died than have pink towels in a blue bathroom). 'You'll have to find someone else. I think I'm busy that day.'

'But I haven't even told you which day—' I began.

'I wonder if they've got these towels in blue?'

I tried talking to Michelle again that evening. It wasn't easy, really, because she was in the bathroom for about an hour and when she came out she had her head wrapped in a towel and something bright green plastered all over her face.

'Want a cup of tea?' I asked her. 'Come into the kitchen, away from the telly, and we can chat while I make it.'

'Chat? What about?' she said. Well, I thought that was what she said, but it was difficult to be sure because she couldn't move her mouth very much on account of the green plaster. She looked through the lounge door at the TV as if she was weighing up her options. There was football on again, and Archie was talking to the referee, asking him whether he was fucking blind and fucking stupid. She shrugged and followed me into the kitchen, perching on a stool and patting her facemask cautiously.

'Washed your hair, love?' I began as I switched on the kettle.

'Coloured it. Warm Honey Pink.'

'Oh, Michelle! Whatever for? You've got such lovely blonde—'

138

'All right, Mum, I'm not a baby – I just fancied a change, OK?'

I blinked in surprise. It was so unlike my Michelle to be snappy with me. I turned away and put the tea bags in the mugs, but she was right behind me straight away, putting her arm round me.

'Sorry,' she said. 'But I feel a bit nervous about it already, Mum. I don't know what it's going to turn out like. It says on the packet that it adds depth and rich warm tones to blonde hair. I've always fancied a bit more depth.'

'How can hair be deep? And how can honey be pink?' I asked, mystified, but she was busy getting the biscuit tin out of the cupboard.

'I wonder if I can eat a custard cream without cracking my face?' She touched her cheek again gingerly and looked at her fingers to see if the green had come off.

'Why's it green, anyway?'

'Cucumber, mint and avocado.'

Well, yes, there's plenty of green there, I suppose. It'd only need spinach in it and you could probably get all your nourishment for a week just by licking it off your face.

'What's all this in aid of, Chelle?' I put our two mugs of tea down on the table. 'The hair, and the face? You look lovely already, you know you do.'

'You only say that because you're my mum. It's part of your job, isn't it.'

'Just because Robbie cleared off – it doesn't mean ...'

'Robbie?' She looked at me as if I was completely mad, shaking her head. 'I keep telling you, Mum, I don't care any more about Robbie. He's not worth worrying about.'

'So what *are* you worrying about?' I asked her straight. 'Only I'm not daft, Michelle. You've been moping around the place, looking upset, and crying. Has anyone been upsetting you? You can talk to me, you know. That's part of my job too.'

'No one's upset me. I've just been feeling a bit fed up, I suppose.'

'What about going out with your friends a bit more, then? You had a nice night out for Nicole's birthday the other week, didn't you?'

She looked back at me with such an intense stare that I wondered for a minute if she'd guessed that I'd heard some gossip.

'It was all right,' she said. I thought I heard a bit of a wobble in her voice, but I might have imagined it.

'Only all right? Maybe you can't remember much about it!' I said with a little light laugh. 'Maybe you had a bit too much to drink, eh!'

'Yeah. Maybe,' she said. 'Look, Mum, it's cracking my face to talk, if you don't mind. I think I'll just go and watch the—'

'You'd tell me if there was anything wrong, wouldn't you, Chelle?'

For just a second she hesitated, standing halfway to the kitchen door with her mug of tea in one hand and her custard cream in the other.

'Nothing wrong,' she said, trying not to move her mouth. 'I'm OK. Stop worrying. Anyway I'm going out tomorrow night.'

'With Kim and Nicole? That'll be nice ...'

She shook her head.

'A bloke.'

I sighed. 'Not Darren Barlow'

'No. I'll leave him to you, as Dad doesn't seem to be bothered about it.'

'Don't be ridiculous! He's not .... I'm not ...' I waved my hands about a bit, flustered and annoyed at this turn of the conversation. 'Who, then? A new boyfriend, Chelle?'

She shrugged. 'One of the doctors from work. Probably just a drink. Just a friend.' With this she walked out, pointing at her face and shaking her head. Too late, really. It already looked a bit cracked.

A doctor, I said to myself under my breath. *I've heard they can be very unreliable*. But unfortunately the thought came straight back at me like a boomerang: *Why? Like vets, are they?*

Fantasia Topping's PA, Charisma Vanderpool, sounded remarkably normal. Her accent was South Essex but she spoke very slowly, as if she had to concentrate on not dropping her H's and T's.

'I'm just calling to make sure you got the letter, Mrs Peacham? About the date for the makeover.'

'Yes. Yes, thank you ... er ... Charisma. I got it on Monday.'

'And is that OK for you, Mrs Peacham? The Tuesday after next, the ... um ... ninth of December?'

'Yes. Yes, that's absolutely fine.'

'And you'll keep your receipts for the train fare, yeah ... yes? *Woman Today* will reimburse all your expenses. And we'll send a car to meet you from Liverpool Street station.'

'Wonderful. It all sounds very exciting.'

Actually I was crapping myself with nerves about it. How was I ever going to know what to talk to these people about? It was bad enough them having names like Fantasia and Charisma, never mind introducing me to people who had pierced nipples and did headstands in the nude.

'And will you be bringing a friend along, Mrs Peacham? Only we need to know for catering purposes, you see.'

Blimey. How many fatted calves were they going to bring in?

'Yes, yes, of course,' I said, vaguely. I was thinking about Maureen saying she was too busy, and being so huffy about the whole thing. And I was thinking about Archie suggesting we made a day out of it, and probably hatching up ideas to tell everyone about my bread pudding and embarrass me by touching my thigh in public. Not that it wouldn't be nice to make a day out of it. I hadn't been to London for years. If there was time afterwards, it'd be fun to do some Christmas shopping in Oxford Street. I imag-

141

ined myself in the bright lights of the West End, swinging in and out of the gaily decorated shops with bags of gift-wrapped parcels on my arms. Nothing like a bit of shopping to cheer you up. And, instantly, I knew just who I wanted to take with me.

'My daughter,' I told Charisma firmly. 'I'm bringing my daughter Michelle with me.'

'Lovely, Mrs Peacham. We'll see you and Michelle on the ninth, then. The car will be at Liverpool Street at ten o'clock.'

'Great. I'll look forward to it.'

And the thing was – I actually *was* looking forward to it now, after all. It'd be so much better, going with my Michelle. We'd have such a laugh! Why didn't I think of it before?

Chris Filbey had tormented me rotten every day since I'd had the phone call from Fantasia Topping.

'You must be crazy if you believe these tarts are really working for a women's magazine,' he said, leaning a bit too close to me as he reached into the cupboard behind my desk for a fresh pack of sterile needles. He gave me a lazy smile and shook his head slightly. 'With names like Fantasia and Charisma! I'm telling you, Penny, they're not going to be taking photos of you in a tweed skirt and twinset.'

'I don't know what you're talking about. It's all above board and proper. Look – here's the letter – see? Headed notepaper – *Woman Today*.'

'If you say so.' He shrugged, ignoring the letter and turning to walk away. 'Just don't say I didn't warn you when they dress you up in black leather and chains and ask you to pose bending over a chair with a whip in your hand.' At this, he turned back and winked at me. 'Just make sure you show me the photos,' he added in a soft growl.

I turned my attention to an old lady carrying a tiny black kitten in her handbag. She'd got the bag zipped up almost all the way, to stop him jumping out, and you could just see his little fluffy head and tufty ears sticking up.

'What's the matter with him?' I shouted, for the benefit of her hearing aid.

The old lady stared at the door of the consulting room that Chris had just disappeared into.

'Oversexed, by the sound of him,' she declared in a loud, clear voice that carried all round the waiting room.

'No! I mean ... ' Oh, shit. I thought she was supposed to be deaf? There were several snickers from behind the heads of a Great Dane and a Dalmatian. 'I mean the kitten,' I said miserably. 'What's the matter with the kitten?'

'Pardon? You'll have to speak up, dear. I'm a bit deaf.' She pulled the unfortunate kitten out of the bag by his neck and set him down on the desk between us. 'I've brought Sooty to get his nuts taken off, please, dear. I can't have any of that how's-yer-father going on outside my windows at night. Not at my age. It sets my nerves on edge.'

I could quite understand it. My own nerves felt as if their edges had been cut with steel. It was alarming, and scary, and exquisite all at the same time. I couldn't take my eyes off Chris's door, waiting for him to come out again. I couldn't stop thinking about the way he'd smiled, the way he'd winked at me, the way he'd described the black leather and the chair ...

'When you're ready, dear? Shall I hold him still while you cut them off?'

What with her selective hearing problem, it took me so long to make Sooty's owner understand that I wasn't the vet, that I was in no way qualified or even inclined to cut off a kitten's testicles, that he'd probably die of shock if we attempted it without an anaesthetic, and that out of fairness to him and consideration of the fact that we could hardly even see them yet, we might prefer to wait until he was more than a couple of weeks old before we set about his genitals with a knife. By the time she'd left, grumbling

143

about not letting him get old enough to start doing how's-yer-father outside her windows, there was an impatient queue of corgis and guinea pigs to deal with, and it was lunchtime before I was free to indulge my mind with images of Chris Filbey again.

I was doing exactly that, on my own in the staff kitchen, gazing out of the window while I waited for the kettle to boil for my Cup-A-Soup and listened to the dog in the pre-op cage whimpering quietly to himself in fear. I was just imagining how it would feel to pose for Chris in black leather and fishnet stockings; how he would look at me with that slow smile, his eyes narrowed, how he'd walk towards me, unbuttoning his shirt, and . . .

'The kettle's boiling,' said a voice very close behind me.

'Oh!' I jumped, and turned, and blushed, and jumped again as he held me, very briefly, by the shoulders as he reached across me to turn the kettle off.

Then, instead of moving back, he stayed there, leaning across me, and he took hold of me again, and ran his hands up and down my arms very, very gently from my shoulders to my elbows, making every nerve in my body tingle with a terrible, terrible desire.

'You ... are ... a ... very ... sexy ... lady,' he whispered slowly against my ear. The feel of his breath made me tremble. 'Do you know that?'

I didn't answer. I couldn't speak. I closed my eyes and thought: If he kisses me now, I won't be able to help it. This is how people start affairs. I always wondered why they do it, and now I know. It's impossible not to.

There were footsteps outside the door. Chris dropped his hands from my arms and stepped away from me with a look like a wince of pain.

'Chris!' called Debbie, pushing the door open. 'Are you in there? Are you ready for the bull mastiff now, or did you want to have your lunch first?'

I pretended to concentrate very hard on pouring boiling water over the lumpy orange powder in my mug that was

144

promising to become minestrone soup.

'Yes, I'm ready,' said Chris. 'I'll be right with you, Debbie. Get him prepped for me.'

'I've kind of lost interest in my lunch now, anyway,' he added quietly to me as Debbie left the room again.

The soup was looking fascinating. It was amazing how long you could spend in silent contemplation of a cup of minestrone. I knew the shape of every piece of vegetable and had counted all the noodles twice.

'I think I've discovered something much more interesting,' he continued, reaching out to touch my arm again. The mug of soup shook violently in my hand.

'Chris! Are we going to be shaving the whole of his hindquarters or just the anal area?'

Just as well, really. It's difficult to stay aroused when you're faced with the question of a bull mastiff's arse.

145

Michelle

I'd done two pregnancy tests. They were both negative. It was ridiculous, but I still couldn't accept that I was really, definitely, safe. I think I was kind-of punishing myself. I almost thought I deserved to be pregnant because I'd behaved like such a tart.

It didn't help, Mum giving me the big Is There Something You Want To Talk About thing, and looking at me with the same look she used to give me when I was little and she knew perfectly well I'd done something naughty but she was waiting for me to own up to it. This time she didn't know, she couldn't know. But it still made me feel uncomfortable. As well as bloody miserable.

It was horrible feeling so down. I'm not like that, normally. I get on and get over things – I don't like going in for all that moping around. Life's too short, as Mum always says. But I just couldn't seem to snap out of it now. What was there to be happy about? I'd tried going out with my mates and having a good time, and I'd ended up making a complete arse of myself, possibly getting raped and pregnant and catching AIDS and dying. Or getting some horrible sexual diseases that would eat away at my insides or make me scabby and itchy and smelly. I kept checking, and so far everything looked normal, but who was to say it wouldn't lie dormant for months, or even years, and suddenly go rampant when I was middle-aged and married?

You hear about marriages breaking up over things like that.

So that was one of the reasons I'd agreed to go out with Fraser Willoughby. After all, he might specialise in elderly people, but he was still a doctor, wasn't he? It stood to reason he'd have learned stuff about pregnancy tests and AIDS at medical school as well, and with luck he'd still remember some of it. I'd have to ask him in a roundabout sort of way, of course – I didn't want him thinking I was a tart. Even if I was one.

Not that I didn't want to go out with him anyway. He was nice; I'd always liked him. And I was kind of flattered that he wanted to go out with me. I know I'd gone off men lately, but I had a feeling Fraser would be different from what I'd been used to. He didn't seem the type to walk out on me in the middle of a pub lunch, or (possibly, possibly not) have sex with me outside a nightclub and never even bother to tell me about it. And definitely not the type to ask me to an Italian restaurant and end up taking some other bird and ogling my mother. No, I reckoned Fraser had more class than all of them. And I wanted to make an effort to look good for him.

I was a bit disappointed with the hair colour, to be quite honest. As Mum so rightly said – how can honey be pink? I suppose I never thought about it till she said it. I just liked the sound of it. I left the stuff on my hair for ten minutes longer than the maximum recommended time, in the hope it would add even more *depth and rich warm tones*. Then I panicked and rinsed it off quickly in case it went bright pink. But when I dried it, it wasn't pink at all. And it wasn't blonde any more, either. It was the sort of colour that peaches go, just before they go off, turn brown and then go mouldy. I wasn't sure whether I liked it at all, and it didn't help one bit when Jessica asked me why my hair looked orange.

'It's not orange,' I said snappily. 'It's honey.'

She put her thumb in her mouth and eyed me very doubtfully.

147

'That's silly,' she said.

'Why? Don't you think it looks nice?'

I was desperate for someone to like it, even Jessica.

'No. Honey is for eats. Not for putting on hair. Nanny, Nanny! Chelly put honey on her hair!'

Silly me.

I got a new blue top, special offer in New Look, and wore it with my best jeans.

'You look nice,' he said when he came to pick me up.

That was a good start. He didn't specifically mention the hair, but on the other hand at least he didn't ask why it looked orange.

He held the car door open for me and he helped me with the seat belt, which I thought was very gentlemanly and made me feel a bit flustered, being much more used to getting in on my own while moving empty Coke cans, old car-park tickets, sweet wrappers and CDs off the seat and kicking a couple of maps and a bottle of de-icer out of the way at the same time.

'Thank you,' I said. 'Where are we going?'

'I thought perhaps the Old Grey Mare in Duffington? It's nice in there, and if we get hungry we can always get a bar snack.'

Oh, shit. Hadn't been in the Grey Mare since Robbie's disappearing act.

'OK.'

He laughed. 'You don't sound keen. Don't you like it there? We could go somewhere else ... '

'No ... you're right, it's nice there. Let's go there. That'll be lovely.'

I smiled at him and he laughed again, looking slightly puzzled.

Well, I had to get over it, didn't I. Couldn't spend the rest of my life avoiding places I'd been with Robbie Nelson.

They had a log fire going in the pub, which was really

148

nice as it was such a cold night. We got a table near the fire and I warmed up so quickly I had to take my coat off.

'You look so different out of uniform,' he said. 'If you dressed like that for work, I'd never be able to concentrate on the patients.'

I wasn't sure if this was a compliment or if he was implying I looked like a tart. I gave my top a bit of a tug, just in case, to try and cover up my cleavage, and noticed he was looking. He took a gulp of his beer.

'I wasn't being insulting. You look great. I like the hair, too.'

'Oh! You noticed!' I smiled. 'It's supposed to be Warm Honey Pink but I think it's ended up kind of Rotten Peach. I was thinking of asking for my money back.'

'Warm Honey Pink,' he mused, looking at it with his head on one side as if he was considering a work of art. 'I think I'd call it Soft Golden Apricot.'

Better than orange, anyway. I was quite tickled by the way he was taking an interest, talking about hair colours as if they were a serious matter for discussion. Robbie wouldn't even have noticed – and if I'd asked him what he thought of it, he'd have said, 'All right,' without even looking. Robbie. My heart took a dive down to my boots at the thought, and I sneaked a glance over my shoulder at the table by the window where we'd sat that Friday lunchtime when he walked out on me. I didn't care any more. I didn't miss him one bit. If he walked through that door now, I'd walk straight out without even talking to him. But it still hurt just to think that he'd *done* it to me. The bastard! The *bastard*!

'Are you all right?' asked Fraser.

I realised with a start that I'd been staring across the pub, pulling a really savage face and possibly even muttering under my breath.

'Sorry! Yes, I'm fine, I just ...'

'Seen someone you know?' He looked vaguely in the direction I'd been staring. 'You looked a bit upset.'

149

'No. No, honestly, I'm fine. Would you like another drink?'

'No – I'll make this one last, thanks, as I'm driving. But I'll get you another one. Vodka and tonic again?'

'Thanks. But I'll pay this time.'

He waved my purse away as if it was something embarrassing he shouldn't be looking at.

While he was up at the bar, I sneaked another look at the table by the window. I don't know why. Did I think Robbie was suddenly going to jump up from under the table, shouting 'Boo!' and laughing that he'd been there all the time? Or was the Ghost of Robbie going to float across the pub to me? There was a barmaid collecting glasses from the table. As I watched her, she turned round and caught my eye, and I recognised her as the girl I'd asked about Robbie on the day he vanished.

'Hello, love!' she called as she made her way back to the bar, pausing at my table just as Fraser arrived with my drink. 'You found your boyfriend, in the end, then?'

I muttered something and took a mouthful of my drink, waiting for her to go away. I wanted to explain to Fraser, but I didn't know where to start. He was giving me a funny look again, but I think he was too polite to ask if I wasn't going to tell him.

'I think she muddled me up with someone else,' I told him awkwardly.

He just nodded and changed the subject.

We were getting on so well, with him telling me lots of funny stories about his days as a medical student, and me telling him all about my mum and her protest group, and her bread pudding, that I was beginning to wonder how I was going to bring up the subject of pregnancy tests and sexually transmitted diseases.

'How do you get on with the other girls in Outpatients, Michelle?' he asked suddenly.

'OK,' I said. 'We always have a bit of a chat at lunchtimes, you know. Actually,' I added, kind of nonchalantly, 'One of the girls was telling me about a friend of a friend of hers who thinks she might be pregnant.'

It sounded false, even to me, but he didn't seem to notice.

'Oh yes?'

'Well.' I leaned a bit closer to him and lowered my voice. 'Apparently she's had two pregnancy tests that were both negative. But she still can't help worrying that she might be pregnant.'

'Why? Does she have any symptoms of pregnancy? Nausea? Frequent urination? Breast changes?'

I felt myself blush bright red, but he seemed to have gone into doctor mode, looking very serious and considering the subject as if he had the patient there in front of him.

'I ... er ... don't think so. My friend didn't say.'

'She's worried because she or her partner didn't use contraception?'

'Um ... yes, I think so.'

I couldn't look at him. I kept swishing the ice cubes around in my drink and watching them as if they were fascinating.

'And she's missed a period?'

Gulp.

'It's two days late,' I said very quietly. 'And it's never usually ... I mean, my friend says her friend is never usually ...' I tailed off miserably.

Fraser was quiet for a few minutes, as if he was thinking about it.

'Sometimes,' he said eventually, 'If someone is very anxious about the possibility of pregnancy, this can upset the hormonal balance and cause a period to be delayed.'

'Can it?' I asked hopefully. 'Do you think that's what's happened with ... this person?'

'Very likely. Especially given the two negative results. If I was ... your friend ... I'd tell ... her friend ... to repeat the test after another week if she still hasn't had her period. But the tests are usually reliable.'

151

'Oh!' I smiled with relief. 'Yes, I'll tell her. Thanks, Fraser.'

'You're welcome. But your ... your friend's friend ... should go to her own doctor, really, if she's got any other worries.'

'Well. I think ... according to my friend ... from what I can make out, the only other thing she's worried about is – well, you know. Having done it – without using anything, as it were ...'

'She's worried about having caught an STD or AIDS?'

'I think so,' I whispered miserably.

'Does she know her partner's sexual history? Has he told her he's got an infection, or been treated for anything?'

'I don't know ... she didn't say.'

'Has she got any discharge? Itching? Burning?'

'NO! Sorry. I mean, I don't know. I'll have to get my friend to ask her.'

'OK,' he said quite gently. 'That's a good idea. Tell her to go to the clinic if she's still worried. And hopefully she ... or her partner ... are using contraception now.'

'I expect so. Probably scared her shitless, I shouldn't wonder,' I said.

I drained my glass, put it back down on the table and looked back at him, trying to arrange my face into an expression of non-embarrassment.

'Well now,' he said. 'Would you like some chips?'

We chatted about hospital stuff for the rest of the evening. Which consultants were good to work for, which ones were bad-tempered and made their registrars do all the work while they concentrated on their private practice. Which nurses he could trust to look after his patients properly. Who was going to the Christmas party. Who was upset because they'd been put on-call.

'Thanks, Fraser. I've had a really nice time,' I told him when we arrived back at my house. 'Do you want to come in for a cup of coffee?'

'No. I ...er ... think I'd better be getting back,' he said. 'Thanks all the same.'

He got out of the car and came round to open my door for me. ''Night, Michelle. Take care.'

Was that it?

I was so surprised, it was as much as I could do to get out of the car without slamming the door.

I was pretty sure he'd fancied me, the way he looked at me and stared at my cleavage and said all that about my hair being like soft apricots. I thought we'd got on well; we'd had a laugh and shared a plate of chips. I'd offered to pay for my drinks. What had I done wrong? Why didn't he even want to kiss me goodnight?

'Goodnight,' I said, lifting my face towards his slightly, hoping for a last-minute clinch.

He gave me a smile and a little wave of his hand, got back into the driver's seat and started up the engine.

Well, wouldn't you just know it? It looked like Fraser Willoughby was going to be another one to add to my growing list of men who weren't interested in me.

'Michelle,' said Mum the next evening. 'Do you want to come to London with me on the ninth of December? I'm allowed to take a guest to the makeover at the magazine, and I thought you might like to come.'

'I thought Dad wanted to go with you?'

'He can't,' she said quickly. 'It's only for women. They'll be dressing us up for photographs, and doing our make-up, and stuff, and men would get in the way.'

I could quite believe that, even if Mum was making it up. Did I want to go to London? I sighed. I didn't feel like I wanted to do anything, at the moment.

'Come on, Chelle. It'll be a nice day out. We can go Christmas shopping in the afternoon. It'll cheer you up.'

'I suppose so.'

It was true I hadn't started any Christmas shopping. And it *would* make a change to have a day out in London. A day away from work, away from Fraser Willoughby and his apologetic little smile that was already telling me he was very sorry but he had no intention of going out with me again.

'OK,' I said with a shrug. 'If you want. I'll ask Sister tomorrow if I can get the day off.'

'Lovely,' said Mum, looking really excited.

Ah, bless her. I suppose I should have been happier for her, but to be honest, it was getting difficult to be happy about anything.

'Have you got your period yet?' asked Nicole on Friday night.

We were in the pictures, waiting for the main film to start, and I wished she'd keep her voice down about my periods.

'No,' I whispered back. 'And thanks for telling everyone in the cinema.'

'I don't suppose you are pregnant,' she announced cheerfully. 'And anyway, there's still plenty of time for an abortion.'

Several heads in the row in front of us turned to look at me. I shrank down in my seat.

'Kim says she can't understand why you didn't get the morning-after pill.'

'Kim should mind her own fucking business,' I hissed angrily. I put some more popcorn in my mouth and mumbled through it: 'Anyway, why are you talking to Kim about it? I told you not to tell anyone. If her mum gets to hear about this, it might as well be in the *Duffington Echo*.'

'Ssh!' said someone behind us loudly as the film started.

'Sorry,' whispered Nicole. 'I'll tell her you're not pregnant, shall I? I'll say he used a condom. That'll shut her up.'

I wouldn't mind if I even *knew* whether he'd used anything. Or even if we'd done it at all.

I spent a long time in a hot bath the next morning, hoping it would bring on my period, if it was ever going to come. When I went downstairs, Mum came out of the kitchen wiping her hands on a tea towel and saying:

'Someone phoned for you a few minutes ago.'

'Who?'

'I don't know. A man.'

Fraser? Realised he couldn't live without me after all and desperate for another date?

'Didn't he say who he was?'

'No, love. He was quite rude, actually. He just asked if you were in, and then he said he'd come round. Then he hung up.'

'*Come round*?' I squawked, dropping the slice of bread I was just about to put in the toaster. 'What, *now*?'

I was in my dressing gown, my hair wrapped in a towel.

'Well, he didn't really say. But I suppose ...'

I flew back upstairs, pulling the towel off my hair as I went, yanking my dressing gown off as I ran into my bedroom, and just about managed to get my knickers and jeans on when there was a ring at the doorbell. I listened, holding my breath, as Mum walked to the front door and opened it.

'Oh, hello, dear,' I heard her say.

Dear?

'We haven't seen you for a long time, have we? You haven't got any news of that Robbie, by any chance, have you?'

I froze, half in and half out of my jumper.

'No, 'fraid not, Mrs Peacham. I've come to see your Michelle.'

Killer. I knew it. He'd come to kill me.

'Michelle!' Mum called up the stairs. 'Visitor for you!'

She made it sound like he was Prince Charming come to fit me with the golden slipper. If only she knew. Luckily, my mobile phone was by my bed. Trembling with fright, I dialled Adam's number. Shit! It was on Voicemail.

155

'Adam, quick, I need you!' I said desperately. 'Come round as soon as you get this message! Killer's here!'

'Michelle!' called Mum again, gaily.

I listened to his heavy footsteps going down the hall. What could I do? What sort of a daughter would hide in her bedroom and leave her mum to the mercy of a murderer? I crept downstairs, my heart hammering against my ribs. Mum was showing him into the lounge.

'There you go,' she said brightly. 'Take your boots off on the carpet, please, Killer dear.'

Killer *dear*? A psychopath comes to the house to kill me, and my mum's probably going to bring him a nice cup of tea and a plate of digestives. I tried frantically to catch her eye, shaking my head violently, but she was tripping back out to the kitchen chatting away about putting the kettle on.

Fuck. It was just him and me, standing in the hall, looking from his big old boots to the lounge carpet and back at his boots again.

'You'd better take them off,' I said in a little mouse-squeak of a voice, trying to be braver than I felt. 'My mum really, really freaks out about boots and carpets.' I made it sound like a threat. *Touch me, buddy, and you'll have my mum to reckon with*.

'Well, now,' he said with a sneer, 'We wouldn't want to freak your *mum* out, would we, eh?'

But he still bent down and took his boots off.

'What do you want?' I said, watching him. 'Robbie's not here. I told you, I haven't seen him since we were waiting for a chicken roll in the—'

'Save it, Michelle. I don't give a fuck what kind of a roll you were waiting for. I'm more interested in what *I'm* waiting for. You understand?'

By now he'd left his boots in the hall and was padding across the lounge carpet in his socks. They were black and fluffy and he had a hole in the toe of one of them. He was pulling a really mean face at me but it was kind of hard to take him seriously while I could see his big pink toenail

156

sticking out of his sock.

'Two thousand pounds,' he said, standing over me and spitting his foul breath into my face. 'Two thousand pounds, plus interest, OK? I don't want to have to keep on asking, Michelle. I don't want to have to get *nasty*.'

'Here we are. Nice cup of tea and some custard creams,' announced my mum, elbowing the door open and bringing in her best tray laden with the proper china cups. 'I wasn't sure whether you take sugar, Killer, dear, so I've brought in the sugar bowl. All right?' She put the tray down on the coffee table and turned to give me a meaningful look. 'Watch the biscuit crumbs on the carpet, Chelle, there's a good girl.'

'Mum ...' I said, trying to make her look at me. I was raising my eyebrows, grimacing, winking, doing everything short of jumping up and down waving a banner saying 'THIS MAN IS A DANGEROUS NUTTER!' but she just smiled at me, said 'Drink it while it's hot,' and walked back out of the room.

'Two thousand pounds,' Killer said again in a horrible, menacing voice. 'Plus interest. Or else, Michelle.'

'Plus interest?' I said. 'So how much would that be, then? In total?'

The thing is, you see, I wasn't bad at maths, at school. It was actually one of the only things I passed at GCSE. And even though he was really scaring me, it still kind of irritated me, Killer going on like that about 'plus interest' when I had the definite feeling he had no idea what it was.

'Eh?' He looked completely blank.

'What percentage are we talking about? Only I need to know, to work it out. It's no good just demanding interest, if you don't tell me how much.'

'The usual, Michelle, obviously,' he said, sounding rattled.

'And that would be what? One per cent? Two per cent?'

'Yeah. Two, yeah, two purse sent. What you said.'

'OK. So that's two thousand pounds plus ... um ...

157

forty pounds interest. Have I got that right?'

'Whatever!' he said impatiently. 'Just get me the money, right?'

'If I knew where Robbie was,' I said, trying to make a move towards the door, 'then I'd tell him. But being as he owes *me* money too, there's no way you're getting it off me, so why don't you just—'

'*I want my money, Michelle, and I don't care how I get it, right!*'

Considering he was in his socks, he looked pretty big and frightening when he stood right up close to me like that. The red hair in his nostrils was really disgusting.

'And what exactly are you going to do if you *don't* get it, Julian?'

Adam! Thank God! I'd been so scared I hadn't even heard the front door.

'*Julian*?' I said in disbelief.

'Yes. Julian and I were in the same class at school. You weren't such a big brave boy in those days, though, were you, *Killer*? Where did that nickname come from? Killed a fly once, did you?'

'Piss off, Adam. I—'

'*Piss off*?' Adam's voice suddenly got really, really loud. I'd heard him shouting often enough over the years, but I'd never, ever heard him shout quite like that. I cringed nearly as much as I had when Killer was breathing over me. 'Who do you think you're talking to, Julian Sparrow? Who the *fuck* do you think you are, coming into *my mother's house* and threatening my little sister?'

'I ... look ... it's all very well for you, Peacham, but I just want my money back.'

'That's your problem, wanker. If you want your money back, you can go and find Robbie Nelson yourself – he's not here, and he's got nothing to do with this family any more. Got it?' He squared up to Killer – who was much bigger than Adam but he backed away, blinking like an owl. '*Got it*?'

158

'Yeah, right, well, like I said, I just ...'

'You're *just* going to get out of here, fast, and if you ever come back, *Julian*, I'll rip your stupid chains off you and stuff them sideways up your arse. Got that, too?'

'OK, OK, no need to ...'

He backed out of the room, grabbing his boots as he went, and stumbled down the hall in his fluffy socks.

'Thank God you came! He was really scary and he didn't even know how to do percentages,' I blubbed, as Adam put his arms round me protectively.

'Oh, dear!' said Mum, coming back in from the kitchen. 'Has he gone, Chelle? He never even drank his nice cup of tea! Do you want a custard cream, Adam? Only mind the crumbs on the carpet, there's a good boy.' She looked from me to Adam as we both started to laugh slightly hysterically. 'What have I said now?'

'Don't worry, Mum,' I said. 'Adam's just rescued me from being beaten up, tied up and thrown in the river, but as long as there aren't any crumbs on the carpet, we'll be fine.'

'Honestly, Chelle, your imagination!' she said, shaking her head. 'It'll get you into trouble one day, you mark my words.'

Trouble? I was already in enough of that. Trouble was my middle name these days, wasn't it – as my mum would say.

Penny

It was only the first week of December, but some people had had their Christmas trees in their windows and flashing lights over their porches for weeks already. When I pulled up on the big sweeping driveway of Elizabeth Baxter-Simpson's house in Panbridge Mount, I was so dazzled by the bright white lights hanging in her ornamental Japanese cedar, I nearly crashed into the garage wall. Inside the house, there was more greenery than there was in the garden: holly and ivy twined artistically over the banisters, wreaths of evergreen leaves, interset with pine cones, perched on every door like vulgar oversize knockers and, hanging from the ceiling beams, huge bunches of mistletoe, tied up with blood-red ribbons that contrasted shockingly with their bulbous drippings of fertile white berries. In pride of place in the bay window of the lounge was the seven-foot tall Christmas tree, staggering under the weight of several tons of solid wooden lanterns, snowmen, angels, robins, and stars – all artfully pretending to be roughly hewn out of an lump of old firewood by a humble craftsman working his fingers to the bone, apart from the fact I'd seen them in Habitat for £25 a box of four, and topped by a sprinkling of those irritating fairy lights that flicker in a sequence of fast, slow, very fast, demented, and then stop for a minute to get you checking whether the bulbs have blown.

'Sit yourself down, Penny, come along,' said Elizabeth, bustling around behind me as if I was in the way. Her lounge was about thirty feet by twenty and there were only five of us in there. 'Go and sit by the fire if you're cold.'

I felt obliged to obey, even though I'd been warmed up plenty by the heat given off by a thousand flashing lights.

'Well then, everyone – shall we recap for Penny, now that she's joined us?'

'Oh! I'm, er ... sorry if I've missed anything?'

How was I being made to feel like a naughty schoolgirl? The meeting was supposed to start at eight o'clock and it was still only five to.

'Not to worry, Penny. We've only just started. You just sit there and get warm, and let Roger read you the minutes of last week's meeting.'

'Last week's?' I frowned myself into silence, as Roger creaked to his feet and began shuffling papers awkwardly. I didn't remember there being a meeting the week before. Had I missed it? Had I forgotten the date?

'Minutes of the Special Meeting of the Peace for Panbridge Park Pressure Group Committee, held on Friday the twenty-eighth November at Elizabeth Baxter-Simpson's house ...' began Roger in a shaky voice.

Special meeting? I frowned even deeper. If it was so special, why hadn't I known about it?

'Get on with it, Roger,' snapped Elizabeth abruptly. 'Never mind about all the headings.'

'The purpose of the meeting,' he continued hurriedly, his voice shaking even more, 'was to discuss the matter of the adverse publicity being given to our group by the media attention attracted by Penny Peacham and her pudding.'

'Hang on a minute!' I jumped to my feet and for some reason felt the need to wave my arms at Roger as if it was difficult to attract his attention. 'Stop, stop reading! What the hell is all this about? Are you telling me you lot held a meeting last Friday *behind my back*? A meeting to discuss *me*, without me being here? Are you joking? Please tell me

161

you're fucking joking?'

I don't normally use the 'f' word in public like that. Roger, who hadn't met my eyes since he stood up to start reading his bloody minutes, went a delicate shade of puce and studied the backs of his hands very carefully. Elizabeth coughed discreetly and fluffed her hair up. The only other two members who'd had the guts to turn up – Beryl and Doris, a couple of retired schoolmistresses who lived together and wore tweed skirts with socks – both got up and dashed for the kitchen, making flustery noises about a cup of tea.

'I'm sorry, Penny,' said Elizabeth. 'But as you can probably imagine, it would have been very embarrassing to discuss this in front of you. Certain members ...'

'Who? What certain members?'

'*Certain* members,' she said again firmly, 'wanted to hold a vote. They're entitled to a democratic decision, so ...'

'A *vote*? A vote on what?' I sat back down with a thump. 'You voted to chuck me out of the group, didn't you? That's what you've brought me round here to tell me.' I stared at Elizabeth. 'I thought you *agreed* with me giving these interviews? You said ...'

'This isn't personal, Penny,' she replied, giving me a very direct look. She looked from me, straight across at Roger. I knew what she was telling me. It wasn't Elizabeth who wanted me out, but she'd been outvoted. And we both knew who had led the hue and cry against me.

'A motion was proposed,' Roger began reading again, 'that Penny Peacham should refrain from any more dealings with the media, which should be left to the group's nominated PR officer ...'

(*guess who*)

'... and that if Penny was unwilling to accept this, she should be asked to leave the group. The motion was put to the vote and was carried by a majority of five votes to four. It was therefore agreed ...'

'Agreed? Agreed by whom – you, Roger? You and those

162

two in the kitchen who haven't got half a brain between them? And your senile neighbour Harry, I suppose, and his wife Edna who's too deaf to know what anyone says at any of the meetings? Between you, you've *agreed* to boot me out . . . '

'Not necessarily,' said Elizabeth quickly. 'We don't want to lose you, Penny. Surely it would be easier to just do what Roger suggests – leave all the media dealings to him, and— '

'*Fuck* what Roger suggests! Fuck the lot of you!' I grabbed my bag and swung out of the room, knocking against the Christmas tree, making all the little wooden bells jangle and sending the flashing lights into overdrive. I collided with Beryl and Doris carrying in their tray of teacups, and I'm ashamed to say I told them to fuck off as well.

As I stomped towards the front door I heard Roger crowing:

'You see? Would you *want* the group to be associated with that sort of language and behaviour?'

And Elizabeth Baxter-Simpson replying in a tired voice:

'Penny's quite right, Roger, as a matter of fact. Shut the fuck up.'

I was crying by the time I got home; but it was humiliation more than anything else. Who ever heard of anyone being banished from a protest group? I couldn't believe it. I'd never been in trouble for anything in my life – not even a speeding fine.

'They can't do that!' protested Archie, staring at me in amazement.

'They can. They voted. It's democratic.'

'But they've got no grounds to get rid of you!'

'They voted to stop me talking to the media, not to get rid of me. But I'm not having Stupid Roger telling me what I can or can't do!'

'Too right, Mum!' said Michelle crossly. 'He's just

163

bloody jealous, that's all. He's supposed to be your PR man, but *he* never got interviewed on the radio or got his picture in the paper or anything.'

'Maybe I shouldn't have done, either,' I said gloomily, accepting the cheer-up cup of tea Michelle was handing me. The fighting spirit was beginning to drain out of me, leaving me feeling a bit silly. 'All it seems to have done is cause trouble.'

'That's *so* not true!' said Michelle stoutly. 'Is it, Dad?'

'No, it's not,' he agreed, to my surprise. 'If your group had any sense, Pen, they'd realise your publicity is the best thing that's happened to them. Without you, they'll just fade back into obscurity and we'll never get the bypass. Trouble is, people like Roger care more about their own insecurity than they care about the cause they're supposed to be fighting for.'

This was such a long speech for Archie, who normally only managed more than two sentences if he was talking about a football match, that I was completely lost for words.

'Never mind, Pen,' he went on, giving me a sudden hug that made me splash my tea over the edge of the mug. 'If they've kicked you out of the group, there's nothing to stop you carrying on with your interviews. And you can say whatever the hell you like, can't you!'

Strange how things happen, sometimes. The very next day, when I got home from work, there was a message on the answerphone from someone with the unfortunate name of Jodie Turk, who sounded about fourteen but declared herself to be a features writer from *Woman Today*. She wanted me to give her a ring suggesting a convenient time for us to have our 'little chat'.

'Would now be OK?' I asked when I called her back.

'Oh, gosh!' she said, sounding completely thrown. 'I mean, well, Penny – now would be *super*, but are you *quite sure* you don't need some time to prepare?'

164

'Should I?'

Not being funny, but look: I'd spent days, weeks even, preparing for the interview on East Coast Radio, and where had that got me? I'd come to the conclusion that it was better to just do it off the cuff, and hope for the best.

'Well, gosh, no – I mean, that's fine, Penny, if you're ready to roll now, as it were! You don't want to make yourself a cup of tea? Get yourself comfortable?'

'I'm quite comfortable, thanks.'

To be honest, I wanted to get it over with while I was on my own. If Archie or Michelle, or even worse, Jessica, were in the house listening to me talking about myself to a complete stranger on the phone I wouldn't feel comfortable at all.

'OK, super, Penny. Well then, let's start off by talking about this little protest group you're involved in, shall we?'

Oh, shit.

'How did you come to be on the committee for your little group, Penny?'

'I volunteered,' I said flatly. 'But to be quite honest, it's probably not—'

'And you hold regular demonstrations, don't you? Holding up the traffic, standing in the road waving banners? That kind of thing?'

'No, no, we ... it's only been done once. It was quite successful, but ... look, er, Jodie – I think I ought to explain.'

'It's OK, Penny – I *know* you want to get onto talking about your famous *pudding*! But we've got plenty of time, don't worry. I just wanted to get a bit of background information'

'Yes, but you see—'

'How long has your little protest group actually been campaigning for the bypass?'

'Nearly two years. But it's not my little group. I'm not in it any more.'

'Oh! Oh, gosh!' I could hear Jodie frantically flipping

through sheets of paper. Had she got the wrong set of questions? Had she been given the wrong information by Fantasia Topping?

'Sorry – sorry to mess up your interview,' I said miserably. 'But I thought I'd better tell you. I've left the group, you see.'

'Oh, I *see*! Can't spare the time now that you're so busy with your *pudding*, Penny?' she said, brightening up, thinking no doubt that this was going to make a much more interesting story.

'Something like that. Call it a ... well, a conflict of interests, I suppose.'

'Absolutely, Penny! I'm sure it *must* be very difficult for you – as a mum and ...' (I could hear her consulting her notes again) '*and* a grandma – my goodness, you don't sound old enough, ha ha! – as well as working at the vet's – is that right, Penny?'

'Yes. Yes, I work three days a week at Tail Waggers. Sometimes I do Saturday mornings too, but then I get an afternoon off during the week. It depends on how many dogs are being—'

'*Super*! Well, with such a busy life, as I say, Penny, I'm sure it must be *very* difficult to find the time to make your *famous pudding*, and still have lots of fantastic sex!'

'Pardon?'

'Sex,' she repeated very loudly, adding for good measure, in case I wasn't sure what it meant, 'Lovemaking. Going to bed and—'

'Yes, yes, OK, I know what it is,' I said hurriedly. For some reason, instead of conjuring up images of Archie and myself engaged in our usual, comfortably familiar (albeit occasional) routine, she'd sparked off my fantasy about Chris Filbey and the operating table. 'What makes you think I have lots of fantastic sex?' Chance would be a fine thing ...

'Now, then, Penny!' she said with a silly giggle. 'No need to be coy! We know all about your *Passion Pudding*

166

and its reputation. Remember, this feature is all about mature women with sexual vitality – that's why you've been chosen, Penny!'

Oh, yes. Bugger. I'd forgotten that. How do I pretend to be someone with sexual vitality? Close my eyes and think of ...?

Chris and me in the kitchen. Chris stroking my arms. Whispering in my ear, calling me sexy ...

'Well, yes, maybe my pudding really *does* make people passionate!' I said.

To be honest, it had only just occurred to me. Maybe it wasn't such a silly idea after all. Maybe I ought to be taking it seriously – all this stuff about the pudding that I'd dismissed as nonsense. Let's face it: since Chris heard about my pudding, and especially since he ate a bit, he'd shown a lot more interest in me, hadn't he? And what about Archie – the more he ate of the stuff, the more strangely aroused he seemed to be getting lately.

'*Excellent*, Penny!' said Jodie excitedly, having obviously been told exactly what she wanted to hear. 'Now – is it true that your ingredients are top secret, an ancient family recipe that's been handed down through the generations?'

'Oh, absolutely.'

'So your mum and your grandma must have been right little ravers too, eh?' she giggled. Not a nice thought. 'And what does your husband ... um ... Archie ... think about your pudding? I bet he likes it, eh, Penny?'

I was beginning to think she was getting off on this.

'Yeah. Loves it.'

'Tell me a little bit about your relationship with Archie, then, Penny. So. You've been married for *thirty-two years*! Wow! There certainly must be some – shall we say – *sexual chemistry* there, to keep it going for as long as that, eh? And you put it all down to your bread pudding?'

I sighed. There were so many things I could talk about in an interview. Quite apart from the Peace for Panbridge Park Pressure Group that I'd just been thrown out of. I

167

could talk about fuchsias. I could talk about working in a vets' surgery. I could talk about bringing up children, and looking after grandchildren, and running a home, and (seriously, without the pudding connotations) holding together a marriage when sometimes staying married is the last thing in the world you want to do and you'd like nothing better than to walk out, run away, start again, be on your own, have some space, be yourself, not have anyone else to look after. I could talk about myself. I could talk about life. But I was being asked to talk about sex. They were using the pudding as an excuse; all they really wanted me to do for this magazine was to titillate their readers by telling them some absolute crap about my sex life which they might, or might not, be stupid enough to believe. In return, I was going to get a makeover. And treat Michelle to a day out in London.

Everything has its price.

I took a deep breath, and proceeded to tell young Jodie Turk enough outrageous fibs about my *sexual vitality* to make her ears go red. And to earn me my place in the *Woman Today*.

Michelle

'So how are you doing now without your man? Are you back home now with your mam and dad, God bless your heart?' asked Claire as we worked together on a patient's terrible leg ulcers on Friday morning.

It was always a good thing to try to get a conversation going while you were dealing with leg ulcers. It helped to take your mind off the smell. The first time I was confronted with one, I had to go outside to the toilets and be sick, but the others told me everyone has to go through that, and I was beginning to get used to it now.

'Yeah. Maybe I should never have moved in with Robbie,' I said, shaking my head. '*You* wouldn't have, would you, Claire? I mean, where you grew up in Ireland, it probably wasn't allowed, was it?'

'Oh, 'tis true we're a backward lot with regard to the modern way of things, child. The folk back home in Killarney have a mortal fear of the wrath of God, to be sure. If I'd so much as kissed a boy without a ring on me finger, why, me mam would have taken a belt to me, so she would.'

'Don't you think that's a bit harsh, though? Not even kissing?'

'Well it sure as hell beats being a single pregnant mother and going to live with the nuns, so it does.'

'I think I'd rather live with the nuns than live with a man

again. They're a waste of space, aren't they?'

'Find yourself a good one, my love. You will, in time. You'll see.'

'Huh. Not sure I believe that any more.'

Fraser Willoughby looked in on us just at that moment.

'Are you nearly finished with Mrs Armstrong's leg?' he said, looking straight at Claire as if he hadn't even seen me.

'Yes, doctor – she's all yours now,' said Claire.

I got up and walked away to wash my hands.

'Are you all right, child?' asked Claire when Fraser had gone.

'Fine,' I said.

But she looked from me, out of the door where he'd gone, and back to me again, and went 'Hmm, so,' to herself, and shook her head. And I wished I could tell her how he didn't want to see me any more. She might have known what was the matter with him.

It was no use talking to any of the other girls about it. They were all at fever pitch by now, about the hospital party.

'I'm going to get a dance with Michael from the children's ward, if it's the last thing I do,' declared Julie.

'I fancy that new A & E house officer,' giggled Karen. 'Have you seen him? Tall, blond hair, nice bum ...'

'I've still got the hots for Charles, in Orthopaedics,' sighed Melanie. 'But I'm not sure whether he's going to the party. What about you, Michelle?'

'Eh?' I'd been eating my lunch, lost in my own thoughts about pregnancy tests and single parenthood.

'Who have you got your eye on? You're a single girl again now, aren't you? About time you got off with someone new.'

'Yeah, it *is* about time!'

'Good point – who do you fancy, Michelle?'

'Let's set her up with someone at the party, girls! What about Trevor from the labs?'

'No! He's horrible!' laughed Karen. 'Why not Alec the paediatric registrar?'

'He's married. Although you wouldn't think it, the way he carries on ...'

'Well, how about Simon from Personnel? I know he's not very tall, but you never know, he might make up for it in other areas.'

'Do you mind?' I retorted. 'Do you have to discuss me like I'm on the shelf and I need a man to pick me up?'

'Yes, leave the poor child alone,' said Claire. 'She's had enough of a bad time with one man recently to last her a lifetime. Do you think she's after getting herself into more trouble and getting her poor heart broken all over again?'

Claire had to raise her voice really loud to say the last bit, because all the girls were giggling so much. And just as she was giving it some welly about my poor broken heart, Fraser Willoughby walked directly behind us, with his sausages on a tray, on his way to find a table. He glanced at me but didn't say anything. Melanie and Karen nudged each other and winked at me.

'What about him, then! You had lunch with him the other week, didn't you!'

'Yeah, I reckon he fancies you, Michelle! I bet you could have him as soon as look at him ...'

'Shut up!' I hissed. I could feel my face burning red. 'He might have heard you! Can't you just give it a rest?' I got up and took the rest of my lunch over to the bin. 'I'm going back to work.'

'Now do you see what you've done there? Didn't I just tell you so?' I heard Claire saying to the others. 'You should leave the poor girl alone, so you should. You and your mickey-taking!'

But they were still giggling as I went out the door.

'I take it you haven't heard any more from Julian Fuckwit Sparrow?' said Adam when he came round with Jessica on Friday evening.

'Killer? No, thank God. But I can't see him giving up that easily, Adam. At the end of the day, he still thinks

Robbie owes him loads of money.'

'Nothing to do with us. Don't worry, Chelle – he's probably still pissing himself at the thought of me stuffing his chains up his arse.'

'Look, Chelly! Look!'

Jessica came bounding into the room, wearing her pink pyjamas and waving Red Bed-Ted at me. Red Bed-Ted was wearing pink pyjamas too. Mum had obviously been busy with her sewing machine. How the hell did she ever learn to do things like that? I mean, did girls get *taught* to make teddy-bear size pyjamas out of a bit of pink material, when Mum went to school? Or does she do it by instinct? It frightens me sometimes, when I think about having kids of my own. I mean, I'd never be able to make cute little dollies' clothes, or knit nice little toddler-size jumpers, or even make lovely fancy birthday cakes like Mum made for Jessica's third birthday, all in chocolate with a pink bow on it and a big pink icing number three. Where do I go to learn stuff like that? It's a shame they don't teach it at antenatal classes along with all the breathing exercises.

'Is she staying the night? Are you off away for the weekend again?' I asked Adam irritably.

'Yes. Hopefully should be back Sunday morning.'

'Well, thanks for nothing. Supposing Killer *does* come back again? Supposing he comes while Mum and Dad are out, and just me and Jessica are here on our own?'

'He won't. I'm telling you, Chelle, he's a big fat coward.'

'If you really cared about Jessica ...'

'That's not fair!' he snapped. 'I have to go away. It's important.'

'Well, have a nice time, then,' I said crossly, 'with your new girlfriend, whoever she is. Don't you worry about us!'

'It isn't— ' he began, then broke off, with 'Oh, what's the point?' and went out to say goodbye to Mum and Jessica.

I was left feeling like it was me being unreasonable. But

I'm sorry; Adam was taking the piss, and he knew it. That was why he was getting so stroppy about it. A guilty conscience, as Mum would say.

On Saturday evening, Dad went out to have a drink with one of his old mates from the car dealership. Mum said she was glad of the break. She'd been looking a bit tense when Dad was around, as if she wasn't quite sure what he was going to do next.

'Let's have a girls' night in, Chelle,' she said. 'Get a video and a takeaway, shall we? And a bottle of wine?'

I *was* going to ask Nicole and Kim if they wanted to go up the Cloud. I thought it might take my mind off the baby that I might, or might not, be growing inside me – a baby who, as if it wasn't bad enough to be born with the genes of some bastard who couldn't even stay with me long enough to help me get my knickers back on, would also be going through life with a mother who couldn't make birthday cakes or knit dolls' clothes. And also, I thought it was about time Kim and I started being friends again. She'd been bitching away at me for weeks. I was pissed off with it. What was I supposed to have done wrong?

'Unless you were planning to go out?' added Mum, seeing me hesitate.

I nearly said yes, I was. But then I saw the look on her face. She couldn't go out, could she – she was lumbered with Jessica again. After all the years of being stuck at home because of me and Adam, it just wasn't fair.

'Tell you what,' I said. 'I'll ask Nicole and Kim if they want to come round and join us, shall I?'

'Oh, yes!' said Mum, looking really pleased. 'That'll be lovely. Do you want to phone for a Chinese, or some pizzas? Shall I make a pudding for afterwards?'

'Yeah.' I grinned at her. 'Make some of your Passion Pud, eh, Mum? Us girls could probably do with it!'

It was a joke, right? For a start, I don't normally eat Mum's bread pudding. I'm trying to lose a bit of weight, so I try not to eat cakes or puddings, unless it's a special occasion – and after eating a takeaway, I couldn't really imagine we were going to have any room left for pudding of any kind. Also, personally, I was fed up with the whole idea of passion. It always seemed like a good idea at the time. Like sex with Robbie – it put him in a good mood so that he took me out for a pub lunch, but look what he did then – buggered off as if I was just a bit of old rubbish to be dumped when he'd had enough of me. And look at the episode with Luke: that was even worse. I should never have got passionate with *him*, that was for sure. I might be paying for it for the rest of my life.

But the next thing I knew, there was Mum, in the kitchen, kneading away at her bowl of bread and weighing out sultanas and raisins and stuff, looking all pleased with herself. I didn't have the heart to tell her not to bother. I watched her put the pudding in the oven, and I thought to myself: That's something else I won't know how to do, if I ever have children. The poor things won't get puddings unless my mum makes them. Maybe she'd better give me some lessons.

Nicole and Kim brought the Chinese takeaway with them. Kim's dad drove them round, and they said they'd get a taxi home so they could have a drink. We had a set meal: king prawns in black bean sauce, sweet and sour pork, chicken chop suey and special fried rice, and everyone got stuck into the white wine. Everyone except me. I just had a little glass and kept hiding it, pretending to fill it up when they weren't looking. Well, it wasn't good for the poor baby I might, or might not, be having, was it? We didn't bother getting a video in the end because it was quite good on telly, but believe it or not we didn't even watch it, because we spent the whole time yakking.

It started off with Mum asking the other two what they were up to – you know, the normal mum-type thing – How are you getting on in your jobs, how are your parents keeping, what are you doing for Christmas, have you got a boyfriend at the minute? Mum had known Nic and Kim since we were all at school, and she always liked it when we all got together and she could join in the chat like she was one of the girls.

'No,' said Nicole mournfully, wiping sweet and sour sauce off her mouth with the back of her hand. 'No, I haven't got a boyfriend, Mrs Peacham ...'

'Penny,' said Mum.

'Penny. Well, I did go out with someone a couple of times, Penny, but I haven't seen him since.' She shrugged. 'Maybe I'm better off without.'

'Yeah. You are. Definitely,' I agreed, taking a little sip of my wine.

'It's so different now for you girls,' said Mum. She was slurring a little bit, and I looked at her carefully, wondering how many glasses of wine she'd had. 'So different from when I was your age. We had to get married, really. It was the expected thing to do, if you wanted regular sex.'

'Mum!'

'Well, it's true. You have so much more freedom, and I think it's a good thing. If you don't want to live with a man, you don't have to, do you? Look at Michelle; she—'

'Don't start on about Robbie, Mum, please. Nobody wants to talk about that.'

'I wasn't going to. I was going to talk about that new chap of yours.'

There was a sudden silence. All eyes were on me.

'New chap?' said Kim. 'I didn't know about this, did I, Chelle?'

Thanks, Mum. Thanks a million.

'Nothing to tell.' I shrugged. 'Just someone at work I had a drink with. Just as friends, you know.'

'Are you seeing him again?' asked Nicole at once.

'No. Well ... yes, of course I see him at work, you know. But it was just ... nothing ... just a drink ... and we didn't plan anything ... we haven't ...'

'He hasn't asked you out again?' said Kim a bit nastily.

'Join the club,' said Nicole, sighing loudly. 'I really thought Scott was The One. I was going to have it off with him the next time I saw him – if you don't mind me saying so, Mrs Peacham. Penny, I mean. I thought we were ready. It was kind of going that way. But then he never turned up. And Kim says she saw him up the Cloud with Angela Atkinson.'

'Angela *Atkinson*! She's a right old slapper!' I protested.

'I'm sure she's not as pretty as you, dear,' said Mum, patting Nicola's hand sympathetically. 'Never mind, plenty more fish in the sea. That's what I keep telling Michelle.'

'I don't *want* any more fish in the sea! I'm fed up with them, all of them! They can just bloody well ... swim off!'

'Never mind,' said Mum again. 'What about you, Kim, dear? Have you got a boyfriend at the moment?'

'Er ...' Kim looked down at her plate and seemed to be concentrating on pushing the last bit of chop suey around with her fork. 'Not really, not as such, you know, not actually seeing anyone, like, just you know, just kind of hanging around, kind of with everyone, mostly, if you know what I mean.'

I stared at her.

'What's *that* supposed to mean?' Then I noticed that Nicole was looking down, too, and concentrating very hard on the one grain of rice that was left on her own plate. 'Is there something going on here that I don't know about?'

'Course not!' said Kim, still playing with her noodles. 'Just, you know, Chelle – you haven't been up the Cloud with us for ages, so ...'

'Only because you've been such a bitch ever since Nic's birthday night.'

There was a bit of a tense silence for a minute. Mum glanced around at us, looking a bit lost, then she got up, nearly knocking the bottle of wine over, and said all bright and breezy:

'Anyone like a piece of my bread pudding?'

*

I don't think any of us wanted it, to be honest. We were all full up with the Chinese, and they were all a bit pissed on the wine. But it was probably a good thing to change the subject. I wanted to have it out with Kim: find out why she'd been so off with me, and why now, all of a sudden, she seemed to be all right again. And what the big secret was about. Was she seeing someone, or wasn't she? I suppose, to be fair, I hadn't told them anything about Fraser either. Maybe it was difficult, with my mum there. Not that she'd disapprove or anything, but the others might find it a bit embarrassing if, for instance, they wanted to tell me all about some particularly good sex they'd had. Or even particularly bad sex.

Anyway, just to change the subject, we agreed to have some bread pudding, and it was quite funny the way everyone got excited about it, like they hadn't been coming round to my house ever since they were about ten years old and eating it at various times of day or night, hot, cold, and even fried for breakfast.

'Ooh! The famous Passion Pudding!' squealed Nicola, giggling and grabbing the dish of pudding as if she wanted to cuddle it. 'Maybe I should eat a *big* piece of it, Penny! Maybe it will bring me luck in the old *passion* business, eh?'

'You never know!' smiled Mum, dishing it out and plonking it onto our plates a bit unsteadily.

'P'raps you should give some to Scott. Then maybe he'll dump Angela Atkinson and come back for what you promised him,' laughed Kim.

'Maybe,' said Nicola, looking slightly uncertain as to whether Kim was taking the piss out of her.

'And maybe your *friend* at work might take you out for another *friendly* little drink, Chelle,' added Kim, a bit spitefully I thought.

I pulled a face at her, watching her tuck into the pudding.

'And maybe you might decide whether you're seeing somebody at the moment, or not!' I said.

She put down her spoon and opened her mouth to reply. Perhaps she was actually going to tell me who she was, or wasn't, going out with. Or she might have just been going to tell me to fuck off and mind my own business. We'd never know. Because just at that minute Mum looked up at the window and let out a blood-curdling scream.

'What?' I shouted, looking round in a panic. 'What's the matter?'

Kim and Nicola had both stopped eating and sat back in their chairs, looking at Mum with their eyes popping out of their heads.

'There was someone out there!' said Mum, pointing shakily at the window. 'A man! Staring in at us! AAAAAAH! There's another one! There's two of them! Chelly, quick, quick! Phone the police! Phone your dad on his mobile! No, call nine-nine-nine! Quick, they're in the garden! Tell them they're in the garden!'

'All right, all right – where's the phone? Why doesn't anyone ever put it back? Stop shouting, Mum – they've gone now!'

'No, they're still out there. I can see them!' She was standing at the window, staring out into the darkness. 'Two of them!'

'What were they like?' I asked, trembling slightly at the thought of Killer possibly lurking around the house, waiting to murder me while I looked for the phone under all the cushions on the sofa.

'How would I know? It's dark! I could only see their eyes, looking in. Oh! Oh, Chelle!' She grabbed my arm, gripping me so hard I had bruises for a week afterwards. 'They're coming in the front door!'

'Don't be silly! The door's locked. They can't … '

Nicole and Kim were on their feet by now, standing close behind me and Mum like we were going to protect them. There was a 'click' as the front door opened, and all four of us froze into silence as we heard it quietly close again, then listened to the footsteps coming down the hall.

'Hello, girls!' boomed my dad, swaying into the room and breathing his beery breath over us. 'Having a nice evening? Oh, lovely – bread pudding! Can I have a bit, Pen?'

'*Archie*!' said Mum, almost crying. 'Oh, thank God it's you! Thank God you're home!'

'What's the matter, Pen? Aren't you feeling too good? What – had a bit too much to drink, have you?'

'Don't be stupid! There are men out there in the garden! Two of them! I saw them, looking at us through the window!'

'I'm trying to call the police,' I told him, 'But you've left the bloody phone somewhere again, Dad'

'Me? *Me*! I never use the damn' phone ...'

'Never mind about that!' shrieked Mum. 'Archie, get out there in the garden and find them! Go on, find them and chase them away!'

'No, Mum! It's dangerous! Let me call the police. I'll get my mobile!'

'Police! Bollocks to them!' retorted Dad. 'They won't come round for at least twenty-four hours. We could all be dead, and buried in our own garden, by the time *they* get off their arses. Leave it to me!' He grabbed a full bottle of wine off the table, unlocked the patio doors, and strode out into the darkness.

'What's he doing?' asked Nicole in a scared little voice. 'Is he going to hit them with the bottle?'

'What do you think?' said Kim scathingly. 'He's not going to sit down and have a nice little drink of wine with them!'

Nicole sniffed a couple of times as if she wanted to cry. The rest of us stood in shocked silence, staring at the open patio doors.

'Archie!' wailed Mum. 'Come back!'

'Give me a torch!' I said, pretending to be brave but shaking all over. 'I'll go out and help him.'

'NO!!' everyone shouted together.

179

Fortunately I didn't have to argue about it, because just then in came Dad, swinging the bottle and whistling.

'Mission accomplished!' he said breezily. 'All clear!'

'Did you hit them?' sniffled Nicole.

'Was there a lot of blood?' asked Kim, looking very impressed.

'Oh, Archie!' said Mum, putting her arms round him. 'Are you hurt? Did they put up a fight?'

'Who the fuck *were* they?' I said. 'What did they want?'

'Nothing to fuss and worry about, girls!' he said, loving every minute of it. 'I just had a quiet chat to them, and off they went'

'But who . . . ?'

'Just a couple of friends of old Robbie. Terry Johnson, I think the big dark lad was called – remember, Chelle? With the accent? And the short one with big ears, they used to call him Muggs. I told them: "Boys," I said, "No use you looking round here for old Robbie. We haven't seen him for over a month, now. Disappeared into thin air, he has." I asked them if they wanted to come in and have a drink, but they seemed to be in a bit of a hurry. Said to tell Robbie they were looking for him, if we heard from him.'

'That was nice of them,' said Mum.

'Yes. Nice lads. You see? All that fuss about nothing! Ha! Can't go out and leave you ladies on your own, without a man to look after you – can I?'

'Oh, Archie!' said Mum, going all silly and girly. 'You're so brave and capable!'

'Give us a bit of your pudding, then – eh, Pen?' He winked at her. 'That'll do for starters!'

'Oh, please!' I said, pretending to be sick. 'Keep it clean, you two.'

I mean, it wasn't very nice, having my parents carrying on like that in front of my friends and all. Kim and Nicole looked well shocked.

*

Tell you what, though. I think the fright must have brought on my period, at last. So at least I wasn't going to be a single mother after all. I could have had a couple more glasses of wine, couldn't I?

Penny

Darren Barlow phoned me on the Monday, just as I was leaving for work.

'I'm in a hurry,' I snapped. 'What is it?'

'Penny, Penny, calm down, my dear! What's the rush? You'll give yourself a heart attack. Take time out to smell the daisies!'

'Have you got anything important to say? Only I'm late for work, and I don't think my boss would be too impressed if I said it was because I was talking to you about smelling daisies.'

'I get the impression you're a little bit antagonistic towards me, Penny, my love.'

'Yes, well!' He really was the most exasperating person. 'What do you expect? You invite my daughter to restaurants ...'

'She's a delightful girl. I always like to eat in the company of delightful girls.'

'So it seems! Who's the one you were with the other week? Your girlfriend? Or your wife?'

'Cecilia? Lovely lady, isn't she?'

'And lovely Cecilia isn't bothered by you making obscene gestures at me all evening? Even though I was with my husband and quite *clearly* not interested?'

'Come along, now, Penny. You were enjoying every minute of it. When are you going to let me take you out for a nice little meal on our own? Mm?'

'What!' I couldn't believe the cheek of him. 'I'm *not* having any little meals with you, and neither is my daughter! Now, unless you want to pay me for a day's lost wages ...'

'I've got an important proposition to put to you, Penny. But I don't want to be rushed about it. I need to talk to you when you're in a calm, sensible, frame of mind.'

'I'm not interested in any propositions from you ...'

'I think you might be.'

'What is it? Another radio interview? I'm telling you, I'm not interested. I don't belong to the PPPP any more.'

'*Really*? Well, that *is* interesting news. Resigned, did you, Penny? Getting too famous to bother with their silly little meetings now? Too busy with your public image?'

'No!' I retorted, stung. 'If you must know, they kicked me out. And it's probably your fault, to be quite honest. They didn't like all the publicity about the bloody pudding! Now, I'm hanging up, and I'm going to work.'

'You're lovely when you're angry, Penny.'

I slammed down the phone.

I arrived at work at the exact same moment as Chris Filbey. At least he couldn't complain about me being late.

'Tomorrow's the big day, isn't it?' he said with a wicked grin, as we walked to the door together.

'I'm going to London for the makeover day, yes.'

'*Makeover day*!' he scoffed. 'I'm telling you, Penny – it'll be black leather and—'

'Have you ever seen a copy of *Woman Today*? It's got recipes in it. And articles about gardening.'

'And true life stories. 'I Married My Mother-In-Law'. 'I Had Sex With A Corgi'. All nice clean family entertainment.'

'You've just got a dirty mind,' I said, laughing.

'Yes, I have.' He looked at me very steadily, his smile fading. 'You've got no idea just *how* dirty.'

I tried to ignore this. And I tried to ignore him purposely brushing against me as he opened the door to the surgery and ushered me in. The waiting room was empty. I could hear Debbie talking to Glenn in the kitchen, probably making coffee before the first clients of the day turned up. Chris pushed the door closed behind us and pulled me towards him, with one hand across my shoulders and the other clasped firmly to my bum. I couldn't pretend to ignore this. I had a fleeting thought that this was the point at which a respectable married woman should gasp with shock and horror and utter something along the lines of: 'Mr Filbey! Whatever do you think you're doing?' Well, a gasp was about all I managed. But I wasn't about to protest. I wasn't going to try and stop him. I'd already known, hadn't I – known perfectly well that this would happen at some point. It was just a question of when, and where, and whether I was going to feel guilty about it.

'Someone might come in . . . ' I muttered as we stopped for breath, our lips still resting against each other's. I hadn't kissed anyone like that apart from Archie. Not ever. I was trembling all over with excitement and fright.

'We'll hear them. The dogs will bark,' he whispered back. We had two Jack Russell bitches out the back, waiting to be spayed. 'Jesus, Penny, I need you so badly. I think about you all the time. When can we go to bed together?'

'Bed?' I echoed. I was still recovering from the kiss. I could hardly breathe. My heart felt like it had taken on a life of its own and gone for a dance all round my body.

'I want to go to bed with you. I'm desperate.' He pulled me closer so that I could feel him. He wasn't joking – he felt big, hard and desperate. I closed my eyes, feeling myself melt.

'Oh, yes . . . ' I sighed.

'When? Don't make me wait, Penny. I've got to have you. I'll make you scream for more, I promise you . . . '

Bloody hell. My eyes flew open at the thought of it.

Scream for more? I'd seen films like that. It never seemed very realistic. I always wondered who they were kidding.

'You'll beg me. I'll have you begging for it. I'll fuck you like you've never had it before.'

He was grinding himself slowly and rhythmically against me as he was saying this into my ear. He was making me believe it. I was getting very close to begging for it already.

'On the table,' I gasped. 'The examination table. I've always wanted to—'

'Excuse me!' With a jolt, I realised someone was trying to push open the door we were leaning against. 'Excuse me, are you open? Can I come in? Only my rabbit's ear got caught in his cage door and it's bleeding all over my coat.'

'Bollocks,' said Chris softly, straightening up and shaking his head. He stood back as I walked shakily to the reception desk, sat down and fumbled in my handbag for a mirror and lipstick.

'You look gorgeous,' he whispered. 'Totally shaggable. Come in, Mrs Hodgson. We'd better have a look at Buster's ear, hadn't we!'

'Hello, Penny. Long time no see!'

'Oh, Maureen – hi.' I moved the phone into the crook of my neck so that I could turn the gas down under the potatoes. And whose fault was it, that it had been such a long time? I'd left messages on her answerphone about having lunch, and texts on her mobile about meeting up after work. I was beginning to think she'd changed her numbers. 'How are you?'

'OK. I was just phoning about tomorrow. The makeover. To wish you good luck.' This was quite a surprise, considering that she seemed so scathing about it when I told her. 'Although you know how I feel about it,' she added. Aha.

'How? How do you feel?'

'To be quite honest, Penny, I wish you weren't doing it. I think you're being exploited. I think you're being made a bloody fool of.'

'Well, thank you very much!'

'Sorry. But as your friend, I think you need someone to be straight with you. You've got carried away by all this business. All this media attention – the radio, the papers. It's all very well, but at the end of the day, they'll just drop you like a hot cake when the fuss has all died down, and leave you high and dry.'

'I know that. I didn't ask for all the fuss. I didn't even want it. I was trying to publicise the bypass ...'

'And as for leaving the PPPP! Well, I couldn't believe it when I heard.'

'Who told you?'

'Everybody's talking about it. How you stormed out of the meeting. Honestly, Penny, I do think all this fame has gone to your head. When it's all blown over you're going to need your friends.'

'Maureen, I need my friends *now*! Where were you, when I asked you to meet me for lunch? Why didn't you call me back? It's not *me* that's neglecting my friends! It wasn't me that stormed out of the meeting! Well, yes, I did, but it wasn't like that – they voted me out! They—'

'Just a friendly word of advice, that's all. Don't say I didn't warn you. And just be careful tomorrow – taking Michelle with you.' She said this with an audible sniff. 'Your own daughter!'

'What's that supposed to mean? I wanted *you* to come!'

She sniffed again.

'Just be careful what you're getting Michelle into. She was always an impressionable girl. Vulnerable. Very *susceptible*, if you know what I mean. To the men.'

'Maureen, I haven't got a clue what you're implying, but if you can't say anything nice, I wish you hadn't phoned, to be quite honest.'

'Don't be like that. I just called to wish you good luck,'

'Well, thank you,' I said, not really mollified. 'I'll tell you all about it afterwards, shall I?'

'If you like,' she said, sounding totally uninterested. 'See you later.'

The potatoes had gone all mushy. I poured them down the sink and threw the saucepan in after them.

I'll tell you the truth. Part of it was that I was hurt; she was supposed to be my best friend. She was meant to be sharing all this with me – the laughs, the excitement, the 'fuss' as she called it – not making me feel anxious about it, as if I were doing something highly dangerous and disreputable instead of going for a trip on the train to the *Woman Today* offices. But the other part of it was that even while I was talking to her about the makeover, the forefront of my mind was taken up with thoughts of Chris. Oh, sure, I felt guilty about what I'd done, and about what I wanted to do. But much more than that I felt alive with it – buzzing with it, fizzing with it. There was so much energy and excitement inside me about it, I couldn't sit still. I felt like dancing, like singing, like running a marathon. What I *didn't* feel like doing was talking to Archie, because I could imagine that all the time we were talking, he might see straight into my head and find pictures in there, pictures of me and Chris kissing against the waiting-room door. And it was even worse talking to Maureen – because she'd been proved right, hadn't she? She'd suspected all along that I was going to turn my fantasies about Chris into reality. She'd have a field day if she knew I'd already invited him to have sex with me on the examination table.

'What sort of photos do you think they'll take of you, Mum?' asked Michelle.

We were on the train on the way to London the next day. We'd had a good chat, first about what Christmas presents we were going to buy for Jessica, and for Archie, and Adam. Then we'd got onto the subject of Michelle's Christmas party at the hospital, and what she was going to wear, and whether she ought to buy something new while we were in the West End. We were coming through the

187

built-up area of the East London suburbs before we finally got onto the subject of the makeover itself.

'I don't know,' I said, trying to smother the thoughts of black leather and fishnet stockings that instantly came rushing into my mind – swiftly followed by thoughts of Chris. 'Just normal boring pictures, I suppose. You know: women's magazine-type pictures. Sitting in an armchair, or standing at a kitchen sink.'

'Yeah, probably in a kitchen, making your pudding!' laughed Michelle.

I was pleased to see how much more cheerful she seemed today – positively looking forward to the day out. In fact, she seemed a lot happier since Saturday night. The evening with Kim and Nicole must have done her good, even despite the fright we got from those friends of Robbie's – silly boys.

We were both feeling giggly with a kind of nervous excitement when we got into the big black BMW at Liverpool Street station and were whisked smoothly through the streets of London. Michelle sat with her nose almost pressed up to the window, staring at the sights. She'd only been to London a couple of times since she left school. (They used to have a lot of educational trips when she was at senior school, but she was usually sick on the coach which took a lot of the shine off it. The trip, I mean, not the coach.)

'Oh, look – St Paul's Cathedral!' she said, and 'Oh, Mum, look! The Houses of Parliament!' I had to smile; it was like being with a very impressed American tourist or an awestruck ten-year-old.

'Here we are, ladies,' said the driver at last, pulling up outside a quite ordinary-looking modern office building. 'Sign the chitty for me, please, love.' He thrust a clipboard and pen under my nose, pointed to where I had to sign, waited for us to get ourselves out of the car and roared off to his next assignment.

'Well!' said Michelle, looking around her a bit uncer-

188

tainly. 'I suppose this must be it.'

'Yes, look.' I pointed to the plate on the wall. 'Third Floor: GOLDSTEIN PUBLICATIONS: *Your Health; Budget Home; Woman Today*. That's us, Chelle. Ooh – I'm dead nervous, now! Shall we forget it, and just go shopping instead?'

'No! Don't be silly. Come on – you're going to have a great time.' She propelled me in through the glass doors and across the lobby to the lifts. 'Third floor! Going up!'

Unlike my heart, which had sunk down into the pit of my stomach. What the hell had I let myself in for? Maureen was probably right: I was about to be made a complete prat of.

'Penny! *Wonderful* to meet you!'

We'd been ushered, by the receptionist on the third floor, to a nice little sofa by a window with copies of *Woman Today* on the coffee table, while somebody came to meet us. I knew it was Fantasia Topping, even before she called out to me in the same breathless, excited tones that I remembered from our phone conversation. Somehow it just had to be. Her hair was jet black, wavy and very, very, long, flowing loose behind her like a cape. She wore several huge hoop earrings in each ear, and about eight or ten rows of very chunky beads of assorted lengths – some fairly tight to her throat, others hanging as low as her waist. Her skirts – she seemed to be wearing two or three – were also of varying lengths, the longest flapping around the heels of her lace-up black boots. But most disconcerting was her bright luminous yellow T-shirt, with cutaway sleeves and a smiley face logo, which seemed completely at odds with both the romantic gypsy style, and the heavy-duty winter weight, of the rest of her outfit. You could easily imagine that she'd got dressed in the dark and accidentally chosen things from her child's dressing-up box.

'Fantasia!' she introduced herself, grabbing me by the arms and kissing me enthusiastically on both cheeks. 'And

189

this is your daughter? Wonderful! HELLO!' she shouted at Michelle, who flinched and gazed back at her in bewilderment. 'I'm Fantasia Topping, and I'll be looking after you both today and making sure your mum gets through it all in one piece – ha, ha, ha! Come along!'

Michelle and I both laughed politely and duly followed Fantasia along the corridor to a door at the end, which she flung open with a flourish and a cry of 'Here we are!'

I was evidently the last to arrive, because seated around the table in that room was such an assortment of people as I hope never to have to encounter again. At the back of the table, facing me, was a very large elderly woman with a tight grey perm, wearing a judo outfit. Next to her was someone of, probably, about my own age, looking extremely stern and wearing a blue dressing gown. She was talking across the table to a small, thin man in cotton pyjamas who looked scared to death. But most worrying of all was the woman to my right, who was dressed entirely in motorcycle gear, including a crash helmet. This wouldn't have been so bad if it wasn't for the fact that her tight-fitting leather jacket was unzipped all the way down to mid-boob-level – and it didn't look as if she was wearing anything underneath. I was reminded so sharply and forcefully of Chris Filbey's warnings about black leather that I lost the power of speech and movement.

'Come along! Don't be shy!' encouraged Fantasia gaily, tugging me into the room by my arm. 'We're all just getting to know each other!' She pushed me into a chair and beckoned Michelle to sit next to me. 'Now, ladies! This is Penny Peacham, our *Passion Pudding* cook!' There was a ridiculous little flutter of applause, as if Fantasia had pulled me out of a hat as an act in a magic show. 'Now, then, Penny: would you and Michelle like a nice cup of tea or coffee, before we get you into your outfit?'

I'd actually have liked a nice cup of arsenic rather than even *think* about what sort of outfit she had in mind for me.

'Tea, please,' said Michelle faintly. I could see that she

190

was trying desperately hard not to stare at the other occupants of the room and their strange attire. Dressing Gown Woman was the only one who had brought her husband. The one in leathers seemed to be on her own, while the judo lady had a girl of about fifteen with her.

'My eldest grandchild,' she told us, proudly, as we sat politely sipping our tea. 'Piety.'

'Pleased to meet you, Piety,' I said, feeling sorry for her.

'Right,' said Piety without looking at me. She spat a piece of chewing gum into her hand, looked at it for a while and then put it back in her mouth.

'I've got ten, you know,' said her grandmother. 'Three boys and seven girls. Two of the girls are twins.'

'Lovely,' said Michelle. 'Must keep you busy.'

'Busy?' she scoffed. 'Don't talk to me about busy. I teach two judo classes every day except Sunday.'

I didn't want to ask her what she did on Sundays. Presumably that was the day she practised her nude headstands.

'OK, ladies,' called Fantasia. 'Now you've had a nice rest, shall we get down to business – yah? Penny, we need to do your hair and make-up, dear, and get you into a *lovely* little outfit. These other ladies were all here a bit earlier – not so far to come, you see – so they're ready to go up to the studio now and meet *darling* Ber*nard*.' She grinned excitedly at the others. 'Charisma will take you all up there, ladies. We'll join you in a little while. Come along, Penny! Bring your daughter!'

She swept out of the room. Michelle and I glanced at each other as we hurried after her.

'They're not having their photos taken dressed like *that* – are they?' asked Michelle in horror.

'Of course not! They've probably chosen their outfits and got them hanging up in the studio.'

'Well, I hope you're right. The one in the leathers looked like her boobs were going to pop out at any minute.'

191

'Not a pleasant thought!' I chuckled.

Fantasia led us into another room. It looked like a very small downmarket hairdresser's salon. Three fairly battered leather chairs sat facing a mirror that ran along the length of one wall, and on the opposite wall were a couple of sinks and two large trolleys laden with pots, bottles, spray cans, brushes, cotton wool balls and powder puffs.

'Have a seat, Penny, dear. Gabby will be with you in a sec. She's going to make you look *absolutely stunning*!' she enthused, looking at me as if it was a near impossibility, but someone of Gabby's supreme talent would be able to manage it somehow.

Fantasia bustled out of the room, muttering about deadlines and darling Ber*nard*. Michelle sat down in the chair next to mine. For a minute or two we were both silent, and then we caught each other's eyes in the mirror and started to giggle. By the time the door opened again and Gabby, who was a six-foot blonde with cropped hair and multiple tattoos, came marching into the room carrying a hairdryer and an armful of towels, we were both creased up, crying with laughter, unable to sit up straight or utter a word.

'Good morning, ladies,' she said disapprovingly. 'Which of you is my victim?'

I think it was at that point that I kind of lost interest and started looking forward to lunch.

Michelle

I'm not as dim and naïve as Mum seems to think I am. Let me tell you something: I had a good idea what they were up to, Fantasia bloody Topping and her gang, even if Mum didn't. As soon as I clocked the one in the motorbike leathers with her tits hanging out, to say nothing of her in the dressing gown with probably not much underneath and hubby in his jimjams, I thought, OK – what's going on here, then? I was glad I was there, to tell the truth, to make sure Mum didn't get talked into posing in a bikini or anything tacky like that. We did have a laugh, though, and when that big lesbian stylist marched in, barking her orders, I thought I was going to wet myself. You should have seen what she did with Mum's hair. She's got nice hair, my mum. She used to be blonde like me, but now she has it done a kind of ash colour, and she wears it parted on the side and straight down to not quite shoulder-level, with a fringe. This Gabby put it up on top of her head, tied up in a sort of silky black scarf thing. Then she did her make-up with lots of rouge, which looked really odd 'cos Mum's naturally quite pale-skinned and personally I don't think it suited her. What with the bright red lipstick, I thought she looked a bit like a clown, but Mum was going, 'Oh, yes, lovely, Gabby!' so I thought I'd better keep my mouth shut. Soon wash off, anyway.

Well, all this took about half an hour or so, and then

Fantasia came back in the room, skipping up and down with excitement and giving it lots of Oohs and Aahs about how fantastic Mum looked, and what a natural, and how *darling* Ber*nard* was going to capture her film star quality. Mum pretended not to be pleased, but I could see her blushing even under all the rouge, glancing at herself in the mirror and having a little smile to herself – and who could blame her? I mean, at her age, and being married to Dad all those centuries, I don't suppose she often got anyone saying anything nice to her.

'Now, I've got some *lovely* little outfits for you to try on, Penny,' she said, dumping an armful of clothes onto a hanging rail and swishing them from one end of the rail to the other like she was opening the curtains. I watched Mum's eyes light up. Obviously, this was going to be the most exciting moment for her. She'd told Charisma her dress size already, and we were both expecting a lovely array of designer clothes for her to choose from – a bit like going on a shopping trip but without spending any money or bringing anything home at the end.

'How about *this*!' said Fantasia, lifting one of the garments off the rail with a flourish and waving it in Mum's face. '*Cheeky* little number – but I *like* it, Penny, I *like* it!'

It was terrible. For a start, it looked as if it was only just about knicker-skimming length. And ...

'Why's it so *white*?' I asked, looking at the thing with disgust. Mum's face had dropped. I could see she was trying really hard not to be rude.

'It's a chef's outfit, of course! Isn't it *cute*?' giggled Fantasia. 'Or – look, Penny!' She fished another one off the rail. 'A French maid's dress and apron! Now, I think that would *really* suit you.'

Sometimes rudeness is the only thing available.

'You've got to be joking, haven't you!' I said, grabbing the French tart's dress with one hand and the chef's minidress with the other and bundling them both back onto the hanging rail. 'What do you take my mum for? She's not wearing fancy dress! She hasn't come here to dress up like a trollop, in silly little dresses, pretending to be a chef or a waitress like she's in a pantomime! Where are the proper dresses?'

'Proper dresses? I'm sure I don't know *what* you mean, Michelle,' said Fantasia, flashing me a look that made me feel like she wanted to kill me. 'How about this one, Penny?'

'It's an apron!' I said. 'Why would you want to photograph her in an *apron*?'

'Or this?'

'That's an *overall*!'

'Michelle, I'd really like your mum to make her own decision about this. Why don't you go and get yourself a nice cup of tea from the machine down the corridor? And a nice bar of chocolate?'

I only just stopped myself from telling her to stuff her nice bar of chocolate up her arse.

'I'm staying here,' I told her flatly. 'I want to see what else you've got for Mum to wear. Where are all the designer clothes? The nice dresses and blouses and trousers?'

'Oh, dear, Michelle!' she said with one of her silly little giggles that were beginning to get seriously on my tits. 'I don't know *where* you got the idea that this was *that* sort of a photo shoot. Didn't your mum explain to you? Penny, you must have explained to Michelle about the *theme* of this feature?'

'Mature women, yes,' said Mum, looking embarrassed. 'Something to do with mature women and ... er ... vitality.'

'Exactly!' said Fantasia, looking pleased with herself. 'And your mum, Michelle, stays vital and alive and fascinating, as I'm sure you know, by making her *famous pudding*! Your mum is our *little chef*!'

'Are you supposed to be pleased that she's comparing

195

you to a motorway café?' I asked Mum crossly. 'Shall we just go home now?'

'Oh, Chelle!' she said sadly. 'I've been looking forward to this . . . '

So what was I supposed to do? Act like the wicked witch and spoil her day? Or grit my teeth, smile sweetly and pretend I thought it was all great fun?

'OK, then,' I said, after a moment's hesitation. 'OK, this'll be great fun.'

'So which shall I choose, Chelle?' Mum was looking at me hopefully. I *knew* she was disappointed that she wasn't getting to try on any designer outfits, and felt silly about being asked to dress up as a Little Chef. But she wasn't going to admit it.

'Maybe the apron,' I said, trying to sound enthusiastic. I only suggested it because it wasn't as short and tarty as the other things. 'It's quite pretty.'

It wasn't. It was awful. It was white, with a big frill all round it, and it tied up at the back with a bow.

'What does she wear underneath it?' I asked.

'A nice little dress,' said Fantasia excitedly, producing the nice little dress from the rail. It was blue, and about six inches shorter than the apron. I suddenly realised what the whole outfit reminded me of: Alice in Wonderland. They must have got all this gear as a job lot from an amateur dramatics group!

By the time we headed up to Darling Bernard's studio for the photos, the other women had apparently all finished, and gone to make a start on the buffet lunch. I was beginning to feel my stomach rumbling. We'd had an early breakfast, and a long journey, and I hadn't had anything to eat since. I found myself hoping they were going to leave some grub for us.

'Michelle,' said Fantasia as if she'd read my mind, 'Why don't you go along to the lunch while your mum has her photos done? We'll join you in a few minutes – yah?'

196

'Well . . . ' I felt a bit doubtful about leaving Mum with this madwoman and some creepy photographer, but I *was* starving, and I was thinking maybe I could get Mum a plate of food in case all the others were gannets and didn't leave her anything.

'Go on, love,' said Mum. 'I'll be fine, honestly – he's only got to take a couple of quick pictures, hasn't he, Fantasia?'

'Oh, yah, Ber*nard* is the most *amazing* photographer – he's an absolute *fiend* with the camera!' She demonstrated. 'Snap, snap, click, click – *fait accompli*!'

If that's the case, I could do it myself, and do Ber*nard* out of a job.

I was shown back to the room where we'd had our cup of tea earlier. It must have been some kind of meeting room: the long oval table in the middle was now covered in a white tablecloth and spread with plates of sandwiches, sausage rolls, bowls of salad, things that might have been chicken nuggets or garlic mushrooms, it was difficult to tell, and little cakes. I was a bit disappointed, to tell the truth. I don't know what I was expecting – something more cosmopolitan I suppose, being as we were in London, in the offices of a national magazine – not just a replica of every birthday party buffet I'd ever been to at home. But I *was* very hungry. The relief of not being pregnant had given me back my appetite.

The woman called Charisma who'd been introduced to us as Fantasia's 'PA' handed me a glass of something orange and fizzy.

'Buck's Fizz,' she said. 'Or there's plain orange if you prefer?'

'No, that'll be fine,' I said. Not pregnant. No ban on alcohol. I smiled to myself happily. 'Thank you.'

'Help yourself to the buffet, Michelle.' I started moving towards the table, my mouth watering. 'Oh, but first – let me introduce you to Janine, our Beauty Editor, and

Rashmi, our Features Editor. 'Rashmi, this is Michelle – Penny's daughter. Penny the Passion Pudding chef, you know?'

'Mum's not a chef, actually,' I said, irritated again. 'She works in a vet's. And really, what she wanted to do was publicise the appeal for a bypass ...'

'But it's so *wonderful* to meet all these lovely ladies!' said Rashmi, completely ignoring me. 'All these *amazing* ladies who've all found their own ways of keeping their sexual spark alive, despite their age ...'

'Mum's not old!' I frowned. I took a gulp of my Buck's Fizz. 'And she's *not* into anything *sexual*!'

'*Wonderful* for our readers to see,' she went on regardless, 'How they can bring a bit of fun and excitement into their lives, however old they are ...'

'She's only fifty-two!'

'Middle age, the menopause – it doesn't have to be the end of anything, you see. That's the message we're trying to get across to our readers. Great sex can carry on into old age, with a bit of effort and imagination.'

'I *don't* think Mum would like you putting all this emphasis on sex in your feature.' I took another gulp of my drink and realised I'd nearly finished it. 'I don't think she would have agreed to be in it, if she'd known you were going to—'

'Another drink, Michelle?' interrupted Charisma, approaching me with a tray of full glasses. I drained my glass and handed it to her in exchange for a new one.

'Thanks.'

Rashmi had moved on to talk to someone else. I made another move towards the table.

'Hello, Michelle – I'm Janine, the Beauty Editor,' said a very slim girl with lovely glossy copper-coloured hair. 'I've just popped into the studio to see the result of your mum's makeover. Doesn't she look *great*!'

'Well, I suppose so. Although I don't really like the rouge. Or the red lipstick.'

'It's a bold look, I know. Very dramatic. Very sexual.'

This was beginning to piss me off. I took another mouthful of my drink before I answered her.

'My mum doesn't want to look *sexual*. She wanted to look nice, look attractive, but ...'

'You mustn't be uncomfortable about your mum being a sexy woman, Michelle. It's *wonderful*. People don't stop being sexual when they get older, you know ...'

'She's not old!' I snapped. 'And she's not sexual! She's my mum, for God's sake!'

'Well, of course, I understand that it could make you feel threatened ...'

'What!'

'Your own sexuality ...'

I drained my second glass of Buck's Fizz in one go. The edges of everything in the room began to look slightly blurry. This was not good. I needed to eat.

'Excuse me,' I said a bit rudely. 'I'm very, very hungry.'

I picked up two plates and plonked a couple of sandwiches on each of them, followed by a sausage roll and a couple of the mushroom/chicken nuggets, and went to sit down in the corner of the room where I hoped I could quietly sober up without anyone else going on at me about sexuality.

'Wotcha.' Someone sat down heavily in the chair next to me, almost unbalancing the spare plate of food for Mum, which was resting on my knees.

'Oh – hello.' It was Piety, the stroppy-looking granddaughter of the judo lady (who was now, surprisingly, dressed in a fairly normal-looking skirt and blouse and chatting excitedly to Rashmi at the other end of the room). 'Are you enjoying yourself?'

'Am I, fuck!' she muttered. 'This is fucking awful, isn't it?'

'Well, I must admit ...'

'They're all fucking perverts. I told Gran she was out of

199

her tiny fucking mind getting involved in all this.'

'I know what you mean. They do seem a bit obsessed with—'

'Gran was hoping they were going to give some publicity to her stray cat charity. That's what she did the headstand thing for. She's ever so athletic – comes from all the judo, you see. But they're determined to make out she did it in the nude. Fucking perverts.'

'She didn't?' I took a bite of ham sandwich. 'She didn't do the headstands in the nude?'

'Course not. What do you take her for? She did it in her judo suit. She said something stupid in the interview about practising in the nude, and that was it!'

'Sounds a bit like my mum. She wanted to publicise our bypass appeal, but when she went on local radio, she got nervous and said all this stuff about her pudding. Now that's all anyone wants to hear about.'

'Well, you can just imagine what this feature's going to be like!' said Piety, shaking her head.

'Yeah. But it's such a shame. Mum was so excited about today – I don't want to spoil it for her.'

'I know. Gran thinks it's wonderful. I only came with her to keep her out of trouble.' She helped herself to a sausage roll off my plate and took a large bite out of it. 'They're such a worry, aren't they, when they get older?'

Mum was a bit quiet when she came back from the photo session. She sat down on the other side of me and said hello to Piety.

'I got you some buffet,' I said, handing her the plate. 'Get stuck in because there's not much left. You were ages having your picture taken!'

'I know. Bernard was a pain in the neck. He must have used about twenty rolls of film. He got me looking in one direction, told me it was *absolutely super*, took dozens of shots, and then made me look in another direction and put a different expression on my face and went, "Oh, that's fabulous, that's amazing!" and took dozens more!'

'They're a load of nutters,' I said. 'I wouldn't be too hopeful about this feature if I were you, Mum.'

'I know.' She picked up a sandwich off the plate, looked at it suspiciously and put it down again. 'It's not exactly what I imagined, Chelle, to be perfectly honest. Still, never mind! Let's go and do some shopping, eh? Come on! I don't fancy this lunch. We can have tea and cakes later in Harrods or somewhere. Pretend we're rich and famous.'

'You *are* famous!' I told her, laughing.

We spent nearly forty minutes saying goodbye to everyone. But it was worth it. By the time we'd got out of there and had a taxi take us up to Regent's Street, even though it was only the middle of the afternoon, it was getting dark, and the streets looked all bright and Christmassy and exciting. We went in and out of the shops getting loaded down with bags of lovely presents for everyone, and for the first time that day we both started enjoying ourselves. And to be honest, for the first time since Robbie disappeared, I felt really happy again. So I think I must have finally got over it – mustn't I.

Penny

Michelle and I were both tired out by the time we got on the train home from London. To begin with, I thought I was going to fall asleep and not wake up till we were back at Duffington. But we'd bought ourselves some Coca-Cola and a couple of bars of chocolate for the journey, and it's surprising how it perks you up. I didn't really want to talk about the *Woman Today* thing. I needed a bit of time to mull it over on my own, to decide what to make of it all. I'd had enough of it. So instead, Michelle and I started talking about how they'd voted me out of the PPPP.

'I couldn't believe it when you came home and told us!' she said. 'I thought it was terrible that those stupid morons pushed you out.'

'Well, they didn't really leave me a lot of choice. If I'd stayed, I'd have had to promise not to do anything with the media. Anything like today.'

She gave me a look, and I knew what she was probably thinking: maybe not such a bad idea.

'What with them,' I sighed, 'and what with Maureen – seems like everyone except me knew it wasn't going to be a good idea coming today.' And how did we get back on the subject of today, after all?

'What do you mean, about Maureen? What did she say?'

'Oh, nothing much. Just gave me the impression she thought I was getting carried away with it all – you know, all the fuss about the pudding. As if I *wanted* any fuss in the first place!'

'Don't worry, Mum. She's probably just jealous.'

'No,' I said stoutly. 'Not Maureen. We've been friends too long for that sort of thing, Chelle.'

'Well, that's what I thought about Kim. You know, we were best friends at school, and shared that flat together too, didn't we. But she got really funny with me the other week, after I— ' She stopped short, shook her head, and looked out of the window for a minute before going on, 'After I had a dance with someone on Nicole's birthday. And Nic said to me – "Chelle", she said, "She's just jealous. She fancies him herself."'

'So – what do you think, then? That Maureen wishes it was her getting all this attention? Getting interviewed on the radio and having her picture in the papers and everything?'

'Probably, Mum. But she'll never admit it, will she?'

'I wish it *was* her, in a way.'

'Aren't you enjoying it, then?'

I thought about it. Thought about Archie treating me as if I was suddenly a different woman, a woman he actually looked at, and took notice of, and not just someone in the kitchen doing the ironing. Thought about Chris Filbey. But as soon as I started thinking about him I shuddered all the way through, and had to give myself a little shake and have another drink of Coke.

'Yes. Yes, I *am* enjoying it, I suppose. But I wish Maureen would have a bit of excitement in *her* life, too. It's no fun for her at the crematorium. There's not a lot of life there. And she doesn't do anything else, much, apart from crosswords.'

'And look at who she's married to!' Michelle grinned.

Tony wasn't exactly anyone's idea of a bundle of fun. Even Archie couldn't stand him. He was such an all-round misery-guts, he made Archie look like a stand-up comedian.

203

'So maybe she *is* jealous,' I said wonderingly. 'Maybe that's why she's been a bit funny with me, after all.'

'Jealous of you and Dad!' chuckled Michelle.

Or jealous of what I'd told her about Chris Filbey?

Or – more to the point – of what I *hadn't* told her, but she was imagining.

'So what's the score with Darren Barlow?' asked Michelle when we'd finished all the chocolate.

'Score? What score? There *is* no score with him. I don't know what his problem is. He asks you out, even though he's old enough to be your father and he's already got a wife or a girlfriend ...'

'I thought it was *you* he fancied, Mum. You were flirting with him!'

'I wasn't! I was trying to keep him away from *you*.'

'And *I've* told him to leave *you* alone!'

'Well, he phoned me again yesterday morning.'

'He never! You didn't say.'

'Oh, I couldn't be bothered with him. I was late for work. He was going on about a *proposition*. Probably another bloody radio show! He can stick it up his—'

'Yeah. Specially now you're not even in the PPPP any more, eh!'

'He knows that. I told him.'

'Hm. See what I mean, Mum? It's *you* he's interested in. Face it; you've got all the men after you now you're the media star!'

Michelle was teasing, of course, and I laughed along with her. But I was thinking to myself, desperately, desperately – *there's only one man that I want to be interested in me*. And I knew it was wrong. Wrong and dangerous. But I wanted to carry on from where we'd left off.

It was late when we got back to Duffington. I'd parked the car in a side street a few minutes' walk from the station, and it was as much as Michelle and I could do to stagger back there with all our shopping, dump it in the boot and drive home. As we pulled up outside the house, she jumped with surprise.

'My car's not there!'

'Maybe Dad's borrowed it,' I said.

'Why would he? His is here.'

'I don't know. Maybe his wouldn't start, or something. Come on, give me a hand in with these bags, and we'll see if he's in.'

Archie was not only in, he was watching football with the sound turned up so loud we both flinched as I opened the front door.

'Where's my car?' shouted Michelle, marching straight into the lounge and turning the TV down by about 500 decibels.

'Leave it alone! I'm watching it,' he grumbled.

'Yes, and half the bloody town is listening to it,' said Michelle. 'Where's my car, Dad?'

'Your car? How should I know? Where did you leave it?'

'What! What are you talking about! I left it outside, like I always do!' She sank down on the sofa, putting her head in her hands. 'Don't tell me my fucking car's been fucking nicked from outside the fucking door!'

I didn't say anything to her about the swearing. Even Archie just blinked a couple of times.

But when she looked up at him and went on: 'While you were sitting there with the fucking football blaring!' he said, quite sharply:

'OK, OK, calm down. When did you last see it?'

'Last see it? It's not a missing cat!' I said, getting cross with him myself now. 'It didn't wander off by itself!'

'It was there when Mum and I went out this morning,' said Michelle. 'Have you been out today, Dad?'

'Yes, I've been out! What, do you think I've been sitting here on my backside all day just because you two have been off on your jaunt?' No comment. 'I've been wallpapering Mrs Brown at number sixty-five.'

'And was my car outside when you went out? Was it there when you came home?'

'I don't know, do I! I don't go checking cars, counting them, every time I walk in and out of my own house! What do you think I am?'

'Blind?' retorted Michelle rudely.

'I'd have thought you might have noticed, Archie,' I agreed.

'Oh, great!' He got up and turned off the TV. 'That's just great, that is. Everything that goes missing in this house is my fault. Everyone else goes out gallivanting down to London having their *hair done* and their *make-up done* and their *photos taken*,' (he said all of these with a really nasty sneer) 'while Muggins here has to get up and go to work like normal, earning a crust, feeding the family, keeping the wolf from the door – and when the car gets nicked it's *my* fault! Maybe you left the bloody keys in the ignition, Chelle! Maybe you left the car door unlocked! Eh? Have you thought of that? Eh?'

'No need to shout,' I told him. 'You did lock it, didn't you, Chelle?'

'Course I did. I always do.'

'Better report it to the police, then. No point us all shouting at each other,' I said, suddenly feeling very tired.

'Have to do it in the morning,' muttered Archie, still disgruntled. 'Won't be anyone at the police station now. Not that they'll be interested. Not that they'll do anything. Waste of bloody time.'

'Robbie,' said Michelle, suddenly, leaning back in the armchair and letting out a long, slow breath.

'What about him?' said Archie.

'Just like when he went missing. That what you mean, Chelle?' I put my arm round her. 'First him, now the car, eh? Not your year, is it, love? Never mind, don't be upset, we'll claim on the insurance ...'

'No. I mean, Robbie's taken the car. He still had the key. He's sneaked back and taken it, hasn't he!' She sounded almost excited. 'You know what this means, Mum!'

'He's an even bigger bastard than we all thought?' said Archie sarcastically.

'No! Well, yes, but listen. It means he must still be in this area! He can't have gone far – he must have been around here all the time, watching, knowing I had the car here ... waiting for a chance to take it back.'

'But normally you take it to work every day,' I said reasonably.

'Exactly! So today, for once, it was outside here all day – nobody at home watching ...'

I couldn't help wondering why she sounded so pleased about it. I thought she was supposed to be over Robbie Nelson? Why all the sudden excitement about him supposedly being in the neighbourhood?

'Even if it was him, it was still your bloody car,' said Archie. 'And don't you forget it. He owed you the money! He's still nicked your bloody car, Michelle, and you still want to report it to the police tomorrow!'

'I know,' she said quite calmly, getting up to go and put the kettle on. 'I know that, Dad. Why do you think I'm pleased about it?'

'I forgot to ask you,' said Archie as we were getting ready for bed, 'How did it go today?'

'All right,' I said a bit guardedly.

'Only *all right*? Didn't you enjoy it? I thought you were looking forward to it, Pen?'

'I was.' Shit, how much was I going to tell Archie? He would find out anyway, when the stupid magazine appeared. 'It was a bit disappointing, really,' I said. 'I think they were looking for cheap thrills.'

'Cheap thrills?' he echoed.

'Making innuendos. Portraying me and the other women as kind of sex icons for the older generation.'

'*Sex icons*, eh?' he said, raising his eyebrows. And I

207

could see from where I was standing, his eyebrows weren't the only things being raised either.

'Still, never mind,' I said quickly, getting into bed and pulling the duvet up to my neck. 'I had a nice time Christmas shopping with Michelle ...'

'Sod the Christmas shopping,' he said, getting hold of me quite roughly and pulling the duvet back off me. 'Let's see about this *sex icon* stuff, shall we?'

Bugger. I was too tired, really. But it seemed like Archie was bloody insatiable these days.

The next day was a Wednesday and, as usual, at about half past five or six o'clock, just as everyone was coming home from work, getting their dinners on and their kids fed, putting on the TV and their slippers, and getting settled down for the evening, the *Duffington Echo* was posted, completely free of charge to everyone except its regular advertisers, through the letterboxes of all the residents of Duffington, Panbridge Park and the surrounding villages.

'Paper, Mum,' said Michelle, dumping it on the kitchen worktop next to where I was chopping onions for a stew.

'Thanks, love. Take it into the lounge, can you, and ...oh!' I broke off, gasping in surprise, at the exact same moment as Michelle grabbed the paper up again, straightened out the front page, and shouted:

'Blimey, Mum! You're in it *again*!'

I was on the phone to Darren Barlow before I'd even finished reading the article.

'Penny!' he greeted me, too enthusiastically for my liking. 'How lovely to hear from you. And may I say what an inspired piece of journalism I've just had the pleasure to read about your good self in our local rag?'

'No,' I snapped. 'You may not. Don't be so facetious! I know it was you.'

'Sorry, Penny. I'm not quite with you there. What was me?'

I sighed with impatience.

'All that stuff about me being "tactically removed" from the PPPP. You're the only person I told!'

'The only one? Well, I must say I'm very flattered. You consider me trustworthy, obviously.'

'No, I don't, and I've been proved right, haven't I? How dare you tell the paper about it? "Passion Pudding Penny dropped from Panbridge Park Pressure Group!" And "No Comment," says Roger Clark, PR Officer of the PPPP! Hardly surprising, is it? They'll kill me! They'll chop me up in little pieces and feed me to the lions!'

'Don't be melodramatic, Penny, dear. It doesn't suit you. Of course they won't kill you. Whether they like it or not – and I quite agree they probably won't – it's more publicity for their pathetic little cause: publicity that their mealy-mouthed cowardy-custard Roger couldn't generate if he tried. Everyone loves you, Mrs Passion Pud – and everyone will be up in arms about you being forced out of the group. It's a scandal. And a nice whiff of scandal never did anyone's publicity any harm. Trust me, I'm a radio presenter.'

'*Trust* you!' I said furiously. 'That's a joke. I can't believe you did this ...'

'Exactly. Of course you can't believe it, because I didn't. Sorry, Penny, darling, but much as I love you, I've got better things to do with my time than to phone up silly little reporters on the local paper about you. I've got bigger fish to fry.'

'Meaning?'

'I'll tell you all about it over dinner. The Italian restaurant. I know you like it there.'

'Get stuffed, Darren. I've already told you ...'

'Still not interested in my little proposition, then? OK; I can wait. Just give me a ring when you change your mind.'

'What makes you think I'm going to?' I spluttered. 'Oh, this is ridiculous! Why am I bothering to even speak to you? Don't phone me again!'

I heard him laughing as I hung up the phone, and remembered with annoyance that it had been me phoning *him*. Bloody man! Bad enough that he'd given the *Echo* a field day again, he couldn't even admit it and apologise. *Bloody man!*

'Well,' said Archie, folding the paper carefully and handing it back to me, 'At least this time it's fairly tasteful.'

'Tasteful!' I exploded, still feeling too rattled by my conversation with Darren Barlow to be pacified by Archie's attempt at tact.

'Yes – I think so. I mean, at least they've stuck to the facts, haven't they?'

'What – "Penny Peacham, Panbridge Park's famous pudding creator, was given her marching orders recently by the organisation she helped to set up ...?"' I read out. 'That's not factual, Archie. It's almost libellous!'

'But it gives the whole story further on. It says they voted democratically. It says you could have stayed in the group if you agreed not to get involved with the media any more.'

'Yeah. I bet they *loved* that.'

'They love *you*, Penny,' he replied, smirking smugly. Anyone would think it was because of him that 'they' loved me. Whoever 'they' were. Everybody, according to Darren Barlow – not that I'd ever believe a word *he* said.

'Anyway,' added Archie, suddenly more serious, 'it serves that load of wankers in the PPPP right. If they wait for that old fart Roger to get the media interested, we won't get a bypass until we're all in our graves. He needs to wise up to the fact that any publicity is better than no publicity.'

'That's what Darren said,' I conceded.

'Darren?'

'Darren bloody Barlow. I've just phoned him and given him a piece of my mind for giving the story to the *Echo*. Not that he'll admit it. *Stupid* man.'

'Hm,' said Archie. 'Well. Like I say, Penny, I think it's a

210

pretty good story. You could end up being pleased about it.'

Yeah, right. Like a mouse ending up pleased about being caught by the cat. How is *that* supposed to happen? I screwed the *Echo* up viciously and chucked it out with the paper recycling.

'How did the modelling assignment go?' Chris Filbey asked me as soon as I walked into the surgery the next day. 'Plenty of shots of your stocking tops and suspenders?'

I hadn't been at work since my trip to London. But that morning when I got up and started getting ready, I'd suddenly become aware of something. Without even consciously thinking about it, I'd got my flimsiest, sexiest black underwear out of the drawer to put on. And my tightest-fitting, low-necked blouse. And a short, straight skirt. And ... stockings and suspenders. I hardly ever wore that kind of stuff. What made me decide to wear it today? Some subliminal message I was giving out, by any chance? Surely not?

'Oh, it was all a bit of a waste of time, really,' I told him, slipping off my coat, feeling him watching me. 'I don't suppose they'll even bother running the article.'

'But they took photos?' he persisted.

'Yes, but ...'

'Kinky ones?' He leaned across the reception desk, grinning at me. 'Whips and chains?'

'Oh, for God's sake!' I said, trying to ignore how flustered and hot I was feeling. 'Go and buy yourself a copy of *Playboy*!'

'Why would I want to do that?' he said very quietly. 'I don't want pictures. I want the real thing.'

'Ssh!' There was a client already sitting in the corner of the waiting room, a very large man in a yellow anorak, with a tiny black puppy on his lap. 'Ssh, someone will hear ...'

'No they won't,' he whispered. 'They'll think we're having a very serious discussion about a sick animal. Come

211

with me now. Quickly, before the others turn up.'

He turned and walked into his consulting room, without looking back to see if I was following him. My heart was beating so fast I had to take a couple of great gulps of air to try to steady myself down. Glenn and Debbie could both arrive at any minute. It would be completely crazy to go after him. Crazy, reckless, dangerous ... to say nothing of bad, wrong, and downright stupid.

As I walked into the room he looked up and gave me a very smug smile. He'd known perfectly well I was going to follow him.

'Shut the door,' he said.

'OK.' I leaned on the door to close it. 'But ... isn't it ... a bit dangerous?'

'That's what I like about it.'

He pulled me towards him. I was trying to keep my ears pricked for any possible sounds of Glenn or Debbie coming in – the outside door opening, footsteps, voices, puppy in the waiting room yapping or howling – but with Chris looking at me like that, as if he was ravenous and I was a three-course dinner, it was kind of hard to concentrate on anything else.

'Penny, you don't know what you're doing to me,' he groaned softly, pressing himself against me. 'I'm desperate for you. When are you going to let me ...?'

'Well, right now could be a bit awkward,' I hedged. 'Debbie might come in, or Glenn, it's nearly time to start the clinic, and there's a puppy ...'

'Say you will,' he persisted. 'Say you'll come to bed with me. I'll make all the arrangements. A nice hotel room. Champagne. Anything you like.'

He was saying all this right close against my ear, breathing into my ear and kind of nibbling at it at the same time. But it was making me feel very uncomfortable. Not the ear thing – that was nice – the stuff he was saying. Hotel rooms, arrangements. It all sounded too much like ... well, too much like *adultery*. So what did I expect? That

212

it'd be OK to have a quick shag in the consulting room, like my fantasies – that somehow if it wasn't prearranged, with a room booked and champagne ordered, it wouldn't count? That I could tell my conscience it had *just happened* – like I was a teenager getting carried away and going further than I meant to? *I didn't plan it. It just happened.* Wasn't I a bit too old for that kind of excuse? A bit too old, and a bit too *married*.

I pulled away from him just as he was about to kiss me.

'What's the matter?' he asked, looking surprised.

'Nothing. I'm just not sure . . . '

Behind me, the door handle suddenly turned and Debbie's voice called out cheerily, 'Morning, Chris!'

My ears obviously hadn't been pricked enough. I'd missed every sign of her approach, yapping puppy or otherwise. It's surprising how quickly two people can jump apart, move to opposite sides of the room and pretend to be very interested in bottles of antiseptic and sterile drapes.

'Morning, Debbie!' said Chris without any sign of having been interrupted.

I smiled at her a bit shakily, not trusting myself to speak, and walked past her out of the room, uncomfortably conscious of her eyes on me.

'Penny,' she began, turning quickly and following me. 'Penny!'

'What?' I didn't want to meet her eyes. She was looking at me very carefully, very anxiously.

'I just think . . . ' she began, and hesitated, still watching my face as if she was looking for inspiration.

'You think what?' I asked, trying to sound innocent.

'Oh, nothing.' She sighed. 'Never mind.'

Phew, that was a relief. For a minute, there, I thought she'd guessed something was going on. How could I be so stupid? I wasn't going to risk anything like *that* again. However tempting it might be.

Michelle

It was a pain in the arse, not having the car. I'd got used to driving to work – I didn't have to leave so early in the morning. Now it was back to hanging around at the bus stop in the cold and the rain like before. And as you can imagine, the police were about as much help as nothing: just like my dad said. I had to take a morning off work to go to the police station, and they didn't even seem very interested.

'Unfortunately,' said the big ugly copper behind the desk, not sounding very sorry about it at all, 'this sort of thing happens all the time, love. Probably been taken out of the area by now.'

'Probably been taken abroad,' agreed his mate without looking up from his paperwork.

'Probably been taken to pieces and used for parts.'

'Or it might have been used by joyriders and abandoned.'

'Crashed into a tree.'

'Or burnt out, more likely.'

'Well, thanks very much,' I said. 'You've really cheered me up.'

'Never mind, love. Claim off your insurance. Not much hope of getting it back.'

'But I think I know who's taken it.'

At this, they both looked up, their eyes out on stalks.

'You do?' This was probably very exciting for them. The

214

possibility of a real arrest. 'Can you give us the name and address of the suspect?'

'I can give you his name. Robbie Nelson. But I can't give you an address because he's gone missing.'

'Oh, yes,' said the big guy, staring harder at me. 'I remember you now. The case of the missing boyfriend! You never got him back, then?'

'No, and I don't want to. But if he's taken the car, I want him caught. He never paid me for it.'

'Well, without an address ...' he said doubtfully.

'Can't you try and find him? You've got a description of Robbie, and a description of the car. Circulate the details to all the police forces in the country. What about road-blocks? Have all the ports and airports watched ...'

I've seen enough police programmes. I know what they're supposed to do. How come I was telling them their job?

'It's not like we're after a murderer or a terrorist, is it, love. Can't go wasting police resources just for a stolen car.'

Great. See what I mean? Makes you wonder what we pay our taxes for.

By Thursday, the day before the hospital party, everyone at work was practically hysterical. Everyone except me. I wasn't even looking forward to it, particularly.

'I might not bother coming,' I told Julie as we were getting the clinic ready.

'Not bother coming?' she gasped, staring at me as if I'd said something really disgustingly rude. 'But it's the Christmas party!'

'I know. I just don't fancy it this year.'

'Not fancy it!' She stopped and gave me a worried kind of look. 'Are you not over it yet?'

'Over what?'

'Your boyfriend. The one who disappeared. Are you still upset about it?'

'No, it's not that.'

'It'll do you good to come to the party. Forget about him. Get off with someone new. How about that nice Fraser Willoughby? I've seen him looking at you, Michelle. You could do worse. He's good-looking, isn't he, and I don't think he's gay.'

'No. I'm not interested. I don't want to get off with anyone.'

'You need to move on, love. Put it all behind you ...'

'I have. It isn't that!'

'Plenty more fish in the sea. No good crying over spilt milk. Every cloud has a silver lining.'

'I'm not crying over anything. I just don't see the point of getting pissed, and getting a snog, and then ...'

'Don't see the point?' repeated Julie, her mouth open wide with shock. 'But that's the *whole* point, isn't it? What else is there? That's what Christmas is all about, isn't it?'

She was almost the same age as me, but all of a sudden I felt really, really old.

I hadn't seen much of 'that nice Fraser Willoughby' recently. Someone said he'd been on study leave or something. But to be honest, I didn't really want to see him anyway; it would just make me feel sad and inadequate, like I'd failed at something. I'd kind of managed to put him out of my mind. Well, almost. But isn't it always the way? Someone's name comes up in conversation and the next minute, even if you haven't seen them for ages, up they trot as if they'd been waiting in the wings for their cue.

Sister had sent me up to one of the wards that same afternoon, on an errand for some records, and there he was, sitting on a bed, chatting to a patient, smiling and laughing as if he was the happiest man alive, without a care in the world about any poor girl he might have dumped after only one date and without even telling her she was dumped. He glanced up at me and, really, I'd have liked to walk away with my nose in the air, pretending I'd got something in my

216

eye and hadn't even seen him. But I couldn't. I was too taken aback at seeing who the patient in the bed was: old Mr Partington with the amputated fingertip.

'Oh, hello!' I said. 'I haven't seen you in the clinic lately. Is your finger worse?'

Sometimes they get infected, you see, and the patients have to come into the ward and get put on an intravenous antibiotic drip. I do know these things.

'Hello, love,' he said. 'No, it's not me finger. That's healing up lovely now. It's me chest.'

With that, he went into this terrible coughing fit, like he was about to bring his lungs up. I made a dive for the dish on the bedside table just in time, almost knocking Fraser off the bed. I won't go into details because I know not everyone's got the stomach for this kind of thing, but let me just say I didn't like the look of what he'd coughed up. Nor did Fraser, I could see that. But I didn't say anything, of course. I just wiped his poor old face with a tissue and handed him his glass of water, and called one of the nurses to bring him a clean dish.

'I'm sorry you're feeling poorly,' I told him after I'd settled him back against his pillow. 'Try not to talk too much. Maybe, if the ward sister doesn't mind, I can pop up to see you again a bit later, after I've finished work downstairs.'

I don't know why. I just felt really sad for him. I mean, it was bad enough having his wife die of cancer, and then chopping half his finger off, without winding up in hospital with a bad cough, wasn't it? I thought I might be able to cheer him up a bit, somehow, just talking to him about this and that. He probably didn't get many visitors.

He smiled and nodded at me, looking really tired now, so I just patted his hand and left him with Fraser while I went to collect my records from the nursing station. When I came back, Fraser had got up from the bed and surprisingly (seeing as he'd barely spoken to me since he took me out on a date and dumped me all on the same night) walked

217

out of the ward with me, holding the door open for me and waiting while I cleaned my hands, and everything.

'That was kind of you,' he said as we walked down the stairs.

'What? Well, I like him. I feel sorry for him – no wife or anything, and only half a finger. Doesn't seem fair.'

'No. And now he's got lung cancer.'

'Oh, God!' I swallowed back a sudden, stupid feeling of wanting to cry. I mean, I was a health care assistant, wasn't I; I couldn't start crying over every patient that got cancer. I'd never get any work done, blubbing all over the place.

'Are you OK?' he asked quietly. 'I'm sorry – I know you're fond of him.'

'Yes, but it's probably not a good idea, is it?' I sniffed. 'Getting too fond'.

'People without any feelings would make lousy doctors and nurses.'

'But I'm not. I'm not a nurse. I'm only a—'

'Well, you should be,' he interrupted me, quite fiercely, as if he was telling me off. 'You'd make a bloody good nurse. Think about it, Michelle!' With this he pushed open the outside doors at the bottom of the stairs and strode out into the cold dark December afternoon. 'Think about it, seriously!'

'But I'm not clever enough!' I called after him as the doors swung shut. I thought I heard him shout something back, but it got lost in the wind.

He obviously didn't realise I wasn't clever enough.

Which didn't explain, really, why he dumped me, did it?

Mum was making one of her puddings when I got home that night. I was a bit surprised, really. I thought she'd got sick of making them, when all the fuss started, but now she seemed to be secretly taking a kind of pride in it.

'Well,' she said, wiping her hands on a tea towel, 'Jessica and I have been making mince pies, so I thought, while the oven was on I'd just quickly mix a pudding up,

218

too. Jessica helped me. It's kept her quiet.'

Jessica was probably going to be able to cook a three-course dinner before I could even be trusted to boil an egg. To be fair, though, at the moment anything Mum could do to keep her quiet was good news. She was even more hysterical about Father Christmas coming than the girls at work were about the party. And as usual, she was spending more time at our house than she did at her own.

'Come and sit down with me, Jessica, and let me read you a story,' I said, trying to steer her away from the hot oven. 'Come on. Poor Nanny's tired out after working at the vet's all day and then coming home to mince pies and things.'

I sometimes wonder how my mum manages it all without collapsing in a heap. If I was her, I'd have bought the mince pies at Tesco and given Jessica Play-Doh to roll out instead of pastry. Maybe my generation was born with less energy than hers. It's a bit frightening to think about. If it goes on like this, what will *our* children be like? Maybe they won't have enough energy to get out of bed at all, and us old people will have to keep on working to look after them.

Anyway, Jessica wasn't having any of it. Sitting down nice and quiet with Chelly and a book was not on her agenda, not when there was so much Christmas stuff all around the house to hype her up into such a state of excitement. Dad had got the Christmas tree down from the loft the day before; we'd stopped having a real one because the first Christmas we had Jessica, when she was only a baby, she kept crawling over pine needles on the carpet, and getting them stuck in her legs and crying. They're supposed to be non-drop but you can't rely on it. So this evening, Dad was putting the fairy lights on the tree and then Jessica and I were going to help with the baubles and beads and little hanging Santas.

'You've got to wait till I've got the lights on, Jessica,' said Dad, sounding a bit stressed. He had them all laid out on the floor trying to work out which ones needed new bulbs. 'Put the baubles down, there's a good girl, or you'll break them.'

'On the tree! Put them on the tree!' squealed Jessica, looking like she was going to throw them.

'Jessica, come on, out of Granddad's way.'

Blimey, no wonder mothers always look tired. How do they cope with two kids, or three or four?

'Ding-dong!' she announced suddenly, running to the front door. 'I get it!'

'No you won't!' I ran after her. Fortunately the door handle was still too high for her to open. 'Chelly opens the door, not you. Oh, hello Nic! Come in. Thank God – you can help me keep this one quiet.'

'Don't want to keep quiet! Is Father Christmas nearly here?'

'No, and he only comes to quiet children, so you'd better keep the noise down a bit,' said Nicole, laughing. 'Have you got time for a chat, Chelle?'

'Yeah, course! What's up? You look really pleased with yourself.'

'I am.' She threw herself down on the sofa. 'Guess what!'

'No idea. You've won the Lottery? Got a new job?'

Nicole worked in a furniture shop and she really hated it. She said she thought she was cut out for better things than sofas and wardrobes, really. She was always applying for new jobs but she never seemed to get on very well at the interviews. Robbie used to say she needed to learn to string more than two words together, but that only goes to show what a nasty bastard Robbie was, doesn't it?

'No, haven't done the Lottery, and still waiting to hear about the job at the beauty salon. *Much* better than that, Chelle! It's Scott!'

Scott. I had to think for a minute.

'The bloke you were going out with? The one you were ready to have ...' I glanced at Jessica quickly. Fortunately

220

she'd got interested in a cartoon on telly. 'The one you really liked?'

'Yes! Listen, it was all down to your mum's pudding!'

'Eh? Are you joking? How come?'

'That night we all had some of the pudding, round here, after the Chinese takeaway. Well, I know it sounds silly,' she shrugged and smirked, 'but I made a sort of wish while I was eating it.'

'That does sound pretty silly,' I laughed.

'Well, you were all talking about the pudding making people passionate. So I just made this wish that it would make me so sexy and lovely that Scott wouldn't be able to resist me.'

'And?'

'And the very next day, he phoned and said he'd dumped Angela Atkinson and would I please go out with him again.'

'But he hadn't even seen you! How could he tell you were so sexy and lovely? I'm not saying you *weren't*, but how could he tell, over the phone?'

'Vibes. I must have given off vibes, and he just picked them up.'

'Wow!' I laughed again. It did all seem very silly to me, but how could I say that when Nic was so happy and excited? Good luck to her. It wasn't very often she got a boyfriend, and maybe this Scott would be the one that would hang around for longer than the first time they had sex.

'Have you had sex with him yet?' I whispered.

'No! I'm making him wait for it!' she giggled.

'Wow!' I said again. This was indeed a new concept. 'I thought you said you were going to ...?'

'Yeah, but you know what, Chelle? I really like him, but I don't want him messing me around any more. And my mum said to me: "Nic", she said, "don't think I'm interfering ..."' She pulled a face that gave a very good impression of her mother being interfering, '"But if you

221

want to hold onto a man, don't give him everything he wants straight away."'

We were both quiet for a minute, contemplating this piece of old-fashioned wisdom.

'Bollocks to that,' I said. 'If you really like someone, you have to ... '

'But maybe you *don't* have to, Chelle. Maybe it's true, maybe they respect you if you make them wait a bit.'

'We're not living in the nineteen fifties now!' I said, 'With all due respect to your mum, Nic. They didn't have the Pill in their day, did they.'

'My mum's not *that* old! And anyway, when you think about it, Chelle, you weren't on the Pill yourself when you got drunk and had it away with Luke—' She stopped short, looked at me quickly and shook her head. 'Sorry.'

'No. You're right, I wasn't. I've come off it for a break because the doctor was worried about my headaches, but I keep telling him it's because of Mum's fuchsias. And anyway, I don't think I *did* have it off with Luke. It was just Kim being a bitch.'

Nicole didn't answer. She was looking at the cartoon Jessica was watching, as if there was suddenly a really interesting bit.

'Anyway, I'll never find out now,' I said with a shrug. 'So I'm just going to forget about it.'

'Mm,' said Nicole.

I was a bit offended really. She could have shown a bit more sympathy, after I'd been so excited for her about Scott.

But I didn't say anything. She was probably feeling sexually frustrated, because of her mum's new No Sex thing. But that was hardly my fault, was it?

After Nicole had gone home, and Jessica had finally been allowed to help put the baubles on the tree, and Adam had come to take her home to bed, I sat and watched TV with the tree lights reflecting in the screen – red, white, yellow and green – and instead of concentrating on the TV programme, which was crap, I was thinking about Fraser. I was thinking again about how he obviously didn't like me (or he wouldn't have dumped me), and yet when he talked to me earlier on, on the ward, he was being really nice, smiling at me and saying I ought to be a nurse, like he actually meant it. So what was that all about, then? If he didn't like me, maybe he just felt sorry for me. I didn't want him feeling sorry for me. I felt tears come to my eyes just at the idea of it. Then I gave myself a little shake and thought – what's the matter with you, Michelle? Here we are, nearly Christmas, everyone getting excited about parties and Santa and baubles on the tree, and you're sitting here practically blubbing because some guy feels sorry for you instead of fancying you? Get a grip, girl!

And the thought kind of crossed my mind: You know why you're blubbing really, don't you. The truth is that you really like him. That's your trouble. You keep on telling yourself you're finished with men, but you're not being honest, are you? Underneath it all, that's what's wrong with you, Michelle Peacham. You really, really like him, and you know it.

I didn't have time to dwell on this, though, because just then Mum came into the lounge with a cup of tea for me, and a piece of pudding on a plate.

'Here you are, Chelle – nice piece of my pudding,' she said. 'You all right, love?'

'Course I am,' I said, sitting up straight and fixing a smile on my face. 'Thanks, Mum. Smells delicious.'

'I put a bit of extra spice in it,' she said, 'to make it kind of Christmassy.'

'Delicious,' I said again, taking a bite.

And you know what? It might have been really silly. I might have laughed at Nicole, making her secret wish about Scott, but I took another big bite of my Mum's Passion Pudding and closed my eyes, and wished very hard.

223

Make me gorgeous. Make me irresistible. Make Fraser Willoughby desperate for me. And make it happen quickly.

Now I'd just have to wait for 'the proof of the pudding' – as Mum would say.

Penny

The next day at work, I tried to stay out of Chris Filbey's way. It wasn't easy. I could feel his eyes on me every time he came anywhere near me, but I didn't dare look at him unless I had to, like if he was standing there at the reception desk handing me a vaccination card or an insurance claim form, for instance, making it absolutely ridiculous to avoid eye contact. And when I did, he was giving me these looks, shaking his head slightly and raising his eyebrows as if to say, What's the matter? or, Aren't you talking to me, then? I pretended I hadn't noticed. Those looks were likely to be the undoing of me.

Inside, I was a complete mess. On the one hand, I'd more or less convinced myself that I couldn't help having an affair with him. On the other hand, when he started talking about hotel rooms I panicked. I didn't know whether I was brave enough to go through with it. Could I handle the deception, the necessary lies, the guilty conscience I'd be inflicting on myself for the rest of my life? The fact that Debbie could so easily have walked in and caught him kissing me the other day had suddenly brought home to me, with a sharp smack, the reality of what I was doing. Or, to be more honest, the reality of what it would be like to be found out. I wasn't sure any more. I thought it might be nicer to just enjoy the fantasy without having the actual sex. Less messy, in more ways than one.

At lunchtime I went out to the shops to avoid having any social contact with Chris over the kettle or the sandwich toaster. Debbie was waiting for me when I got back, an envelope and a list of names in her hand.

'Penny, you're the only one I still haven't got,' she told me urgently. 'Come on, pay up!'

'Eh? Got what? Pay up what?'

'The balance of your money for the meal. The Christmas meal next week, Penny!' she added in exasperation when I still looked at her blankly.

'Oh! Oh, I'd forgotten all about that,' I admitted. Had one or two other things on my mind. 'Look, to be honest, Debs, I'm not that fussed about going. I'm really busy at home, and—'

'Don't be silly. Everyone's busy this time of year, but it's only one evening, isn't it. Besides, you won't get your deposit back. Your name's down, you're coming.'

'No, honestly, I ... I'm not bothered about the deposit. I'll give it a miss.'

Debbie looked at me for a minute with her head on one side.

'Is anything the matter, Penny?' she asked quietly.

'Of course not!'

'Nothing you want to talk about?' She looked around her at the empty waiting room. 'Confidentially?'

'No! Absolutely not! I just don't really feel like going out, that's all.'

'But you will by next Saturday! You won't want to be the only one not coming. It's only another twenty pounds to pay, Penny, and I absolutely insist: if the money's a problem, don't worry about it, I'll get Chris and Glenn to chip in a bit more – they're already paying for the drinks and it won't hurt them, they earn a lot more than we do, and I know they wouldn't want you to be left out, so—'

'No! Of course the money's not a problem!' I delved into my purse, hot with embarrassment at the idea of her asking Chris to pay for my meal. 'Here's the money. OK? So you

226

can tick me off the list. And that's the end of it.'

'Yes. OK. Thanks, Penny,' she said, giving me a puzzled look. 'I'll settle up with the restaurant on my way home, then.'

'Good. Yes. Thanks for organising it.'

I put my purse away and got back to work.

Could always cry off with a headache on the night, couldn't I.

I was really busy that afternoon, trying to explain to the owner of a pregnant whippet, on the phone, why the vets wouldn't agree to induce the labour early so she could get the puppies rehomed in time for Christmas – while fending off demands from a distraught woman, with a very definitely dead budgie in a cage, to interrupt the vet in the middle of an operation in order to put the bird on life support.

'God!' I exclaimed to myself when I'd finally managed to deal with both without any loss of temper or life (apart from the poor budgie).

'Magnificently handled, if I might say so,' commented a voice from the corner of the waiting room.

The quiet man in the big black coat, who I'd assumed to be waiting for the cat in the post-op recovery cage to be brought out, was actually Darren Barlow in disguise. Well, OK, not actually in disguise, but ...

'I'm Father Christmas,' he said cheerfully, flinging open his coat in a manner uncomfortably reminiscent of a flasher, revealing (instead of anything less pleasant) the bright red suit with wide black belt traditionally required for the job.

'The white beard looks ridiculous on you,' I said wearily. 'What are you doing here? Getting the reindeer checked out for fleas and lice before you take them down the chimneys?'

'Don't be silly, Penny,' he said mildly. 'I've been helping out at a children's party at the Sunny Smiles Day

227

Nursery. We radio presenters like to involve ourselves in the community, you know.'

'How very noble. And now you're involving yourself in vets' surgeries too? I hate to be the one to tell you, but cats and dogs don't believe in Santa Claus.'

'I came to see you, dear, not the dogs and cats. Although I was rather taken with that little Persian kitten that just went out. I do like a nice little frisky pussy.'

'You're disgusting.'

'And you're very elusive. I've been leaving messages for you, Mrs Many-P's, and you keep ignoring me. So I thought: if the mountain won't come to Mohammed ...'

'I can still ignore you while you're sitting there, you know. I could get you thrown out if I wanted to. An undesirable intruder in the waiting room.'

'Come on. Everybody knows that Father Christmas is a sweet, loveable, huggable guy who loves little kids and little furry animals.'

'Yes, and everybody knows he lives in Lapland and doesn't hang around Panbridge Park wearing a black over-coat and a pathetic cheap false beard.' The waiting-room door opened and two springer spaniels bounded in, laughing, pulling their red-faced owner behind them. 'And I've got clients to deal with,' I added.

'No problem. I'll wait.'

'For *what*?' I hissed at him in annoyance.

'I keep telling you. I need to talk to you.'

'Sorry to interrupt you, love, but Charlie here has eaten a reel of Sellotape and Freddie has swallowed a whole sheet of Christmas stamps. Can the vet have a quick look at them both? Their throats might be stuck to their stomachs.'

I looked at the two lively, dancing spaniels, caught Darren's eye across the room and found myself trying hard to smother a smile.

'Certainly, Mr Rampton. Have a seat, and the vet will call you in as soon as he's ready.' I glanced back across the room. 'And, Mr Christmas? If you're really sure you want to wait, I'm afraid I can't fit you in until the end of surgery.'

'That'll be absolutely wonderful, Mrs Many P's. I'm looking forward to it.'

Glad one of us is.

There were two more minor emergencies before I was free to shut up shop.

'Wonderful to watch you working, Penny,' commented Darren as I turned off the computer and prepared to leave. 'I've seen you in a whole new light this afternoon. Your compassion for that little hamster nearly brought tears to my eyes.'

'All right, all right, it's bad enough having you sitting there staring at me, without having to listen to your sarcasm,' I snapped.

'Goodness me! Well, I can see it's been a stressful day for you, my dear, but really, there's no need—'

'I'm not *your dear*. And I think it's about time you told me what all this is about, quickly, in as few words as possible, so I can go home. All right?'

'Absolutely. That's what I've been *trying* to do, Penny. But I don't want to talk to you while you're all cross and irritable. Come on, get your coat on. I'm taking you to the pub.'

As he was saying this, he was actually taking my coat off the peg and trying to put it on me.

'Get off!' I said, pushing him away. 'Who said anything about going to the pub? Will you *stop* manhandling me!'

There was the click of a door shutting, and then a voice saying very stonily behind me:

'Is everything all right, Penny?'

'Yes, thank you, Chris,' I said without looking round. 'Everything's fine.'

'This ... *gentleman* isn't annoying you?'

Yes, of course he's annoying me, but what's it got to do with you?

229

'Would you like me to take you home?' Chris persisted, hovering, his hand on the door handle, watching me, sizing Darren up, taking in the Father Christmas outfit and the beard and all.

For a split second, I thought about accepting. Thought about telling Darren to piss off after he'd waited here for me all afternoon, and hoping he'd finally take the hint. Thought about getting into Chris's car with him, sinking down into the soft leather of his passenger seat and letting him drive me ... home? Or maybe somewhere else? Somewhere quiet and peaceful – perhaps a hotel room, like he'd suggested, with champagne and thick curtains and low lights and a big, soft bed ...

I only thought about it for a split second. No, I couldn't accept a lift with him. If I did, I'd be done for. I'd be another statistic – an illicit affair, a broken marriage – and I still hadn't made up my mind whether I was brave enough, or stupid enough, or desperate enough, to risk it. Until I decided, I'd rather play safe. I'd even rather go to the pub with Darren bloody Barlow!

'It's OK,' I told Chris, turning away from him. 'Thank you all the same, but Darren and I are going out for a drink.' I pulled on my coat and glanced at Darren. 'Ready?'

'Oh,' said Chris, looking Darren up and down again. 'Oh, well, in that case, Penny, I hope you and *Darren* ...' The way he pronounced *Darren* was only slightly less unpleasant than a sneer. 'I hope you both have a lovely evening together.'

He slammed the door as he left.

'What was that all about?' asked Darren, who'd seemed too surprised at my change of heart to ask any questions until we were out of the surgery and getting into his car. 'Are you having an affair with him, Penny?'

'No!' I retorted hotly, closing the car door with more force than was necessary. 'He's my boss, and he's just ... concerned about me. Can you blame him, seeing me being

230

dragged off to the pub against my will by some ... by some *Santa*?'

'That's a very hurtful insinuation. I'm not doing any dragging, and what on earth could be more innocent than a little seasonal drink with dear old Father Christmas?'

'Let's just cut out the crap, Darren. And for Christ's sake take that stupid beard off. I'm *not* sitting next to you in a pub with you looking like an ancient garden gnome.'

The nearest pub to the surgery was the Fountain's Head, which I always found a strange place. The name, for a start. How could a fountain have a head? And then, inside, there was one very large bar catering for sports fans, with two of those horrible giant screens showing whatever moronic match was being played that night, a billiard table, two darts boards and one of those table football games that get men all excited and competitive and make them think they're real players. There wasn't much room for people who wanted to just come out for the evening and have a drink. But the other bar, through the back, was a tiny narrow room furnished like I remembered my grandmother's best parlour about forty years ago. You weren't allowed in here with muddy boots on. You wouldn't feel comfortable coming here to get pissed, show your knickers and sing rude songs (always supposing you were the type of person who'd do that). It wasn't a bar for rowdiness and pints of ale. It was a place for quiet conversations over a nice glass of wine and a plate of steak and chips. There was music – but it was music without words. Soft music versions of former pop songs. It was irritating because sometimes you thought you recognised a song but without the words, you couldn't remember what it was. Sitting at a corner table with Darren *Santa* Barlow, I was too busy concentrating on whether the old Beatles song being played was 'Hey Jude' or 'Strawberry Fields Forever', too intent on trying to remember a few words of one or the other and mentally fit them to the tune, to be bothered with what he

231

was saying.

'So, you see, it's a tremendous opportunity,' he finished suddenly.

We'd got a glass of white wine each, and a packet of crisps, and as he mentioned the tremendous opportunity he took a swig of wine and tipped a few crisps into his mouth straight out of the packet. Then he put the glass and the crisps down in front of him and looked at me expectantly.

'So what do you think?'

'"Hey Jude"'.

'Sorry?'

'No, *I'm* sorry,' I admitted. 'I wasn't listening. Can you go over it one more time – the ... er ... tremendous opportunity?'

'I don't think you're taking this seriously, Penny,' he said with a sigh. 'If it wasn't for the fact that your success and happiness are so important to me ...'

'Bollocks they are! Whatever crazy scheme you've brought me here to discuss, there's one thing I know for sure – *you're* the one who's going to benefit from it, and *I'm* just the mug who gets to say a few embarrassing words on the radio about the bloody pudding.'

'TV.'

'T ... what?'

'Big thing with a flat screen, stands in the corner of your living-room, has an off-switch that people forget how to use.'

'Why? How come?'

'Well, I suppose they get lazy, and they just watch all the crap and then complain about it.'

'NO! *Why* are you talking about TV? What's happened? Why not radio?'

'Be*cause*, Penny my dear, as you'd know if you'd been listening to me, Yours Truly has been invited to host a spot on the TV show *East This Week* – interviewing local celebrities. Well, to be honest, I've invited myself. And I've been accepted – as long as I can find my own celebrities and get them to agree to being on the show.' He smiled a very smarmy smile. 'Which is where *you* come in, of course.'

'Oh, no. Absolutely not. Not TV. Not talking about the bloody pudding, and all its sexual properties and stuff, not in front of everyone on TV so they can see me! Absolutely no way. And that's the end of it! Drink up! I'm going home.'

'Not just the pudding. That might get a little mention, of course. But don't you want the opportunity to talk about the bypass?'

'I'm not on the committee any more. It's nothing to do with me.'

'And the protest group, and how you got chucked out of it ...'

'I didn't get chucked out. I chose to leave, rather than agree not to talk to the media.'

'Exactly,' he said, and picked up his wine glass again, without looking at me, and took a long, slow drink.

'What? You think I should do this to spite them? To show them they're wrong? Prove that media attention works?'

Darren was still drinking his wine, looking the other way as if something was very fascinating at the next table.

'You think it *can* work? You reckon by talking about it on TV I can get more interest in the bypass?'

He pretended not to hear me.

'You think it could kill two birds with one stone? Generate more support for the bypass – maybe even help to get it approved – and piss off old Roger and his gang good and proper?'

'Penny!' said Darren, putting down his glass and turning back to face me. 'I'd never have thought of all that myself. You're a genius, woman! I always knew it.' He reached into the pocket of his overcoat and brought out a diary. 'So. Which Friday afternoons are you free?'

*

233

I felt disgruntled after I'd finished my meeting with Darren. I'd done it again, hadn't I? I'd allowed myself to get talked into something I really, really didn't want to do. What was the matter with me? A grown woman with two adult children, a grandchild and thirty-eight varieties of fuchsias, and I couldn't say no? Then I thought about Chris Filbey, and remembered that I'd said no to *him* this afternoon.

'Bloody great!' I muttered to myself, feeling even more disgruntled. 'I say yes to a man I can't stand and don't want to be anywhere near, and no to the one I really want to ...'

I had to stop myself thinking about what I really wanted to do with Chris. If I thought about it too much I'd end up changing my mind.

My car was still at the vets', but I'd got Darren to drop me in Panbridge town centre. I thought a bit of retail therapy might stop me feeling disgruntled, but it was odd: the longer I wandered through Marks & Spencer, Woolworth's and BHS, pushing my way through the crowds of Christmas shoppers, looking at all the red party dresses, sparkly jewellery, shiny new toys and bright silly trinkets, the more fed up I felt. Why was I drifting around the shops on my own at Christmas time? Why didn't I have any friends? This was no fun without a friend to share it with. Where the bloody hell was Maureen when I needed her?

I found her number on my mobile and punched 'Call' crossly.

This is the Voicemail Service for 077 ...

'Well, sod you, then!' I told the phone, cutting it off and putting it back in my bag. Almost immediately, it started to ring.

'Hello!' said Archie. 'Are you out shopping?'

Surprisingly, I felt a rush of warmth for him. At least somebody loved me. At least good old Archie still cared enough to give me a call and see where I was, what I was up to, whether I wanted any company ...

'Only we've got no potatoes left, and only one egg. And the milk's gone off.'

So much for caring.

I made him come and meet me, and we went to the supermarket together. He didn't seem to mind.

'Couples who shop together, stay together,' he pronounced cheerfully.

'Since when?' I said morosely. 'We never do normally.'

'Then maybe it's time we started. When we both retire, Penny, we'll be spending all day every day together. Lots of time to go out to the supermarket.'

Jesus. I just can't wait.

Sainsbury's was even worse than M & S and Woolworth's. People seemed to be on a mission to pile as much as they could get into their trolleys. They were barely looking at what they threw in: Christmas puddings, satsumas, wine, lemonade, boxes of crackers, pots of pâté, family size packets of nuts and raisins, party size bags of sausage rolls ...

'There's still two weeks to go!' I complained, watching a man load two crates of lager onto the top of an already full trolley. 'Where are they going to keep it all?'

'In a stable, with the cattle and the oxen?' suggested Archie, nudging me and grinning. 'Come on, Penny, what's up? You always like Christmas!'

'Yeah, but it's beginning to wear a bit thin. It feels like we're all worshipping at the temples of Tesco and Sainsbury.'

'*We* don't go to church.' He reached between two red-faced plump women to grab a tin of tomatoes from the shelf. 'We're no different from any other family – just enjoying the fun and the traditions. It's become a commercial festival. You can't change the world.'

'No. Maybe I've just started wishing I could.'

He looked at me in surprise.

235

'Had a bad day?' he asked unusually gently.

'I suppose so,' I admitted. 'And I've just agreed to be on TV. A regional news programme, with bloody Darren Barlow. I think I must've let go of my senses.'

'TV, eh?' he said, with a kind of unnatural gleam in his eyes. 'Well! I don't think you've let go of your senses at all, Penny Peacham. I think you've just begun to find them. Cheer up, Pen! Think about it: you're going to be famous. This time next year, we could be filling the trolley with champagne and bloody caviar!'

So maybe I'm ungrateful. But I don't want to be famous, thank you very much. And as for bloody caviar – it's crap.

Michelle

I changed my mind about the hospital party. You can probably guess *why*. The girls in Outpatients said Fraser Willoughby was going to be there. Even though he obviously didn't like me, and had dumped me without even saying so, I couldn't miss an opportunity to see him, now that I'd realised how much I liked him. Even if he wasn't very nice to me, even if he ignored me, it would be better than sitting at home not seeing him, wouldn't it?

I didn't sleep very much the night before the party. This was partly because of my mum's Passion Pudding. I'd gone back for a second bit, thinking maybe twice as much pudding would be twice as much luck for my wish coming true. Don't get me wrong – Mum's pudding is delicious, but if you eat too much of it just before going to bed, it lies on your stomach something chronic. Then there were the dreams. I woke up twice, sweating and shaking, from dreaming very strange dreams about being chased by animals. Tigers, mostly. I read a book once on how to interpret dreams, and it was amazing to discover how many dreams are actually about sex. You might think you've had a perfectly normal nice little dream about lying on the beach, or walking in the forest – but trust me, once you've read this book you realise you were actually, subconsciously, wishing in your sleep for your next-door neighbour to shag you, or to have sex with a fireman or a lesbian or an Alsatian dog or whatever. It's very eye-opening. I wished I still had the book, so I could look up what it means to be chased by a tiger; but I had a sneaky suspicion I could guess.

It was bad enough being knackered from having hardly any sleep, but then I had to spend the whole day at work in a constant state of nerves in case I saw Fraser. Every time I caught a glimpse of a white coat or a stethoscope I felt my heart jumping into my throat. Sister told me off twice for not paying attention. I'd called the wrong patient in to see the wrong doctor, which was quite embarrassing for everyone when he started asking the lady whether her foot was better, when it was her ovaries she'd come about. And then I wheeled this nice little old lady down to the blood test department, in her wheelchair, when I was supposed to be taking her to the toilet. Luckily she was quite all right mentally, and when the phlebotomist came towards her with the needle, she shouted out that she only wanted a pee, so it all worked out fine except that I felt a complete failure as a health care assistant. And that only made me feel more desperate, because if I was useless as a health care assistant, how could I take Fraser seriously when he said I'd have been a good nurse? I wanted to take him seriously, you see, (even though it was rubbish because I wasn't clever enough), because it was the nicest thing he'd said to me.

In the end, I didn't see him at all – not a single time, all day. I went home feeling worn out from the possibility of seeing him, and with a stiff neck from keeping on looking over my shoulder in case he came up behind me.

When I got home, Jessica ran down the hallway to meet me, pushing Pink Bunny in her doll's pram straight into my legs, and I shouted at her and made her cry.

'I'm sorry, Jessica, but you've just hurt Chelly really badly.'

'Where? There's no blood,' she sniffed.

238

'There doesn't have to be blood, to be hurt. I'll have a big black bruise on my leg, there.'

She rolled up my trouser leg.

'Where? *Not* a big black bruise. You're *not* hurt, Chelly.'

Well, in the time we've stood here arguing about it, my leg's probably dropped off for all I know.

'What's she crying about, Chelle?' asked Dad, putting his head round the kitchen door. 'What have you done to her now?'

'Oh, great! Everything's always my fault, isn't it? I've only just walked in, too.'

'Yes, and she was fine before you came in. Don't start winding her up – I've only just calmed her down about You Know What.'

'Christmas, Christmas!' sang Jessica at once, her crying immediately forgotten, and not fooled for one minute by *You Know What*. 'Nearly nearly Christmas! Nearly nearly Christmas!'

'Now look what you've started!' groaned Dad.

'Shall I just go out again?' I said crossly. 'I get more bloody grief here than I do at work! Where's Mum, anyway?'

'I don't know. Shopping, probably, with your Auntie Maureen.'

'Doubt it.' I stepped over a pile of Lego that looked like it had just been thrown together haphazardly, but would probably turn out to have been a masterpiece of creation if I accidentally kicked it. Nasty Chelly strikes again. 'I don't think Mum sees much of Maureen these days.'

'No – I noticed that,' said Dad thoughtfully. 'She hasn't been round here for a while, has she, or even phoned.'

'I think she's jealous of all the attention Mum's getting – you know – about the pudding.'

'Hm,' said Dad. 'Maybe you're right. Women are funny like that, aren't they.'

Are they? I left Jessica talking to Pink Bunny about being

239

a good boy because Father Christmas was coming, and went upstairs to start sorting out my wardrobe for an outfit to wear to the party. I heard Dad talking on the phone to Mum, and the next minute he was bounding up the stairs like a five-year-old, running into his bedroom to change his shirt, and running back down the stairs, calling out to me as he passed my door:

'I'm going to meet Mum in town, Chelle. She's shopping all on her own. I thought she might like some company.'

Lovely. Anyone would think he was a teenager on his first date instead of an old married man going to the supermarket with his wife. What the bloody hell had got into him?

'Look after Jessica till we get back,' he yelled from the front door as an afterthought.

'Gandad!' shouted Jessica as the door slammed. 'Gandad! Where you going? I come!'

I stared miserably at the contents of my wardrobe as the noise of Jessica's crying drifted up the stairs. Great. I had the distinct feeling that my life was pants, these days.

It took me nearly as long to narrow the choice of party outfit down to three possibilities as it did to shut Jessica up, and by then I was cross with both her and myself for not realising sooner what the solution was. Obviously, I should have let Jessica choose my outfit! As soon as I stopped running up and down the stairs like a lunatic between the lounge and my bedroom, offering her colouring books, videos, biscuits and even (sorry, but I was desperate) sneaky looks inside one of the wrapped-up Christmas presents, and picked her up under my arm, carrying her kicking and wailing upstairs where I plonked her down on my bed, she stopped crying and stared open-mouthed in amazement at all my clothes lying on the floor.

'Oooooh!' she said, breathless with excitement. 'Chelly's playing dressing-up!'

'Yes.' Great idea. 'Do you want to help me, Jessica? I'm

going to dress up as a beautiful princess,' (I didn't much like the way she giggled at that) 'and I need to wear the most beautiful dress to the Royal Ball.'

'Is there a handsome prince?' she asked, sliding off the bed and trampling all over my best black trousers.

'Yes,' I said, with a genuine sigh of longing. 'Yes, Jessica, there is. So you see, I have to be the most beautiful princess at the Ball.'

'Chelly's an ugly sister!' she said, splitting her sides with laughter at her own joke. Kids these days are too bloody lippy by far, if you ask me. '*I* want to be a beautiful princess! Can I? Can I wear this dress? Can I? Can I?'

It was the red dress I'd worn to last year's Christmas party, and even though I liked it, I'd already rejected it for tonight, in case people recognised it. It was shiny and sparkly and Jessica was holding it up and looking at it as if it'd dropped out of heaven.

'All right. It's not a little girl's dress but I'll see if I can pin it round you somehow, OK? And put some glitter in your hair?'

'Glitter!' She jumped up and down with excitement.

'Yes, but first you've got to help *me* be a beautiful princess. I've got to choose the prettiest dress, out of these three.' I piled all the discarded clothes roughly back into the wardrobe, and carefully laid out on my bed a red and gold diagonally cut dress with a handkerchief hem; a black slinky shift with tiny shoestring straps and a sweetheart neckline; and a soft, royal blue one with a halter neck and silvery beads across the bodice.

'Blue! I like blue! Put the blue dress on!' shouted Jessica, hopping from one foot to the other in her impatience to get on with her own transformation into a princess.

Secretly, I liked the blue dress best, too, but I wasn't sure whether it was very fashionable. Would I look more like a little girl going to a birthday party than a beautiful princess hoping to nab her prince? I tugged off my trousers and jumper, pulled the dress over my head and squirmed around behind my back to do up the zip.

'What do you think?' I asked Jessica, looking at myself doubtfully in the mirror.

'Oh!' said Jessica, her eyes big in her face. 'Chelly's a princess!'

So the blue dress it was, then. Jessica had never said anything flattering to me before in her life!

I hung it back up while I took Jessica and last year's red dress downstairs. Finding Mum's tin of safety pins took about ten minutes. Putting the dress over Jessica and trying to pin the yards of excess material out of the way so that she still thought it looked something like a princess's dress, or any sort of dress at all to be honest, took nearer to half an hour, and by this time I was beginning to worry about the time. I still had to have a shower, wash my hair, do my make-up and get dressed, to say nothing about choosing jewellery, shoes and nail varnish.

'Am *I* a princess now?' asked Jessica very doubtfully, and who could blame her? She looked more like something out of the ragbag. Thinking about how easily Mum would have been able to convert that dress into something stunning for Jessica just made me panic even more. See? Not only would my kids, if I ever had any, not get puddings or birthday cakes – they wouldn't even be able to play at dressing up. Perhaps I really should stay single.

'You look lovely,' I told her, with my fingers crossed behind my back. 'Just like a proper fairy princess.'

Luckily she was still young enough to think a fairy princess was one step better still than a bog standard princess. Give her a couple more years, probably till she started school, and she'd be turning up her nose at fairies and wanting to be a catwalk model.

'Fairy princess!' she shouted, looking like she was going to faint with happiness. 'I'm a fairy princess! I want a magic wand!'

It was getting on for seven o'clock and I really, really

needed to get my arse in gear if I was going to be ready for this party. Magic wands were just a tiny bit lower down on my schedule of priorities than a shower and hair wash.

'Here,' I said, putting one of Mum's wooden spoons in her hand. 'Magic wand.'

'*Not* a magic wand!' she said in disgust, throwing it on the floor and folding her arms across her chest. Jesus, there was no pleasing some fairy princesses, was there?

'All right. Look, I'll make a deal with you, OK, Jessica?'

'*Princess*.'

'OK. I'll make a deal with you, Princess ... you play nicely with Pink Bunny while I have a shower ...'

'Don't *want* to ...'

'And teach Pink Bunny some good fairy magic spells, yeah?'

She looked at me with her head on one side, considering. I moved on quickly: 'And while I'm in the shower, I'll be inventing a magic wand for you.'

'What's *inventing*?'

'I'll magic one up for you. While I'm in the shower, and getting dressed, and doing my hair, and my make-up, and ...'

'That'll be *ages*.'

'Magic *takes* ages.'

Have you ever seen a three-year old look suspicious? They do it really well. They don't hold back. They give you this look that says, Yeah, right. And I'm the fucking Queen of Sheba, am I?

'So I'm going up to have my shower now, OK, Jessica?'

'I come with you. I watch you doing magic.'

'OK. Bring Pink Bunny and you can play in my bedroom while I'm in the shower.'

'I hear you doing magic? Saying magic spells?'

'Absolutely. Course you can.'

Trust me. It's not easy showering and washing your hair,

243

and getting dressed for possibly the most important party of your entire life, while continually chanting: 'Abracadabra, hocus-pocus, thunder and lightning, frogs and toads – make me a fairy wand!'

Jessica wasn't best pleased with the hairbrush I gave her when I came out of the bathroom.

'*Not* a magic wand,' she said, refusing to even touch it. 'Silly hairbrush.'

Shit. I'd sprayed it with glitter, too.

But to be honest, despite her stamping and scowling (which I told her was most unattractive in a fairy princess), I was by now a lot less worried about Jessica's wand than I was about Mum and Dad not being back from shopping. What the bloody hell were they playing at? Dad hadn't even *asked* me whether I was OK to stay with Jessica – just gone rushing out of the door like he had no cares in the world. Who was supposed to be the young, free and single one, here? How come *I* was stuck at home looking after the baby on a Friday evening while they were gallivanting around town together and Adam was – where? Good point, eh? Off out boozing and Christmas partying, I supposed, never mind who was looking after his daughter! Never mind who might be left at home like Cinderella, missing the ball, while he enjoyed himself probably until all hours, coming home drunk and expecting me to give up *my* life for *his* child – his child that he should never have had with that stupid cow Julia, if he'd only listened to everyone else when we told him not to get involved with her!

'Thanks a bundle, Adam!' I muttered bitterly, looking anxiously at the clock for the thirty-first time in ten minutes. 'Thanks, Mum! Thanks, Dad! Bloody thanks, everyone, for ruining my life! And shut up about the fucking wand, Jessica!' I added, very quietly (don't worry) – quiet enough for her to not hear. And then, of course, I felt horrible for thinking that she shouldn't have been born, and felt sorry for her, having such a nasty cow of an auntie as well as a selfish father and no mother to speak of, and I had to sit down and give her a cuddle to show her I still loved her whatever horrible thoughts might be going through my head.

At ten to eight, I phoned Dad's mobile. Switched off. Bloody typical. I tried Mum's mobile.

'Hello?' she said. 'Who's that?'

Doesn't realise you can look at the caller display. Still getting to grips with technology.

'Mum, it's me – Chelle. Where are you? What's that music in the background?'

Were they in a pub? A fucking pub, while I missed the start of the most important party of my life?

'Music? Oh, it's just the radio, Chelle. The car radio. We're stuck in traffic.'

'What? I thought you'd only gone to Sainsbury's?'

'Yes. We did. And it was packed – honestly, people were buying up whole legs of ham, and cases of wine, and—'

'Yes, but where are you now? What time will you—'

'And it was *awful* getting through the checkouts, and then you should have seen the car park! Nose to tail, all the way out, and all the way back up to the roundabout, and then by the time we'd got back to the vet's ...'

'What? Why did you go back to the vet's?' Not that I really wanted to know.

'Because I'd left my car there, dear. Darren Barlow came up to the surgery this afternoon and insisted on taking me to the pub. It was the strangest thing – he was dressed up as Father Christmas.'

'But where are you *now*?' I persisted desperately. Bugger Darren Barlow and whatever he was dressed up as. Nothing would surprise me.

'Like I say, dear, we're stuck in traffic, coming back up the Panbridge Road. We didn't even get back to the vet's. The traffic was too bad. I've had to leave my car there!'

'It'll be fine, dear,' I could hear Dad soothing her, above the dulcet tones of Coldplay on the radio.

Fine? It was only a bloody car, wasn't it? Who cares!'

'So how long do you think you'll be?'

'Oh, God only knows, at this rate. I tell you what, Chelle: this just goes to prove it, doesn't it?'

'What? It proves what?'

'The need for a bypass, of course! See – just a bit of extra traffic, for Christmas shopping, and the whole town is brought to a standstill. I hope those people at the Highways Department are stuck in this jam! That'll show them!'

'But, Mum ...'

'I don't know *how* long it's going to take us, Chelle. We've got the engine off at the moment. We've only moved a couple of yards in the last twenty minutes. What's that you say, Archie? Yes! Yes, Chelle – Dad says, to be quite honest, we might be better off turning off down Green Lane and going for a drink at the pub in Potts End till this all gets moving.'

'No!'

'What? Sorry, Chelle – I lost you there. The reception's not too good. Oops, I think my battery's had it. Archie, I must remember to charge this ...'

With that, my mum's battery died; and my hope died with it.

I kept the blue dress on while Jessica and I made a magic wand out of an old Weetabix packet and stuck foil over it. I think she'd picked up on my mood, or else she'd just tired herself out, because she was quiet and docile for the rest of the evening and finally went to bed, without a murmur, insisting only on sleeping with the red sparkly dress and the silver wand laid out on the end of her bed.

'Chelly going to the ball?' she asked sleepily as I kissed her goodnight.

'Maybe another time. Goodnight, Fairy Princess.'

Not her fault, after all, if my life was ruined.

I'd fallen asleep on the sofa by the time Mum and Dad

came home. I woke up when they shut the front door. It was gone eleven o'clock.

'Ssh,' I heard Dad saying as he peered into the lounge. 'Chelle's asleep, Penny.'

'No I'm not,' I said.

They both came into the room, turning on the light, making me blink and rub my eyes as I sat up.

'Have you had a nice eve—' started Mum, and then she stopped, looked at me more closely and carried on, 'You look lovely, dear?'

It was spoken as a question – a question about why I was lying asleep on the sofa on a Friday night wearing one of my best dresses that was now all creased up and spoiled, wearing make-up that was now all splodgy from sleeping in it.

'I was going out,' I said dully. Did it matter any more?

'So why ...?' She stared at me, and for a minute I thought she must have had so many glasses of white wine in the pub at Potts End that she'd lost the plot. Was she really going to ask why I hadn't gone out? Had she actually forgotten about Jessica completely?

'Is Adam not here, then?' put in Dad.

'No. Dad, you knew he wasn't here when you went out ...'

'But we phoned him!' said Mum, and to be fair to her, she looked stricken. 'We called him on his mobile, from the payphone in the pub. He said he was on his way ...'

'We thought it'd be nice to stay in the pub and have a bit of dinner,' said Dad.

And make a night of it, by the look of it.

'Lovely,' I said, plumping up the sofa cushions and throwing myself back down.

'But, Chelle!' Mum came and sat down next to me, and tried to turn me to face her. 'Chelle, we wouldn't have stayed! We would've just had one drink to wait for the traffic to ease up, and come straight home. I said to your Dad – "Archie,' I said, "we mustn't be too long because

247

it's Friday night and Michelle probably wants to go out clubbing."'

'It was the hospital party.'

Mum clapped her hand to her mouth.

'But we only stayed because Adam said he was on his way!' she insisted. She glanced at her watch and added anxiously, 'Where has he got to, Archie? That was *hours* ago. I hope he hasn't had an accident. You know how he drives ...'

'He's probably in some pub, with some bird,' I said, tears of self-pity pricking my eyes.

'Who's in a pub with some bird?' asked Adam, looking into the room. He was wearing his underpants and an old T-shirt, and looked like he'd just got up. 'Want a cup of tea, anyone?'

I was the only one not speaking. I drank my tea and listened to them all arguing around me.

'How was I supposed to know she was waiting to go out?' shouted Adam. 'She was asleep on the fucking sofa when I came in! Sound asleep!'

'In her best dress! And don't swear!' snapped Mum. 'You could *see* she was all dressed up for the party, Adam. Where's your common sense?'

'I didn't look at what she was wearing! She's my fucking sister!'

'Don't swear about your sister!' said Dad. 'You promised your mum you were coming straight home.'

'I *tried* to come straight home! The traffic was all snarled up, all the way back past Panbridge! I sat in the fuck— in the bloody car for two hours, and I was so desperate for a pee, I came in and went straight upstairs to the toilet. Michelle was asleep, Jessica was asleep, so I lay on the bed upstairs and watched TV. Probably dozed off. For Christ's sake! Next thing I know is you come in and have a go at me for not waking Chelle up for her party! *I* didn't know she had a fuck— a sodding party!'

248

'Have you all finished talking about me?' I said, putting my mug down on the coffee table with a crash. 'Because I'm going to bed.'

'Don't be stupid,' said Adam. 'Get in the car, I'll take you to your party.'

'Oh, yes, sure!' I stood up and shook the folds of my dress out. 'Look at me! And look at the time! It's half past eleven, Adam – it'll be all over. '

'Course it won't! I know what hospital parties are like ... '

'How?' demanded Mum.

'Couple of nurses I used to know ... years ago, ' he said vaguely, not looking her in the eye. 'Chelle, it'll only just be getting going. Look, I'm *sorry* I didn't wake you up. But don't sulk, it's not too late. '

'I'm not sulking. And it's not your fault. It's just ... ' I sighed. 'The moment's gone. And my dress is ruined.'

'Nonsense! Of course it isn't,' said Mum, snapping into housewife mode. 'Take it off, Chelle, and give it to me. Come on, don't argue. All it needs is damping down, and ironing on the wrong side with a soft damp cloth. '

'How do you know?' I asked her, smiling for the first time. 'What?'

'How do you know all that stuff about soft damp cloths and ironing on the wrong side? Where did you learn it all? How am I ever going to manage, if I ever get married and have kids? I won't know how to do *any*thing.'

'Chelly,' she said briskly, but she was smiling back at me at the same time. 'Chelly, if you don't get out of that dress double-quick and go upstairs and fix your make-up and hair, you needn't worry about getting married 'cos you'll never even get out of the house. Hurry up – I'll go and warm up the iron.'

Sometimes, even with all the shouting and swearing and blaming each other and carrying on, I get a nice warm feeling about my family. Get on my nerves at times, but they're all right really.

*

'Tell you what,' said Adam, twenty minutes later, as we were driving to the hospital at breakneck speed down the now quiet roads. 'Mum's not wrong.'

'About what?' I was using the vanity mirror in the car to finish doing my hair and lipstick. It wasn't easy at the speed Adam was driving. I was probably going to end up with lipstick all over my cheeks, like a clown.

'About the bypass. Never realised how bad the traffic gets through here now, at rush hour.'

'It's got worse, I s'pose, since you moved out. More people with cars all the time, aren't there. And now, with the Christmas shoppers ...'

'It was a complete nightmare tonight. Fucking ridiculous. The council ought to be doing something about it. We pay our taxes ...'

'Well, write a letter, Adam! Or phone up the radio about it! Yeah, that'd be cool. You could say you're the son of Mrs Passion Pud! Go on *Daytime with Darren*!'

'Fuck off!' he laughed. 'Anyway, what's the score with this Darren geezer, Chelle? Is he all right? What's his fucking game, with Mum? Is he trying it on with her?'

'I thought so at first, to be honest, but now I'm not so sure. Mum thought he was after *me* – but I just wanted him to take me to the Italian restaurant. I don't know what he's after. I think he's just a bit weird.'

'Yeah, well – you want to watch yourself, Chelle, leading on some weirdo like that, just to get an Italian meal out of him. What's the matter with you? Can't you get anyone decent to take you out for a meal for Christ's sake?'

'No,' I muttered into the mirror, but he wasn't listening.

'And as for Mum, you better keep an eye on her. She doesn't know what she's getting herself into, playing around with these weirdos. She's not, you know, worldly wise about these things, is she. She's been married to Dad all these years. She wouldn't know what to do if a man started trying it on with her. The shock would probably kill her.'

'Yeah, I know. Don't worry, Adam. I've talked to her

about it. I don't think she likes him. Although come to think of it, she did say something on the phone tonight about him coming to her office dressed as Father Christmas and taking her to the pub.'

'Fucking weirdo,' said Adam, shaking his head. 'Keep an eye on it, Chelle, for Christ's sake. Might be worth getting Dad on the case.'

'Jesus, no. Dad's already acting funny enough with Mum these days. It's embarrassing. All kind of lovey-dovey and yucky. I'm beginning to think it's all down to her pudding.'

'Yeah, right!' laughed Adam.

'Really! I think there might be something in it. Nicole made a wish when she was eating a bit of it, and this Scott phoned her up and asked her to get back together with him.'

'You don't say!'

'All right, you don't have to believe me, but let's just wait and see ...'

'What?' We were pulling up outside the hospital social hall now, and he turned to look at me. 'What's that supposed to mean, then? Have you been making wishes yourself, eh, Chelle? Eating Mum's Passion Pud and wishing for some hunky doctor to ask you out – eh? Is that what the new hair colour's all about? And the special dress and everything? What's his name, eh, Chelle?'

'Shut up!' I felt my face burning red. 'Shut up, Adam – there isn't anyone. OK?'

'If you say so,' he said, laughing. 'Off you go, then. Have a lovely time.'

'Thanks. See you.'

I got out of the car and shut the door, and was just starting to walk away when he wound down the window and called after me:

'Hope he appreciates the dress. All the ironing ...'

'Piss off!' I hissed at him, but he'd wound the window back up and driven off. I could see him still laughing. Bastard!

*

251

Of course, it was true what Adam said about hospital parties. The DJ was still playing dance music and the place was still heaving. But the table where the buffet had been laid out looked like a swarm of locusts had been over it and left nothing but the paper plates, screwed up serviettes and chicken bones. And at the other side of the hall, the drink table looked even worse. When my eyes got used to the dark and I looked more closely at the sorry state of the people leaping drunkenly about to 'Love Shack', it was obvious where the contents of all the empty bottles and cans had gone. If I'd arrived at the beginning of the party, I'd probably have been in exactly the same state by now, joining in the shouting of the chorus with the best of them and probably falling over at the same time. But it's funny how it doesn't look like fun when you're dead cold sober. I wandered over to the drinks table, picked up a few wine bottles and shook them but it was no good – not a drop left.

'Hello, Cinderella,' said a voice behind me.

Him.

I turned to look at him. He was wearing jeans and a black shirt, with a leather jacket slung over his shoulder, and by the look of his eyes was either very drunk or very tired. Either way, he looked gorgeous. I tried not to stare.

'Cinderella *left* the ball at midnight,' I said lightly.

'So what do you call someone who *turns up* at midnight, when all the booze and all the food has gone?'

'Unlucky!' I said with a sigh.

He laughed.

'That makes two of us, then. I've only just got here myself.'

'Oh!' I reassessed him. Definitely not drunk. Definitely very, very tired. 'Where have you been, then?'

'On the ward.'

'I didn't think you were on call?'

I stopped, realising this was a dead giveaway of the fact that I'd checked the on-call rota specially, before I decided to come to the party.

'No,' he said. 'No, I wasn't on call. Just had ... a job to do.'

'Oh. I see. Well ...'

I didn't really know what to say. The crowd, by now, were giving it large to 'Sisters Are Doing It for Themselves!' and a couple of nurses were taking their clothes off to the music. Blokes were pushing each other out of the way to get a better look, and there was a definite possibility of a fight breaking out between a porter and a male nurse.

'Michelle!' shouted Julie, who'd just caught sight of me for the first time. 'Come and dance!'

'Yeah! Come and have a boogie, Michelle!' joined in Karen and Melanie, screeching at me above the noise of the music and the drunken singing.

'Do you want to dance with your friends?' asked Fraser.

'No. Not really. I don't feel drunk enough.'

'I know what you mean. It all looks a bit ridiculous when you're sober, doesn't it.'

The two nurses were down to their bras and pants. They were going to feel terrible when they saw all the photos after Christmas. The porter was gripping the male nurse by the arm and telling him to watch who he was fucking pushing or he'd fucking lay one on him. His mate was telling him to calm down and come outside for a fag. A young nurse flung her arms round him giggling and asking if he'd said come outside for a shag. Then her eyes glazed over and she slid gracefully to the floor and started to be sick.

'Shall we go?' said Fraser.

'Go?' I stared at him. This was the man who'd taken me out for one date, and then ignored me ever since. Why should I go anywhere with him? Why should I want to?

'OK,' I said. 'OK, yes. Let's go.'

I didn't know where, but did it really matter?

See? My mum's pudding was working already.

Penny

We sat in the lounge for a little while on our own, just me and Archie, after Adam had gone with Michelle. It seemed funny, without the telly on or anything.

'What you were saying earlier,' said Archie, 'about Darren Barlow ...'

'Forget it. I'm going to phone him tomorrow and tell him I'm not doing it. I don't know why I even let him talk to me about it. It's just a big ego-trip for him – he wants to be on TV. Well, he can find some other mug to—'

'But, Penny, it'd be great! Look how popular you were on the radio.'

'I wasn't! It was just all that nonsense about the pudding.'

'Darren knew what he was doing, Pen. Whatever we might say about him, he knows about the media. He understands how people react. He must have thought the gods were smiling on him that day you did the first radio show and all those people started phoning up.'

'But Archie, I'm *not* a media person. And I don't want to be. The only reason I listened to him at all was I liked the idea of proving stupid Roger wrong.'

'Yeah – wouldn't that just be perfect? If it was you, not the PPPP, that persuaded the county council to approve the bypass? Come on, admit it! Wouldn't that make you feel good?'

'Why are you so desperate for me to do this?' I said, looking at him in puzzlement. 'I didn't think you'd *like* to see me looking like a prat on TV talking about Passion Pudding. I thought you'd find it embarrassing.'

'To be honest, Pen,' he said, inching a bit closer to me on the sofa and putting his arm round me, 'I find it all quite a turn-on.'

'Do you?' I squawked, too surprised to move away.

'Yes. Definitely. Listening to you saying all that stuff on the radio, about older women being sexy – it was great. Knowing everyone was listening to you, but *I'm* the one that gets to go to bed with you.'

'But ... I ...'. I swallowed hard. It was hardly the time to mention the fact that until recently we normally only went to bed to drink our cocoa and fall asleep. It was also not really an appropriate moment for my thoughts to start straying to Chris Filbey's offer of a hotel room and champagne.

'In fact, shall we go to bed now?' continued Archie. 'Just thinking about you being on the TV, Pen, talking about your passion pudding – it's doing things to me.'

I could see. It certainly was. Blimey.

It actually even took my mind off Chris Filbey.

Archie was up early the next morning, singing along with the radio and bringing me a cup of tea in bed, with the papers. I was beginning to think it was worth having sex more often.

'Keep the music down a little bit, though, love,' I said. Not that I wasn't grateful. 'Michelle is still asleep.'

'Yeah – wonder what time she got in!' he chuckled. 'I didn't hear her, did you, Pen?'

'No. Leave her be. Good luck to her. Nice to see her going out enjoying herself again.'

'Absolutely!' He sat down on the side of the bed with his own cup of tea. 'Adam says he thinks she's seeing someone. A doctor, probably.'

255

'She went out with someone a few weeks ago, didn't she. But I didn't think it was anything serious. She hasn't mentioned him since.'

'Well, I'm only telling you what Adam's just been saying, downstairs. He said when he dropped her off at the hospital she was all flushed and excited and when he teased her about a hunky doctor, she didn't exactly deny it.'

'Honestly, you two! Men are worse than women! Leave the poor girl alone – she was probably just having a good time dancing with her mates.'

'Well, like you say, she's still dead to the world this morning, even with Jessica running up and down the stairs squealing on about Father Christmas.'

'That child will make herself ill before we ever get to Christmas Eve.'

'Adam and Michelle used to be just the same, though. Do you remember?'

'I do. I always loved Christmas when they were little, didn't you, Archie?'

'We had some great times,' he agreed. 'Do you remember when we bought Adam his first bike? When he was so happy he cried?'

'Yes. And Michelle – when she got the dolls' house. She wouldn't go to sleep Christmas night in case Father Christmas came down the chimney again and took it back!'

And for just a minute, sitting there together, sipping our tea and sharing those memories, I thought to myself – we don't say much about it; I don't often think it, either. But maybe we *are* happily married. We've survived this long, after all.

'Chelle still not up?' asked Adam with a grin when I went downstairs a bit later.

He was sitting in the lounge with the TV on, watching cartoons with Jessica. She'd been up since the crack of dawn and tired herself out already.

'No,' I said. 'And leave her be, Adam.'

256

'I am! I was just wondering whether to take Jessica home, or stay till Chelle gets up. I want to hear all the goss about last night.'

'Goss? What's the matter with you? I thought it was us women who were supposed to be the gossips? What makes you think there's any goss to hear? Poor girl, can't have a nice night out partying with her mates, without everyone starting . . .'

'*Nice night out with her mates*, my arse! All dolled up in that sexy blue dress, all lipstick and high heels, right? I'm telling you, Mum, she's got some grubby little doctor on the go, sniffing round her, I bet you any money you like . . .'

'Adam! Don't talk like that about your sister, please!'

'Well, she has, I bet you. '

'There's no need to make it sound so . . . well, so *sordid*, thank you very much.'

'Well, it's all down to you, Mum, if she *did* score last night,' he retorted. 'All down to you and your pudding!'

'What are you talking about?'

'Chelle was telling me about her friend – whatsername – Nic. Ate a ton of your pudding, apparently, hoping to get her old boyfriend back, and what do you know? The next night he's knocking on her door begging for it!'

'Don't be silly!'

'That's what Chelle said. So I reckon she's been helping herself to a portion or two of your Passion Pud herself, Mum. Testing out its . . . special qualities, you know! Seeing if it can get her a bit of— '

'That's enough, Adam. For goodness' sake, I get enough of all this nonsense about the bread pudding from everyone else, without you starting. Although I'm pleased for little Nicole,' I added. 'She never seemed to have much luck with the boys.'

'No, well. Shame. Nice girl. Fit enough. But no conversation.'

'Since when did that matter to you young men? I never

257

heard you or your mates discussing girls' conversations, when you were living at home, Adam.'

'I've grown up a bit now, Mum, in case you hadn't noticed. Life's about more than a quick sh— a quick bit of the other,' he finished, glancing sharply at Jessica. 'Sometimes, you know, now I've got a little girl, I think about her growing up and going out with some horrible spotty little oik who's going to try and have his way with her – and I want to punch his lights out.'

'He's probably still in nursery school himself at the moment,' I said, laughing. 'But I'm glad you realise what it feels like to be a parent. Now maybe you can see why I don't like you talking like that about our Michelle.'

'Yeah, but I'm still saying ... no way was she wearing that dress for the benefit of her mates.'

'Chelly's a princess,' put in Jessica, suddenly sitting up and taking notice. 'A lovely princess!'

'Yes, darling, she is, isn't she,' I agreed. 'She looked beautiful last night.'

'And me! *I*'m a beautiful fairy princess!' She jumped down from the sofa. 'Want my dress on! Want my dress on now!'

'Ssh!' I called after her as she went charging out of the room. 'You'll wake Chelly up!'

'No danger,' said Adam. 'She'll sleep till lunchtime. Probably knackered herself out last night!'

Just as Adam was finally talking about giving up on the 'goss' from Michelle and taking Jessica home, there was a knock on the door.

'It's Maureen!' said Archie in surprise, looking out of the window.

'Haven't seen you for a long time,' commented Adam as he opened the door. 'Thought you'd left the country.'

'Come in, Maureen,' I told her. 'Don't take any notice of him. Were you going home now, Adam?'

'Oh, nice! Don't want me around now your mate's here

258

to hear the gossip, eh? Come on, Jessica, we know when we're not wanted, don't we.'

'Gossip?' said Maureen, who hadn't even said hello yet and was barely over the doorstep. 'What gossip?'

'There isn't any. Take no notice. Come in and I'll get the kettle on. Bye, Adam. Bye, Jessica, darling. Oh – Adam! You can't let her go home wearing Michelle's dress.'

'I thought Chelle had given it to her?'

'No. Don't be silly. It's her nice red dress from Warehouse. She only bought it last year. Lift your arms up, Jessica, and Nanny will take it off for you. Where's your jumper and trousers?'

'No!' shouted Jessica at once. 'Want my fairy dress on! Don't want trousers!'

'But Chelly will want it back, sweetheart. It's not yours to keep.'

'*Is* mine!' she said, bursting into tears. 'Chelly gave me! I'm a fairy princess! Where's my wand? Want my wand!'

'Dearie, dearie me! What a fuss!' said Maureen, who never did have much patience with children crying (never having had any of her own). 'Come along, Jessica, do what Nanny says, there's a good girl.'

'No!' shouted Jessica, stamping and sticking her tongue out at Maureen.

'Don't be rude,' said Adam, smacking her bottom. Which was right, really, even if Maureen did deserve it for interfering. You can't have children sticking out their tongues like that just because they want fairy dresses on. You have to have some discipline.

With that, Jessica's crying reached screaming pitch. Adam got hold of her very crossly and held her still, yelling and going red in the face, while I tried to take the dress off her – it was a lot easier once we'd managed to get some of the pins out, because after all it was a dozen times too big for her and just kind of fell down round her ankles.

'Want ... my ... dress! Want ... my ... dress!' she sobbed pitifully, while Maureen turned her back disap-

259

provingly and went into the kitchen to put the kettle on.

'Her own bloody fault,' muttered Adam. 'Ought to mind her own bloody business.'

'All right, Adam,' I said with a sigh, picking up the dress and trying to hide it from Jessica while he sat her firmly down on the sofa, still crying. 'Just leave it, please.'

'What the hell's all the noise about?' demanded Archie, who'd been upstairs in the bathroom when it all let rip. 'You tired, Jessica? Want to go home to bed?'

'No!' she screamed. 'No bed! Want my fairy dress!'

'Shut up, Jessica, we've all had enough about the fairy dress,' retorted Adam, beginning to lose his temper. 'Come on – in the car.'

'Father Christmas is listening to you – all this bad temper and crying!' Archie warned her. 'He won't bring you any nice presents if you're not a good girl.'

'Oh, for goodness' sake, she's just tired,' I said, as the crying promptly got louder. 'She'll probably fall asleep in the car, Adam.'

I went out to join Maureen in the kitchen as he carried her out of the front door.

'She's normally a good kid really,' I said, getting the milk out of the fridge. 'Just a bit excitable and overtired, what with Christmas coming ...'

I don't know why I felt like I had to apologise to Maureen for my granddaughter's temper tantrum, but that was how things seemed to have gone, between us. A bit stilted and unnatural.

'I know,' she said surprisingly. 'And it's not been much fun for her, has it – no mum, and being packed off to child-minders and nurseries.'

'We all do our best ...'

'I know you do.' She put down the mug of tea she'd been holding and, even more surprisingly, came to give me a hug. 'I wasn't being critical, Penny. I actually really admire your family, the way you all rally round and help out.'

260

'Oh!' I said. I didn't know what else to say to this. 'Oh! Well, you have to ... you know ...'

'Adam's very lucky. You all are.' There was a pause of several minutes during which I heard Adam's car pulling away from outside the house, Archie changing channels on the TV, and the floorboards creaking upstairs as Michelle finally got out of bed and padded across the landing to the bathroom. Several minutes for me to watch Maureen's face as she stared at her mug of coffee, and realise something for the first time in all the years I'd known her. She was very, very unhappy.

'What's wrong?' I asked her quietly.

'Nothing. Well ... everything. But nothing special. Nothing new.'

'You and Tony?'

Well, what else could it be?

She shrugged.

'Normally I just get on with it. You know, get on with my life, and leave him to get on with his. Ignore him. Otherwise he'd get me down, the way he goes on – moaning, grumbling, miserable all the time.'

'But now?'

'Oh, it's just because it's Christmas time. I see families like yours, Penny, and it makes me want to cry. You probably think I'm an old ratbag, but the truth is that I envy you – even all the hard work, and the mess, Adam and Michelle and their friends coming and going, and Jessica's tantrums. I thought it was hard when Tony and I were young and we found out we couldn't have children; but it's harder now. At least, then, we had each other. We still loved each other. Now – oh, now I feel so lonely, Penny! I wish I had a family! You don't know how lucky you are.'

'I do,' I said, putting my arms round her. 'Although I suppose we all forget it, at times. Daft thing, you don't have to be lonely. You can come round here any time. You're part of the family, you know.'

'Tony and I should have split up years ago, really. We

don't *talk* like you and Archie do. We don't laugh. We don't go out anywhere together. We don't even argue. There's absolutely nothing left.'

'Then why don't you go your separate ways?'

'Why? I don't think either of us have got the courage. Starting again – at our age – I couldn't face it. Our generation ... we grew up differently, didn't we. I never learned how to fix the car, or mend a fuse, or work an electric drill. Tony never learned how to cook. He can't use the washing machine. I don't think we could manage ...'

'You could. Of course you could! If you're so unhappy!'

She shook her head.

'Too late. Never mind. I'll be OK. Sorry.'

'Don't be silly. I had no idea things were quite so bad.'

She smiled sadly.

'It's why I've stayed out of your way lately. You've been so happy – with all the excitement about the pudding and everything – and I've been so bloody miserable. I'd have spoiled it all for you.'

'Of course you wouldn't!'

'And I'd have nagged you constantly about what you were about to do,' she added, dropping her voice to just above a whisper.

'What? What was I about to do?'

'The thing you were most excited about. Sleeping with your boss.'

'Oh. That. Well, I haven't.'

'Yet.'

'No. Look, I don't know if—'

'OK, I'm not saying another word. Except that you'd be mad to risk what you've got here.' She waved her arm around the kitchen as if it was the whole world and all its riches. Maybe it was. 'For a quick bonk? Absolutely bloody mad.'

'I know. I *know*, but it's so—'

'I'm not saying another word,' she repeated, drawing a hand across her lips. 'Now – shall we have this cup of coffee, Penny, and pretend I never said any of that stuff?'

'Yes, of course – if that's what you want.'

We didn't even get to drink the coffee. At that moment, Adam's car screeched back to a halt outside the house and he came hurtling down the path, thumping on the front door and yelling.

'Chelle! Chelly, quick, get up! Hurry up – out of bed, you lazy cow! Come on, quick! I've just seen your car going down the Panbridge Road!'

There was pandemonium for a few minutes. Archie ran to let Adam in at the front door just at the moment he found his door key and let himself in, so that he practically fell into Archie's arms and they both started pushing and swearing at each other; Maureen stood up too quickly and splashed her coffee all down her trousers; Jessica, asleep outside in her baby seat in the back of the car, woke up and started shouting for Daddy, and Michelle came charging down the stairs, still in her pyjamas, squealing about the car and whether Robbie had been driving it.

And in the midst of all the noise and fuss, Maureen caught my eye and nodded towards my daughter. When I followed her gaze I could see why her eyebrows had shot up into her hairline. Michelle had obviously gone to bed very late and hadn't bothered to take off her make-up. She hadn't bothered to have a shower, either. There was a trail of what looked very much like sand behind her all the way down the stairs. And her feet and ankles were a funny colour – the kind of funny colour of the mud that you get at low tide at Duffington Sands.

Michelle

For December, it wasn't really a cold night, but after the heat of the disco lights and all the drunken dancing bodies, I shivered a bit when we first went outside.

'Didn't you have a coat?' asked Fraser.

'No. My brother drove me here and dropped me right outside, and I thought I'd phone for a taxi to take me home. I *thought* I might have had a lot to drink,' I added with a smile, thinking about all the empty cans and bottles on the table.

'Here.' He draped his leather jacket round my shoulders. I hugged it close to me and breathed in the scent of him. Lovely.

'The pubs will be shut now,' he said, looking at his watch.

'Oh – I didn't mean it like that! I'm not desperate for a drink. It doesn't worry me.'

I didn't feel like anything in the world would worry me, as long as we could just stand there like that together, outside the hall, with him looking at me as if he liked me again.

'Shall we go for a drive, then?' he said.

'Yes. Yes, that'd be nice.'

'Down to the beach?'

'Oh! Yes, lovely!'

His car was parked round the back of the hall. We got

in and I slipped his jacket off, laying it carefully on the back seat.

'Don't worry about it,' he said lightly, starting up the engine. 'It's just an old thing. You'll need to put it on again when we get to the beach.'

'You told me before that you like going there,' I remembered.

'Yes. I like to breathe the sea air. Specially after a bad day.'

'And it's been a bad day today?'

'Up till now,' he said, giving me a quick smile.

I felt a big jolt of happiness inside me. He *did* like me! He *was* pleased to be with me! Then I remembered how he'd cut me dead after we'd been out before, and the happiness faded away again. I'd better be careful. I knew what my mum would say: I'd end up getting hurt. And she'd probably be right; who was to say he wasn't going to turn his back on me again after tonight?

'What sort of day have *you* had?' he asked as we pulled out of the hospital drive and onto the main road.

'Awful. I was trying to get ready for the party, and Jessica threw a tantrum about dressing up as a fairy princess and I had to pin her into a dress of mine, and make her a wand. I'm useless at making things. It'll probably fall apart when she's waving it, trying to do a magic spell or something, and she'll be left holding half a Weetabix box.'

He laughed.

'Kids, eh!'

We drove the rest of the way to Duffington Sands in silence. I was watching his hands on the steering wheel. They were nice hands – big and strong-looking but not too hairy. He was concentrating on the roads, even though there wasn't much traffic. I wanted to ask him what he was thinking about but maybe it was none of my business. Perhaps serious things to do with his patients were occupying his mind. Making life or death decisions. So I kept quiet.

265

When we parked at the beach I put his jacket round me again.

'Put it on properly,' he said, helping me to shrug my arms into the sleeves. 'It'll be breezy down by the sea.'

In fact it wasn't very cold at all. I took off my shoes – no point trying to walk on sand in high-heeled party sandals – and we climbed over the dunes. Once, when I stumbled a bit, he grabbed my hand to steady me and I felt a kind of thrill go all the way up my arm. I was hoping he'd carry on holding my hand but he didn't. In fact he dropped it quickly as if it was burning him.

The tide was on its way out, and as we walked onto the damp sand the moon came out from behind a cloud and shone a low shaft of light shimmering across the waves. We turned to walk along the beach, following the edge of the sea.

'So why was it a bad day?' I asked eventually, as I was beginning to think he wasn't going to talk any more.

I don't know what I was expecting him to say. Maybe one of the consultants had grumbled at him, or a nurse had made a mistake or some of his patients had been cross and grouchy. I know the elderly patients can get irritable sometimes. Mostly I put up with it and don't rise to it, because the way I look at it is, who can blame them? It's probably bad enough getting old, without being ill too and having to come to the hospital.

'That patient we saw on the ward yesterday,' he said, staring out to sea.

'Old Mr Partington?'

'Yes. He died tonight.'

'Oh!' I stopped dead in my tracks. I felt tears spurt to my eyes.'But it was only yesterday ...'

'I know. He developed pneumonia. In a way, he was lucky – it was very quick.' He stopped, too, and turned back to face me. I could only see the whites of his eyes in the moonlight. 'But very unpleasant.'

'Is that where you were tonight? Instead of the party?'

'I was on my way to the party and I thought I'd just look in on him. Then I didn't have the heart to leave him.'

'That was nice of you,' I said, swallowing back my tears. 'Poor old chap.'

'Yes. Doesn't seem fair, does it – but there you go. I chose this specialty.'

'It's what I like best, as well. Working with the old people.' Funny, but I hadn't even thought about it until I said it. 'They seem ... more deserving. And more *grateful*. Mostly!' I added with a smile, thinking of one of the grumpy ones the other week who'd told me to sod off and leave him alone.

'I think so, too.' He paused, and then, suddenly and to my complete surprise, took hold of my hand again and held onto it, before going on: 'And I meant what I said yesterday.'

'What?' I said. It came out as a bit of a squawk, because I was still so surprised by him holding my hand.

'That you'd make a good nurse. You would. And I don't know why you're not considering it.'

'I tried to tell you, though – I'm not clever enough.'

'Rubbish.'

'I'm not! You have to have loads of GCSEs, don't you, and go to college, and I ... well ...' I hung my head, regretting it for the first time in my life, 'I didn't work very hard at school, to be quite honest. I messed around a lot with my mates, and bunked off lessons to drink cider in the park.' Shit. Why did I have to tell him that? What must he think of me? 'I only passed two exams,' I added. 'Maths and drama. They were my best subjects.'

'I bunked off lessons too,' he said. 'My mate Joe and I used to go down to the river, share a joint and use my dad's binoculars to watch the girls from the girls' school the other side of the river playing netball in their little short skirts, showing their knickers. When my dad found out, he told me I'd go blind. I was so scared, I got a load of medical books out of the library to find out if it was true.'

267

'And did you find out?'

'No, but at least I didn't go blind. And the books were so interesting, I decided I wanted to be a doctor. And then I stopped bunking off, because I knew I'd have to work really, really hard to pass all the exams I needed, to go to medical school. I wasn't particularly clever, but I was determined.'

'That's nice,' I said, because I didn't know what else to say.

'And that's why I know you should do your nurse training. It's not about being clever – it's about having the right aptitude.'

'How do you mean, aptitude?'

'I think you're *suited* to nursing.'

I raised my eyebrows to myself in the darkness, chuffed with the idea that he thought I had aptitude.

'But I can't go back to school and take all those exams again,' I said sadly. 'I just couldn't hack it, honestly.'

'You wouldn't have to. You take NVQs – I'm not sure exactly how it works but I think you have assessments while you're working, doing your normal job. Talk to Sister. Then when you pass those, you go to college.'

'But I couldn't ...'

'Of course you could! Talk to some of the other nurses – loads of them have come into it by that route. It's a shorter college course, because you'll have learned some of the stuff on the job. You pass modules on different subjects.'

'How do you know?'

'I asked Sister for you. She said to tell you to talk to her about it.'

'Oh!' I was shocked. He'd actually talked to Sister about me! He must really mean it. 'Well – thank you. I'll ... think about it.'

'Promise me you'll talk to her?'

'Well ...' I supposed I'd have to, now. I felt nervous just thinking about it. 'OK. Maybe after Christmas.'

'No. On Monday. Don't put it off, or you'll change your mind. Promise?'

'OK.' Blimey. 'Why are you so keen for me to do it?'

'I told you. I just think you'd make a good nurse. I think you're wasted, doing what you do now.'

Wasted? Blimey.

'And you know what else I think?' he added.

He had his back to the moonlight, so I couldn't see his expression. But his tone of voice had changed, and he was talking very close to my face.

'What?' I asked shakily.

'I think you look lovely tonight. Absolutely lovely. You look gorgeous in blue. You were wearing blue when we went to the pub that night. You should always wear blue.'

And then he kissed me.

I suppose when I first got together with Robbie, when we first started having sex, and when we moved in together – I suppose I thought I was in love with him then. But I don't even remember what it used to feel like when he kissed me. I don't remember our first kiss at all. It might have been on the dance floor at the Purple Cloud, or it might have been on the sofa in Mum and Dad's house after he gave me a lift home. Which only goes to show that it meant nothing to me at the time, and that would have been a bit sad really if we'd ended up staying together. I'd have been useless on something like *Mr and Mrs*. You know: 'When was the first time he kissed you?' – 'No idea'. 'Did you enjoy it?' – 'No idea'. We'd never have won a Mediterranean cruise or a holiday in the Bahamas.

This kiss with Fraser, though, was a kiss that I'd never forget. If I lived to be a hundred, I'd still be able to remember the moonlight shining on the sea, and the feel of his leather jacket on my arms, and the sea breeze blowing in my hair, and his hands holding my face, and the feel of his lips on mine, and the way it went on, and on, and on, and only stopped eventually because ...

'Oh!' I yelped, trying to regain my footing in the soft muddy sand. 'Oh, fuck, I'm sinking!'

And he picked me up in his arms as if I was a little kid like Jessica, and carried me back up to the dunes, setting me down in the soft, dry sand where the spiky grass scratched my legs and my bum through the soft material of my dress, and I didn't care. It was perfect. I'd never forget it.

He sat down next to me and I waited, hoping he was going to start kissing me again. Maybe we could lie down here in the dunes and really get into it.

'Are you cold?' he asked, looking at my bare feet and legs.

'A bit,' I admitted. I glanced at him. God, I was so desperate for him to carry on kissing me.

'Never mind – we'll soon warm up,' I said. I lay back and put my arms round the back of his neck, pulling him down towards me. 'Come on, Fraser, warm me up!'

For a minute he looked like he was considering it. Then, suddenly, he turned away, sighed, and peeled my arms off his neck as if he had a scarf on that was strangling him. He sat up straight and stared at the sea.

'We'd better go back to the car,' he said abruptly, 'if you're cold.'

It was like a slap in the face. What had I done wrong?

'What's the matter?' I asked, sitting up and brushing the sand out of my hair.

'Nothing. Come on – let's go. It's late, and you're cold, and muddy, and— '

'I don't care about that. I just want to know what's going on!' I was almost shouting.

'Nothing's going on. I'm sorry. I shouldn't have ... given you the wrong impression, that's all.'

'Wrong impression? What do you mean – the impression that you liked me? Liked me enough to take me out on a date and then ignore me ever since?'

'I'm sorry. I *do* like you.'

270

'Yeah? You liked me tonight, did you, enough to say all that stuff about my apti ... whatever, and tell me I look lovely in blue, snog me almost senseless, carry me into the sand dunes, and then ...'

'Look, I shouldn't have ...'

'And then act like suddenly, I'm so disgusting you can hardly look at me!' I finished furiously. 'What is it with you? Don't you like women really, or what?'

I felt like kicking him, to be honest. My mum would have said it served me right, wouldn't she? I should never have come to the beach with him.

'Of course I do,' he said quietly. He held out his hand to help me up, but I ignored it and got up on my own. I started striding off towards the car without waiting for him. 'Of course I like you, Michelle! I like you a lot – that's the trouble. But I'm not the sort of guy who plays around.'

I stopped dead.

'You're married, aren't you.'

Shit. Why didn't I guess? Just because all the girls at work had told me he was single – what did they know? He probably had a wife and six kids somewhere up in Yorkshire or down in Devon.

'No,' he said, sounding surprised. 'I'm not married.'

'Attached, then. Whatever. Well, thanks very much for telling me, Fraser. I think *before* the kiss on the beach might have been a better time, but at least now I know where I stand. Don't bother about taking me home – I'll ... I'll get a taxi, or ...'

'Don't be ridiculous. There aren't any taxis at Duffington Sands, and I'm not letting you walk the streets at this time, in that state.'

I looked down at my legs. They were thick with mud, almost up to the knees, and the skirt of my nice blue dress was stained from the sand and torn by the gorse. I felt like crying. My feet had gone dead with cold and, to be honest, the last thing I wanted to do was walk anywhere at that time of night.

'OK, then,' I said stiffly, heading towards the car again. 'If you'll just drop me home, thank you, and then ...'

Then what? I wanted to say something melodramatic and final about never seeing him again, but I knew that wasn't possible unless I changed my job.

'Then we'll say no more about it?' he finished for me.

'If that's the way you want it,' I said, the words almost choking me.

'You can give me back the jacket on Monday at work,' he said.

The bastard! I mean, how much more of a bastard could he possibly be?

I crept into the house and tiptoed up the stairs, muttering under my breath the whole time about what a pig, and a shitbag, and a nasty piece of work he was and how much I hated him and how I never wanted to see him – or any other man – ever again as long as I lived and how I'd rather be on my own anyway, and never have sex, and in fact perhaps I'd become a nun, and live in a nice safe convent with all the other nuns and sing hymns all day. I took off his leather jacket and kicked it into a corner of the room, took off the ruined blue dress and got into my pyjamas without bothering to wash or even brush the sand out of my hair.

But when I lay down and closed my eyes, all I could see was his face and all I could feel was that kiss. I really, really hate to admit it – but for the first time for a very long time, I cried myself to sleep.

I didn't rush to get up the next morning. I felt a bit of a wreck and a bit stupid. I mean to say, if any of my friends was to tell me that they'd been for a walk on the beach and had a snog with someone who'd already treated them like shit, someone who was probably married or had a partner or was in love with someone else, I'd tell them to their face that they were a bloody idiot.

272

I heard Jessica running around the house and yelling. I heard Adam telling her off and I heard Maureen's voice, so I thought it was probably time I got up, otherwise everyone would be talking about me. I'd only got as far as the bathroom when Adam came back shouting about seeing my car.

'Was it Robbie?' I demanded. 'Was Robbie driving it?'

'Never mind about Robbie,' said Mum. I think she was worried that I still wasn't over him. Little did she know that not only was I *so* over Robbie Nelson but also, I was planning on joining a convent. 'Never mind about him, Chelle – let's just concentrate on the car.'

'It wasn't Robbie,' said Adam at once. 'You know who it was? Fucking Julian Sparrow!'

'Killer?' said Mum and I together. She didn't even tell Adam off about the *fucking* in front of Auntie Maureen.

'Yeah, Killer!' he sneered. 'Come on, Chelle – in the car! We'll follow him.'

'Don't be bloody stupid, lad,' said Archie. 'He'll be miles away by now.'

I'd been just about to run back upstairs to get dressed, but I stopped and sat down on the bottom step. Dad was right. It was a waste of time.

'No ... I'll put me foot down – burn up the road ...'

'Not with Jessica in the car, you won't,' said Mum.

'Dad's right, anyway, Adam,' I said wearily. 'There's no point. But at least we know who's got it.'

'Yes. We'll let the police know.' Dad smiled with satisfaction. 'Silly little fool must have been crazy to think he could get away with it.'

'Yes.' I frowned. Something about it didn't quite add up. 'How can he have been driving it around Panbridge all this time, and not expect to get picked up by the police?'

'The police don't bother to look for stolen cars at all, if you ask me,' said Adam.

'And anyway,' said Mum suddenly. 'Where have you been with all that mud on your legs, Michelle?'

*

273

It took a while, what with all the ribald comments from Adam, to explain to Mum that the party was more or less over by the time I got there so some of the girls and I decided to go for a walk on the beach.

'Why?' she asked, looking at me slightly puzzled, with her head on one side.

Shit. Never was much good at lying to Mum.

'Well, a couple of the girls had had a bit too much to drink. They wanted some fresh air. And someone else had a car – no, they hadn't been drinking – so they offered to take us to the beach. That's all. It was a nice night for a walk.'

Adam was looking at me with amusement, shaking his head very slightly. I flushed a bit red. Well, so what? So what if I was actually lying in the sand dunes with my arms stretched out waiting to be ravished by someone who didn't even want to? I was over the age of consent, wasn't I? No one else's business. I turned my back on him and went back upstairs to have a shower.

'If you ask me, Penny,' Maureen's voice floated up behind me, 'and I know I shouldn't say it, but I think your Michelle has been *canoodling* in the sand with someone. You mark my words!'

Canoodling? Chance would be a fine thing.

Penny

Chris Filbey was a bit funny with me at work.

'How's the new boyfriend?' he said, sounding very irritable. 'Getting ready to come down your chimney, is he?'

'Don't be vulgar,' I said. 'And he's *not* my boyfriend, and he doesn't normally dress up as Father Christmas.'

'Just when he wants to sit you on his lap and give you a special present, eh?'

'I told you, he's not ...' Oh, what was the point? Why should I care what he thought?

'He's that stupid local radio presenter, isn't he?' said Chris with a face on him that almost matched the pug he was taking in for its vaccinations.

'Darren Barlow, yes. And he wants me to be on a TV programme with him!' I couldn't resist adding.

'I bet he does,' snarled Chris, closing the consulting room door with a slam, almost trapping the pug's owner's fingers.

Debbie, who'd been following us and obviously listening, looked at me and shook her head slightly. I shrugged and smiled at her to show her that I hadn't got a clue what was wrong with him.

'Got out of bed the wrong side, I reckon!' I whispered.

But she didn't smile back.

We spent our lunch break putting up decorations in the

waiting room. We did it every year, but sometimes I did wonder whose benefit they were for. Did the dogs and cats care whether we had a miniature silver Christmas tree in the corner with red baubles on it? Did their owners really care, when they brought their sick pets to the surgery with their untimely injuries or bouts of diarrhoea, whether we had loops of tinsel trailed across the room and a fake holly wreath on the door?

Still, normally it was a cheerful occasion, with all of us joining in the fun, a bit of good-natured banter going on and the singing of a few raucous Christmas carols. But this year, for some reason, it was a lot more subdued. Chris was in a foul mood, I was annoyed with him for being in a foul mood, and Glenn just kept staring from one of us to the other with a thousand questions in his eyes that he wasn't actually prepared to ask. Debbie had obviously made up her mind it was best to keep quiet and say nothing whatsoever to anyone, and the other nurse, Hazel, was completely unaware that anything was wrong and kept up a constant barrage of chitchat that no one was listening to. Just as I was putting the finishing touches to the tree and Chris was climbing down from the chair he'd been standing on to pin up the tinsel, the door burst open and in stormed Kim, the other receptionist. Kim and I job-shared, but because she had young children she mostly did the evening surgeries, while her husband looked after the kids. We usually only saw each other on social occasions but she did like to turn up for the decorations. When I say she stormed in, I don't mean she was in a temper. That was just the way Kim always arrived anywhere: like an avalanche. She was a big girl, and she was usually carrying about six carrier bags full of shopping. This particular day, she seemed to have come straight from buying up the entire stock of Toys 'R Us.

'Bloody kids!' she shouted as she dumped all the bags in the middle of the waiting room and threw herself into the nearest chair. 'Next year they're not getting bloody anything, I don't care what they say!'

As her children, Forest and Sky, were only about six months and eighteen months old, I doubted whether they'd been saying an awful lot, but I sympathised with the sentiment.

'There's a lot of pressure from the TV adverts, isn't there,' I agreed. 'Jessica wants everything she sees, but she's not getting it.'

'Bloody buses!' she went on as if I hadn't spoken. 'Bloody full, all of them. Had to walk from the town centre with all this lot. Bloody Christmas! Am I too late to help?'

'Well, we've just about finished. But stay for a cup of tea now you're here. There's ten minutes till we open again. Where are the kids?'

'With me sister. Her bloody kids are just as bad. Damon wants a motorbike.'

'He's only four, isn't he?'

'Yeah. She was going to get one off e-Bay for him but his father put his foot down. Not that it's any of his business if you ask me. Never even sees the bloody kids. Bloody men!'

'Oh, well,' I said with a shrug. 'It'll all be over in a couple of weeks' time.'

'I know,' she said gloomily. 'All this bloody money, just for a couple of bloody days.' She followed me out to the kitchen and watched as I put the kettle on and got out the mugs. 'What's the matter with all that lot? They've all got the bloody hump, haven't they? Hazel's the only one talking, and she won't bloody shut up!'

'Don't ask me,' I told her wearily. 'Chris is in a bad mood, and I don't think anyone else wants to risk annoying him, so we're all keeping quiet.'

'That's bloody ridiculous. What's the matter with him? He's acting like a spoiled brat!'

'I know, but it's not worth—'

The kitchen door opened and Chris looked in.

'Am I interrupting something?' he asked tersely. 'Or can

I make myself a coffee when you've finished chatting?'

'I'll do it,' I replied equally tersely. 'I'll make one for everybody.'

Kim looked from him to me and back at him again.

'Who's rattled *your* cage?' she demanded. 'Got the bloody hump, have you?'

'Kim ...' I warned her.

'No, Penny – I don't care if he *is* the boss, there's no need to be bloody rude – especially not at bloody Christmas. Cheer up, Chris, for God's sake! It might never happen!'

Chris glared at her, turned and walked back out.

'Some woman,' said Kim, nodding her head at me. 'Definitely.'

'What?'

'That's what's wrong with him. Some woman's turned him down, and bloody good luck to her, whoever she is! Bloody serves him right!'

'Why?' I kept my eyes on the coffee mugs and concentrated hard on keeping my voice neutral and normal. 'What do you mean?'

'Oh ... nothing.' She looked round the kitchen door cautiously as if to check that Chris was out of sight, hesitated for a moment but then added quickly, 'I'd better not say any more.'

'Why not?'

'Nothing,' she repeated firmly. 'Forget I spoke! Where's me bloody tea?'

I was busy for the rest of the week. You'd think a vet's surgery would get a bit quieter near Christmas, wouldn't you, but no such luck. I suppose a dog or a cat or a rabbit doesn't know it's the middle of December when it suddenly gets a foreign body in its ear or a gammy paw or whatever. They don't know their owners are going to think: Oh, bloody hell – still got half the Christmas shopping to get, all the cards to write, the turkey to order and the presents

278

to wrap up, and now the bloody dog's gone and got an infected anal gland. They just get ill and need sorting out, whatever. Fortunately we're just a Small Animal Clinic (fortunately because I'm scared of horses), but our other surgery a couple of miles away had a major emergency with a pony falling and breaking its leg and some horrible skin problem affecting a herd of cows, so Chris was called away to help out over there. I wasn't sorry, even though it meant Glenn was absolutely rushed off his feet and the waiting room was heaving with irritated people who were having to wait much longer than normal. I wasn't sorry because I didn't really want to see Chris while he was in that vile mood. I didn't like the thought that it might be something to do with me; although if it was, Kim had got it wrong. I hadn't exactly turned him down. Not yet. And was I going to, or not? I was trying not to think about it.

There was enough to think about, at home. The Christmas cake and Christmas pudding had all been made months before; I'm always very particular about doing them early. It's all very well buying them in Marks & Spencer or Tesco but really, you can't beat homemade, at the end of the day. The mince pies were in the freezer but I wanted to make a couple of quiches and a few sausage rolls so I could be sure of having plenty for supper on Christmas Day and Boxing Day. And then, because Christmas Day was on a Thursday, we'd be at home for two more days – Saturday and Sunday – and I'd got no doubt that Archie, Michelle, Adam and Jessica would be enjoying their extended holiday, slumped in front of the TV or playing games, while meals and snacks appeared in front of them as if by magic. I was buggered if I was going to spend the whole time in the kitchen, so the freezer and fridge needed to be stocked full to the brim with stuff I could just heat up and stick on their plates. Sometimes I had dreams about going off on an exotic holiday somewhere for Christmas. Not the whole family. Just me.

'Can't you come and sit down, woman?' called Archie

when I was in the middle of rolling out another lot of pastry. 'There's a good film on TV.'

'I'll be there in a minute,' I said.

But the truth was that I didn't really want to go and sit on the sofa with Archie. It was already difficult trying to decide whether or not I was brave enough, or stupid enough, to have an affair with Chris, without being distracted by Archie's sudden new interest in me. I'd lived with him for thirty-two years without him showing much interest in me. Why did he have to start now, just as I was teetering on the brink of a possible extramarital adventure?

I kneaded the pastry as hard as I could and tried not to think about either of them. Maybe Kim had a point: bloody men; and bloody Christmas!

By Saturday, the date of Tail Waggers' annual staff dinner, I hadn't seen Chris for five days, and had barely spoken to him for over a week. I'd almost convinced myself I didn't care. My life had been all right before I'd started getting myself into this silly adolescent state – a bit boring at times, I supposed, but generally all right. I could easily go back to that. I could pretend I'd never kissed Chris Filbey passionately on the lips in the waiting room, never been held close against him and offered hotel rooms and champagne, to say nothing of the chance to scream and beg for more. Maureen was right. All that stuff was fun if it was only a fantasy. I should never have tried to turn it into reality. If Chris didn't like it, if he was going to sulk and show off every time I spoke to another man, even someone as pathetic and ridiculous as Darren Barlow, then it was tough. The sooner I put an end to it all, the better. Which was why I'd changed my mind about the Christmas meal. I wasn't going to make excuses and miss it. I would go, and I would bloody well enjoy it. And if I got the opportunity, I'd tell Chris tonight that I wasn't interested any more. It might be easier with a couple of drinks inside me.

I had a long, hot bath, sprayed myself all over with Paris, put on my best underwear, my red silk blouse and tight black trousers. I wasn't going to let Chris think I was moping around, disappointed or frustrated just because of not going to bed with him. I was a woman who was getting on with my life; my life was fine. I didn't need him.

'Bloody hell,' said Archie when I came downstairs. 'You look ...'

'Tarty?' I asked, suddenly nervous.

'Bloody gorgeous. Don't go out. Stay here and make passionate love to me.'

'Shut up, you fool!' I laughed, dodging around his outstretched arms. 'The cab's waiting. I'll be home late, Arch. Don't wait up.'

He actually walked to the window to watch me getting into the taxi.

Kim and Debbie were already in the cab; we were meeting the others at the restaurant, as they lived in the opposite direction.

'You look really nice, Penny,' said Debbie, who'd put silver glitter in the purple part of her hair for the occasion. She had a kind of anxious look in her eyes. 'I'm glad you decided to come. You didn't seem very keen last week.'

'I know. I'd just forgotten about it and I was worried about sausage rolls and stuff. But you're right – we all need a night out, don't we.'

'That's what I told my Joe,' agreed Kim. 'I told him straight: "If I don't get a fucking break, I'll end up murdering you and selling the kids. You won't live to see bloody Christmas."'

'Who would you sell the kids to?' asked Debbie, sounding genuinely interested.

'Highest bloody bidder, Debs. You've got to look at it from my point of view. I'd have my Joe's funeral to pay for, wouldn't I.'

'You crack me up, you do,' said Debbie, not laughing.

'I need a bloody drink, I know that much. As soon as I set foot in that restaurant, I'm getting a Bacardi Breezer inside me, with a white wine chaser.'

'Me too,' I said, even though I'd never drunk Bacardi Breezer before in my life. I took a deep breath. 'I really, *really* need a drink tonight, girls.'

'Bloody good for you,' said Kim predictably.

Debbie didn't say anything. She just raised her pierced eyebrows at me.

We sat at our table, ordered drinks and waited for the others. I was annoyed with myself for the way I kept looking over my shoulder, watching the door. Glenn arrived, and then Hazel, full of apologies for being late – the traffic had been bad on the Panbridge Road. Tell me something I didn't know. A full-scale debate erupted, about the need for a bypass and how I'd been involved in the pressure group and got kicked out. Everyone was looking at me, waiting for me to join in and agree, but I couldn't. I couldn't take my eyes off the door.

'Right, I think we'd better tell them to bring our starters, guys,' said Debbie eventually. We'd pre-ordered and, as the organiser of the event, she was getting twitchy about keeping the restaurant staff waiting. 'If Chris turns up, he'll just have to catch up.'

If he turns up?

I realised my toes were screwed up inside my shoes and I was clenching my hands into fists on the table. Debbie glanced at me.

'You all right, Pen?'

'Yes! Course I am. Roll on the starters, then, Debs! We're all starving.'

What was the matter with me? I didn't even *want* to see him, did I! It'd do me a favour if he didn't turn up, especially if he was as moody as he was at work earlier in the week. I picked up my spoon and tucked gratefully in to my spiced parsnip soup.

'Lovely!' I said. I broke off a piece of my roll, and looked up to see Debbie's eyes on me. 'What?'

And then I saw him.

I dropped the roll in the bloody soup.

'Sorry – did I give you a shock or something?'

He'd sat down opposite me, which only served to make me more flustered. I'd spent a horribly embarrassing couple of minutes fishing the roll out of the soup bowl, trying to wipe up the splashed soup from the table and finally allowing a waiter to place a clean napkin across the stained part of the tablecloth while I looked the other way and pretended it was nothing to do with me. And now Chris was looking across the table at me with a look in his eyes that said he knew exactly why I was so flustered, and a smile that said he knew how to deal with it.

'No! Of course not.'

Just that you walked into the restaurant looking like a Greek god out of a Hollywood movie, with your shirt unbuttoned just far enough, and your hair casually tousled as if you'd just got out of bed ... and I'd come here tonight trying to convince myself I didn't want anything more to do with you, and now I'm sinking fast. And you know it. You bastard, you know it!

'You look kind of anxious,' he said softly. We were at one end of the table. The others were deep into a heated discussion about New Year's Resolutions and whether it was worth making them. 'What's the matter, eh, Penny?'

'Absolutely nothing!' I retorted, trying to remember how annoyed I was with him. It was no good him looking at me like that! He'd been rude and horrible last time he'd spoken to me. And I didn't want an affair with him. I had a perfectly nice husband, who suddenly seemed interested in me, and I was quite happy without Chris Filbey leering at me over the table ... wasn't I.

'Have you missed me while I've been at the Potts End surgery? You haven't forgotten all about me, I hope, while

283

I've been mending horses' limbs and treating cows' udders?'

'Been too busy to miss anybody!' I assured him.

I took a huge gulp of my wine, and tried unsuccessfully to move my chair away from him slightly, which only resulted in me doing a kind of awkward wriggle and attracting everyone's attention to me.

'What about you, Penny?' asked Kim.

'What?'

'Are you making any New Year's Resolutions this year?'

'Yes – come on, tell us what your resolutions are, Penny!' joined in Chris, laughing into my eyes.

The waiter leaned discreetly across my shoulder to collect my soup bowl from my messy place. I had a brief, mad urge to get up and say very calmly but very loudly: *Yes! My New Year's Resolution is NOT to have sex with Mr Filbey!*

Instead I tried, feebly and without any success, to avoid looking at his amused and challenging gaze across the table.

'New Year's Resolutions?' I said shakily. 'Well, er ... I think ... um ...'

'Maybe you should resolve to make your famous pudding more regularly,' suggested Chris smoothly. 'So we can all eat it and become more passionate – what do you say, everyone?'

There was a general murmur of laughter and a few ribald comments. I drained my glass and reached for the bottle to top it up again.

'So is that a promise, Pen?' he persisted. 'More pudding? More passion?'

'Leave her alone, Chris,' said Debbie, looking worried. 'Stop teasing.'

'Teasing?' he said very quietly, 'Who's teasing?'

The waiter brought our main courses, and I picked up my knife and fork gratefully to start on my turkey-with-all-the-trimmings. *Concentrate on the stuffing. Concentrate on the chipolata.* Everything on the plate seemed to be taking on

284

a sexual connotation. Chris was busy with his salmon and I thought, thankfully, that he'd forgotten about me for the time being. I gulped back the wine and attacked my roast potatoes. Ate a mouthful of turkey. Started on a Brussels sprout. Then I glanced across the table at Chris again, to find him staring at me again. He smiled lazily and mouthed silently but very plainly: *Beautiful.*

I wasn't beautiful.

I'd never been beautiful; but here, tonight, someone thought I was.

Come on, be honest – it's a turn-on, isn't it. I didn't *want* to be excited by it, but I was only bloody human.

I drank another whole glassful of wine, straight down, and felt the room tilt.

I couldn't finish my dinner. I was slurring by the time the Christmas pudding was served up.

'Are you OK, Penny?' I heard Chris ask. His voice sounded as if it was coming from a long way away.

'I'm not used to ... very much wine,' I tried to say, but the words got mixed up and I was put off badly by the way the table was swaying and the walls were moving in towards me.

'Maybe a little fresh air ...' he suggested, pushing back his chair and coming round to help me to my feet. 'Come on, you'll be fine, let's just get some air.'

Outside, it had turned chilly and was starting to rain. Chris put his jacket round my shoulders and took my arm, guiding me towards the car park.

'It's too wet out here. Maybe we should sit in my car for a little while. Just till you feel better?'

'I feel a bit better already, actually. The cold air must have helped.'

'Come and sit in the car anyway. Just to make sure. No knowing, with that white wine. It's a bastard. Hits you suddenly. I never touch the stuff.'

'OK. Just for a minute, then.'

285

He held the car door open for me and I sank gratefully into the front seat while he walked round to the other side. Within two seconds of getting into the driver's seat, he'd grabbed me round the back of the neck and started kissing me. Not gently like I'd secretly been hoping he might. Hard and insistently. Like he wasn't going to take no for an answer.

'No ...' I muttered, trying to pull away. The kissing was making my head spin again. 'No, Chris, I don't ...'

'*No, Chris!*' he mimicked. 'Come off it, Penny. You're bloody gagging for it, you know you are.'

He pulled roughly at the buttons of my blouse. OK, I admit it: I'd had fantasies like this, but now, I felt giddy and nauseous and I didn't like it.

'Stop it!' I said, struggling with him. 'I don't want this, Chris. I want to go back inside.'

'I'm not hurting you, you silly girl. Let's just have a quick shag. No one's looking. Come on, you know you want to.'

'No!' I managed to wriggle out of his grasp and straighten up my clothes. 'I'm *not* a silly girl: I'm a married woman, and I *don't* want a quick shag in your car, for God's sake – what do you think I am?'

'You wanted it badly enough before,' he said crossly. 'On the examination table, you *said*.'

'It was just a fantasy. I'm sorry if you took me seriously.'

In fact, I was sorry I took it seriously myself. Getting sorrier by the minute.

'All talk!' he retorted in disgust. 'All the fucking same, you women.'

'Sorry,' I said again. 'But I'm going back to the restaurant now. The others will be wondering where we are.'

I opened the car door, stepped out and walked straight into Debbie.

'What are you doing here?' I asked stupidly.

'Came to make sure you were all right.' She glanced at

the car, where Chris was leaning back in his seat with a look of resignation. 'What did you expect? I wasn't going to leave you out here in *his* clutches.'

'He was just making sure I wasn't going to be ill,' I said defensively, walking back to the restaurant with her. 'Too much wine, you know. I'm not used to it.'

'It's OK, Penny,' she said, softly, taking my arm. 'I know. I know all about it.'

We went to the Ladies and talked, leaning against the sinks.

'Nothing's happened between us,' I told her, watching her reflection in the mirror. 'Whatever you might think. Whatever it looks like.'

'Good.'

'Why should you care?'

'I like you.'

'And not him, obviously.'

'Trust me, Penny; you don't want to get involved. I know you've been flirting with each other. Everyone knows. Everyone's been watching it coming. It's been kind of inevitable.'

'What do you mean?'

'You're a challenge, because he hasn't had you yet.'

I held her gaze in the mirror for a long time.

'So ... who *has* he ...?' I asked finally, very quietly.

'Most recently? Hazel.'

'Shit.' I stared at her. 'What do you mean – most recently?'

'Before her, it was Janice.'

'The nurse who left earlier in the year?'

'Uh-huh. Why do you think she left? She was upset because he was still seeing Kim at the same time.'

'Kim? Shit.'

'He's a good-looking guy, and he puts it around. Did you think you were the only one who's been tempted?' She laughed. 'I'd probably still give him one myself, given half a chance, if ...'

287

'*You too*?'

'If it wasn't for one thing.'

'What?' I asked faintly.

'Well – did he give you all that crap about screaming for more? Oh – it's OK, you don't have to answer. It's written all over your face. Well, don't worry. You haven't missed anything, love. The only screaming you'd have been doing would have been with frustration. He might look like sex on legs, but trust me; I've had more fun in bed with a book and a hot-water bottle. I couldn't believe it. He's absolutely fucking useless, Pen!'

I didn't go back to the table. I called a cab, and asked Debbie to tell the others I was still feeling ill. To tell the truth I did feel a bit sick, but only with disgust at myself, and relief that I hadn't let anything happen after all.

'You're early!' said Archie, sounding pleased. 'Good time?'

'Not bad,' I said.

'What's wrong? You look a bit rough.'

'Oh, just a bit too much to drink.'

'Want a coffee?'

'Yes. That'd be nice. Thanks.'

He got to his feet and started to lumber out to the kitchen. I watched him, feeling suddenly, strangely, fond of him.

'Archie?'

'What?'

'I've made such a stupid idiot of myself.'

He stopped and looked at me, smiled and patted me on the head as if I was a small mischievous dog.

'Don't worry about it. We all do it. Everyone will have forgotten about it by the time they wake up tomorrow.'

I'm not talking about getting drunk. I'm talking about nearly, nearly, agreeing to have sex with someone who just wanted to add me to his list. And who wasn't even any good at it.

288

'I suppose so,' I said. 'Thanks, Arch.'

It was going to take more than coffee, though, to take away the nasty taste in my mouth. It was the taste of shame.

Michelle

I woke up early on the Monday morning, and couldn't work out why. Everything seemed unnaturally bright. Something had lightened the sky, but it wasn't sunshine. I threw back the curtains and blinked with surprise. Snow!

'Snow!' I shouted, running down the stairs in my pyjamas. 'It's snowing! It's settled!'

'Yes. Your dad's already outside, clearing the front,' said Mum, pouring me a cup of tea. 'You'd better get going a bit early, Chelle. The buses will probably all be running late. You know what the traffic's going to be like on the Panbridge Road.'

I showered and dressed quickly and came back to the kitchen for a quick slice of toast. I wasn't looking forward to going to work this morning and facing horrible Fraser again, but what could I do? I liked my job and I wasn't going to let some man spoil it for me.

Mum was eating a bowl of cereal in the kitchen. She watched me buttering my toast.

'What?' I said, feeling her eyes on me.

'Is everything all right, now?' she said. 'Only ... you looked a bit upset Saturday morning, after your party. I haven't really had a chance to talk to you about it.'

I'd spent most of Saturday and Sunday round at Nicole's, whingeing away at her about men in general and Fraser Willoughby especially, going over and over the story of how he'd acted as though he really liked me and then told me he wasn't the type to mess around.

'Married,' Nicole had pronounced firmly. 'Whether he admits it or not. Married, or as good as.'

'I know,' I'd said miserably. 'I can't understand why he's trying to deny it. If he doesn't want to see me then he could at least be honest about it.'

But it was difficult, really, moaning to Nicole about men at the moment, while she was all loved up about Scott.

'Oh, it's nothing, really,' I told Mum now through a mouthful of toast. 'Just – a bloke I thought I liked. And now I don't.'

'Oh,' she said.

I thought she might be going to offer me a bit of her usual mum-type advice. You know – plenty more fish in the sea, pick yourself up and dust yourself down, don't cry over spilt milk, or whatever. But instead she just stared at me as if she was looking right through me.

'Same old story, eh?' she said, shaking her head and looking like she understood.

Which, of course, she couldn't do, having been married to my dad for a hundred years and never having to bother about all the shit men can put you through.

Still, it was nice of her to pretend she did.

I'd only been at work for ten minutes when Sister called me into her office. I didn't think I'd done anything wrong. I'd got in on time despite the snow, and the chaos on the roads.

'Michelle,' she said, 'I understand you might be interested in doing an NVQ.'

'Oh!' I said. I went very hot with embarrassment. 'It was only a sort of *idea*. I was just kind of *thinking* about it. I was ... well, I was wondering whether there was any chance of ever, one day, possibly, trying to become a nurse, you see, but I realise I haven't got any qualifications and I'm not very clever, and I expect you think I've got a cheek even thinking about it, and you'll probably tell me

291

not to be ridiculous, so I'll just get on with my work, shall I?' I gulped and took a breath. 'I forgot ... *someone* ... had been talking to you about it.'

'Well, it's a good job *someone* did talk to me, isn't it, Michelle? Otherwise you'd probably have kept on making excuses to yourself about not being qualified or clever. Of *course* you should do your NVQ, you silly girl, and as soon as you pass it I'll personally put you forward for a nursing course. You'd make a very good nurse.'

'I *would*? I mean, you think so? Really?'

'Really,' she said, smiling. 'Don't put yourself down. It's going to be hard work and you'll need to believe you can do it.'

'Thanks, Sister. I don't mind working hard.'

It might take my mind off other things. I could devote myself to my work and become one of those single career women who don't need a man. I could have my own apartment and live on my own with a cat. I didn't really like cats but I could probably get used to them. The worst they can do is scratch you. They can't break your heart, like certain other species.

I went to the canteen at lunchtime. It'd stopped snowing and the snow that had settled had mostly been worn away by people walking and driving on it, but the rooftops and grassy places were still white. I sat down with my omelette and chips, and turned on my mobile phone to call Mum and tell her about my news. But as soon as I turned it on, it rang with a message from Voicemail. It was the police station. They'd found my car.

'Abandoned on a factory estate just outside Ipswich.'

'Ipswich? What was it doing there?'

'Well, people will drive anywhere to dump a car ... '

'But you followed the lead I gave you? When I phoned on Saturday? About my brother seeing it being driven down Panbridge Road?'

'Of course. We called at the address you gave us for Mr

... er ... Julian Sparrow. But his mother said he was no longer living there.'

'She *would*.'

'Well whether he lives there or not, I suspect his mother warned him we were looking for him so he took fright and dumped the car. So you're very lucky. Apparently it hasn't been damaged at all. Often, you know, they're burnt out or smashed up by the time we find them.'

'So you said. But are you going to arrest him now? Take him in for questioning? Because I tell you what, he's also been harassing me, saying I owe him money, which I don't, and threatening me. If it wasn't for my brother saying he'd stuff his chains up his ar— up his bum, he'd probably still be coming round my house, frightening me ...'

'That sounds like a serious allegation, Miss. You need to make a separate complaint if you want us to interview the young man about these additional matters. But unfortunately, we haven't been able to track him down, and his mother's claiming she hasn't got an address for him.'

'Lying cow,' I muttered.

Still, it was good news about the car. Two bits of good news in one day. What next?

I put the phone down and looked up straight into the face of Fraser Willoughby.

'I don't think you and I have got anything to say to each other,' I told him stiffly.

Sounded good, didn't it? I was proud of myself for saying it.

'I just wanted to make sure you spoke to Sister about doing your NVQ,' he said. 'That's all.'

'Oh. Well, yes, I did. And I suppose I should say thank you for talking to her.'

'I thought you might ... forget. Or not bother.'

We stared at each other. I wanted to get on with my omelette and chips, to be honest. I wanted him to go away. I didn't like looking at him. It reminded me that I used to

293

like him. I used to find him attractive. Very. I even started thinking I might be falling a little bit in love with him. I still might be, even though I hated him as well.

'Well,' he said. 'I'd better go and get some lunch. I expect Jessica was all excited about the snow this morning, was she?'

My first instinct was to ask him where he got off talking about my family like he knew them, like he cared. But the way he smiled when he said her name, I actually felt a kind of jolt of pleasure, despite myself, that he'd remembered it. If he hadn't been so horrible, I'd have thought it was sweet of him.

So instead of biting his head off I just shrugged and said, 'I don't know – didn't see her this morning. But she's already so excited about Christmas, I expect the snow will have just sent her over the top.'

'How's her fairy wand holding up?'

'It isn't. She dunked it in her bath water, trying to magic the water into lemonade. It went soggy and collapsed.'

'I suppose she's lost faith in magic now, then?'

I nodded. And she wasn't the only one.

All day, I kept turning the conversation over in my head. I wished we hadn't talked at all. Not about Jessica, not about anything. What was the point? It just made me upset all over again. Why did he have to act as if he was so nice, when he was actually such a bastard? Why didn't he just piss off, like Robbie did? Piss off back to his wife or his girlfriend or whoever it was he didn't want to be unfaithful to. See if I bloody cared. Good riddance to bad rubbish, as my mum would say.

But I knew I was lying to myself. I still fell asleep remembering the kiss on the beach. And I thought I always would, forever.

By Christmas Eve, the snow had all gone and it was back to being mild and miserable. I finished work early, as there weren't any clinics in the afternoon. It had been quiet all day, and it was nice to have time to chat to the patients and each other without flying around like mad things the way we normally do when everything is always running late. I'd finished wrapping all my presents up the night before, and set off home to help Mum pick up the turkey and the last-minute vegetables and stuff. If it hadn't been for the sick feeling in my heart, caused by Fraser bloody Willoughby, I'd have been quite happy really.

'Honestly!' said Mum as we drove home from the shops down the Panbridge Road, 'Even on Christmas Eve this bloody road is a nightmare! Where does all the traffic come from?' She glanced over at me. 'Michelle?'

'Sorry, Mum. What did you say?'

I hadn't answered her because I'd suddenly recognised the car two ahead of us in the traffic jam. It was him – Fraser. We were crawling nose-to-tail and every now and then when the driver of the car in front moved slightly to the left or right, I got a good clear view of the back of his head. Not that I wanted to look. I just couldn't help it, could I.

'What are you looking at?' asked Mum as I slid sideways in my seat trying to get a better view.

'Nothing. Just ... oh, just someone I know, a couple of cars ahead.'

'Oh. That's nice, dear.' But I could tell her mind was elsewhere. 'If we don't get going in a minute, I'm never going to get time to stuff this turkey tonight.'

'I'll help you. Here we go – we're moving now.'

The traffic up ahead surged forwards and within a couple of minutes we were indicating to turn off the main road and head towards our street. And so was Fraser.

'Is that the person you know?' asked Mum as we followed him down Panbridge Crescent.

'Yes,' I squeaked, watching in alarm as he pulled up outside our house. What the hell?

I was out of the car before Mum had even put the brake

on. He was waiting in his car, with the window down.

'Bit out of your area, aren't you?' I said. 'Did you get lost, or what?'

'No. I came by on the off chance that you'd be in. I only noticed you were behind me as we turned the corner.'

'I thought we agreed that there wasn't any more to say?'

'I know. It's just that I've brought you something for Jessica.' He reached for a package off the back seat and handed it to me through the window. It was wrapped in a Woolworth's carrier bag and was a long, thin shape. I felt it. Magic-wand-shaped. 'Sorry it's not gift-wrapped.'

'I don't think . . . ' I began, trying to hand it back to him.

'Please. It's such a little thing. I thought it might help . . . to brighten up her Christmas.' He finally met my eyes. 'And yours,' he added.

I shook my head, staring at the Woolworth's bag. It wasn't fair, was it?

'I don't know what you're playing at,' I said quietly. 'I thought you didn't want anything to do with me, but you keep on . . . '

'I don't think this will hurt, will it? Just a gift for the child, from a friend. He won't be upset by that, will he?'

'He? He, who?'

'Your boyfriend.'

'Boyfriend? I haven't got a—'

'Partner, whatever.'

'No. I haven't got a partner. I haven't got anyone. I live with my mum and dad. What are you talking about? It's *you* that's got a partner.'

'No, I haven't. I told you I haven't.' He stared at me. 'You're single, then? Unattached?'

'Of course I bloody am!' I wasn't talking quietly any more, as you can probably imagine. All the neighbours could probably hear me, to say nothing of my mum who was taking a very long time about unloading a turkey and a few bags of Brussels and parsnips from the boot. 'What do you take me for? Do you think I'd be snogging you on

296

the beach if I had a bloody boyfriend? I never said I had a boyfriend!'

'Jesus!' He slapped his head and then hung it. 'I'm sorry, Michelle. I've completely misread the situation. Misinter—preted and misunderstood.'

'So *you* haven't got anyone else, either?'

'Me? No, I'm free as a bird. I just don't like seeing people who've got ... strings attached, and I ... wrongly assumed ... ' He got out of the car, slammed the door shut and leaned against it. 'I'll be honest with you. When you told me that story, when we went out to the pub, about your "friend" who thought she might be pregnant ... well, I have to tell you, doctors get that sort of thing all the time, and the friend is never really a friend – it's always the person themselves. And then that barmaid asked you about your boyfriend, and you looked ... well, to be honest, Michelle, you looked kind of shifty the whole time we were in that pub. I just put two and two together. I was sorry, because I really liked you.'

I felt a nice warm feeling, like the sun was coming out. It wasn't, of course. It was getting dark and it felt a bit like rain.

'I know I was acting funny in the pub,' I admitted. 'I didn't really want to go there, because it was where I used to go with my ex. We were in there when he pissed off, you see. I'll tell you about it some time.'

'Was he her father?'

'Sorry? Whose father?'

'Jessica's father. Your ex-boyfriend – is he her father?'

I blinked. Was he for real?

'Are you serious?' I said. 'Did you really think Jessica was mine?'

There was a ten-second pause. It was only ten seconds, but it was enough for me to know. It was my own fault, I suppose. I obviously hadn't explained. I'd appeared with Jessica on the beach, and he'd just assumed ...

'She's my niece,' I told him, and I saw the look on his

297

face, and I felt this kind of sigh go all the way through me. 'She's my brother's little girl. We look after her a lot.'

'Oh. Oh, Michelle, I'm really sorry . . .'

'Not your fault. I thought I'd said . . . but obviously, I didn't. How funny! How funny that you thought I had a child! I mean, I'm just too bloody useless. I can't make cakes, or dolls' clothes, or stop her crying. I'd be a useless mum. I'd have to go to night school first, or something, and have lessons.'

'No you wouldn't. It'll all come naturally, when it's the right time.'

'Do you think so? That's nice.'

'So, what about your "friend"? Did she take a pregnancy test?'

'Oh, that friend, yes! She was just a bit worried about a one-night stand. It's OK. She's not pregnant.'

'Pleased to hear it.' He smiled.

'So was I,' I said.

He looked around quickly. Mum scuttled indoors with the last bag of shopping pretending she hadn't been listening. He leaned towards me and kissed me on the lips – just once, very lightly, very gently. He was still smiling.

'Happy Christmas, Michelle,' he said.

'Happy Christmas, Fraser.' I felt myself smiling too.

Maybe I'd never stop smiling again.

Jessica nearly collapsed with pleasure when she unwrapped the magic wand the next day. Well, it did help that I'd taken it out of the Woolworth's bag and wrapped it in the very last bit of Christmas paper that was left over.

'A *real* fairy wand!' she trilled, skipping round the room waving it around her head, only just missing the TV and a lamp. On the word *real* she gave me a look that spoke volumes. Weetabix-packet wands just weren't in the same league as this baby. 'Thank you, thank you, lovely Father Christmas!'

The wand was pink and glittery with silver streamers.

'Actually,' I said, 'It wasn't Father Christmas. It was—'

'Careful, Chelle,' said Mum.

Careful? I'd forgotten *careful* when Fraser kissed me outside our house on Christmas Eve. *Careful* was for people who didn't know whether they liked someone, or didn't know whether that someone liked them back. *Careful* was for people who weren't sure if they were going to see the other person again, or whether the other person was married, or attached in some way, and might end up dumping them. I'd done with *careful*.

But for Jessica's sake, OK.

'It's a present from a friend,' I told her. 'A nice, nice friend of Chelly's, Jessica. Isn't that kind?'

'Yes,' she said happily. 'Nice friend, Chelly!'

'"Nice friend, Chelly,"' mimicked Adam. 'Nice for snogging in the sand dunes, eh? *Well* nice!'

'Shut up, Adam,' I said, and threw a walnut at him, closely followed (when he ducked) by the nutcrackers. But I was laughing. How could I not laugh? How could I not be happy?

'*More* presents?' asked Jessica, suddenly bored with the wand for the moment and tugging at my hand expectantly.

'Oh! Oh, so Chelly's suddenly back in favour, is she? Well now, let me see! Can I find a little present somewhere here for a good little girl? Oh, yes – is this it?' I held the parcel up too high for her to reach. 'I can't see the label. Is this Jessica's, do you think?'

'Me see! Me see!' she squealed, jumping up and down. 'Me have the present, Chelly! Lovely Chelly!'

Oh! For once, Useless Chelly was the favourite auntie! I dropped the parcel into her arms and watched as she tore off the paper.

And for once, Jessica was reduced to silence.

'A *real* fairy princess dress!' she whispered hoarsely. She held it up, pink and gold and glittery, with silky silver wings. I thought for a minute she was going to cry. Instead, she climbed onto my lap, put her little chubby arms round

299

my neck and buried her face against me.

'Say thank you to Chelly, then, Jessica,' Adam reminded her gently.

'Thank you, Chelly,' she repeated. 'I love you, Chelly. Specially mostly of all of everybody!'

That had to be worth something, didn't it?

Everyone else in the room had gone quiet. They almost looked like crying. Load of old softies!

Mum was on the phone to Maureen a lot over Christmas. I didn't hear much of what she was saying. She was talking quietly and sounded kind of sad and serious. Still, at least they seemed to be on speaking terms again. It made me think that maybe I should make a bit more effort with Kim. We'd been mates for such a long time, it seemed a shame to fall out now.

'Want to go up the Cloud on New Year's Eve?' I asked Nicole. 'Me, you and Kim – like the old days, eh?'

'It's tickets only,' she said. 'They sold out weeks ago, and anyway, they were twenty quid. I couldn't afford it, not till I start my new job.'

Nicole had just heard she'd been accepted for a job at a hairdresser's. It was shampooing and sweeping up, and I was a bit worried that she thought she'd be doing cuts and highlights in a couple of months' time. But at least she was going to get a share of the tips so hopefully she'd be a bit better off. And it'd make a change from furniture, obviously.

'And sorry, Chelle, but to be honest I'm seeing Scott on New Year's Eve,' she went on. 'We're going for a romantic meal. But we could go out on Tuesday if you like – the night before?'

Romantic meal? I felt a little twinge of jealousy. Robbie never used to be interested in romantic meals. That chicken roll at the Grey Mare was probably about as romantic as he got – and look what happened then! I thought, very briefly, about Fraser, and found myself wondering whether he liked romantic meals or not. But it wasn't a good idea to get carried away.

'OK,' I said. 'Yeah, that'd be nice – we'll go on Tuesday night, then. I'll ring Kim. I haven't seen her for a while. Have a nice time on New Year's!'

Lucky thing. And all because of my mum's pudding, apparently. Maybe I should eat some more of it myself.

He phoned on the Sunday, the day before I went back to work.

'I couldn't wait any longer to talk to you,' he said. 'Have you had a good Christmas?'

'Lovely, thanks,' I said. My heart was right up in my mouth, making my voice come out all wobbly. 'And Jessica *loved* her magic wand; thank you! How about you?'

'Fairly quiet. Went home to my parents in Kent for Christmas Day and Boxing Day. Then I had to come back because I was on call yesterday.'

'Oh.' I paused. Should I? Shouldn't I? 'What are you doing tonight, then?' I asked all in a rush.

'Nothing, yet. I wondered ... '

'I was wondering ... '

We were both talking at once, then suddenly both laughing together, feeling a bit silly for being so nervous.

'Do you want to come round?' I managed to get out, eventually. 'And we can go for a drink?'

'That sounds great,' he said.

I hung up the phone and ran up the stairs two at a time to get changed.

'I think lover boy must be coming round,' I heard Adam comment to my dad as they watched the news on TV.

'Good for her,' said Dad, to my surprise. 'Just hope he treats her better than that bloody Robbie. If I could get my hands on him ... '

'Don't you worry about Robbie,' said Adam. 'Just leave him to me.'

Which was a funny thing to say really, being as he'd

gone missing; but I didn't have time to think about it. I needed to decide which jumper to wear and whether to have my hair swept back or falling across my face. I needed to try both out in the mirror and see which looked sexiest.

'Pleased to meet you, Dr Willoughby,' said my mum.

She looked like she was tempted to curtsy. Honestly!

'His name's Fraser,' I told her sharply. And I felt like adding 'Hands off!' because she was gawping at him as though he was a film star. Well, obviously he was gorgeous-looking but did she have to do that whole *Dr Willoughby* thing as though she was in awe of him? Mum worked with vets, after all, and they're much the same at the end of the day, lancing boils and treating constipation, whether it's a cat or a human. And I bet she didn't look at her vets as though they were film stars, did she.

'I've just got to get my shoes and coat on,' I told Fraser. 'I won't be a minute.'

'There's no rush, Chelle. Why don't you have a seat, Fraser, and I'll make you a cup of coffee while you're waiting? And you could have a piece of my Christmas cake if you like?'

'Not your famous pudding?' he asked with a beaming smile.

'Oh! No, no, just Christmas cake!' said Mum, laughing all kind of pretend-embarrassed, obviously loving it. There are times, just occasionally, when my mum really does annoy me.

'Well, another time, Mrs Peacham ...'

'Call me Penny, please, Fraser!'

'Penny, then – another time, I'd love to try some of your cake, or your pudding – I've heard all about what a great cook you are. But I think, if you don't mind, that Michelle and I are waiting to go out, just now. Have a nice evening – it's been good to meet you.'

'You handled that well,' I told him, admiringly, as we got in the car. 'I think she would have liked you to stay

302

there all night, sat on the sofa complimenting her on her cake or her bloody Passion Pudding.'

'Oh, well,' he said with a smile, 'look at it from your mum's point of view, Michelle. She's been married to your dad forever, and probably doesn't get a lot of attention. A little bit of flattery doesn't cost anything and might make her day. She's probably forgotten what it's like to be young and beautiful – like her daughter.'

'Now you're handing *me* all the old flattery!'

'But I mean it, though. And I don't need Passion Pudding to make me feel the way I do.'

'How? How *do* you feel?'

'Like stopping the car in the middle of all this traffic and kissing you till you beg for mercy!'

I started to laugh. But before I had time to recover, he pulled over to the side of the road and proceeded to do exactly that. Except that I didn't beg for mercy. The only reason we stopped was that so many cars were honking us, I was worried we were going to get arrested.

Penny

Maureen phoned me a few days after Christmas.

'I'm leaving him,' she said. She sounded like she'd been crying for days and only just about managed to stop. 'You were right, Penny. It's what I should do. I've been a coward much too long.'

'You're not a coward. Are you really sure this is what you want? You mustn't take any notice of me. It's easy for me to talk – it's not me who's got to make the decision.'

'Well, I've made it. I can't stand it any more. Tony hasn't spoken a single word to me, all over Christmas. Didn't even buy me a present. Just sat glued to the TV, waiting for his dinner to be put on his lap. I nearly threw it over his head. I want a life of my own, Penny, before it's too late.'

'Have you told him?'

'Yes. He laughed at me.' She paused. 'It's the first time I've heard him laugh for years. It made me even more determined.'

'Well, good for you. But what will you do? Where will you go?'

'I don't know. I told him the house will have to be sold, but he's not taking me seriously. He says I'll never manage on my own and I'll come creeping back to him after a few days.' She sighed. 'I hope he's not right, Pen.'

'Of course he's not!' I said crossly. 'Of course you can

manage without him – and be ten times happier! He's sapping your confidence! Come and stay with us.'

I said it without thinking, but even though I realised there would have to be some reorganisation of the bedrooms, what with Michelle, and the fuchsias, I knew it was the right thing to say.

'I couldn't. I'd be in the way. Archie wouldn't like it.'

'Yes he would. And it'll only be temporary, till you get yourself sorted out. Just long enough to show Tony you mean business.'

'And that I'm not going creeping back to him?'

'Exactly.'

I went straight upstairs and looked at how much room the fuchsias were taking up. Maybe I could put some of them in the bathroom. The steam might do them good.

'I need to talk to you,' I told Archie that night when we were getting ready for bed.

He looked at me, very worried.

'What about, Pen? I don't like it when you say that. It normally means we haven't got enough money to pay the bills.'

'No, it's not that – although we probably haven't. What do you expect, straight after Christmas?'

'Is it about our Michelle? 'Cos you shouldn't worry, Penny – I think Adam's right: now she's got herself a new boyfriend, she's not bothered at all about that bloody Robbie.' He watched my face in the mirror as I brushed my hair. 'Or is it about what you did the other night, at the Tail Waggers' dinner?'

I stopped, frozen, with the hairbrush in my hand.

'It's all right,' he went on calmly. 'We all make mistakes. Don't feel bad.'

'What do you mean?' I asked in a croak.

'Getting drunk. We've all done it, Pen.'

'Oh! Oh, yes, I suppose so.' I hung my head and tried to look suitably humble. 'But that wasn't ...'

305

'Look at me, for instance. I've made a bit of a stupid mistake myself, recently.'

My head flicked up again.

'What sort of a mistake?'

Oh my God. How ironic was this? I'd just avoided committing adultery by the skin of my teeth, and now Archie was about to make some kind of sordid confession. I didn't really want to know.

'Don't tell me!' I added hastily, putting down the hairbrush and turning to face him. 'I don't want you to ...'

'But I think I should, Pen. It's been bothering me, you know – preying on my conscience.'

I could hardly believe what I was hearing. Surely he wasn't having an affair? Good, solid, dependable old Archie? Who the hell could it be? Surely not Mrs Gardener from number forty-seven? He'd spent a lot of time down there during the summer, repointing her patio. She might have been over seventy but she wasn't looking bad on it. Or that Julie Branksome, the daughter of the old lady at number nineteen? She was a feisty looking piece of work, and I'd heard some of the neighbours saying no man was safe in that house if she was around. Had Archie been getting more than he bargained for when he painted their ceilings?

'You see, Penny – it wasn't Darren Barlow.'

'What wasn't?' I asked, staring at him in confusion, thoughts of him illicitly entwined with Mrs Gardener or Julie Branksome slipping away from my mind.

'It wasn't him who told the *Duffington Echo* about you leaving the pressure group. It was me.'

'You?' I realised I was still standing gawping at him. I sat down next to him on the bed, where he was sitting with one sock on and one sock off, his arms dangling between his legs, watching me. 'You phoned the paper up? Talked to them about me? Why, Archie? Why the hell would you do that?'

'I didn't phone them up. They phoned me. Well – they

phoned here asking for you. Quite a few times, they did. I always told them to ring back when you were home. Then this one time, the woman said she'd heard a rumour about you being thrown out of the PPPP, and was it true? I couldn't help myself, Pen! I was just so annoyed for you that these stupid people had got hold of half the story; I had to put them straight and tell them it was you who left.'

'But they still published it with a screaming headline about me getting my "marching orders"!'

'You know what the press is like for a bit of scandal. But look at the sympathy vote it got you!'

I had to admit it was true. Even now, weeks later, people were still stopping me in the street and saying how silly it was that I'd had to leave the group, considering all the publicity I'd generated for them.

'Well, I suppose you did it for the best,' I said grudgingly. 'But really, Archie, I think you could have told me. I was all for giving Darren Barlow a smack.'

'Maybe I just wanted to watch you do it!'

'Yes, I know what you mean. He's the most irritating man I've ever met. I can't believe I agreed to appear on that bloody TV programme with him. What the hell was I thinking of? I was scared enough on radio ...'

'You'll be brilliant, Pen. You're a natural.'

I still hadn't got used to Archie saying things like this to me. He never used to notice me, really, never mind saying I was brilliant.

'You're only saying that 'cos you want me to make some more pudding for you,' I teased him.

'Partly that, yes. But also ...' He pulled off his other sock and studied it carefully as if there was something interesting in its toe.

'What?'

'Well, also, Pen, to be perfectly honest, I did kind of encourage the TV thing.'

'You what?'

'Darren kept on phoning ...'

'I know! I couldn't get rid of him! Then he turned up at work dressed as bloody Santa!'

'Well, that was only because I said you probably wouldn't mind.'

'*Wouldn't mind*? Archie, have you gone raving mad? Why the hell ... He didn't exactly need any encouragement!'

'Well, actually, he did. He was about to give up. He thought you'd never agree to talk to him about it. I thought you'd be pig sick if you missed this opportunity. TV, Penny! Have you thought about how many people are going to be watching?'

'Of course I have, you idiot! I've thought of nothing else since I let him talk me into it. I'm terrified!'

'It's the best opportunity you'll ever get. Push home the message about the bypass for all you're worth. Darren's so grateful that you've agreed – it's his big career opportunity – he's not going to mess you around this time. You can make this happen, Penny. You can change the course of history for Panbridge Park, and stuff Roger and his stupid committee right up the ... '

'You make it sound almost exciting.'

'Well, there's another thing about it, too.'

'And that is?'

'The pudding. Promote the pudding again, on TV this time, and we'll have got it made. I bet you anything you like.'

'Got what made? I don't know what you're talking about, Archie!'

'Penny's Passion Pudding. I think it's true what everyone's saying about it. It's got certain sexual properties. I think I should market it. We should go into business, Pen.'

I grabbed the smelly sock out of his hand and threw it into the laundry basket.

'And I think,' I retorted, 'that you're stark, staring mad. It's the most ridiculous thing I've ever heard in my entire life.'

The trouble was, I was so completely taken aback, I clean forgot to tell him about Maureen.

We all went back to work on the Monday. Even Archie. He had a toilet seat to fit for a lady in the next street who'd been perching on the edge of the pan all over Christmas and had told Archie quite brazenly on the phone that she had red rim marks on her bum. I'd been dreading going back. I'd tried not to think about Chris Filbey over the holiday, but it wasn't going to be possible to ignore him at the surgery.

'Tough it out, Pen,' Debbie whispered to me almost as soon as I got to work. She touched my hand very briefly, looked me in the eye, and said, 'Just act like nothing's happened. It'll do him good.'

That was all very well. But something *had* happened. I'd made a complete prat of myself, and it was going to be difficult to put it behind me.

'And don't be too hard on yourself,' she added with a grin. 'Remember you're the one who got away ... '

I suppose that much was true. All the other female members of staff, and ex-members of staff by the sound of it, could have formed a Chris Filbey's Sexual Conquests club. They could all have met up for lunch and discussed his prowess in the sack. Or lack of it, if what Debbie said was true. In a way, I felt quite left out.

'Morning, all,' said the man himself five minutes later, striding through the door and walking straight past me as if I was invisible. 'Nice Christmas, everyone?'

'Lovely, thank you,' I called after him. But he'd closed his consulting room door behind him without even waiting for an answer.

'Prick,' said Debbie under her breath.

I was actually beginning to wonder what I'd seen in him.

Maureen was arriving on New Year's Eve, and it wasn't until the day before that I suddenly remembered to tell Archie.

'Bloody hell,' he said. 'Who'd have thought it, eh? I bet old Tony never dreamed she'd finally work up the courage to walk out on him.'

'No, well – it serves him right, if you ask me,' I retorted sharply. 'He should have paid more attention to her, years ago.'

'Absolutely, Pen. Not every woman is lucky enough to have a wonderful husband, like you have. Just you think on!'

'No, *you* bloody think on, you cheeky sod!' I laughed. 'I might just take a leaf out of her book and walk out myself, one day!'

'Yeah, Mum might just find herself a nice handsome toyboy, mightn't you, Mum!' joined in Michelle.

'Don't be silly, Chelle,' said Archie. 'Your mum isn't interested in younger men. No match for experience! Isn't that right, Pen?'

'If you say so,' I replied, suddenly not liking the conversation any more. 'Anyway, what I'm trying to tell you all is that you'll have to make allowances. Maureen's staying here till she sorts herself out somewhere to live. So just be a bit considerate, please. No wandering around in your underpants, Archie. And clean the bloody toilet.'

'Christ, woman – is it my home or not? Maureen's seen worse things in her life than a man's underpants ...'

'Not with you in them, she hasn't!' joked Michelle.

'And the fuchsias will have to go in the bathroom. So please be careful. I don't want the stems broken when you're cleaning your teeth.'

'Bloody house is turning into a home for waifs and strays.'

'My fuchsias are not waifs and strays. They are things of beauty. They keep me calm.'

This shut them all up for a moment, until Adam suddenly piped up:

'So is it still OK for Jessica to stay over the New Year, then?'

'Adam!' said Michelle. 'You've just heard Mum! We've got to be considerate, and make allowances. Maureen's going through a rough time. She needs peace and quiet, not Jessica running around the house screaming!'

'She won't be running around screaming. Not if you don't get her overexcited.'

'Oh, great – so it's *my* fault if she misbehaves?'

'It's all right, Chelle,' I said. 'Maureen won't mind. She likes having everyone around her. She told me only the other week how she wishes she had a family like ours.'

'Bloody hell,' joked Archie, 'She must be in a bad way.'

'But even so, Adam,' persisted Michelle, 'I don't see why you think it's OK to keep dumping Jessica on Mum all the time.'

'And *I* don't see why you think it's OK to keep sticking your nose into it ...'

'You've got a bloody cheek! I live here now, don't forget!'

'Yes, and whose fault is that? If you hadn't lost your stupid boyfriend ...'

'Oh, that's very nice, that is! It wasn't *my* fault the bastard walked out! I didn't *ask* him to vanish into mid-air without eating his fucking roll!'

'Michelle ...' warned Archie.

'Well, I'm sorry, Dad, but Adam's *fucking* asking for it! It makes me so angry the way he just pisses off for jolly weekends with some *bird* and expects everyone else to look after Jessica.'

'Mum doesn't mind!' shouted Adam.

'No, I don't, really ...' I tried to intervene, but by now nobody was listening to me.

'Adam, Michelle has got a point, you know,' said Archie unexpectedly. 'I mean, we don't mind looking after Jessica, of course we don't. But it is kind of taking liberties, you know, all these weekends – and you need to be careful she doesn't feel a bit insecure, too – what with her mother buggering off ...'

311

'Oh, great!' said Adam, standing up and looking round the room at us all. 'So that's the majority verdict, is it – that I'm a fucking useless father who dumps his kid at every opportunity to go off on the pull?'

There was silence for a minute.

'No, Adam, of course not,' I started to say. But he didn't hear me, because Michelle was already speaking:

'If the cap fits, Adam,' she told him loudly, 'if the cap fits, as Mum would say – then bloody wear it.'

He slammed the door so loudly on the way out, the house shook.

Michelle

It had to be said, didn't it?

Although, to be honest, I did feel a bit mean after he stormed out. He hadn't had it easy, bringing up Jessica without that cow of a Julia around. But I just couldn't sit back and see him taking the piss out of Mum any more. He'd have to find someone else to mind Jessica for change. Or take her with him. Or bloody well stay at home – it wouldn't hurt him, for once.

'Well, I don't blame you, Chelle. Your brother needed telling,' said Nicole as we queued to get into Purple Cloud.

It was heaving – everybody seemed to have decided to come out for the night before New Year's as well as the actual thirty-first. Or maybe instead of it, if they didn't want to pay the ticket prices, and who could blame them? Trouble was, almost everyone in the queue except for us seemed to be about fourteen. I had a horrible feeling we were the only ones there who'd left school.

'It's not under-sixteens' night, is it?' I whispered.

'No. It's always like this. Where have you been?'

Half asleep, apparently. I looked around me at the sea of teenage faces and suddenly felt very, very old.

'Half of these won't be allowed in,' she said. 'What's the matter with you? Don't you remember having to borrow ID from my cousins and Kim's big sister, and memorise their dates of birth in case we got asked? Don't you remember how often we got turned away and had to go home crying?'

'Yeah. Yes, of course I do. But did we really look as young as this lot? Why haven't I noticed before?'

'We normally get pissed before we come here,' Kim reminded me.

Oh yes. That'd be it.

'We've been saying, actually,' admitted Nicole, 'that maybe we're getting too old for this place. Maybe we need to find somewhere else?'

'Bloody hell,' I said sadly. 'It's the first time I've been too old for something since I left the Brownies.'

We forgot about it, though, once we got inside the club. It was good to be out with the girls again, having a couple of drinks, having a laugh, catching up on all the goss.

'So how's *your* love life then, Chelle?' asked Nicole when she'd finally had enough of telling us all about Scott – how gorgeous he was, how much she loved him, how much he loved her, how she was still holding out on him and not having sex but thinking about doing it on the tenth of January for his birthday, because she couldn't think what to buy him.

'Good, thanks,' I said, trying not to grin too widely.

'What?' demanded Kim. 'So there *is* a new man, is there? You wouldn't tell us, that night round your house.'

'No, well, I didn't think I'd be seeing him any more. We had a kind of misunderstanding.'

'What kind of?'

'Nothing much. I thought he was married, and he thought I had a kid and might be expecting another one.'

'Oh, nothing important, then!' said Kim sarcastically.

She took a swig of her drink, looked up across the dance floor and suddenly froze.

'What?' I said. I followed her gaze and gasped with surprise. 'Bloody hell! It's him! Luke! I never thought I'd see *him* again! He lives in Yarmouth and ... oh, he must

314

have recognised me! He's coming over! Oh shit!'

'Oh shit!' echoed Kim quietly as Luke approached us. Then, to my surprise, she called out to him, 'What are you doing here? It was supposed to be a girls' night.'

'I know,' he said with the slow, lazy smile that I remembered only too well. 'But I was missing you, baby. You didn't mind, did you?'

And to my absolute amazement, he pulled Kim close to him and proceeded to kiss her. And it wasn't the kiss of a casual acquaintance.

'They're going out, aren't they!' I exclaimed to Nicole behind their heads.

She nodded, her face a grimace of anxiety.

'She wanted to tell you ... but it was difficult ... she didn't want you to be upset ... I told her you might have been pregnant ... she didn't know what to do ... '

'She could have tried bloody talking to me!' I said. Kim surfaced, spluttering, from halfway down Luke's throat.

'I'm sorry, Chelle ... I told him not to come tonight. I was going to tell you – honestly.'

'Yeah, sorry, Michelle,' echoed Luke. He smiled at me. 'No hard feelings, eh, babe?'

No hard feelings? What, when you left me in a club doorway with my knickers in my pocket? When I spent weeks worrying myself to death about my late period, to say nothing of any frightening diseases you might have given me? When I spent good money on pregnancy tests and nearly ruined my new relationship because he thought I was having a baby?

I stared back at him in disbelief. How dare he talk about no hard feelings?

'It's not Luke's fault,' said Kim defensively, holding onto his arm and stroking it. 'You weren't an item, or anything, so when he asked me out ... '

I sighed. Did it really matter? I didn't want to go out with him anyway. Sure, he was a good dancer. Sure, he had a good body, and a nice smile. But at the end of the

315

day, was he funny and loving, kind and clever, gentle and sweet, as well as good-looking and the best kisser I'd ever met? Because I had all those things now with Fraser. So to be quite honest, Luke could get stuffed, with or without Kim's help, for all I cared.

'Don't worry about it,' I told her. 'I just wish you'd talked to me, instead of ignoring me. I didn't know what I'd done wrong.'

'I was scared to,' she said. 'I thought you'd hit me.'

Yeah, like I'm suddenly a heavyweight boxing champion.

'Daft cow.'

'Want a drink?'

'OK. Thanks.'

'I'll come to the bar with you, Kim,' said Nicole, rushing off behind her, obviously wanting to squeal and giggle together and say wasn't it awful, the way I'd found out, and hadn't I taken it well, without even hitting anyone.

'So,' said Luke when we were on our own, 'how have you been?'

I fought the temptation to retort: Two months pregnant with a nasty sexual disease. How about you?

'I thought you lived in Yarmouth?' I said accusingly.

'I do. Did. I came here again a few weeks after the night we ... met ... and ended up staying.'

'Staying? What, as in – with Kim?'

'Well, not exactly. But her parents helped find me a flat. And a job.'

'How very, very lucky for you!'

'Look, Michelle – it wasn't quite the way it sounds.'

'Oh no? You mean it wasn't that you dumped me outside a nightclub after you'd finished with me, and then decided to go out with my friend and take advantage of her parents ...'

'No. That wasn't how it was. You were very drunk that night, so I'm not surprised you don't remember. But I didn't dump you outside the club. I took you out there for

316

some fresh air. Then after a while you went back in, to the toilet, and came out giggling with your panties in your hand. In fact, if you really can't remember, you were waving them around your head. I was pretty embarrassed, so I grabbed them off you. Then I saw Kim and Nicole, coming to look for you, so I stuffed them in your pocket quickly, before they could see and get the wrong idea. Nothing happened between us, Michelle, and I can assure you nothing was ever going to.'

'Oh,' I said, quietly, feeling the shame welling up in me and burning my face red. 'Why? I thought you liked me.'

'I did. I really fancied you. But if there's one thing I can't stand, it's girls who drink too much. They make themselves look stupid and leave themselves open to all kinds of abuse. It's such a big turn-off.' He paused, shook his head and smiled at me. 'But sorry – maybe you don't normally do that sort of thing. It's a pet hate of mine.'

'Oh! Well, if it's *such* a pet hate of yours, maybe you shouldn't encourage it!' I retorted. How dare he! 'I wasn't buying *myself* all those drinks, you know.'

'I guess I kind of assumed you knew your own limits. You could have said no, Michelle. It's really hard to respect girls who can't say no. My religion teaches us that women should be quiet and gentle and obey their menfolk.'

You what?!?

'Good for you!' I said. 'Mine teaches me that men like you are patronising and full of shit.'

I turned away from him and watched Kim coming back from the bar with Nicole, carrying the drinks between them, chatting and laughing and eyeing up the guys on the dance floor.

'He's religious,' I whispered to her. 'He hates women drinking. He likes them to be quiet.'

'I know,' she whispered back, 'but I'm working on him!'

I sighed and shook my head. I should have been worried about Kim. She was definitely, definitely, with the wrong guy and it was going to lead to tears. But all I could think about was what a lucky escape I'd had.

'You know that girl I told you about?' I said to Fraser the next night.

We were at a pub in Potts End – a little village pub where there was no New Year's Eve buffet, no ticket entrance, no dancing, no silly hats and whistles and 'Auld Lang Syne' – just a nice menu of bar meals and a cosy corner for a romantic evening.

'What girl?'

'My friend? The one who was worried about being pregnant or having ... caught something nasty?'

'Oh yes,' he said calmly.

'Well – guess what? She went through all that worry for nothing. She didn't even *have* a one-night stand!'

'Really? So why did she think she did?'

'God knows. Maybe she was very drunk. Or very stupid,' I said, shaking my head sadly at the stupidity of the stupid person. And well I might do, as my mum would say.

'Never mind,' he said, covering my hand with his on the table and smiling at me. 'Everyone does something stupid now and again, don't they. At least your friend is OK.'

'Yes,' I said, smiling back at him and thinking I must be the luckiest stupid person in the world. 'Yes, she's definitely OK now.'

'Happy New Year, Michelle,' he said, raising his glass and clinking it with mine. 'I've got a feeling two thousand and four is going to be a good one.'

'Me too,' I said happily. 'I think it's going to be fantastic.'

I was still in two minds about whether to make a complaint to the police about Killer threatening to kill me. I tried talking to Mum and Dad about it.

'At least you've got the car back, Chelle,' said Dad, which really annoyed me.

318

I'd only had it back a few days. It had been picked up from where it was dumped in Ipswich by a recovery company, and towed away somewhere for the police to fingerprint it, and of course, what with Christmas and New Year, by the time I was allowed to go and pick it up I'd almost forgotten what it looked like. It had been very annoying, and inconvenient, and I wanted to see Killer get done for it. His fingerprints were bound to be all over it – he was too stupid to think about wearing gloves or wiping his prints off. Why did it make it all right, just because I'd got the car back again now?

'So what?' I snapped. 'I still don't see why I should let him get away with it – stealing the car *and* coming to the house like he did, scaring the shit ... the crap out of me ...'

'I don't think he could have meant it, Chelle,' said Mum. 'He always used to be such a nice little boy. I remember when he and Adam were at school together, he always wore lovely clean shiny shoes, and a nice white shirt.'

'Oh, that makes all the difference, then, doesn't it! Never mind if he threatens to kill me, Mum, just as long as he wore clean shoes and a nice shirt when he was eleven years old! For God's sake!'

'They don't call him *Killer* for nothing, Pen,' agreed Dad.

'So why are you saying you're not sure, Chelle? If you think he really wanted to kill you, why haven't you told the police already?' Mum still sounded as though she thought I was exaggerating the whole thing wildly. Let's face it, she did bring him a nice cup of tea and a plate of biscuits while he was talking about murdering me.

'I know it sounds silly,' I said with a sigh, 'but I was kind of hoping he'd track Robbie down. Not that I want to see him!' I added quickly as Mum and Dad raised their eyebrows at each other. 'But I think he should pay me back for the car. And pay everyone else what they're saying he owes them. Even Killer. And I want to tell him what I think of him, too – walking out on me, leaving me with the rent to pay and everything. That's all.'

'It's unfinished business, isn't it, Chelle,' said Dad.

'Absolutely. And while Killer's desperate to find him, part of me thinks I should let him get on with it. Maybe he *will* find him. Then maybe I can get Killer locked up afterwards.'

'Locked up?' said Mum. 'Oh, Chelly, I'm *sure* he doesn't deserve that! He was always so polite, and his mum was secretary of the PTA ... '

'That's all right, then. As long as his mum was secretary of the PTA, I can forgive him anything.'

'I don't know *why* they started calling him Killer,' she said, half to herself, half to Maureen, who'd been listening to all this (surprisingly) without comment. 'Julian is such a nice name.'

Maureen had moved in with us on New Year's Eve. She wasn't herself at all; in fact I'd never known her to be so quiet. She spent quite a lot of time upstairs in the bedroom on her own, and when she was downstairs she didn't seem to want to watch TV, or do anything, just sat staring into space. Once or twice I heard her say to Mum, 'Do you think I've definitely done the right thing? Are you sure?' and I felt sorry for her, really. She wasn't my bossy Auntie Maureen any more. She was just a sad, lonely woman. Why hadn't I noticed it before?

'I wish I'd got myself a new job, now,' she said one day, staring out of the kitchen window with a saucepan in her hands as if she'd forgotten what it was for. 'I should have done it years ago, same as I should have left Tony years ago. Then I might have had a decent career by now, something a bit more interesting. The crematorium's all very well, I've got a good pension to look forward to, but there isn't much excitement, and people tend to be miserable.'

'Maybe Mum could get you a job at the vet's, Maureen,' I said, thinking I was being helpful.

But Mum shot me a terrible look, gave a kind of shudder like someone had walked over her grave, and changed the subject quickly.

Funny. You'd have thought she'd like the idea of having her best friend working at the same place.

The other thing that made it strange at home during January was not having Jessica around. In fact it wasn't just strange, it was horrible, and what made it even more horrible was knowing that it was all my fault.

'I wish I'd never said anything, now,' I told Mum. 'Adam says he's never going to leave Jessica here any more.'

'Oh, take no notice of him, Chelle. He'll come round. He'll forget all about it in a little while. He's just showing off.'

Yes, and meanwhile Jessica was getting older every week, and learning new words, and playing new games, and soon she'd be going to school, and learning to read and write, and taking her exams, and getting her first job, and my poor mum, who'd practically brought her up, would never see her again, and it would all be down to me and my big mouth.

'Stop fretting, girl,' said my dad. 'It'll all come out in the wash.'

But would it? You know what normally happens in the wash – when I do it, anyway? Things shrink, or stretch, or go pink when they're meant to be white. So I wasn't in the habit of looking forward to seeing how things came out of the wash, and this wasn't any exception.

321

Penny

I didn't think much of the New Year. It was miserable and wet; we were waking up every day to cloud and drizzle, or gale force winds and belting rain. Maureen moped around the house barely talking and Archie kept asking me when she was going to find a place of her own. The only one who seemed really happy was Michelle. Even that worried me; I was just a bit afraid that she was so seriously smitten with this new boyfriend of hers, she was going to end up getting hurt. Having said that, he did seem really nice. Very polite, and very complimentary about my cooking. But I kept thinking these thoughts about doctors being like vets. I tried warning Michelle to be careful and take things slowly, but what can you do? She wasn't a teenager any more. I was only her mother – why should she listen to me?

We didn't even have Jessica running around the house, with her funny little giggle and her sweet silly chatter to liven things up a bit. I know it was sometimes annoying the way Adam took it for granted, but to be honest I did love looking after Jessica, and I missed her really badly.

'Let's go round to Adam's place and see her, then,' suggested Michelle. She was worried that Jessica would never come round again and thought it was all down to her. 'Give Adam a ring, Mum, and ask if we can go over tonight.'

But whenever we tried ringing him, Adam had the

answerphone on. I left messages but he didn't call me back. Archie kept saying to leave him be, that he'd come round once he'd finished sulking, but I was beginning to think we were going to be one of those families with rifts in them that go on forever.

At work, Chris Filbey ignored me for about two weeks and then suddenly started to act as if nothing whatsoever had happened. This was such a relief, as it'd been so unpleasant while he was giving me the cold shoulder – what with everyone else noticing and even dogs beginning to howl because of the atmosphere in the surgery (dogs are very susceptible to people's moods) – that I decided I should just go along with it and pretend I'd forgotten all about it too. I consoled myself by thinking about how rubbish in bed Debbie had said he was. It would have been bad enough jeopardising my marriage, without doing it for a totally disappointing experience.

The TV show with Darren Barlow was scheduled for the twenty-third of January; and the edition of *Woman Today* magazine that was carrying 'my' feature was coming out the week before. I got a complimentary copy of it a few days early. Archie was out, laying floor tiles for Mrs Gardener, when the big brown envelope arrived in the post.

'Aren't you going to open it?' asked Maureen, as I sat down opposite her and stared at it on my lap.

'I don't know if I dare. I think the pictures are going to be tacky and the article's going to be awful.'

She gave me a look that was very clearly saying, What else do you expect? I ignored her. After all, she had her own problems now, worse problems, perhaps, than having dodgy magazine features written about you – so it was understandable that she might be a bit unsympathetic.

'Do you want me to open it, then?' she asked eventually when I'd sat with the envelope on my lap, drumming my fingers on it, for about ten minutes. 'Would you like me to look at it first, for you?'

'All right, then. Yes, please.' I handed it across to her. 'I think I'll go and make a coffee while you're looking at it.'

I took my time with the coffee. I loaded the washing machine and set it off. I tidied the fridge and wiped the work surfaces over. Eventually when I couldn't think of anything else to do, and the coffee was probably getting cold, I took a deep breath and carried the cups into the living room.

'Well?' I said to Maureen, hardly daring to look at her.

She looked up at me, and she was smiling. It wasn't a smile of derision; it wasn't the kind of smile that says: Jesus, what a complete arse you've made of yourself! It looked like a normal, pleased type of smile. I put the coffee cups down and waited.

'It's really good, Pen,' she said. She sounded surprised, and who could blame her? 'It's not smutty. It's funny.'

'*Funny?*'

'Yes. What on earth did you think, when they dressed you in that Alice in Wonderland gear and made you pose with the your leg up on the chair and the mixing bowl on your knee? Did you *really* think it was going to be a serious article?'

'Well, I ... I didn't know what to think. What with the grandma doing the nude headstands ... '

'The picture of her is funny, too! She's not nude; she's standing on her head in her judo suit, with a couple of cats winding around her arms. I haven't read the article properly yet but apparently she was publicising her cats' charity.'

'And the Latin teacher sleeping in the garden? And the motorcycling woman with pierced nipples?'

'Read it yourself, Penny! Yes, they've taken the piss in a very gentle way, but ... '

'It's not all about sexual vitality and stuff?'

'It's more about having a life, whatever your age. The way you were telling me about it, I was expecting it to

324

portray you as a kind of sex goddess.'

'And it doesn't?'

I wasn't sure whether to be relieved or disappointed.

'No. It's portrayed the four of you as ... well, as rather amusing eccentrics!'

The rather amusing eccentric in our family was sitting in the lounge reading her own article when Archie came home. I heard him talking in the kitchen to Maureen. He never was any good at whispering.

'Is it OK? Is she upset?'

'I don't know,' said Maureen. 'She hasn't said anything yet.'

They both crept back into the room and sat on the sofa opposite me, watching me.

'For God's sake,' I muttered. 'I'm not about to suddenly have a fit and throw the magazine across the room.'

'It's good, isn't it, Pen?' Maureen said breezily. 'What do you think?'

'I think,' I admitted honestly, laying it down and looking up at them both, 'that I feel a fool. First of all I was expecting to be taken seriously; then I thought I was being ... I don't know; *cheapened*, I suppose. But who was I kidding? I'm not famous, or important, enough for either of those, am I. I've just been ... *teased*.'

'It's a *gentle* teasing, though, Pen,' said Maureen. 'It's quite nicely done.'

'Let me have a look,' said Archie. 'Well: the front cover is all right, isn't it? *Life In The Old Girl Yet: Four Older Women Tell Us About Their Obsessions*. Nothing wrong with that, Pen!'

'Not if you don't mind being called an old girl and an older woman,' I said miserably.

'Just a turn of phrase, Penny,' soothed Maureen. 'They have to sell the magazine, don't they!'

'And the picture is *very* nice,' went on Archie, flicking through the pages. 'I've always thought blue suits you well.

325

And the mixing bowl matches your eyes!'

'Don't take the piss!' I said. But I was beginning to laugh. I had to admit, it was quite funny. And quite a relief not to be served up as some kind of ancient dominatrix beating men with a wooden spoon, after all.

'Have you read the article?' Archie added, scanning it quickly and beginning to look quite excited.

'Yes. It's just more piss-taking.'

'Well, it might be a bit tongue-in-cheek, but it's very good. It describes quite openly how this all came about because you went on the radio to try and promote the bypass, and ended up talking about your pudding. I know it makes a funny story, but at least it's getting the facts across. Look at the little box at the bottom – it actually gives details of the PPPP, how long they've been pressing for a bypass, and how long the Council's been promising to look into it! Honestly, Penny, there's no way Roger could ever have got such good publicity.'

'I suppose so. But all the stuff about the pudding ...'

'It's brilliant! It's going to make a lot of people laugh, yes – all these silly little sniggers about how it's supposed to make people passionate, and how you won't reveal the secret ingredients – and I specially like all the stuff about how the pudding's improved our sex life, Pen! But when they've finished laughing, how many people are going to wonder whether there's actually something in it? How many people are going to try and get hold of the recipe, or a piece of the pudding for themselves?'

'Well, they won't be able to, will they – so hopefully that'll be the end of it.'

'Don't be so sure,' he said. 'Penny, I think one day we're going to look back on this day and thank Fantasia Topping and her crew of nutcases for giving us just the break we needed.'

'And *I* think you've gone slightly off your head,' I retorted. 'And I think it's time I put the chicken in the oven.'

*

It didn't take long for word to get around that the magazine was due out, and by the Thursday, the day it hit the newsagents, all the staff of Tail Waggers' and apparently half the population of Panbridge Park who owned cats, dogs, rabbits, guinea pigs or pet spiders had got hold of it. People came in through the doors waving their copies of *Woman Today*, telling me what a good picture it was of me before they'd even told me what was wrong with their animal. I wasn't sure whether I was flattered that everyone thought it was a good picture. In one way it was reassuring. In another way, it was a bit of a bummer that all these years I'd taken time and trouble over my appearance, having my hair done, buying nice clothes, looking after myself – when all I needed to do all along, apparently, was dress up in some ridiculous gear out of someone's fancy dress box, hold a pudding basin and a wooden spoon and I was sorted.

The only person who didn't say anything complimentary was Chris. He did, however, give me a quick smile and comment: 'That wasn't what I wanted you to do with the chair,' before walking quickly away. I was pleased, really, because for one thing it made me think that perhaps we were getting back onto a normal friendly footing again, and for another thing it didn't make me feel remotely excited or turned on. Thank God: I was cured.

The other interesting thing was that lots of people had obviously taken the trouble to read the article properly. Even during the first few days, I lost count of how many people commented on the piece in the magazine about how long the PPPP had been fighting for the bypass, and how often the council had promised to look into it. Mrs Boggins with the vicious tomcat who terrorised the neighbourhood said she'd write to them, threatening to sue them for breach of promise. Mr Aston, whose children's pet mouse had fallen into the fish tank and had a near-death experience floating on the back of a startled guppy, said he was going to visit the Council offices and ask them what they were playing at. It was heart-warming, the support I suddenly seemed to have generated. And for every person who talked to me about the bypass, at least another two or three were asking about the pudding.

'It's just a plain old bread pudding!' I tried to tell the first few, but eventually I realised it was just a waste of time – they weren't having it.

'Yeah, right – don't give us that, Penny!' leered old John Carter who regularly brought his budgie in to have its beak trimmed. 'It says quite plainly in the magazine that you put some *special ingredients* in it, to make you sexy. Come on, don't be mean – tell us what the ingredients are, there's a good girl. I want to get my Doreen to make me some!'

I was tempted to tell him to stop letching over women's magazines and get himself some Viagra, but it probably wasn't worth the unpleasant experience of having to watch his reaction.

By the day of the TV programme, I'd got used to being a minor celebrity again in Panbridge Park.

'Couldn't be better timing, Penny!' exclaimed Darren Barlow on the phone, the night before the show. 'I've been plugging the show *shamelessly* on the radio all week, and they've given it a mention in the *Echo* as well. Your name's being bandied around town already because of the magazine article – which, if you don't mind me saying so, was a brilliant piece of gentle satire. And the photo! Such wit! Such irony! Such—'

'Oh, shut up, Darren. A picture of someone looking daft in an apron holding a mixing bowl isn't witty.'

'Ah, but Penny, you're not seeing the *facetiousness* of it, the *playfulness*, the ...'

'The piss taking. Yes, thank you, I'm well aware that I'm being mocked. It serves me right for taking myself too seriously. I'm getting over it. Just don't keep on about it, and *please* don't mention the mixing bowl on the show.'

'Fair enough, Penny. Whatever you say, my darling.

You know how very grateful I am to you for agreeing to this. I'll be forever in your debt.'

'All right, all right, no need to be ridiculous. What time are we kicking off?'

'I'll pick you up about four, sweetheart, and drive you to the studios. Don't worry. Just be yourself. Wear something alluring but not revealing. You're good at that.'

Are we talking blue frocks and white aprons here, or what?

When people ask me now what I remember about that TV show, I have to admit that it was all a bit of a blur. Think about how nervous I was on the radio, and multiply that by a hundred, and you'll begin to have an idea of my state of mind that day. I have trouble even remembering what I was wearing, until I watch the video Michelle made, and cringe when I see myself sitting on the cream leather sofa at the TV studio in Norwich, looking like an air hostess in my dark green suit and white blouse, grinning maniacally at Darren, crossing and uncrossing my legs as if I had a fly crawling on my knees or an itch somewhere very embarrassing. I try, on the whole, not to watch this video. Archie thinks we should keep it forever because it marked a turning point in our lives. I think we should dump it because it makes me look a prat.

Darren, for once, *doesn't* look a prat in the video. He's ditched the silly T-shirts in favour of an open-necked casual blue shirt with beige trousers. He's not even wearing a baseball cap, and his hair's grown back, a kind of pale rusty shade that might be his natural colour. He looks almost normal.

'Hello, Penny,' he says after he's introduced me to the world (or at least, that part of the population of East Anglia with the time and inclination to watch a silly regional chat show programme). 'Welcome to the show – and let me be the first to congratulate you on the very nice article about you in a national glossy women's magazine this week!'

It isn't glossy. It's cheap and really quite nasty, and everyone knows it.

Then you see me stammering a hello and a thank-you, crossing and uncrossing my legs, fingering the buttons of my jacket, stroking my hair, eyeing the camera nervously and having a cough.

'Penny,' says Darren then, fixing me with a serious *I'm very interested in you* look that is so unlike him, it makes me want to giggle. 'You've already attracted a lot of attention locally because of a certain pudding recipe.' Well, that's got that out of the way, anyway. 'But making puddings isn't all you're interested in, of course, is it?' He says this with a condescending smile like it's doubtful I should be allowed out of the kitchen. 'You're also, I understand, a strong believer in the need for a bypass for Panbridge Park. Tell us a little bit about the background to this, Penny.'

He sits back and looks straight into my eyes. This is the moment when he must be thinking that I can either make his career, or wreck it. You can see me, in the video, take a sharp breath as if my chest is hurting. Here goes.

Considering everything, I think I give the PPPP a very good press. I describe how we set up the group, and why, and what we'd done to try to convince the council about the bypass. I talk about how many times we'd been promised it would be given consideration. How many times we'd been told it had been on an agenda at a meeting of some committee or other, only to be passed over for lack of time, or lack of funds, or lack of interest.

Look at me in the video. I look like a real politician now I've got into my stride and lost the squeaky nervous voice I started off in. I'm giving it this sincere, caring, expression that would have had Maggie Thatcher eating her heart out. When Darren asks me why I'm not a member of the PPPP any more, I trot out the reply we discussed on the journey up to Norwich.

'I wanted to do my own publicity. As you saw in the

330

magazine article, it's perhaps not the average run-of-the-mill publicity you'd expect for a bypass campaign – but I think it works. I think anything that draws our cause to the attention of the public, and ultimately the council, is worth doing.'

I'm proud of that speech. Darren probably should be, too, as it was him that wrote it, and rehearsed it with me on the car journey till I was almost word perfect. But it gets better. Look at me now: I'm dropping my gaze as if I'm about to cry. Now, this is embarrassing. I'm not much of an actress.

'But let's not forget the serious issues here, Darren,' I'm saying in my Maggie Thatcher voice. 'Let's remember that the Panbridge Road, through Panbridge Park, is an accident black spot. There have been twenty-four fatalities during the last five years, from accidents along the stretch of road between the Potts Hill turn-off in the north, and the Safeway roundabout in the south. Twenty-four people killed, Darren, mostly pedestrians – eleven of them children – and many more seriously injured, of course. What we're saying is that those accidents were avoidable. Those people should not have been injured. Those children shouldn't have died. The traffic that killed them should have been taken out of the Panbridge Road, away from the local shops, the local schools and the housing estate where they were living. Let's do it now, before more children are killed!'

Darren's nodding at me sympathetically.

'Absolutely, Penny – absolutely. Well, if anyone from the county council is watching this programme – I'm Darren Barlow and I'm bringing you Penny Peacham today, Penny Peacham from Panbridge Park who's been telling us all about the need for a bypass there. Come on, what's the hold-up, guys? Is there a *reason* why these people are still waiting for their bypass, still waiting for their children to stop being killed on that busy road? Or is it just a matter of mindless bureaucracy?'

331

The camera zooms in to show Darren's grave, concerned expression. There's a pause, and then we break for commercials. Because Michelle wasn't sure about working the video, and didn't want to risk pausing it in case she couldn't start it again, we then get five minutes of hard sell for the latest Vauxhall, for vegetable oil spread that tastes so much like butter it makes cows dance and sing, for toilet paper so soft it makes people hold it up to their faces and swoon with joy, and for holidays to Greece where young couples walk hand-in-hand on a beach in the moonlight wearing white flowing robes like something out of a religious order.

After the break, we get another close-up shot of this new, serious-minded, blue-shirted Darren Barlow, talking in his new sensible voice, welcoming us back and telling us that the wonderful Penny Peacham is still here with us (camera swings to show me, unprepared, shuffling in my seat, trying to smooth down my skirt and showing too much leg in the process), and that Penny is now going to tell us all about the pudding that's caused such a stir (he laughs at this very obvious pun and makes a gesture of stirring a pudding, which still makes me cringe even now I've watched it so many times). Then I'm on camera again, close up, full face, terrified.

I'd already decided what I was going to say about the pudding. I was going to follow the same line as the magazine article, and tell the true story about how everyone got to hear about it on the radio show. I even managed to make it sound funny. This is one part of the video I don't feel too horrified at watching. I like the way I'm shown joking with Darren about how he let the callers on the first radio show manipulate me into talking about the pudding instead of the bypass. I even joke about how cross I was with him and how I'd never have believed I'd ever appear on a radio show with him again, never mind TV.

'So – come on Penny! Tell us about the pudding,' says Darren. 'You do realise, don't you, that all over the region right now, everyone has got their pens and paper ready to write down the recipe!'

'Sorry, Darren,' I say, and you can almost see me squirming with embarrassment, 'but it's a secret, an old family recipe handed down through the generations. I promised my grandmother never to reveal the ingredients ... '

Listening to all this crap now, I almost hate Darren for suggesting I come out with it. And all the inevitable stuff that followed, about whether or not any of the ingredients had special hormonal effects and anti-ageing properties. I'd drawn the line at telling outright lies, but I did a lot of smiling and smirking and agreeing that people had told me the pudding seemed to have helped their love lives.

'Well, Penny,' he said finally, when I was beginning to feel like the smile was hurting my face, 'It's been an absolute pleasure talking to you; *very* interesting to hear about the good fight you're putting up for a bypass for Panbridge Park – I think you've convinced us all here in the studios, at least, that it's *got* to happen; and *fascinating* to talk to you about your amazing Passion Pudding. I'm sure we'll hear more from you in the future, Penny Peacham – thank you again for joining us here today on *East This Week*.'

This is followed, on our video, by another five minutes of adverts and then twenty minutes of *Emmerdale* before Michelle remembered to stop it recording.

'I think I prefer the adverts,' I told Archie, the first time I watched it. 'It's a close thing whether I even prefer *Emmerdale*.'

'Nobody likes watching themselves,' he soothed me. 'Even on holiday videos, even in photos, you know it's true. But if you want *my* opinion, Pen ... '

Did I?

'You were brilliant! And didn't Darren say the same thing to you?'

'Yes, well. He's just chuffed that he's got his big break in television. I could have sat there the whole time reciting

333

a nursery rhyme and picking my nose and it would still have been brilliant for *him*.'

'Hmm. Well, if it's *that* easy, I think I'll give him a ring and ask to be on his next show!'

'You don't know any nursery rhymes!' I laughed.

'I'll get Jessica to teach me one,' he said – then he stopped short, and bit his lip. Adam still hadn't brought Jessica round.

Still, Archie was right about the TV show being a turning point in our lives.

Four days later, Roger from PPPP phoned me. He was obviously so pained to have to speak to me, it sounded as though something nasty had crawled into his trousers and was gnawing his bum. He'd heard from the county council; the bypass was due to be discussed by the planning committee three weeks later and, unofficially, he'd been told there was no way this time it was going to be dropped from the agenda – and there was a very good chance of it being approved.

Three days after that, we had a phone call from Darling Desserts, a Norfolk-based company producing locally inspired cakes and puddings. They wanted to buy the recipe for Passion Pudding, and market it under my name. And they were offering a lot of money.

Michelle

It might have worked for Nicole, but that whole thing of putting off having sex wasn't for me. It was absolutely fantastic with Fraser. I suppose, looking back, it had only been about three months since I last did it, with Robbie on the kitchen floor on top of the dirty washing, but it was so much better with Fraser, it almost felt like up till I met him I must have been doing it wrong. We couldn't get enough of it. We could hardly keep our hands off each other. Sometimes, at work, we had to try not to be too close together or it would have been terrible, we'd have been jumping over patients to get on top of each other – and you just can't have that sort of thing going on in an outpatient department, really, especially with elderly patients and the possibility of cardiac arrests.

Luckily, Fraser had hospital accommodation, and when he wasn't on call, I used to stay over in his room. I thought Mum and Dad would be pleased to have a bit more space at home, what with Maureen staying there and the fuchsias still not ready to go outside – but Mum made a bit of a fuss about whether I was rushing things.

'I'm *not* rushing,' I told her. 'It's not like we're getting married, or anything.'

I must admit, though, that the thought of getting married had begun to cross my mind. It never had before. But then, had I ever really been in love before?

*

335

On Valentine's Day, which was a Saturday, Fraser had made sure he wasn't on call, and we went out for the day. He drove me to Cambridge; we strolled around the city, had a pub lunch and then went on a punt down the river. It was so romantic, snuggled together in the back of the punt with a blanket over our knees.

'I want it to go on for ever,' I said with a sigh.

'The punt ride?' said Fraser softly, pulling me closer to him so that our faces were touching. 'Or ... us?'

'Both.'

'We ...ell,' he began, shaking his head doubtfully. 'Forever is a long time ... '

I felt my heart sink. I shouldn't have said that, should I; people say you shouldn't start talking to men about things like 'forever' – it frightens them off. Maybe he didn't really love me after all. Maybe he was getting fed up with me already. Maybe ...

'The punt would start to rot after a few years,' he went on, smiling at me, 'And the poor punter would get a back-ache.'

'But what about *us*?' I said in a whisper.

'Us? Oh, I don't see us rotting. Or getting backache. I think there's a pretty good chance of us going on forever.'

'Really?'

He didn't bother to answer. He just kissed me. The punter, who'd been describing the Bridge of Sighs as we passed under it, saying it was even better than the Bridge of Sighs in Venice, looked at us and shut up, in mid sentence. I suppose he thought he was wasting his breath.

And like the kiss on the beach, it was a kiss I was never going to forget. Ever.

We didn't hear from Adam until the end of February. By then, lots of things had happened. The county council had approved the bypass, and announced that work was going to start on it during the spring of the next year.

Mum had signed contracts with Darling Desserts, who

336

were going to manufacture her special version of bread pudding under the name Penny's Passion Pudding and call it a Norfolk speciality, even though we lived in Suffolk. She was earning so much money out of this deal, she was going to retire from Tail Waggers and concentrate on entering her fuchsias for shows, and also spend time experimenting with other recipes to market under the Penny label. Apparently Darling Desserts had suggested Penny's Lustful Lemon Pie, but she had doubts about it and was working on Penny's Fruity Fruit Cake. She said she was more at home with fruit cake, really, although I had a feeling it wouldn't be long before we saw her branching out into lustful lemons and randy raspberries and God know's what else, and bloody good luck to her.

Dad said he would spend a bit less time working on people's toilets and ceilings, so that he could look after the *business*, as he called Mum's pudding deals. He said he'd been looking for a new interest since he retired, and had realised he preferred doing accounts and promotions to tiling and plumbing, so he became a sort of agent for Mum, taking all the phone calls from nutty people who wanted to tell her about their sex lives or ask what the ingredients were, and answering the letters from other nutty people who wrote to thank her for saving their marriages or making them irresistible to the opposite sex. Sometimes I heard them laughing together over a particularly funny letter, or listened to them getting excited about their plans for the future – holidays they hadn't been able to afford before, meals in nice restaurants, even one day perhaps a new house in one of the villages along the coast – and I thought: Well, bugger me. I never realised before, but Mum and Dad are actually quite happy together.

Maureen dropped a bombshell just after Valentine's Day. Apparently she'd be moving out the following week – not to rent a little flat of her own, which we'd all been expecting, but to move in with someone called Sidney from the

337

crematorium. They'd worked together for nearly ten years but it wasn't till she split up with Tony that Sid plucked up the courage to tell her he'd been secretly in love with her the whole time. He took her out to dinner on Valentine's night and apparently that was it. I don't know what he gave her to eat (she joked with everyone that it was actually the Passion Pudding she'd had the night before), but within hours she'd agreed to move in with him. Mum was worried, needless to say, that she was being very hasty and might live to regret it, but Maureen just looked her in the eye and said:

'Penny, I've known Sidney for ten years – how can that be hasty?'

Even Mum had to admit this was true, and she was better off with him than with bloody Tony. I thought it was all quite romantic, really, and surprising to see how Maureen looked all soft and fluttery when Sidney was around. Dad just thought it was good that someone was taking her off his hands and he was getting his favourite armchair back.

Fraser and I started looking for a place of our own. There were some nice new flats only about a ten-minute walk from the hospital, which we could just about afford. Of course, once I became a nurse I'd be earning a lot more money, but I had all the training to go through yet, so we didn't want to overstretch ourselves.

'One day,' said Fraser, 'I'll be a consultant, and you'll be a staff nurse, and we'll be able to afford a big house in the country, and have two dogs, and the kids will go to a good school, and— '

'Kids?' I said in a sort of a shriek.

'You do want kids, don't you?'

'Yes!' I hadn't realised it before, but I did. Yes, I did! 'But I don't think I'd be very good at it. I'm useless with Jessica . . . not that we ever see her now.'

'No you're not. You're great with her. That was one of the things I first loved about you – that time you drove her

338

all the way to the beach to try and stop her crying! It was crazy – and sweet, and special. I think I fell in love with you on the spot.'

Blimey. If I'd known, I'd have worn better pyjamas.

Adam phoned on a Friday night, the last week in February.

'Thought you'd left the country,' I said.

'Not quite. Been to the other end of it, though. I'll tell you when I come round.'

'You're coming round? Great! Are you bringing Jessica? I'll tell Mum!'

I know what you're thinking. After two months, he just phones up and says he's coming round? Shouldn't I have been angry? He'd upset Mum, and kept her from seeing her only grandchild, who was probably by now learning to drive, reading Dickens and playing the clarinet. Shouldn't there have been some sort of an apology? Or at least some kind of discussion about it – not just 'I'm coming round'.

But you've heard the story of the Prodigal Son, haven't you. When it happens in your family, you don't care about all the apology bollocks – you just want everyone back together, on speaking terms again, never mind what's gone before. So Mum didn't exactly kill the fatted calf, but she did cook Adam's favourite shepherd's pie, and Jessica's favourite sausages, and she did make one of her brand-new Fruity Fruit Cakes.

And then Adam arrived, with a bottle of something for Dad, and a big bunch of flowers for Mum, and a box of chocolates for me, and Jessica dressed in her nicest little pink cord jeans and white jumper, looking very cute and very excited to see us all. And Killer.

I was completely speechless when I opened the door and saw him standing behind Adam. I couldn't even manage *What the fuck?*

'I've brought Julian with me,' said Adam unnecessarily. 'He wants to talk to you, Chelle. How you doing, anyway?'

He bent down to kiss me but I shook him off, which was

339

a shame really considering this was meant to be a family reunion and everything.

'Where did you find *him*?' I demanded. 'And who says I want to talk to him? Does he know the police are looking for him? He stole my bloody car, Adam!'

'He didn't, actually. We'll explain, Chelle, if you'll just let us come in.'

I stood back, holding the door open, watching resentfully as my brother, who'd stayed away from us for nearly two months, allowed a car thief and potential murderer into our house.

Jessica had already been picked up and cuddled and kissed and was now playing happily with some of the toys Mum kept for her. Mum and Dad hugged Adam and said how good it was to see him again and everyone kept very clear of the subject of looking after Jessica and the row we'd had after Christmas. Meanwhile Killer kind of sloped into the corner of the room and sat on his own, looking at the floor, and I sat opposite him, glaring at him.

'Well,' said Mum eventually, 'I think what we all need is a nice cup of tea, don't you, everyone? Is it one sugar or two, Killer, dear?'

'Do the police know you're here?' I growled at him as soon as Mum had gone out of the room.

'It's OK, Chelle,' said Adam quickly. 'We've talked to the police. We've told them it's all a misunderstanding. They'll be phoning you in the morning to make sure you're happy for them to drop the case.'

'Drop the case? What do you mean, misunderstanding? How can you misunderstand seeing him driving up the Panbridge Road in my car? Why are you trying to defend him?'

'Because he didn't steal your car. He found it.'

'Oh, yeah, right! Is that what he told you?'

'No. It's what *I* told *him* to do. Didn't I, *Julian*?'

'Yeah,' said Killer, barely raising his eyes from the

340

floor. He was obviously still terrified of Adam. He was pathetic. I couldn't believe I was ever frightened of him.

'I've been trying to help you, Chelle,' said Adam, with a huge sigh.

'Help me? What, by letting violent criminals use my car?'

'Just *listen* for a minute! I wanted to find your car for you. But I couldn't do it on my own. It was bad enough finding time for ... everything else ... getting Jessica looked after, trying to hold down my job. So I told Julian it might be a nice way for him to show you he was sorry for the way he frightened you and made threats to you. A nice way for him to avoid the police being told about all that stuff.'

'Yeah. Like, sorry about that, Michelle,' muttered Killer without looking at me.

'We had a ... suspicion ... a lead, if you like, about where the car might be. So Julian went off for a week or so and tracked it down. He did well. But basically, he's a prat.' He shot a look at Killer, who flinched as if he'd been struck. 'I told him to keep in touch with me and let me know when he found it, but of course, he didn't bother. I was beginning to think he'd buggered off. Then I saw him driving it down the Panbridge Road.'

'I was on my way home with it! I'd just found it the day before!' protested Killer.

'Yes, OK, but did I have much of a reason to trust you?' shot back Adam.

'You could have told Michelle not to go to the police, though,' he whined, shuffling his feet.

'Don't be bloody stupid! *You* should have told *me* you were driving with no insurance and no fucking licence!' Adam looked at me, shaking his head. 'Fucking idiot panicked when the police turned up at his mum's place, did a runner and dumped the car in Ipswich.'

'No thanks to you that I got it back at all, then,' I told Killer angrily. 'So much for helping!'

'No; but he *did* help,' said Adam grudgingly. 'He did find it in the first place.'

'Where?' I asked. 'Where did he find it? And what was all this *lead* business about? Why did you have suspicions about it? You're making yourself sound like some sort of bloody Sherlock Holmes.'

'He found it in Liverpool.'

'Liverpool? How did you guess *that*? Why Liverpool? Who stole it? Who took it there?'

'Don't you know?' Adam looked at me, shaking his head as if I was stupid. 'You were right in the first place. Robbie Nelson. He made it easy for us by nicking the car. If we found the car, we'd find him. If we found him, we'd find the car.'

'Robbie. Yeah. Of course.' I sat up, suddenly realising what I was saying. 'So ... are you telling me you know where he is? Did you find him? Is he in Liverpool?'

'No. He's sitting outside in my car, Chelle, waiting to talk to you.'

He was stretched out on the back seat, his feet in Jessica's car seat, headphones on, listening to music. He looked as if he didn't have a care in the world.

'Michelle! You're looking great!'

'Shut up! You bastard!'

'Come on, babe!' He sat up quickly, dropping the head-phones on the floor. 'We need to talk ...'

'I'm *not* your *babe*. And the only thing I have to say to you is—'

'Let me explain. Please, I can explain ...'

I looked around me. I'd stormed out of the house leaving the front door wide open. Adam was standing at the door, holding Jessica back, watching me. At the lounge window, Mum and Dad were both peeking round the curtain, Mum's mouth a huge 'O' of surprise and worry.

'Not here,' I said curtly. 'Get out. We'll walk.'

He ran to follow me down the street. I was walking so fast, he had trouble catching me up.

'Don't just run off,' he called after me.

342

'That's great, coming from you!'

'If you'll just let me explain!'

At the corner of the road I turned into the park entrance. It was a cold evening. We'd had snow again earlier in the week, and although it'd stopped now the wind was whipping through the trees with a horrible noise like someone crying very badly. I was only wearing jeans and a thin sweatshirt. I sat down on the first bench we came to, hugging myself for warmth, shaking with cold, shock and anger.

'Well?' I demanded as he sat down next to me. I couldn't look at him. 'Make it quick. I'm freezing.'

'We should have gone indoors ...'

'No, we shouldn't! I don't want you in my house. I don't want you anywhere near me, or my family, ever again.'

'I can understand how you feel ...'

'No you can't. If you understood me, even one little tiny bit, you'd never have walked out on me like that, in the middle of a pub lunch, without even a word, without even leaving a note, without even phoning, or anything.'

'I didn't. I didn't walk out on you.'

'Oh, I see,' I said sarcastically. 'You didn't walk out. What, you were abducted by aliens, were you?'

'Yes.'

I snorted. It wasn't very attractive. I was so cold, the snort actually made my nose run, and I had nothing to wipe it with.

'I know you're going to find this hard to believe, Michelle, but ...'

'You're telling me that while I was in the Ladies, while you were sitting there in the pub waiting for your chicken roll, you were abducted.'

'Not while I was in the pub. When I went outside to the car to get my cigarettes.'

'You went out to the car, and you were abducted by aliens.'

'Not exactly aliens, no. Although they might just as well have been. I was abducted by my family.'

*

343

It took a bit of believing. It took so much believing, to be honest, that by the time he'd finished telling me, I'd gone through being cold, being completely frozen and numb, and was starting to warm up again.

Once I started to believe him, I could almost have felt sorry for him until I heard the rest of the story. His family had been trying to track him down, apparently, ever since he walked out when he was a teenager. There had been some terrible family row, and he'd never forgiven his mum and dad for some of the things they'd said. This made me shudder a bit, thinking of the row I'd had with Adam and how, in some families, it might have caused a rift that could have gone on forever. Anyway, lots of things had happened since he'd left: his brother had got married, his sister had had a baby, and now his mum was very ill, and she was asking for him. So they made a really determined effort to find him, and I suppose, if people are determined enough, they can find anyone eventually. His brother and his uncle came down from Liverpool and drove around, looking for him. They knew the area we lived in but not the address. They saw him by chance that day, outside the pub, just as he'd grabbed his fags out of the car and locked the door, just as he was coming back in for his chicken roll. They didn't want to waste time talking to him, arguing with him – they bundled him into their car like something out of a gangster movie and drove off with him shouting and hollering all the way up to Liverpool.

'When we got there, when I saw my mum looking so poorly, I felt different about it,' he said. 'I thought then – they've done the right thing. I was glad they'd done it because I'd never have gone home voluntarily.'

'Fair enough,' I said. I'm not unreasonable. I'm not about to deny his mum the chance to see her son. And I didn't really like to ask, but: 'And did your mum ...? Is she OK?'

'She's fine. It was chickenpox.'

'*Chickenpox*! That's a *children's* illness! I thought you

said she was very ill!'

'She was! Aren't you supposed to be a health care assistant? Don't you know how bad chickenpox can be for an adult? She was terrible! We were all worried sick!'

'But she recovered,' I said levelly, trying not to lose my temper. 'And you still didn't bother to come home. Or to even phone me, or anything, to let me know where you were. Where you'd been *abducted* to. You just left me to carry on, on my own, with all the worry of the rent, and the bills, and no washing machine, and everyone in Panbridge Park screaming for money you owed them, and Killer threatening to murder me. You *knew* you owed all these people money, Robbie, and you never said a word to me, and you just decided to stay up there in Liverpool and let me get on with it all!'

'No. It wasn't like that. It wasn't because of the money. All right, I admit it. You *know* how useless I am with money; I didn't realise it had all got so out of hand. I was, like, in denial, hoping it would all go away. I didn't realise people were going to come after *you*, Michelle – I didn't think Killer was that bloody stupid and ignorant ...'

'You didn't think, full stop. Well, to be honest, Robbie, you did me a favour, because if you hadn't disappeared like that I might never have realised what a complete prick you are.'

He hung his head.

'Sorry, Michelle.'

'*Sorry*'s not bloody good enough. What about my car? You stole my bloody car! You came all the way back from Liverpool, stole my car, and took it back with you? I can't believe you did that!'

'I didn't. Well, OK, I did – but not intentionally. I was coming home. Honestly – I'd made up my mind to come home. I didn't know you'd moved out of the flat. I went round there, and these two girls were living there, and they told me you'd gone back to your parents'. When I got to your parents' house, I stood outside for two hours trying to

345

pluck up the courage to knock. I started thinking about what you must have gone through, having to give up the flat and everything ... '

'Oh! Fine time to start thinking about it!'

'And I was thinking about your mum and dad, and how they must have hated me, and how I didn't deserve to come back to you. So I changed my mind.'

'You what? You changed your mind, so you nicked my car, and drove back to Liverpool?'

'It was my car too, Michelle.'

'I bloody *paid* for it! You borrowed money from Killer, told him it was for the car, but it bloody wasn't! *I* paid for it!'

'Yeah, I think I kind of forgot that.'

'Very conveniently,' I sniffed. 'So why didn't you come straight back when your mum recovered from her chicken-pox, then, if it wasn't because you owed half of Panbridge Park money? Your brother and your uncle kept you locked up in your room, did they?'

'Of course not. We spent a couple of weeks catching up with each other, you know – building a few bridges. It was good. I feel like I've got my family back again.'

'Well, I'm very pleased for you, I'm sure.'

'And then I fell in love.'

Everything went so quiet; even the wind seemed to stop howling. The only thing I could hear was this weird kind of beating in my ears, like a heartbeat. Can your heart beat in your ears? Even as I listened to it, I was fascinated, you know, from the medical point of view. Was I going to faint?

'Michelle? Michelle, are you all right? Did you hear me? I said, I fell— '

'Yes! Yes, I fucking heard you!' Ouch, that was loud. I even made myself flinch. 'Let me get this straight, Robbie. You got abducted from outside the pub when you went to get your fags, you got driven up to Liverpool where your mum was calling out to you from her sickbed, and you didn't get in touch with me or try to come back afterwards until the day you changed your mind and nicked the car instead – because you'd *fallen in love*?' I spat the words out so viciously, he actually moved back from me along the bench. 'Fallen in love with *who*? With *whom*?'

'My second cousin. Sherry. We hadn't seen each other since I was sixteen and she was fourteen. We'd both grown up, you know, and ...'

'Well, how *very* romantic. How absolutely lovely for you both. I hope you'll both be very happy together!' I tried to stand up, but I seemed to have frozen to the spot.

'No! Listen! It's not like that! It didn't last!'

'Oh! Oh, I see! So, first you fell *into* love, and then you fell *out* of love – in the space of ... what? How many weeks?'

'I don't know.' He shrugged, looking very sheepish. 'About four or five, I suppose.'

'That's not *love*, Robbie!' I snapped. 'That's a fling!'

'No! It was deep and meaningful.'

'Yeah, right. I suppose you shagged her ...'

'We had a deep and meaningful sexual relationship ...'

'Of course!'

'And she got pregnant.'

I'd found it almost funny up till then. Almost laughable to think how this guy, that I actually used to think was possibly the love of my life, had turned out to be such a jerk.

'You're not just a stupid jerk, are you?' I said now, suddenly wishing I still smoked. I wanted a cigarette for the first time since I gave up when I was twenty-one. 'You're actually quite a nasty little turd.'

'Don't be like that, Michelle ...'

'You've got this poor girl pregnant, and walked out on her, haven't you. *That* was the only reason you decided to try and come back to me.'

'No! I wanted to come back ... I missed you. But I told you: I couldn't face you. I didn't know if you'd forgive me.'

347

'You were frightened to tell me, more like. You're pathetic, Robbie. I'm glad I've found out what happened. I would always have wondered. Now piss off back to Liverpool and stand by your poor cousin and her baby.'

'She doesn't want me. She says she never wants to see me again and she'll stop me having any access to the baby on the grounds that I deserted her. The bitch!'

'Good for her. Piss off back to Liverpool anyway.'

'Oh, come on, Michelle – I've made the effort to come round and see you, talk it over, try and patch things up . . .'

'What? Are you joking? Patch things up? Did you *really* think I'd want to patch anything up with you after all that?'

'I'll be different. I'll change. I'll look after you. I'll get a good job and we'll get a nice flat. Maybe even a house. We'll get a mortgage. Come on – we'll work it all out, babe.'

'I'm *not* your babe,' I said coldly. 'And there's nothing to work out. You're too late. You might *think* you fell in love, Robbie – but I really *did*. I'm in love with a lovely, lovely man. He's going to be a brilliant consultant, and I'm going to be a staff nurse, and we're going to have our own house, and lots of children, and dogs . . .'

I watched Robbie's mouth drop open in surprise, and I nearly laughed. But part of me wanted to cry.

'And my mum and dad are going to be rich,' I went on, for good measure. 'And they're going to have fantastic holidays every year and buy a big house in the country, by the sea, and Jessica's going to have loads of lovely clothes and toys.'

Shit. I *was* crying. Why? Why was I crying, when I had everything I wanted now, and Robbie was so definitely what I *didn't* want?

'Chelle,' said a voice behind me. 'Chelle, are you OK? You must be frozen. We were all getting worried. I've been looking for you everywhere.'

'I'm OK, Adam,' I said, wiping my nose on the hanky he

was handing out to me. 'I'm coming home now. Robbie's just going.'

'How did you know he was in Liverpool?' I asked Adam eventually, when he'd taken me home, sat me in front of the fire, and Mum had wrapped me in two thick jumpers, put my slippers on my frozen feet for me and made me a cup of hot chocolate. 'How long did it take you to find him?'

'What did you think I was doing, all those weekends I left Jessica with Mum and Dad?' he replied, smiling. Making me feel like a complete cow. 'Did you *really* think I was away having it off with some bird? You silly girl. I was travelling the length and breadth of the country looking for your bloody ex-boyfriend. Perhaps I shouldn't have bothered.'

He nearly fell off his chair when I jumped up, ran at him and kissed him.

'Oh, *Adam!* Why didn't you say?'

'Come off it. You'd have told me not to bother. But it was something I had to do, Chelle. At first, I wanted to drag him back here and make him sort things out with you. Or perhaps just give him a good smacking, for the way he'd messed you about. But once I realised you'd got over him, well, I still thought he at least owed you an explanation.'

'Yes.' Crackpot stupid explanation though it was. 'At least I don't have to go through life wondering what happened to him.'

'You'd better warn Fraser, though.'

'Warn him what?'

'Just what he'll have to deal with if he ever walks out on you. Or gets abducted by aliens, or whatever!'

'Don't worry,' I said. 'I've met his family, Adam, and they're really nice. Not the type of people to wait till someone gets chickenpox and then bundle him into a car and drive off with him.'

'Just as well,' said Adam. 'Or I'd set Killer on them.'

It wasn't really funny. But for some reason we both found this absolutely hilarious. We laughed so much we set Jessica off in hysterics and made Mum cross.

'Now look what you've made me do,' she complained when she'd eventually calmed us all down. 'I've burnt the bloody Fruity Fruit Cake in the bloody oven!'

Might have known it would all be my fault.

Penny

10 September 2005

It's funny, but a cruise was never something I fancied doing before. Well, to be honest, I suppose I never really considered it because we couldn't have afforded it, whether I fancied it or not. Everything's different now. We're not exactly rich but we're certainly a lot more comfortably off, thanks to Darling Desserts.

We're all packed, and I'm just waiting for Archie to put the Jag away in the garage. We were going to drive down to Dover, but then Michelle came round and said she'd drive us there instead. Give us a chance to have a chat on the way, and say our goodbyes. We'll be gone for three weeks. We'll be going to Portugal, Madeira, Morocco and the Canary Islands. It looked lovely in the brochure.

Last summer, before we moved into the new house, we all went on holiday together: Archie and I, Michelle and Fraser, Adam and Jessica and Adam's girlfriend Carly. We took them all to Florida for two weeks. It was lovely, all being together, taking Jessica to all the Disney attractions and watching her enjoying herself. She was a bit young really, but we'll do it all again in a few years' time when she can appreciate it more.

It's different this year, of course, with two babies on the way, and both of them due about Christmas time. Jessica's so excited about having a new baby brother *and* a cousin.

It's all she talks about. I said to Archie – if we're going on holiday this year, it'll have to be soon. I don't want either of those babies coming early and us not being there. So he booked the cruise, and yes, I'm looking forward to it now. Seeing all those lovely places – whoever would have thought we'd be doing it?

'Are you ready, Archie? Should we be getting going, do you think? Or have we got time for a cup of tea? OK, I'll get the kettle on.'

Michelle

I'll just put the TV on for five minutes while Mum's fussing about in the kitchen making a cup of tea. She can't bear to go more than half an hour without one. I hope they supply plenty of tea on that cruise.

I get a bit tired now – you know how it is. The baby keeps me awake at night – he always gets more active as soon as I lie down. I don't want to take more time off from college than I have to, so I'm going to carry on till just before the baby's due in December. Carly and I are going the share the child-minding afterwards. It's worked out perfectly. I can't believe my brother has finally found someone as lovely as Carly. What took him so long?

'Mum – have you made your tea? Come and sit down and watch this before we go – it's the *Darren Barlow Show*. Don't you normally watch it? I'd have thought you'd like to have a laugh at whoever he's humiliating on his show. No – I didn't mean that! He didn't humiliate you, did he. You were his first! You gave him his big break! I always thought he secretly had the hots for you, Mum.

'Come on, come and watch this! He's got Robin Donovan on today!'

The celebrity chef. All the women go mad for him. I suppose he's not bad looking, and let's face it, everyone loves a man who can knock up a superb three-course meal without burning all the pans and turning the kitchen upside down.

I can't quite hear what they're saying. Where's the bloody remote control? Right – that's better.

'Oh! Mum, come here – quick! He's talking about bread pudding!'

'Bread pudding?' Darren Barlow's saying as Mum comes back in the room, carrying two mugs of tea. 'I'm surprised you should choose that as your favourite food, Robin, considering all the recipes you must have tried over the years, all the delicacies from all around the world ...'

'Never forget your roots, Darren,' says Robin, with a cheeky grin for the camera. 'I was born in the East End of London, and when I was a kid my mum used to make a big dish of bread pudding every Saturday. Whenever I smell bread pudding cooking now, it takes me straight back to my childhood in Bethnal Green – sitting at the kitchen table while Mum stirred the fruit and spices into the mixture.'

'That's very interesting, Robin,' says Darren Barlow. 'Coincidentally, my guest on my very first TV interview a year or so ago was Penny Peacham. I don't know if you remember her, Robin – she marketed a very successful range of puddings and—'

'Penny's Passion Pudding! Of course I remember!' exclaims Robin Donovan.

'Blimey, Mum! This is a turn-up for the books, as you would say. Robin bloody Donovan himself, talking about your pudding on TV!'

'Do you know, Darren,' he's saying now – and the camera's zooming in to show his face really close up. He *is* good-looking. I can understand all the fuss. 'That pudding is the *best* version of the traditional bread pudding I've ever tasted.'

'Wow! Praise indeed for Penny's Passion Pudding!' says Darren, looking straight into the camera.

Darren Barlow has made his name, on this TV show, by being quite sarcastic and cutting about people. I'm kind of waiting for him to start taking the piss and making snide remarks. Mum's sitting next to me with her mug of tea halfway to her mouth, just gawping at the screen. She must feel as though Darren's staring into her eyes. I look behind me. Dad's come into the room, drinking his tea, talking about getting the cases outside to the car. Mum looks round at him and he catches the expression of amazement in her face. He stops, looks from her to the TV, and puts his mug down.

'I've actually tried to recreate the recipe for that pudding myself, Darren,' goes on Robin. 'But do you know, I have to admit I can't get the proportions exactly right.'

'I suppose you've heard about the pudding's reputation, Robin?' says Darren with a grin at the camera.

'The stories that were going around about it being an aphrodisiac?' Robin laughs and shrugs. 'Who knows? Let's just say I've eaten it myself and it hasn't done *my* love life any harm, Darren!'

'So I've heard!' chuckles Darren. Robin Donovan features regularly in the gossip pages of the papers – he's been spotted out clubbing with various models and society girls. Only the other week, there were rumours of an entanglement with the girlfriend of a premier league footballer, and currently there's talk about a member of a Scandinavian royal family. 'Well, Robin, let's move on from your favourite food – bread pudding – and perhaps you can tell us a little about your new book *Robin's Real Meals*. What's real about them, then?'

'Turn it off, Chelle,' says Mum in a very faint voice.

'Bloody hell, Mum! Robin Donovan just went into bloody raptures on TV about your pudding! He practically gave you a free advertisement! Do you realise the effect this is going to have on the sales?'

Don't get me wrong. They've sold well, right from day one. But this is going to take things into a whole new league! And obviously, Darling Desserts are going to milk it for all they can get. They'll have Robin's face, and a quote, on the packaging of the pudding before you can blink.

'She's right, Pen,' says Dad slowly. 'I wouldn't be surprised if there's a mention in the papers tomorrow. "Robin Donovan's favourite food ... bread pudding like his mum used to make ... " '

'Well, maybe it's a good job we won't be here,' says Mum, looking worried. 'I don't think I could face all that fuss again.'

'It will have died down a bit by the time we come back from holiday,' says Dad, putting his arm round her. 'But don't knock it, Pen. Your puddings are going to set us up for life. The kids will never have to worry about money ... the grandkids ... '

At the mention of the grandchildren, Mum starts to smile, but she's still sitting with her mug in her hands, staring at the blank TV screen and shaking her head.

'Are you ready then? I don't want you to miss the cruise ship.'

'Yes,' says Dad. 'I've brought down the cases, and I think we should make a move, because the traffic will be building up, especially through the road works for the bypass ... '

'Come on, then.' I take the teacup out of Mum's hands and give her a hug. 'Well done, Mum – I think you're really going to be famous!'

'What a coincidence,' she says wonderingly as she follows me out to the car. 'What a strange coincidence that Robin Donovan should mention bread pudding as his favourite food, on the show with Darren Barlow, of all people.'

'I don't think it was a coincidence, love,' says Dad. 'I reckon media people do each other favours and scratch each other's backs, the same as we all do. And Darren always *was* crazy about you, Pen.' He puts his arm round her and helps her into the car. 'But not as much as I am,' he adds, only just loudly enough for me to hear.

Well, who'd have thought it, eh? In a way, it's quite nice to realise that the old Passion Pudding really does work. Even at my mum's age! How very, very surprising!

Recipe for Penny's Passion Pudding
Ingredients

About 8 slices of stale bread (wholemeal or granary if possible);
2 eggs;
4 oz/110g sultanas (or mixed currants & sultanas);
4 oz/110g raisins;
2 oz/55g glace cherries, halved;
2 oz/55g mixed peel;
4 oz/110g dried apricots, chopped;
3 oz/80g dates, chopped;
2 teaspoons nutmeg;
2 teaspoons cinnamon;
2 oz/55g chopped almonds or mixed nuts (optional);
A sprinkling of brown sugar.

1. Place the bread in a large mixing-bowl, cover with cold water and leave to soak overnight.
2. Squeeze out excess water.
3. Beat the eggs one at a time and stir in with the bread.
4. Stir in the fruit, peel, nuts (if using), and spices.
5. Spoon the mixture into a lightly greased deep pie-dish.
6. Sprinkle with a little brown sugar and a pinch of extra spice.
7. Bake in a moderate oven (350°f/180°c/gas mark 4) for about an hour and a half or until firm but soft.
8. Cut into portions and serve hot or cold.

Author's note:

Penny's variation of the traditional bread pudding contains so much fruit, it does not need any sugar apart from a little to sprinkle on top.

It's healthy and delicious but, unfortunately, I cannot make any promises about its effects on anyone's love life!